Innocent in
the House

Innocent in the House

---◆---

ANDY McSMITH

VERSO

London • New York

First published by Verso 2001
© Andy McSmith 2001
All rights reserved

2 4 6 8 10 9 7 5 3

Verso
UK: 6 Meard Street, London W1F 0EG
USA: 180 Varick Street, New York, NY 10014–4606
www.versobooks.com

Verso is the imprint of New Left Books

ISBN 1–85984–643–2

British Library Cataloguing in Publication Data
A catalogue record for this book is available from the British Library

Library of Congress Cataloging-in-Publication Data
A catalog record for this book is available from the Library of Congress

Typeset by M Rules
Printed by Biddles Ltd, Guildford and King's Lynn
www.biddles.co.uk

Contents

The Prime Minister's Question
1997

He was surrounded on every side by those who wanted to be. Some wanted to be famous, some to be praised, some to be on television every night, some to be outstandingly loyal, some to be famously disloyal, some to be driven by chauffeurs in ministerial cars and some to be Prime Minister. They were breathing down his neck and pressing against his sides; but Joseph Pilgrim's life had been so full of what he wanted to *do* that he had never applied himself to wanting to be anything. He certainly had not expected to be a Member of Parliament, until that singular status rose up one evening and took over his life.

He was listening to the Prime Minister's pleasant, lilting voice, admiring the heroic blandness of those truisms tumbling out undistracted by the jeering faces on the benches opposite, when his mind wandered perilously off the point. He quite forgot that he would be called upon to speak in front of a live audience of a thousand men and women of influence.

It was Prime Minister's Question Time. MPs were squeezed along the green benches of the House of Commons in such numbers that their elbows were locked against their rib cages and their thighs were pressed to their neighbours'. Excitement was high, as always. To nod your head like an overwound clockwork dog and growl 'hear, hear' in unnaturally low tones at the wisdom emanating from MPs on your own side, to interrupt, to point, to laugh, or hold a loud conversation with the person next to you if the speaker be a political opponent is to behave acceptably. Joseph always felt that, when he went into the debating chamber, he left his true self at the door like an outdoor coat hung up in the hall.

Today, he was wedged between one of the catatonically reserved workingmen who even now represent some of the inner-city constituencies in the North, and a younger woman, who was sitting quietly, her hands on her lap. Their silence permitted him to be quiet too, because he was apt to take his cue from those immediately around him. He was also spared his usual agonies of indecision about what he would ask if he was called by the Speaker, because it was all arranged.

It had been brought to his attention by one of the whips, who was in charge of MPs from the region that included Joseph's constituency, an unpopular figure named Neville Reeval, known to the more mutinous of his flock as Never Evil, that the name Joseph Pilgrim was listed third on the printed order paper, making it a certainty that the Speaker would call him to ask a question. Moreover, Never Evil had said, taking Joseph by the elbow and steering him to a discreet location halfway along the book-lined, green-carpeted corridor outside the Commons library, 'My son, you're in a position to please the Prime Minister. Do you want to please the Prime Minister?'

In general, Joseph looked for a middle course between those who so blatantly wanted to please the Prime Minister that they were known as the Androids and others so careless about pleasing him that their chances of holding ministerial office were already wrecked. He tried, as he put it in conversation with his wife, to find a Third Way between rebellion and sycophancy; but Never

Evil's mind did not accommodate such niceties, so Joseph answered with a nod, as if the answer were too obvious to need saying. Never Evil produced a sheet of lined paper on which someone had written in an unfamiliar hand.

'There's a question which the PM would much appreciate being asked,' he said. 'He's got an announcement he wants to make. Should get your name in the papers.'

The question had been written out by hand, in blue Biro on lined paper, a long, winding sentence, opening with the words 'Would the Prime Minister accept that my constituents and the British people everywhere will be heartened by the government's . . .' and so on, until the perambulating sentence arrived at a gentle suggestion as to how the Prime Minister could earn yet more of the nation's gratitude. Joseph said, 'I don't really feel comfortable using someone else's words.'

'Then change the words but make sure you keep the main points,' said Never Evil impatiently.

On the morning of Prime Minister's Questions, there came a message on Joseph's pager telling him to ring a direct line number inside 10 Downing Street. It was the first time he had ever been asked to ring Downing Street. He approached the telephone excited by the prospect of hearing something important, and yet annoyed with himself for being excited. A few clipped sentences later, he had been reminded of how cryptic were the remarks that powerful advisers make to those outside the trusted circle.

The voice at the other end of the line, belonging to an adviser never seen by the outside world, enquired after his health. Joseph was in good health.

The voice remarked that Joseph was likely to be called by the Speaker during Prime Minister's Questions. Joseph confirmed that this was so.

'Well, can I help in any way?' asked the voice.

'But I've already been through this with the whips.'

'And you're happy?'

'Yes, fine.'

'Good. We're very pleased.'

Thus went Joseph's first conversation with a special adviser to the Prime Minister. It was true, though, that he was glad to be given something to do. It meant an end at last to that aching sense of having been left behind as the new government rolled from triumph to triumph. He had been noticed. He had spoken to someone who spoke to someone who sat in the room next to the Prime Minister. He could not help noticing that other new MPs, some younger than he, were being given places on select committees and standing committees, and invitations to meet the Prime Minister or the Chancellor, but for Joseph there had been nothing.

'Yes it's tough embracing change, but we must look to the future not the past . . .' intoned the Prime Minister, speaking without hesitation, boredom or self-doubt, aided by a red folder in which his meticulous staff had listed all the questions he might be asked and set down all the material he needed to give well-informed replies. Ten dozen roaring Tory MPs tried furiously to shout him down.

But why the future? Joseph wondered idly: the future is where we must die; the past is the storehouse of our experience. What a foolish luxury to wish away the past.

He had been surprised at how his own past had been codified since his unforeseen emergence on the outer edge of public life. Joseph had taken very little care over the external facts about his life; he had never collected a job or a position in order to have it on his c.v. yet it was now possible to look up in reference books his date and place of birth, the names of his parents, the family details of his wife, Margaret, the sexes of his children – 1s., 1d. – his school, his Oxford college, his undistinguished career in bookselling and publishing: the facts assembled, checked and made permanent, yet he saw in them nothing recognizable about himself or the life he had experienced.

'It is the intention of this government, unlike that of the party opposite, to govern for the many not the few,' the Prime Minister continued, provoking a new crescendo of catcalls from across the aisle, met with an answering roar of approval from three or four hundred government supporters on the benches behind him. Even the woman next to Joseph raised her attractive head and called out something, but in the enveloping din, he could not hear what.

A witticism came to mind: 'Is it a sign of old age when women MPs start to look sexy?' Could he could risk cracking that while reporting to the general committee of his constituency party? What if he set it in the context of some generalities about challenging the preconceptions about people in public life? He had better consult Margaret first. His wife was good at second-guessing the reactions of party activists.

'Joseph Pilgrim!'

It was the commanding voice of the Speaker. As everyone else remained seated, Joseph rose to his feet, secure in his dark suit, blue shirt and party tie, and in his prearranged question supplied for him in writing by an obliging whip. It was only as the noise died down that he realized he had quite forgotten what the question was.

The handwritten crib was folded away in his top pocket, but an arcane rule forbids MPs to read out questions, even a question prepared by the Prime Minister's own advisers. The very act of taking a sheet of paper from his pocket would have brought a derisive roar of 'reading' from the opposition MPs across the aisle, possibly followed by a rebuke from the Speaker. He began a frantic search through his memory.

The Prime Minister must be invited to congratulate himself, but on what, on what?

Was it the handling of sterling, or a triumph in the world arena?

Was it schools? Was it hospitals? Joseph concentrated so hard that his forehead hurt, but nothing came to him.

Nothing.

There were a thousand people in the chamber waiting for him to begin, among them the Prime Minister and most of the Cabinet, and outside were thousands more watching on television screens, and there was not a word in his head.

Now he was aware of something eerie: the debating chamber had gone quiet. The opposition MPs in front of him had stopped taunting.

Not only was the large chamber silent, but all the lines and colours, the sombre textures of the men's suits, the brilliant scarlets and mauves of women's jackets, the deep brown of the wooden grain of the balustrade above their heads, the slender black wires of the overhead microphones, seemed to slip into focus, as if he had never seen them properly before.

In that moment of near panic, Joseph hit upon the incongruous discovery that, perhaps for the first time, *he knew who he was*. He had a precise sighting of a middle-aged man whose former good looks had been invaded by lines of experience and anxiety, with some hair loss on the crown, who had never succeeded satisfactorily in anything he had undertaken as he stumbled through one life choice after another, making only one undeniably sensible decision, when he married a woman with common sense. Yet he was not a bad man. He knew right from wrong. He had been loved. He had not deliberately wrecked any lives. He had tried to be useful to his fellow beings. He did not have to explain himself to people in authority.

This flash of *Istkeit*, as blissful and inconvenient as the experiences of women who suffer unexpected orgasms in public places, lasted for only a second or two. Though he had a sense of time having stood still, the green numbers on the digital clock above the heads of the MPs across the aisle did not change before he was roused by an inner voice, like a driver who has fallen asleep at the wheel of the car, warning him that blissful though it was to disappear into a reverie, terrible consequences would follow if he did not come round quickly. He was helped by a solitary shout of 'Come on!' From the corner of his eye, he noticed that the Speaker – sitting as usual with her robes of office slung low over her shoulders and her spectacles halfway down her nose – shifted, as if to stand up and tell him to hurry.

There was nothing else to do but improvise.

'The Prime Minister rightly calls upon us to look to the future, not the past,' Joseph heard a voice say. To his relief, it was his. 'But as we gather here to exercise the rights accrued from more than a thousand years of our island's history, from the collective experience of generations who have shed blood to put tyranny to flight . . .'

Where the hell was this sentence going? Must have a question mark at the end.

'. . . should not the Prime Minister be resisting the kind of cultural vandalism which tries to force this country into a world without a history, in a past-free world, a historyless world, because is it not from an understanding of our past that we draw the lessons for the future?'

Was that a question, or not a question? Either way, it would have to do.

Joseph sank back on to the green bench, still struck by the silence in the chamber. He had delivered the whole of his impromptu piece without being heckled. He assumed it was because no one had any idea what he was talking about, for he himself scarcely knew.

He suddenly wished he were at home with Margaret and the children, telling her how he had to spout some drivel off the top of his head. She would pat the back of his hand and reassure him that he should not have agreed to ask a planted question in the first place. She was more optimistic about his political future than he was.

'Bugger!' Joseph whispered, as it came back to him, the question he should have asked. It was about negotiations with the European Commission over the application of additionality to structural development funds for the English regions. How could he have forgotten?

Distracted by this thought, he missed the beginning of the Prime Minister's reply. The noise in the chamber had resumed, at such a volume that it was difficult to hear, and Joseph almost forgot to press his ear to the loudspeaker concealed in the bench behind him.

'Naturally,' said the Prime Minister, 'I of course agree with my honourable friend. My honourable friend is absolutely right, of course we must learn from the past. Of course we must. Nobody would deny that. Nobody would deny it at all. As my honourable friend says, we have a thousand years of democratic history. Of course we have. And we must learn from that. Of course we must learn from the past, but I would say to my honourable friend, we must learn from the past, not be trapped in the past.'

Amid the Mexican wave of 'hear hear' and nodding heads, a hand tapped Joseph on the shoulder and someone in the row behind whispered, 'Good question!' He turned to see who it was. It was a man who had never previously addressed a remark to him, one of the older MPs without a hope of ministerial office, a little man with receding hair and a bright red face which was host to a spider's web of wrinkles fanning out from a point near the bridge of his nose. Joseph acknowledged the compliment with a nod, though he did not at first attach any significance to it, because the little man was hardly one of the parliamentary party's opinion forgers.

Then he noticed to his surprise that his taciturn neighbour had also come to life, and was nodding so vigorously that his greying beard was undulating. Even the demure woman MP sitting on Joseph's other side caught his eye and gave him a smile that implied recognition, if nothing more.

Now he became aware of something else, which he must have taken in subliminally a moment earlier: there had been a change to the mood in the chamber. When the Prime Minister is performing well, the MPs across the aisle will barrack and gesticulate in synthetic fury, but when they think that their quarry is cornered, their anger turns into derisive laughter. They were mocking the Prime Minister now, sitting back with folded arms, shaking their heads in pretended disbelief.

That was Joseph's fault, because he had sprung an unexpected question to which there was no answer laid out in the red folder that the Prime Minister had to hand. Belatedly, Joseph saw what he had done. He had broken a tenet of party discipline. He had caused a surprise. He had irritated the Prime Minister. The repetition of that phrase 'of course', the heavy emphasis – my honourable friend is absolutely right, of course – was a sign that the man who gave the orders was severely irritated.

The cold horror of it. He wanted to leap to his feet to apologize: but he could not, it was not in order. Points of Order come later, after the Prime Minister has gathered up his folder and slipped out through the door behind the Speaker's chair. Meanwhile, the show had moved on; another MP was taking on the Prime Minister.

And even if he could somehow convey a message to the Prime Minister, what would it say: *Terribly sorry, forgot my lines, momentary loss of concentration . . .?* There was no way out. Joseph's last hope that he might one day get to government office had just flickered out.

Or had it? You are never told. You are never certain, until you have seen it in the newspapers, and then it could be wrong.

It was going to be a trying afternoon.

·2·

The Briefing

At 3.30 precisely, Prime Minister's Question Time was over and MPs moved in one heaving crush through the double doors that led out into the division lobby, where conversation could begin. The first remark Joseph heard directed at him came from a Conservative, an ex-minister with a voice nurtured at public school and at Sandhurst who bellowed to him over a sea of heads, 'Good show, Pilgrim!' He must have winced. The looks from the surrounding Labour MPs were mostly sympathetic.

The tide of dark suits carried him through into the next lobby, the one known in parliamentary circles as The Lobby, a large, brightly lit, high-ceilinged, stone room whose most prominent decorations are three black, life-sized, metal statues raised on plinths almost head high. The room also features stone carving stretching up more than twenty feet towards a pointed ceiling, ornate window doors set in each wall, and, on either side of the doors through which the MPs were emerging, two large wooden boards, each divided into 654 individually named pigeonholes and policed by vigilant messengers in black uniforms. These messengers can recognize any and every MP at a glance, and also seem to be able to commit to memory which ones at any given moment have uncollected letters or telephone messages. As the MPs spilled from the division lobby, the messengers moved into action with cries of 'Mr Taylor, Mr Evans, Mrs Smith, Mr

Jones . . .', and messages on slips of pink paper and bundles of mail were rapidly distributed. Joseph listened out for his own name, but there was nothing for him.

The flow of humanity slowed down and broke into groups. Joseph found himself drawn into a crowd of four or five, all Labour MPs, who all seemed to think that his question had touched on an important point. One of the government whips, a woman with whom Joseph had been on vaguely flirtatious terms, walked by. She gave him a long look, shook her head and pursed her lips in mock disapproval, then, vanished into the Whips' Office. Joseph would have liked to go after her and to find out just how much trouble he was in, but at that moment one of the other MPs was in full throat, pouring out complaints about young ministerial advisers fresh from university with no sense of history. Anyway, Never Evil was the proper channel through which official disapproval would be conveyed to Joseph. He should therefore speak to Never Evil, if he could find him.

He hurried away towards the Commons tearoom, along another of the building's numerous green-carpeted corridors, this one lined by two rows of lockers topped by bookshelves full of government documents reaching up to the high ceiling. 'Very brave, Joseph, very brave,' said a quiet voice at his shoulder.

The voice belonged to Sir Peter Draycott, a Tory whose political career was effectively over but who in semi-retirement still enjoyed the luxury of a constituency so safe that he had been able to go to bed at a sensible hour on election night, when so many of his younger, more ambitious colleagues were pitched on to the job market. He knew Joseph as a friend of his wife's, and because they were from opposing parties, they trusted one another in a way no sensible MP would trust anyone on his own side.

'Is that what they're saying?' Joseph whispered. Though there was no one within ten feet of them, it was best to keep his voice down.

'Oh, I don't know what they're saying: they don't talk to me,' Sir Peter replied. 'But I thought it was a good question. Food for thought.'

Joseph took another quick glance around to ensure he was not being overheard, and confessed. 'I have to admit, Peter, that it was a gross balls-up. The whips gave me a plant, but would you believe it, I couldn't remember a single bloody word of what I was supposed to ask. I had to busk it.'

Sir Peter started shaking his head, doing so more and more emphatically as Joseph spoke. He had an almost square face, kindly but featureless, topped by untidy, silvery hair, and usually he had the air of an amiable old bumbler, perhaps to cover the disappointments of a career that had taken him no further than the middle ranks of a failing government; but sometimes his expression would suddenly change, his eyes would narrow, as they were narrowing now, his mouth would purse, and he would take on the appearance of a formidable headmaster.

'I wouldn't say that, I really wouldn't say that if I were you, if you don't mind a tip from an old hand. It's very ill-advised to admit a mistake in this place. I did that in my first year: went through the wrong lobby one night by mistake, owned up; they made me look a terrible fool: the man who rebelled because he got lost in the lobby. With hindsight, I should have said I was driven by my conscience. Rather be a troublemaker than a chump.'

The conversation had to break off as a knot of MPs came down the corridor; a disappointed Joseph knew that this was likely to be the only disinterested piece of good advice he would hear all day. Behind the group of approaching MPs came another figure, rotund and squat, walking briskly alone, a heavy frown on his face. It was Never Evil, who stopped to glare. Being an inch or two shorter than Joseph, he had to raise his chin to give him that eye-to-eye look and, unfortunately, a certain light-headedness had overtaken Joseph. Instead of beholding a fearsome figure of authority, Joseph saw an odd little man with his nose at a rakish angle.

The silence lasted perhaps thirty seconds until Joseph decided to speak, not caring that they were in a congested spot and that other MPs, including Sir Peter, were hovering curiously.

'Afraid I had second thoughts, Neville. Sorry.' Never Evil looked at the other MPs. He was obviously reluctant to speak in front of witnesses, but Joseph went remorselessly on: 'Important though the additionality principle is, as I have often said, I do believe we're in danger of losing our bearings if we lose our sense of history, and I thought it was the right moment to say so.'

Never Evil blinked and walked by without a word. One of the listening MPs tut-tutted and remarked, 'Whoops, somebody ain't happy!' Excusing himself, Joseph took after the whip, and caught up with him in yet another corridor, this one lined on both sides by glass-fronted bookshelves, where there was no one in earshot.

'Neville!'

Never Evil swung about on his heel, but instead of looking into Joseph's face, stared down at his shoes. Since he was a small man, this gave Joseph an aerial view of the bald spot, no bigger than a 50p piece, on his crown.

'Point one, you never, never try to start a conversation like that when people are listening, especially if one of them's a Tory. Point two, if you changed your mind, why didn't you have the courtesy to tell me?' Never Evil spoke quietly, but in a tone of such concentrated fury that Joseph was lost for a reply. 'I repeat, why didn't you tell me?'

Phrases passed through Joseph's mind about this being the Mother of Parliaments, where elected representatives had a historic right to put their questions to the legislature, a right sanctified by the blood of those who had died that Britons might never be slaves, but he knew at heart that so feeble an excuse could only make an angry whip angrier. He had, after all, put poor Never Evil in a difficult spot. The man's job was to ensure that none of the MPs assigned to him stepped out of line, but that was what Joseph had done. Never Evil would have to answer for this to the Chief Whip.

'A bit last-minute, I'm afraid. Sorry.'

'You've caused a lot of bloody trouble, I can tell you,' said Never Evil, waving the written question under Joseph's nose.

'Is the PM annoyed?'

It was, of course, too early for Never Evil to know what the Prime Minister thought. He needed to be told by the Chief Whip, and the Chief would need guidance from Downing Street, where someone would need an indication from the PM, whose life was so crowded that he might already have forgotten that Joseph Pilgrim existed.

'Oh whoa, whoa: you'll know soon enough, my boy. Don't you worry, you'll soon know.'

Pausing just long enough to witness the impact of his words, Never Evil walked away, leaving Joseph to curse himself quietly for the momentary weakness that had made him scuttle after a whip. He reflected glumly that he was now perhaps fated to be like a character out of Kafka, searching every word and every look from anyone in authority for a hint of an official verdict on his misdemeanour, when none had been passed because the meeting at which his conduct should have been an agenda item had never taken place.

Actually, unbeknown to him, there was a meeting, in a room behind the Speaker's chair, where the Prime Minister repaired with a clutch of advisers and officials at the end of his Commons performance. Everyone in the room had an opinion at the ready about each exchange on the floor of the chamber, should the Prime Minister want to hear it; but as ever, he was too busy for retrospection. It was almost four o'clock. Part two of his working day still lay ahead. There was an ambassador to be received in half an hour, meetings with ministers and officials, and a speech to be delivered at a banquet that night, which was only half written. Nevertheless, even prime ministers must pause for cups of tea, and after he had taken the second sip, he looked around the room and asked no one in particular, 'Wasn't I getting a question on additionality?'

There is nothing worse in the life of a Downing Street official than having to explain a cock-up, but mercifully at that moment they were disturbed by the Principal Private Secretary arriving to insist that the Prime Minister must apply his mind at once to the troubled affairs of the faraway country whose ambassador he was due to meet soon. Nothing more was ever said in the Prime Minister's presence about the question Joseph Pilgrim should have asked. Only one or two people in that room even knew the culprit's name.

One was a junior member of the Prime Minister's press team. Some minutes later, he was hurrying along a corridor with the Prime Minister's chief press secretary, rapidly working his way through five things he must tell the chief press secretary before they reached the foot of the winding staircase at the end of the upper committee corridor, which would give him no more than three minutes. The chief press secretary is a tall man who kept fit in his youth and walks with a giant stride. Of the five items breathlessly conveyed during this rapid march, the fourth and second to least important was the Prime Minister's mild surprise at not being asked about the principle of additionality.

'Wasn't someone set up for that?' said the chief press secretary.

'Joseph Pilgrim,' said the aide. 'We don't know what went wrong.' They moved directly on to point five.

Minutes later, the chief press secretary and his assistant were in a crowded room at the top of a turret, their backs against a window that overlooked the Thames and St Thomas's Hospital, confronted by fifty of the country's most influential political journalists. It was the afternoon lobby briefing. Talk ranged over the affairs of the world and the nation, dwelling principally on the upcoming legislation affecting the rights of trade unions. Towards the close of the briefing, the chief press secretary took a question from one of the younger journalists, who worked for a group of provincial newspapers, one of which circulated in the region that included Joseph Pilgrim's constituency. Exploring a possible local angle, she asked what the Prime Minister had thought of the question he had been asked on the floor of the Commons, barely an hour earlier. It had been a long day, and the chief press secretary was feeling a little jaded. The question reminded him that Joseph Pilgrim's unreliability had added one more task to his long working day. 'We haven't a clue what Joseph Pilgrim was asking about,' he said, a little sharply.

It was the terseness of his tone that provoked a second question, to which he repeated, hoping to sound less tetchy, 'I'm sorry, you'll have to ask Joseph Pilgrim: we don't know what was on his mind when he asked that question.'

After that, the chief press secretary gave the matter no more thought, except that he put himself to the trouble of calling two journalists, one on the *Independent* and one on the *Financial Times*, known to him as Bill and Bob, to go through the points the Prime Minister would have made, had he been asked the expected question on additionality, thereby ensuring that the small but important point he wanted to develop was made public.

The lobby briefing came to an end and the journalists moved

out in a single mass, filling the spiral staircase, and spreading out into the corridor beyond, where they began talking among themselves in the hope of extracting the juice to cook a news story from the dry words they had just heard: What about Joseph Pilgrim then, is there a usable line? . . . Did you notice he said 'we'? . . . I've got it in my notes, here: We haven't a clue what Joseph Pilgrim was asking about – we don't know what was on his mind . . . They must know, surely . . . Sounds like they've started a hatchet job already . . . So what was he on about, does anybody know? . . .Who is he, anyway?

An hour later, Joseph was back in his office, feeling better for the reaction he had had from fellow MPs. He was now reassured that he had not made a fool of himself in front of his peer group. The relief felt like alcohol on an empty stomach.

His office was high up in a featureless building on Millbank. It would have been less than five minutes' walk from the Commons, but for the long, crushing crowd of tourists blocking every approach. The building was new and comfortable inside and because he was new, he had not yet collected enough clutter to fill his well-lit office. Among its luxuries were the long shelves around the wall, which allowed Joseph to accumulate a hoard of the documents that are available to MPs free of charge. Six feet of shelf were already full. Never before had he had so much room to file documents, or so many documents to file.

He even had an efficient helper to do his filing and indexing, his research and correspondence. Rachel was only just out of university, very bright and practical, and full of ambition. She was at the filing cabinet as he entered, and did not even look round as he came in and settled in the swivel chair at his desk. It was a struggle to stop his eyes from wandering over her long dark hair, tied back today, and her short, tight dress. He feared that she already despised him, and he did not want to add lecherous

·17·

window-shopping to his list of failings. She had come into his employment believing that it would let her share the excitement of being in government, but sadly the office of a newly elected back-bench MP, upstream and across the road from the House of Commons, was a long way from where the action was. He feared that she was now only filling in time as she weighed up her next move. He often surprised her having long, furtive telephone conversations with people who seemed to understand their world very well.

High up in one corner there was a television equipped with a closed-circuit channel from which Commons debates were broadcast live. It was switched on, with the sound turned down.

'Did you watch it on the monitor?' Joseph asked. She turned and nodded, giving him a smile that did not seem very friendly. 'What did you think?'

'There's already been a reaction in the City to what he said about interest rates. It's on Ceefax,' she replied.

'Is it? That is interesting. Yes,' said Joseph, who had no recollection of any question or answer pertaining to interest rates. 'Um, did you hear me?'

'Yes.'

'What did you think?'

'You caught him out.'

'Yes, but I thought it needed saying. The notion that history is dead is, I think, you know, likely to make us lose direction.'

The telephone rang. 'You've been getting a lot of calls,' Rachel said.

Joseph watched as the answerphone picked up the caller and silently recorded a message. The illuminated panel on the handset informed him that it was his ninth message since he had left the office after lunch. Most, or all, must have been prompted by his question to the Prime Minister.

Rachel looked at her watch and glided across the room to change the channel and turn up the volume on the television set. Joseph frowned, thinking he was to be compelled to hear news of the City reaction to whatever the Prime Minister had said about interest rates, but soon heard, to his surprise, that the news was about him. He gripped the edge of his desk and listened open-mouthed.

The screen was filled by the familiar face of one of the country's most eminent political journalists, evidently answering a question put to him by an unseen newscaster and saying, 'Yes, I can tell you that after Mr Pilgrim asked that question, with its somewhat cryptic reference to history and the past, there was considerable speculation among MPs here as to what it was all about, because it certainly annoyed the Prime Minister.'

Joseph had never before heard himself discussed as an item on a national news bulletin. He felt bizarrely detached, like a man watching himself undergoing an operation under local anaes-thetic. He would have been plunged into self-recrimination if a government whip had told him, face to face, that he had annoyed the Prime Minister, but hearing the statement conveyed to the nation made it impersonal, just like any other news item. He looked at Rachel, wondering if she felt equally detached. She was watching the screen intently.

And have you found the answer?

Well, I can tell you that last night, in a committee room here, there was a private meeting of about fifty Labour MPs with trade union backgrounds. And their concern is that the government shouldn't backtrack on its promise to review trade union legisla-tion. And I can tell you – and this is, I think, the key – that one of the MPs who spoke there, at that private meeting, was Joseph Pilgrim.

'How did he know that?' Joseph exclaimed.

Rachel sniffed. 'Is it true that fifty people were there?'

'About that many.'

'Well, then.'

So this is a first warning shot across the bows from an influential backbench MP . . .

'Influential!' Joseph exclaimed, laughing out loud until silenced by a withering look from Rachel.

. . . don't forget the people who financed the Labour Party and saw you through all the opposition years, don't destroy that relationship, they're saying . . .

A tickling sensation above one hip told Joseph that someone had sent him a pager message. It read: THE CHIEF SAYS DON'T, DON'T, DON'T TALK TO THE PRESS – NEVILLE.

Rachel switched off when the bulletin moved to foreign news. Joseph had been so astonished and excited to hear his own blundering words being received as a statement of national importance that he was tempted to invite her out to get drunk with him. The sound of the telephone saved him from this folly.

'I expect you're going to be busy,' Rachel said, putting on her coat. 'I've drafted replies to all your letters and left them for you to sign, I've cut out something from the *Financial Times* I thought you ought to see, and all the Hansards are in order on the shelf. And there's water in the kettle.'

She slipped out quickly, guessing that he would want to listen to his messages with her absent.

Eight of the ten were from journalists. Joseph meticulously wrote down each name and telephone number. Another was from Neville Reeval, backing up the pager message that exhorted him not to reply to calls from the press. Amid this repetitive litany came the startling sound of a woman's voice.

'Joseph Pilgrim! It's Diana Draycott. I don't suppose you saw me up in the Stranger's Gallery during PMQs, but I certainly saw you. What an odd question. We must meet for a drink and you can tell me what the blazes you were on about.'

A ghastly thought crossed his mind. What if Rachel had heard that message when it first came through, and made the connections between the name Draycott, the sarcastic tone, and the obvious familiarity with Parliament, to deduce that he had had a message from the wife of a Tory? Like many people who suddenly find themselves in the public eye, Joseph was afraid of aspects of his own past, inconsequential secrets which he did not want brought into the open.

On Friday evening, when his wife Margaret was trying to get their younger child to sit down to dinner, and Joseph was becoming anxious about whether he would get to his evening constituents' surgery on time, they could have done without the unexpected sound of the doorbell. Joseph opened the door, unprepared for the flashlight that went off in his face three or four times.

There were two of them: the one taking photographs and a balding man who had both hands in his pockets and an oddly friendly smile, as if it were a social call. He spoke with a south London accent.

'Mr Pilgrim, glad we were able to catch you at home,' he said. 'Could we have a quick word? It's about a man who seems to think you were involved in the death of his wife.'

·3·

The Reporter on the Doorstep

As Joseph's eyes recovered from the flashlights, they focused on the two men on his doorstep. The one who had spoken introduced himself as Dave Drucker. He was oddly dressed, with checked jacket, pale yellow shirt and brown tie, which matched one another well enough, if garishly, but clashed with his black nylon trousers so starkly as to make him look like two halves of different people fitted together by accident. Joseph was not given the name of the photographer, whose opening burst of activity had given way to bored silence. They were from one of the mass-circulation Sunday newspapers. He had no doubt that they were on a mission to ruin him.

Beyond them, he saw one of his neighbours returning home with bursting white plastic bags hanging from the handles of her pushchair. She waved cheerfully at him. He gave only a nod in reply. It was nearing the end of that busy interlude in the normally quiet life of their street, which started with the clatter of children returning from school and was followed by the quieter footsteps of office workers returning home. There was other background activity: the familiar figure of their local road sweeper going slowly about his business, gathering the autumn leaves into pyramids and stuffing them into his blue hand-held cart; a tall, slouching Rastafarian walking by, whistling, head back, hands tucked lazily into his pockets. It was still light. If they stayed here talking, people would notice. Should he invite them into the house? Or would that imply guilt?

Another neighbour was hurrying home, a fat little man whose stomach threatened to rip away the jacket buttons on his dark suit. He waved, though it slowed him down, and then stopped by the gate at the end of the short concrete path to Joseph's door.

'The trade figures are very good, Mr Pilgrim,' he said, as if remarking on the day's weather. He liked to offer his MP neighbour a daily helping of respectful and carefully considered views.

'They are very good indeed, a turnabout in which we can take some legitimate pride, don't you agree?'

'Yes, that's very true, very true indeed, Mr Pilgrim.' And the man went on his way, too polite to notice the strangers at Joseph's door.

The longer the two journalists stayed, the more likely it was that their visit would be talked about by Joseph's neighbours. He did not want that. He considered inviting them in, but that would have made it more difficult to be rid of them.

'I take it you know this gent,' Dave said, in the London accent, his tone pushy but friendly, as if he were striking up a conversation at a party, 'named . . .' He checked in his spiral-backed notebook: '. . . Frank Rist.'

'Yes, I know Fred Rist.'

'Fred? Or Frank?'

'Frank.'

It was a nervous slip of the tongue, which Dave Drucker had picked up at once. Though the man spoke in a slow drawl, and despite the blandness of his round, stubbled face, his mind was obviously nimble. Joseph could feel panic in his gut.

'You were in Newcastle with him, yeah?'

'Yes, in Newcastle.'

'And you were active in politics together?'

'Yes.'

'And you knew his wife, who died, yeah, in Newcastle?'

'Yes. Christine.'

'What can you tell us about the circumstances of her death, Mr Pilgrim?'

He asked his vile question in an everyday tone, as if he were checking the time.

Joseph wished he could summon the will to retreat indoors, but he was afraid that breaking off the conversation might have consequences he could not foresee. He began a listless recital of the findings from the coroner's inquest into that death, so sudden and shocking that the passage of twelve years had hardly dimmed its vividness. It had taken place when the news bulletins were full of images of miners returning to work, defeated, after a year on strike, as if their public event and the private horror of losing Christine were interlinked.

Dave Drucker had done his research. He knew that the police had taken statements from a dozen of Christine's friends who were at her house for an impromptu party that ended a little over an hour before she was killed.

'Were you at that party, Mr Pilgrim?'

Yes, he was, though unlike other guests, he had not given a statement to the police. He did not choose to tell Dave Drucker why not. The police had knocked, but Joseph was away. When he returned, they were already satisfied that they were dealing with a horrible accident, which could never be fully explained. The coroner's jury returned an open verdict.

'What time did you leave the party, Mr Pilgrim?'

'I can't remember. Late.'

'Might you have been the last to leave, Mr Pilgrim?'

'I can't remember.'

'When did you know that Mrs Rist was dead?'

'Before I went into work the next day. Look, I don't mind answering your questions, but this is all very painful and distasteful. Could you get to the point, do you think? It was all very thoroughly looked into at the time.'

Dave Drucker gave him a long, searching look, then consulted his notebook, as if making the point that he was not to be hurried along.

Horrible images were erupting in Joseph's mind: venomous whispering on the dark landing outside Christine's room . . . a house empty, with its front door wide open, letting in an icy draught, as if he had been hearing ghosts . . . Christine, in nightclothes, performing a weird pirouette in the path of an oncoming juggernaut . . . Christine spewed out like a broken toy . . . .

Dave Drucker was talking again, in that low, relentless tone, about his conversation with someone from Christine's family. He was very thorough, this reporter. He had spoken to a parent, aunt or uncle, who had complained that there remained unanswered questions, not satisfactorily dealt with at her inquest.

Joseph should have given a politician's answer. A politician is always on the side of the bereaved. If there are questions, a politician is there to ask. But he was too agitated to play the part, and he feared that it showed.

'The trouble is, it was twelve years ago.'

'But where we're talking about the tragic and partially unexplained death of a human being, yeah, I don't see that it's relevant to say it was twelve years ago, Mr Pilgrim. How well did you know Mrs Rist?'

'Pretty well.'

'Pre-itty well,' the reporter echoed.

'And by the way, she didn't use her husband's name.'

'Why's that? Was there something wrong in her marriage, yeah? Some other party?'

'No, no, Christine was a feminist. That's why she didn't take her name from her husband.'

'Preferred her father's, yeah?'

That was a joke, a light moment in a grim interview. 'That's the bind which feminists find themselves in,' Joseph replied, unable to smile.

'During the inquest, yeah, there's mention of an unidentified witness who was allegedly at the scene until he did a runner. Do you have any idea who that was, Mr Pilgrim?'

'I've no idea, no.'

'Where was Mr Rist?'

'He was in London. He had been there for two or three days.'

'You've agreed that you might have been the last to leave the party, Mr Pilgrim. Didn't you notice anybody hanging about?'

'You'll have to check, but I think there was a long gap between the end of the party and when Christine was killed. Two or three hours, I think.'

'And she was alive and OK when you left the house?'

'I would hardly have walked away if anything had happened to Christine.'

'So you're categorical and definite that Christine Rist was alive and OK when you left the party, Mr Pilgrim?'

'Isn't that what I've just said?'

'To be totally pedantic, no: you answered my question with a rhetorical question.'

'I was in bed when it happened.'

'Whose bed, Mr Pilgrim? If you don't mind my asking.'

'I do mind, actually, and don't misinterpret that. I think you're asking me a lot of intrusive questions for no reason. I don't know what happened to Christine. I've never understood how she died. It has always been a mystery, and I wish you could explain it.'

'What's your theory about this witness who did a runner, Mr Pilgrim? You've had a long time to think about it. You must have a theory.'

'Honestly, my theory was that there was no mystery witness.'

That was true.

The chance of holding a conversation without being interrupted was always low while the children were in the house. Joseph did not hear or see his son arrive, but he felt the small hand take hold of the back of his trouser leg, above the knee. Tom was shy of strangers. Thumb in mouth, he stared resentfully at the two journalists.

He was soon followed by his older sister, Isobel, who marched boldly out on to the threshold, pointed at the black, boxlike object in Dave's hand and demanded to know what it was. Dave, who had a kind of gangsterish charm, explained that it was a 'talk book', to record 'everything your Daddy tells me'.

'Can I hear?'

Joseph intervened: 'No you can't.'

'What's that writing?' Isobel enquired next.

Dave crouched until his head was level with hers, causing the reflected light to shine from his balding skull. Isobel cocked her head to one side and listened, intrigued, as he showed her his notebook, and told her that the hieroglyphs littering its pages were shorthand. Joseph did not like watching his six-year-old daughter being so charmed, but could find nothing in Dave's behaviour to which he could justifiably object.

Straightening up, Dave said, 'Very nice little girl, Mr Pilgrim. How about a picture of yourself and your children?' The photographer nodded dopily, and raised his camera.

'No, absolutely not,' Joseph replied, his hand raised.

'Da-ad!'

'Be quiet! Go back indoors.'

Isobel weighed up whether to stand and argue, but had a better idea. She skipped back into the house, shouting, 'Mummy, Mummy, there's men at the door and one writes with shorthand!' Tom was left clinging in sullen silence to his father's trouser leg.

'Can we wind up this conversation now, please?' Joseph pleaded.

'How friendly are you now with Frank Rist, Mr Pilgrim? Is he at all a mate of yours?'

'You've spoken to him, haven't you? He has given you this information, so how can he be a mate?'

They were interrupted by a sudden, silent visit. Margaret arrived with a face like thunder, swept up little Tom as if he were being menaced by predatory paedophiles, gave the journalists a look of utter contempt, and was gone.

'Why did you and he fall out, Mr Pilgrim?' Dave asked, indifferent to the now-vanished apparition.

'You've spoken to him, haven't you? What did you think of him? His mental state, how did you assess that?'

'I can't say that I've assessed it in any particular way, Mr Pilgrim. What's your assessment of his mental state? Are you inferring that his mental state is in a bad way?' Dave evidently had not mastered the distinction between 'infer' and 'imply'. Joseph noticed that, despite the bland smile on the journalist's wide, stubbled face, there was no smile in his eyes, which watched with hard, unsentimental curiosity. At his side, the photographer had begun emitting little encouraging nods and smiles, as if they were coaxing a nervous examinee to speak up.

'Did I say that?'

'You raised the subject, yeah.'

'Yes, because you have come to me with questions about a very old story because you've been talking to somebody and I think you might ask what that person's mental state is like.'

'Are you inferring that Mr Rist is sort of deficient in his mental state, that he suffers from paranoid delusions, or what is it that you're inferring, Mr Pilgrim?'

He spoke without accusation, like a man trying to make his questions as easy as possible by laying out a range of alternative answers.

'I didn't hear myself suggest anything. I'm asking you a question. You're not answering.'

He could hear the anger rising in his own voice, disobeying his own firm instruction to himself to stay cool. It was made more difficult by Dave Drucker's exasperating calm.

'So, Mr Pilgrim, what you're saying, yeah, is that instead of listening to any complaints and allegations, we should look into Mr Rist's mental state, yeah?'

'I'm not making any suggestion about what you do or don't do.' Joseph sensed that he was being manoeuvred into saying something he would regret when he saw it in print. 'What you do is not my concern: I'm just concerned that you don't listen to stupid stories which could hurt my family.'

'Would you say that Mr Rist is a source of information we can't rely on?'

'If he is the one who is putting about these wild suggestions which you are putting to me, then I would say he is not reliable. And can I add this: what happened all happened a long time ago, long before I was an MP: I've only been an MP for a few months. The idea that a coroner, a British coroner, would cover up . . .'

'Was there a cover-up?'

'Of course there wasn't. That's exactly my point. Now, I've said all I want to say, and the rest is none of your business. OK?'

Dave gave him another protracted look, then gave up: not beaten, but at least fought to a standstill.

'Is this going to make a story for your paper?'

'Not for me to decide,' said Dave.

'But you must have an opinion.'

Dave Drucker tutted. 'I never have opinions, Mr Pilgrim. Dangerous, dangerous things.'

A telephone was ringing in the hallway as Joseph went back indoors. It was Neville Reeval on the line. Hearing a whip's voice gave Joseph such a shock that for a moment he could not breathe properly. While he had been confronted by Dave Drucker, he had pushed out of his mind the seriousness of his predicament, which suddenly came to him in a single, drowning wave. For twelve years, he had harboured a guilty secret whose shocking immediacy seemed to have dimmed each time he took it out for private examination, which he did perhaps once a year. Time and distance had eroded both the likelihood and the consequences of exposure. At worst, there had seemed to be a tiny chance that he might have to travel north to explain himself, suffering this embarrassment away from those who knew him. That, he realized, had changed with his election to Parliament. Suddenly the tiny risk on the far horizon of his worries had grown to a monstrous size and proximity. It threatened utter ruin. And the Whips' Office was already on the phone . . .

Except that Never Evil was talking in a jaunty 'I've got news for you' sort of tone, which under normal circumstances would have been mildly annoying. Right now, it seemed so irrelevant that some moments elapsed before what Neville was saying penetrated the wave of cold panic. There was a vacancy on one of the committees carrying out line-by-line scrutiny of a government bill. After considering several candidates, the whips had decided to offer Joseph that vacant seat. They were sorry it had taken so long to find him a place on a standing committee, but he would of course understand that there were a great many new MPs who had

had to be accommodated. Joseph did not find this explanation at all flattering, suggesting as it did that all those new MPs chosen before him were in some way better qualified, but he did not complain; he thanked Never Evil heartily. Hearing his effusive tone, the whip privately decided that Joseph might not be such a bad fellow after all.

'Yes, well, you'd better remember that this is a favour to you, my boy,' he said. 'Turn up when you're wanted, be helpful, be lively, clear *everything* with me, and don't ever miss a vote. No stunts. You don't fart unless you've cleared it with me. *Comprende?*'

'I hear you.'

'Now, in return, we need a small service from you, old chap. Tuesday night, ten p.m., there's going to be a piddling little vote, a two-liner. Need you there, in the Noe lobby. Sorry to bugger up your evening, but we can't risk a government defeat.'

As Joseph replaced the receiver, he wondered wistfully why he had to allow himself to be ordered around by the likes of Never Evil; why he could not tell them all to take a running jump, in the style of the great parliamentary rebels: a John Wilkes – defiant, principled, immovable; and why, for that matter, he could not emulate the Duke of Wellington by telling Dave Drucker to go publish and get stuffed.

Actually, there were two compelling reasons. One was aged six, the other three. Both were at the kitchen table, eating their fish fingers and baked beans. Margaret, who was strict with them, had them sitting with their backs straight, holding their cutlery properly, but order and calm almost disintegrated when Joseph entered the kitchen. They were bursting to know more about the visitors whose arrival had made their mother so angry, and immediately their high-pitched voices began throwing out unwelcome questions. Isobel's butterfly mind had moved off the interesting discovery that Dave wrote shorthand; she now wanted to see the photograph of herself 'what the 'nother man took with his camera'.

'He didn't take your photograph, Isobel, because I told him not to.'

'Oh, why?'

While Joseph struggled to answer the petulant question, Margaret cleared away the empty plates. Their domestic life centred on the large freestanding wooden table in the middle of the tiled kitchen floor, at which the children were sitting. When they first moved in, Margaret had insisted on removing a wall to double the size of the kitchen by dispensing with an adjoining utility room. She then installed an Aga, and an abundance of open wooden shelves and surfaces, to give the kitchen a farmhouse look.

'I'll be late home on Tuesday night,' Joseph warned Margaret when the children's supper was finished and they had been sent away.

Her face tightened, but she did not complain. She never did. 'What time will you be home?'

'About eleven.'

They might have said more, but Tom toddled back in to announce, 'Mum, Mum, I'm wet!'

Several hours were taken up by baths, bedtime stories and favourite television programmes. There was not a moment in which he and Margaret could talk again, until they were sitting up in bed. By then it was too late in the evening to burden her with an account of Dave Drucker's visit, though the nagging worry would linger for several days as he wondered what to expect to read about himself and Christine's death. He would have known more if he had heard Dave Drucker talking on a mobile phone soon after their conversation ended. *Don't think it's a goer for this week, Ian – couldn't quite see the whites of his eyes . . . Oh yeah,*

yeah, he looked shifty, dead shifty, but he handled himself. I need a second source . . .

That night Joseph had the dream of lying in bed in a room filled with noise and weird, pulsating blue light. It was a recurring nightmare he had first experienced in his teens. It came to pay its respects in times of crisis, so often that he now recognized it as a dream even as he was trapped in it. His shouts and frantic wrestling with the bedclothes woke Margaret, who grumpily poked him with her elbow and told him to be quiet.

Once, when he was a teenager, he had dreamt that he was drowning in the same blue pulsating light and had woken into a drama more extraordinary than the dream. That was one of several stories he did not want to share with the several million people who read the newspaper that employed Dave Drucker.

·4·

The Information Game

Joseph had an informal arrangement with Sir Peter Draycott to meet once a week in a huge tearoom, dominated by large oil paintings of old naval battles, in the depths of the House of Lords. They must have looked an incongruous pair. Joseph had first met Peter Draycott, as he then was, just before he entered Parliament. Then, Draycott had come across as an unappealing father figure, whose conversation was made of pronouncements delivered with the grand finality of a man practising for the dignity of public office; his sole source of appeal was that he had an attractive wife who was much closer to Joseph's age. Now, with his ministerial career behind him, Sir Peter was more avuncular than fatherlike, exuding the contentment that comes of extinguished ambition. His political career had not been a brilliant one, but it had not been a failure either. He expected his own party to be out of office for ten years, so he was collecting seats on company boards to see him through the last years of his children's school and university fees.

'Diana sends her love, as always,' he said.

In one of his reflective moods, Sir Peter had compared the House of Commons to a trading floor on which hundreds of dealers dealt in a nebulous currency. That currency was inside information – any nugget of political intelligence, any little rumour not yet in the public domain. 'Poverty is only knowing what you read in the newspapers,' he had said. This remark opened Joseph's eyes to the seam of calculating self-interest beneath their friendship. Sir Peter gave away the accumulated knowledge of eighteen years in the Commons. Joseph had little inside knowledge to trade with in return, but that did not matter. He was running up an account. Sir Peter believed in Joseph's future. In time, Joseph would be his contact in government circles.

When they met again on the Monday, after Joseph's intervention at Prime Minister's Questions, he now knew that his own reputation was currency in Parliament's internal trading floor. His name had cropped up again in the Sunday newspapers – though not, mercifully, in the one for which Dave Drucker worked: he had slipped out to the newsagent's on Sunday morning, and thence to a park bench, to scour all its news pages one by one, and had been greatly relieved to find that there was not a word about him. Mr Drucker was obviously saving up whatever he had on Joseph. But his name had been in two of the heavier, upmarket Sunday newspapers. It had been strange seeing it there in print and learning by this means that he was a 'generally well-regarded new MP' who was 'tipped for early promotion'.

This slight brush with fame seemed to affect the behaviour of other people. Around the Commons, MPs he scarcely knew had opened conversations with him as if he were an old acquaintance. Most did not trouble to introduce themselves because, with the special egotism of their profession, they expected him to know who they were. One incident among many occurred while he was climbing one of Parliament's main staircases, built around an oblong well so that conversations held at any level were likely to be overheard above or below. An older man with a grizzled face and stubbly beard was descending, followed by two others, all of them Labour MPs.

'Mr Pilgrim, Mr Pilgrim – the very man,' the bearded man exclaimed, in a Brummy accent. 'We were fucking worried about you, we were, but you're OK, brother. You're OK.'

Tapping the side of his nose with a forefinger, the stranger winked at Joseph and went on his way. The men behind nodded in agreement. Joseph did not know any of their names.

'Describe him again. How was he dressed?' Sir Peter asked, when Joseph relayed this incident as they sat at a small table in a corner of the vast Lords tearoom.

'Off-the-peg suit, white shirt, plain tie, and he used the word *fucking* a lot.'

'Very good chap,' said Sir Peter. 'A bit of an Old Labour sort: we on our side never agree with a word he says on anything, but very good chap. His name's Denis Drummond. A good friend of the Deputy Prime Minister, one hears. The DPM must be looking out for you.'

Joseph had no idea what he might have done to make the Deputy Prime Minister 'look out' for him.

'Oh, I expect it was your sparkling performance in the House last week,' Sir Peter said, taking obvious pleasure in the success of his protégé. 'You see, we all like to pretend we're on top of events – Joseph Pilgrim: one to watch, we all say, because your name has been mentioned by distinguished correspondents and we all want to sound as if we're in the know. Actually, none of us has a clue: we're taking a lead from each other, and from the press. You're a bull market today.'

They were briefly interrupted as tea was brought to them on a silver tray, by a waiter whom Sir Peter addressed by his first name.

'How long will it last?' Joseph enquired.

Sir Peter stretched his hands apart and the eyes in his square face widened. 'Oh, I expect that by tomorrow it will all have blown over,' he said.

In fact, an even more extraordinary encounter awaited Joseph the next day. It was almost seven o'clock, and the Commons was filling with MPs who had been summoned to vote. He was in a short stone corridor which resembled a monastery cloister, on his way to the division lobbies, when a voice called, 'Joseph!'

Almost a dozen MPs were within sight but, confusingly, each passed on by without a word, leaving him in a seemingly empty corridor, having been halted by a voice with no body attached to it.

The stone corridor was at least a century old, a busy morass of Gothic colonnades, bosses, ribs and fan vaults and vertical window-tracery, spreading up the walls and across the ceiling in Perpendicular style. Where the vaults intersected overhead there were stone designs: a dragon, a bunch of grapes, or an eroded portcullis. Between the pillars on either side of the corridor were low, green leather benches, and on the left side were windows criss-crossed by ageing lead lattices, casting patches of white light on the corridor floor.

Joseph said 'hello' into the emptiness, and something stirred.

Halfway along on the left, there was a rectangle of sunlight larger than the others, indicating an alcove concealed behind its adjoining pillar. He must have passed it without a sideward glance. From that alcove emerged a youth in a tailored suit. He had a soft, almost girlish face, and his eyes, half-obscured by rimless glasses, blinked continually. He was tall, but he hung his chin forward, which made him stoop like an old man. He was looking at Joseph, as if expecting him to speak.

And out of the hidden alcove, a foot and part of a leg protruded. Someone else was sitting, cross-legged, just out of sight. Only the shine on the black leather lace-up shoe, the woollen sock, and the sharp crease on the trouser leg could be seen.

'Hello, Joseph!' a voice said, again. It was a pleasant voice, neither loud nor harsh but yet confident and commanding. It could have been the Prime Minister's, except that the Prime Minister would never be found sitting in an alcove in a corridor of the House of Commons with only one young adviser in attendance.

There was another movement from behind the pillar, and into view came brown hair rising in a wave, a wide forehead, and the unmistakable face of one of the most talked-about men in public life. When Sir Peter had likened the Commons to a trading floor, he had missed part of the picture; sometimes, the House could be like a magical museum where familiar images took on corporeal life. You could turn a corner and come upon a celebrity, past or present, someone seen on television a hundred times, now walking about or holding conversations like any other human. But these sightings are necessarily rare. For the same reason that an eco-system must have its sustainable balance of predators and prey, no political system can sustain more than a few people at a time who hold real power in their hands. The legendary figure Joseph could now see was one of those few. He had access to that prized bullion, information. His circle of contacts was said to include business tycoons, society hostesses, the Prince of Wales, and every important journalist in the capital, including the Director General of the BBC. More than that, he knew the Prime Minister. It was said that in moments of domestic or international crisis, he was the first to whom the Prime Minister turned for private advice. This living legend was only feet away, and had called Joseph by name.

After an instant the face receded behind its pillar, but the foot yet protruded, proof that what Joseph had seen was not a hallucination. The young man standing in the corridor indicated with an outstretched arm that he should approach.

A hexagonal table and two high-backed, green-upholstered

chairs bearing the portcullis crest of the House of Commons filled the little alcove. The Minister was sitting with a lined pad in front of him, holding a gold pen and making notes in small, sloping handwriting. Having indicated to Joseph to sit at the far side of the little table, he continued writing for a full minute in silence. Joseph was so close by that he could hear the famous Minister breathe.

The young man in the corridor stood with his hands clasped behind his back, blinking frequently and occasionally shuffling his feet. He blinked so often that Joseph mentally christened him the Young Blinker.

After a minute or two of silence, the Minister put away the gold pen in his inside jacket pocket and smiled an open-mouthed smile, which momentarily made him look like one of those theatrical masks with holes for the wearer's eyes and mouth. The combination of a wide forehead, slightly protruding ears and a sharp chin made his face almost triangular. He was reputed to be an extremely difficult man and, like William Pitt the Younger, 'stiff for all but the ladies', yet now he appeared relaxed, and after the false smile had receded, his face seemed alert, even handsome in its way.

'So, what are we to make of the man who is given a *unique* chance to ask the Prime Minister a *germane* question about relations with our European partners but instead, quite without warning, asks something stinkingly difficult?'

The Minister looked at Joseph silently with an amused gaze under which he almost disintegrated. He wanted to tumble out an explanation of how he had simply forgotten his lines, but he remembered Sir Peter's wise advice not to admit to being a fool. Not knowing what else to do, he stared back in silence, until the Minister raised his fine eyebrows and looked away.

'The Prime Minister is sometimes driven almost to despair,' the

Minister said, enunciating each word slowly and distinctly as if he were dictating, 'by a dearth of joined-up thinking. It is not that colleagues don't think. On the contrary, many colleagues think hard and long – though for others thought of any kind might be too demanding. They work hard, they have much to say, all of it worthy, some of it useful in its way, no doubt, but without co-ordination. We are not joined up. How are we to become joined up? Joseph – your suggestions?'

As Joseph ransacked his mind for an answer to this peculiar and unexpected question, his ordeal was worsened by the sudden renewed traffic of MPs on their way through to the lobbies. As they passed, they each stared into the alcove. They were seeing Joseph sitting with one of the great names of contemporary politics, tongue-tied and threatening to break into a sweat. The Minister graciously behaved as if he did not know they were there.

'Yes, it's not a collective, this House: it's like a trading floor for a thousand competing individual enterprises,' Joseph said. It was the first ready answer to come to mind.

'Very apt.'

Thus encouraged, Joseph launched into a case that had been on his mind, a constituent who had come to see him with a housing problem, a tortuously complicated tale of muddle involving a dozen departments and agencies, which was consuming the poor man's life. Joseph was in mid-sentence when the Minister's young adviser noisily cleared his throat. Standing in the corridor with hands clasped behind his back, the young man had one foot forward and with it was tracing a little circle on the floor, his shoe leather scraping the stone surface. He began emitting little grunting noises, looked up, and peered closely at the latticework on the window.

'Sorry, that doesn't even begin to address your question,' Joseph said.

He was on the wrong track altogether, talking about the sort of things MPs can do to make themselves useful, when the Minister's great mind was on the larger question of how to remain in power indefinitely. Suddenly, inspiration came to Joseph in the form of Dave the journalist.

'We must feed the tabloid press, all the time, or they'll feed on us,' he said.

This time he had hit the mark. Something close to curiosity flickered in the Minister's masklike face, while at their side the Blinker stopped fidgeting. Suddenly, Joseph found it easy to talk, because on the day after Dave Drucker's visit, he had wondered whom he could contact for help. Mentally, he had gone through all the MPs and officials he knew – admittedly only a fraction of Parliament's huge contingent, but two dozen people at least, and of them not one had he ever heard say anything to suggest any familiarity with the ways of the tabloid press. If they mentioned tabloid newspapers at all, it was to ridicule them without admitting to having read them. Now, with an apparently interested audience, Joseph gave vent to his frustration without specifying its cause, and made some general comments about the need for like-minded MPs, who appreciated the importance of the vast audiences reached by tabloid newspapers, to maintain contact and exchange ideas.

As he finished, there was an unnaturally long silence. The Minister looked at him without a flicker of expression – for so long that Joseph wondered if he had caused offence. The real reason was that another gaggle of MPs had entered the corridor and was passing within earshot. When they were gone, the Minister looked at the Blinker. The glance lasted only a second, but some silent understanding passed between them. The angle of the Minister's eyebrow must have communicated that he was asking the Blinker's opinion. The younger man responded with a nod so brief that his head barely moved.

'You'll organize this?' the Minister asked. Or perhaps he did not ask, perhaps he used the imperative: his tone was so nicely calculated that either was possible.

'Need to find the right people,' Joseph said.

The Minister nodded again, brought out the gold pen, which hovered for a minute above a sheet of paper, and then he wrote six names in a neat column and he handed the paper across the table.

'You and Gerald should go into a quiet corner to discuss this further.'

Gerald was evidently the true name of the Blinker, who was now standing perfectly motionless, hands still clasped behind his back. He was squinting curiously at the traceries around the window. Supplied with half a name, Joseph now had an inkling of who the young man was: he was one of the small, elite squad of spin doctors who were reputed to have almost supernatural powers over the mass media. The vastness of the new government's majority in the Commons was said to be attributable to its corps of spin doctors. Anyone employing one of these magicians was guaranteed favourable treatment in the daily newspapers; anyone who offended them was damned. Gerald was one. But then, the great Minister had been one too – the greatest of all, in his day, so it was said. It was only to be expected that he would have a younger spin doctor at his side, like a sorcerer's apprentice.

The Minister put away his pen and stood, whereupon Gerald came instantly back to life, but only because the Minister was on the move and Gerald needed to fall in step behind him.

Joseph also rose to his feet, fearing that a rare opportunity to speak to someone at the centre of power was ending too quickly, before he had made full use of it. Desperate to render an offering of inside information, like a tribute to a powerful king, he threw out the only trivial snippet that came to mind: 'One thing perhaps I ought to tell you: I have a tabloid problem of my own. They were outside my house the other day, grubbing about in my private life.'

They were at the top of a small flight of steps by double doors leading into the lobby. Through the grilles protecting glass panels in the doors they could see a milling crowd of MPs waiting to vote. There would be no chance of continuing their conversation in there. The Minister paused for a second to look at Joseph in surprise, as if a complete stranger had started a conversation with him. To judge by the look on his face he was astonished, if not offended, at being burdened with anyone's private problems. Perhaps he intended to give some sort of answer, but that never happened, because the palm of his hand was already pressing one of the doors into the crowded lobby. As soon as the Minister was across the threshold, he was approached by a young journalist, for it is a law of dealing with the famous that you are never allowed more than a few minutes of their time before someone else takes your place.

The journalist had evidently never spoken to the Minister before, because he opened by giving his name and identifying the newspaper for which he worked, which was one of the upmarket dailies. The Minister turned his head slowly to embark upon an extraordinary monologue.

'There is no need to tell me who you are,' he said. 'I know exactly who you are, and I am taking a close interest in your progress. What you wrote this morning, on social security reform, was accurate and fair. Also yesterday's piece and your earlier piece about the Millennium Dome were both reasonable and fair. But I am afraid that the day before yesterday's piece, the day before yesterday's piece . . .'

The Minister was now shaking his head in sorrowful disapproval, as if the word that described the day before yesterday's piece was too painful to utter. Having listened with visible astonishment as the catalogue of his daily output was being retrieved from the Minister's memory, the young journalist tried to interject. To silence him, the Minister raised his voice a decibel.

'There is no division within the Cabinet, as you so wildly claimed. There is no rift – as you put it – between the Home Secretary, the Lord Chancellor, and the Chancellor of the Duchy of Lancaster. We have said we will publish a Freedom of Information Bill, and a Freedom of Information Bill there will be. On that, you may take it from me, the Home Secretary, the Lord Chancellor and the Chancellor of the Duchy of Lancaster are as one. They are always as one. The Cabinet is always as one, which makes it so very unlike the old Conservative Cabinet. And if ever there were a *rift* in the Cabinet, with all respect, I think that the first journalist to come upon it will be someone with more experience of the Lobby than you.'

With those words, the fabulously famous Minister went on his way, walking with long feline strides, head tilted to one side. Even after he had vanished from sight, the journalist continued to stare in the direction of his departure, shaking his head.

'What a fantastic star that bloke is,' a soft voice with a trace of strangulated northern accent exclaimed in Joseph's ear. It was Gerald, free to speak now that his employer had left. 'Do you fancy a jar on the terrace, mate?' he added.

·5·

The Sorcerer's Apprentice

An hour later, Joseph was out on the terrace overlooking the Thames, sitting at a square, wooden latticed table with one arm resting on the balcony. It was pleasant out, though the sun had long set. The mild weather and the brilliance of the lights along the vast wall of the House of Commons above gave the impression of a day artificially extended.

Gerald, who had momentarily disappeared, came back to announce that he had ordered champagne. Blinking four times in quick succession, he settled in a chair opposite Joseph's, produced a notebook and began to write. When a bar steward arrived with an opened bottle and two glasses, Gerald rubbed his hands in pleasurable expectation.

'Bubbly, bubbly, bubbly,' he burbled.

After the first cold sip, his restless eyes settled on Joseph. 'There are days when I think I'm dead,' he announced. 'Do you get that at all? But when I'm dead, I need only a glass of champagne to turn into Lazarus.'

'So you're a champagne socialist,' Joseph said. It was such a weak joke that he immediately wished he had not said it.

'We don't say the S word,' Gerald replied. Joseph could not tell whether that was a joke or not.

Gerald's first glass of champagne went down quickly. He poured himself a second, when Joseph's glass was still half-full, and continued scribbling. 'Could you pass us that list of names he gave you?' he asked.

Joseph handed over the list, though the request surprised him. He watched Gerald copy it into a notebook.

'What are you doing?'

'A memo,' Gerald said, handing back the list. 'I have to. My memory's shit, mate, compared to his. His is like Encarta, as you saw. If I don't remember, I'll get skinned alive. You'll action that idea of yours, won't you?'

'Action it how?'

'Do what you yourself suggested, mate. It was a good suggestion. But the cardinal point I have to underline, Joseph, is that a suggestion is never only a suggestion, when you're with him. He either knocks it down, or he wants it done. So don't misread the situation, mate: have something ready for next time you see him. Get some people together and get them working, but don't use his name. That only sets off waves.'

Joseph now wished he had kept his mouth shut. He foresaw a lot of embarrassment with little prospect of success.

'Just as a matter of interest, Gerald, from what I hear, the Home Secretary, the Lord Chancellor and the Chancellor of the Duchy of Lancaster are having an argument over freedom of information.'

'Having an argument? They're tearing lumps of flesh out of each other, mate. The PM will have to step in.' Gerald took a deep gulp of champagne, then caught the way Joseph was looking at him. 'What, mate?'

'That's not what your employer just told that journalist.'

'Bit of spin, mate, bit of spin, to cover the state the Cabinet's in. No, if he wants a Cabinet rift ventilated – and it is advantageous, sometimes – he won't do it by blurting it out to a junior reporter in a crowded lobby, mate. Not him. He'll be on the phone to a big boy, one of the big-time journos he can trust, one of his captured castles. Here, you said you were getting grief from one of the tabs,' Gerald added, evidently wanting to change the subject. He spread his hands out. 'Ask me anything, mate. That's the spin doctor's job. Sex or money?'

Joseph looked at him in surprise. It took a moment to deduce that 'Sex or money?' was a query about the nature of the newspaper story rather than a sleazy offer.

'Well, it's not money, so – sex, I suppose.'

'What sort? Sheep shagging?'

'No. No, sheep have never been my bag.'

'Woman or man, girl or boy?'

'I'm talking about an adult, heterosexual matter.'

'Shouldn't worry about it then. The only question they'll ask over there' – with a nod of the head he indicated the buildings downstream on the north bank of the Thames, behind which lay Downing Street – 'is can you take it? They all have to go through it: a love affair, a credit card bill, a careless remark – they all go through crucifixion for something, and the whole point is, mate, to show you can take it.'

So that was how he should view Dave Drucker's intrusion into his life, over which he had spent so many hours fretting: it was a rite of passage that went with public life. Such a casual attitude to his problems was disappointing and yet oddly encouraging.

Gerald was staring out over the dark river, blinking approximately every three seconds. 'Here, is it true that dolphins have swum this far up the Thames?' he asked. Joseph did not know. 'I heard they have. We ought to make more of it, press-release it on a quiet day: green government goes swimmingly.'

'Suppose the dolphins got here under the Tories?'

'You're a sharp bloke, aren't you?' Gerald said, with a blink and a sniff. By now, he was enjoying his third glass, while Joseph was nearing the bottom of his first.

Suddenly, Gerald's eyes narrowed. He planted an elbow on the slatted table between them and lowered his head to stare at Joseph over the rim of his glasses.

'Did you ever see the TV pictures of you asking the PM that question? The cameras caught the Deputy Prime Minister, sitting next to the PM, and the expression said bloody volumes. He loves all that stuff about the past and the present: it's his people looking after you, mate. You know that, don't you?'

'So I've heard,' Joseph replied. At once he saw the truth of Sir Peter's remark about trading in inside information. Joseph was grateful to the old Tory for having given him this snippet already, so that he was not indebted to Gerald, whose motive for suddenly releasing it he could not gauge. He was sure, though, that Gerald had a motive.

'Do we have to have all this dichotomy – middle-class/working-class, modernizer/traditionalist?' Gerald continued. 'Take my case, mate. They call me a spin doctor – spin doctor, tin doctor, make-sure-we-win doctor – but actually I'm a traditional social democrat. Can't you tell the Deputy PM for me?'

'But I don't know the Deputy Prime Minister.'

'You will, mate. You're going up. Tell him, tell him that I believe in old values. I've worked for the party since I was in my teens . . .'

'When was that, as a matter of interest?'

'The eighties,' said Gerald. His tone implied that everyone alive had had their teens in the eighties.

Joseph, twenty-one when the eighties began, was revisited by that feeling that he had come into politics too late. 'Late or early eighties?' he asked.

'Well, yes, all right, eighties moving over to nineties – but age is irrelevant. Fuck it, Joseph, my father drives a bus, and they call me middle-class!'

For a moment, there was a look of real anger on Gerald's face.

He poured himself more champagne in such a mood of rage that the liquid filled his glass and overflowed on to the wooden table. He leant forward to slurp from the rim. His attention was then diverted by an electronic pager attached to the belt of his trousers. He unclipped it and read it. 'Fantastic!' he exclaimed, handing the device over to Joseph. The message read: WHERE ARE YOU? PHONE MY MOBILE. RACH.

'Who's Rach?'

Gerald looked at him in such astonishment that for a full minute he did not blink. Then he burst out laughing. 'She works for you, mate.'

'You know my researcher?' Joseph exclaimed. He was surprised by this discovery, though he later realized he had no reason to be. He had already surmised from half-overheard telephone conversations that Rachel had at least one well-connected friend. She and Gerald were close in age and working in similar jobs in the same environment.

'Of course, of course. She's a great kid. I've loved a lot of great Rachels, but she's just about the best. I'm going to call her. Will you wait here, mate? You can read my pager messages, if you're interested. You press this button, right.'

Joseph was alone with an almost empty champagne bottle and an expensive pager which, after a few minutes, began buzzing again. He read the new message on the little luminous screen. It was from Rachel again: RING ME NOW AT ONCE, OR FORFEIT YOUR GONADS.

With nothing else to do, Joseph did as invited and flicked back to read some of the previous messages. He was impressed to see the name of one of the Prime Minister's political advisers. Further back, he uncovered another Downing Street adviser, and a Cabinet minister. Evidently, Gerald's pager number was a must in the Psion organizers of the powerful and famous.

'What do you think?' a voice said unexpectedly close to his ear. Gerald had returned.

'Did you speak to Rachel?'

'Yes, she's on her way. You can read the rest if you want, mate,' he said as Joseph handed back his pager, making it sound more like a demand than an invitation. 'Here, here, this one will interest you.'

At first, Gerald could not find the message that was going to interest Joseph. His eyebrows came together in a look of deep concentration and he blinked rapidly as he scrolled back and forth until he had found it, then he showed it off, grinning proudly.

There was a familiar name on the screen. It was the Prime Minister's name. It was a message to Gerald to ring the Prime Minister. It was mildly alarming to think that this fidgety, mercurial young man had access to the leader of the nation.

'There are only seventeen people who matter in this government, Joseph, and if I told you I know all of them intimately, it would be a gross understatement,' Gerald said. He had temporarily stopped blinking, and was peering at Joseph with a long, wide-eyed stare. Suddenly, he gave a little shudder, as if shaking away an unpleasant thought. He blinked and sat back. His mouth pursed in a resentful expression. 'And I hate it when people call me Moonface,' he said, as if this last remark followed directly from his earlier one.

'Who calls you that?'

'Moonface, Moonie, Moonatic: I've had the lot, mate, because my name's Gerald Moon, but I wish somebody would realize that I'm a socialist traditionalist. I hate spin. Really I do. I went to grammar school, you know. They think I'm a middle-class wanker, when actually – and this'll really surprise you – my old man John Moon drives a bus!'

'You've already mentioned your father.'

'Well, tell him, can't you?'

'Tell who?' Either Joseph was losing his concentration, or his companion was becoming incoherent.

'The Deputy Prime Minister,' Gerald declared, in the raised tone of someone who is tired of having to state the obvious. It was fixed in his mind that Joseph could influence the Deputy Prime Minister, and it was for that reason that he was plying him with champagne and precious nuggets of inside information. As Joseph was weighing up whether he should protest that he had no access at all to anyone in power, his companion's mood suddenly switched from resentment to delight. 'Hey, hey, hey – here she is, a rhapsody in blue!'

In the centre of the terrace was a ramp leading down into the ground floor of the building. Rachel was there, arms at her side, dressed in a dark blue dévorée jacket and trousers. Having stepped out of the light into the evening's darkness, she could not see Gerald, across the terrace, waving energetically. She walked forward uncertainly, an absorbed expression on her face, which suddenly told Joseph something about her. She either did not know that all around her middle-aged men were turning to stare – for there was no other woman in sight who could match her young good looks – or she had simply shut them out from her consciousness. For that minute, she was occupied with her own thoughts. Oddly, it made Joseph feel better about the bored look she had often brought to work with her. After a minute she spotted them, and her manner changed dramatically. She lifted her head, straightened her back, and crossed the terrace like a model on a catwalk. Gerald rose to his feet and pulled back a chair for her.

'Why didn't you tell me you were with Joseph?' she asked, giving Joseph a curt smile, as if he were someone she knew by sight.

'And miss a chance to talk about you behind your back? Here, have some champagne, kiddo.'

Joseph's relations with his young researcher had reached a

point at which he wondered whether he should encourage her to look for another job. It was not that they ever quarrelled, or that he had any valid complaint about her work, simply that her disappointment was all too obvious. But he did not want to lose her: she was obviously bright and, besides, no heterosexual male would want to part company with a woman who looked like Rachel. He wondered whether meeting her in a social setting might help.

'Seriously, I came in with the Boss and we spotted Joseph,' Gerald explained, unaware of that look. 'The Boss likes to test people with impossible questions. Isn't that what he did, Joseph: threw you an impossible question?'

'A tricky one.'

'You handled yourself well though, mate. You won't have done yourself any harm at all. You know, we're changing our mind about you. Those of us that are friends of the very lovely Rachel had been saying, get another job. I mean, who could turn her away? She could be anywhere in Whitehall.' Rachel frowned and gave Gerald a pleading look, but he continued unawares. 'But we now think she's started off in the very best position she could possibly be in, working for you, new MP on the way up. It's good. It's great.'

With that, Gerald disappeared to buy another bottle. Rachel shook her head, looked at Joseph, and rolled her eyes.

'He can be *so* gross. Has he shown you the famous message?' she asked.

'His message from the Prime Minister? Yes, I've seen his message from the Prime Minister.' He could hear himself speaking with the repetitive emphasis that came from too much drink. He was struggling to keep his wits sharp in a sea of champagne, and doing reasonably well, he thought.

'With the giveaway phone number?'

'The Prime Minister's phone number? That's a thought, that's a thought: there might come a day when the Prime Minister's phone number is a very useful thing,' Joseph declared, with a rush of enthusiasm. Rachel shook her head impatiently.

'Give me the pager,' she said.

As she took it from him, her hand brushed his. It was a pleasant sensation. Rachel flicked rapidly through the stored messages until the one bearing the Prime Minister's name was on screen. 'Look at the number,' she said.

It was a seven-digit number. The first three digits were 219, denoting a handset inside the House of Commons. Rachel put the pager down on the table and gave him a smile, as if all was explained, but seeing his look of incomprehension she explained: 'The Prime Minister doesn't have to leave a telephone number. Switch can find him. And he's hardly ever in the Commons.'

'You mean it's fake?' Joseph asked.

Rachel looked at him in astonishment. 'I can't believe you haven't worked it out. The message is years old. It was before the election, when he wasn't Prime Minister. Gerald keeps all the messages he ever gets from anybody famous. He's quite insecure.'

Mildly annoyed that he had not spotted this for himself, Joseph had a quick look through some of the other messages on the pager and came upon one from a politician who had been dead for more than a year. He tried to think of something to say to show that he too had got Gerald's measure, even if he had missed the significance of the 219 phone number.

'He talks a great deal when he's on his own, but when he was with his boss, he didn't say a word.'

'Yes, he's high by now.'

'High on champagne.'

'Or on the old recreational talcum,' Rachel said, half to herself, as she looked out over the Thames.

'Has he a skin problem?' Joseph asked, thinking it might explain why Gerald fidgeted so much.

The look of disbelief on Rachel's face made him wonder if he was missing the point, but before she could reply, Gerald was back.

They talked on. The towering southern wall of the House of Commons gave off strips of yellow light that cast a sheen over the Thames, while across the river, beneath the brightly lit monster that was St Thomas's Hospital, an undulating row of streetlights gleamed like a long string of pearls. Mostly, it was the young ones who talked while Joseph listened. He discovered from their chatter that there was another heaving social world in the same building as the one inhabited by MPs that Sir Peter had described the previous day. This was the world of aides and advisers, who seemed to be endlessly well-informed about each other's ambitions, foibles and love affairs. Though he recognized some of the names bandied about, he did not know their world well enough to join in.

Despite the late hour, there was a pleasure boat passing by. The revellers on its deck waved at the shadows on the House of Commons terrace. Joseph waved back.

How pleasant to be a Member of Parliament, he thought. How agreeable to be sitting on the terrace where the public was not allowed, drinking someone else's champagne, listening to the chatter of these clever, ambitious and well-informed young people. No one could touch him. He was protected by police and by the staff, by his access to the powerful and by all the pleasant privileges of his position. Frank Rist might bear him ill will, but Frank was a little person, far away beyond the security barrier. It was a life that he could get used to.

His reverie was disturbed by the division bell, summoning MPs to vote.

'Don't worry, don't worry: it's only a two-liner,' Gerald said.

That was right: it was a mere two-line whip. A look around the terrace showed that no one else was moving.

Gerald was talking again, but Joseph gave up trying to follow the erratic path of his thoughts, until the expression 'whip them into shape' commended itself to his attention. He did not know who or what was to be whipped into shape, but the words caused some irritant to tug at his memory.

Whip – Never Evil. Never Evil – committee. Committee – two-line whip.

'Shit, is it Tuesday?' he shouted, jumping to his feet, attracting startled looks. 'If it's Tuesday, I'm up the bloody creek. It is Tuesday. I should be voting. They asked me to vote in the two-line whip on Tuesday. Shit! I've missed it.'

'No, you haven't,' said Rachel. 'The bell's still ringing. Come on.'

Rachel was on her feet quicker than he was and led him down the ramp into the depth of the Commons. The way was blocked by a crowd of about twenty people in dinner jackets and smart dresses.

'This way!' Rachel shouted, leading him along the low, wide corridor to the left. They took a wide staircase two stairs at a time and ran across the tiled floor of a high hallway and along a short corridor into the vast Central Lobby. The police here understood immediately why an MP should be running breathlessly as the division bell rang, and shook their heads to indicate that he was cutting it close. A constable politely put out an arm to stop Rachel going any further. From here on, with a vote on, the way was open only to MPs.

He made it through the doors just in time, but then did not know which way to turn – he didn't know whether he was voting Aye or Noe, he didn't even know what the vote was about. There was no time to ask either; but Never Evil was at the door of the division lobby to the right, angrily waving him in. He was through the door, and his name was marked off, only seconds before the bell stopped ringing.

'Sorry, Neville. Got caught in traffic,' he said, panting, as Never Evil glared. 'Do you need me again?'

'No, bugger off home.'

He hurried back to the Central Lobby. It is a vast octagonal hall so high that the columns on either side of the main doorways accommodate three life-sized statues one on top of another, each with its plinth, the feet of the lowest statue as high as a man's head, while above the head of the highest the arch of the ceiling begins. From the point at the centre of the ceiling hangs an enormous gold chandelier. The eight walls are a morass of columns, plinths, statues, gargoyles and large latticed windows. Rachel looked tiny sitting on a low green bench by a far wall, but it was delightful to see her. Hardly knowing what he was doing, he strode across the tiled floor with echoing footsteps, and offered a hand to help her to her feet, which she accepted. He wanted to kiss her on the mouth. He could see by the startled look on her face that she could read his thoughts.

'You saved me from the wrath of the whips,' he said, still clutching her hand.

She frowned and looked past him into the far corner of the octagonal lobby. Looking over his shoulder, he saw what had caught her eye. There was a door that opened on to a passageway leading upstairs to the public gallery, from which a little group of visitors had just emerged, men whose hair had not recently been combed and whose shirts, ties, jackets and trousers appeared to have been lifted randomly from a draper's pick-and-mix. One had stopped to stare across the lobby floor at Joseph. There were streaks of grey in his hair and he wore a black biker's jacket. His lined, weatherbeaten face was familiar.

He nodded to Joseph across the hall – not the casual nod one gives to a stranger with whom one has made accidental eye contact, but a decisive gesture, implying recognition. It was accompanied by a muffled remark, uttered in a deep voice which echoed in the vast lobby, which could have been a none-too-friendly greeting. Without waiting for a reply, the man joined his companions as they passed through the exit, out towards the street.

'What a weird-looking man! Who was he?' Rachel asked.

'Someone I knew years ago. His name is Frank Rist.'

·6·

Frank Rist
1984/85

Frank Rist was a strange one: quick to make friends, quick to lose them, known everywhere yet not in with anyone. He was the one just outside the circle whose hovering presence made other people ill at ease. He did not care much for his appearance, but people's eyes followed him wherever he went. Because of his brooding, almost menacing manner, some women said he was attractive, but they found, as men did, that while it was easy enough to strike up a casual acquaintance with Frank, it was nearly impossible to know him. However, they all recognized an exceptional talent of Frank's: he was very skilled with his hands. While university-educated socialists around him paid abstract homage to the dignity of manual labour, Frank mended things.

Frank's marriage to Christine created a sensation in left-wing circles. She was the better known, her name being on the covers of a number of several well-received books on the case for social- ist feminism. Many of the sisters, like fussy parents, wondered whether Christine was 'making a statement' by marrying such a strange, brooding man. Some thought he was misogynist. They may have overlooked the impact that muscle and Byronic looks can have even on an intellectual who has written lucidly about how women can be complicit in their own oppression. Some of the men, more crudely, guessed that Frank was Christine's 'bit of rough'.

To outward appearances, their partnership worked well. Christine's house on a high bank in west Newcastle was transformed. Uninhabitable rooms were cleared out, floors polished, shelves erected, doors and windows replaced. It had been bought cheaply, and was transformed into a citadel where the various strands of the socialist movement could meet. Within it, Christine and Frank achieved a reputation as a political couple like Eva and Juan, or perhaps more like Rosa Luxemburg and her lover – for it was always understood that Christine was the leader. Those who hung around their house, like Deirdre, or Deirdre's best friend, Marsha, were known to some as 'Christine's chocolate soldiers'.

Joseph, a favourite chocolate soldier, may have been the first to know the secret that the marriage had failed utterly. It was so broken down that Frank had made a room for himself up on the attic floor, leaving Christine to live like a single woman in the large bedroom on the second floor. Joseph knew this because he had a way with older women. He knew that Christine was distressed, blamed herself, and did not want her sisters in the women's movement to know of it. She feared that they might put pressure on her to turn Frank out of the house.

Living only a short walk away, he would often stay late. Sometimes there would just be the two of them, talking away into the night in Christine's bedroom. This was the one room free from evidence of Frank's handiwork. She was an old hippie, one of the four hundred thousand who had been at Woodstock, and everything in the room evoked the sixties: the mattress on the floor covered by a chequered quilt, the oriental rugs, the blue bottles stuffed with dried flowers and joss sticks on the mantelpiece over the wide metal fireplace, the framed pictures by Kandinsky and

Mary Cassatt, and the crowded bookshelves, crudely constructed with bricks and bare planks, on which the distinctive olive green of the Virago imprint featured prominently. Along the floor stood a row of about a hundred LPs, mostly by women singers, arranged alphabetically from Joan Armatrading to Dinah Washington. The large window overlooked a steep grass bank, but because the street was built up and lit only on one side, the bank disappeared into shade after the sun had gone down, when only the main road, at the bottom of the bank, could be seen.

Sometimes, when it seemed that he and Christine were the only people left in the large house, Joseph would be aware of Frank descending from or ascending to his attic bedroom, like the discarded Mrs Rochester. Once, Joseph stayed so late that he fell asleep on Christine's floor, his back resting against the wall. He was woken by voices, and was surprised to see Christine crouching to talk through the keyhole of the bedroom door, which she had evidently locked. She was exhorting Frank to leave them alone.

Frank had another facility, though, which was of great value to those who theorized on behalf of the industrial proletariat: he could walk into a workingmen's club and be at ease with whoever else was to be found there. When the miners' strike began, and groups of eager sympathizers ventured south into the Durham or Nottinghamshire coalfields, they were glad to have Frank accompany them across the cultural divide. The longer and more bitter the strike, the more valuable Frank became. He was impervious to the inconvenience of having to get up during the night to travel south to be on the picket line at dawn. Once, he and Joseph were out in a borrowed van which broke down somewhere in County Durham, far from the nearest telephone. It was then that Joseph appreciated Frank's manual skills. The bonnet went up, and Frank was fiddling with a carburettor when a wasp flew annoyingly close to their faces. Frank brushed it away with the back of his hand, hitting it in mid-flight. The stunned insect landed on its back on the metal rim encasing the engine, where it hesitated for a fatal second to right itself. Frank slapped it, without deigning even to look at it. The wasp compliantly curled and died. For Frank, it was only a short distraction; he did not see anything special in the way he had dispatched the wasp, but Joseph did. It was the first and last time he had seen one of these terrifying insects killed with a bare hand.

Joseph was fascinated by the social life to which Frank had access in the Durham pit villages, where the miners accepted him and remembered his name. He was also struck by the chameleonlike nature of his friend's political opinions. That Frank was married to one of the region's best-known feminists showed when he mixed with the miners' wives and discussed the impact of the strike on family life in the pit villages; in the club, where the men drank, however, Frank would be around when remarks were made that would have made the sisters incandescent, and hear nothing untoward. He could distinguish the moderates and the militants, on sight. In one group, he would speak respectfully of the help and support coming in from the TUC and other sympathizers, while in another, he would assert that the miners stood alone, and stuff the fainthearts. Joseph might have suspected his friend of being a rank opportunist, except that there was nothing in it for Frank, who seemed to switch from one persona to another simply from habit. Joseph watched and learnt.

Still, he was surprised as he listened in to one of the political conversations that struck up at the club, when one middle-aged miner pronounced that it was all the fault of the Poles, selling their coal cheap on the British market. He wanted a boycott of all imported coal for as long as any British pit was under threat, and did not care too much if that caused the families of Polish miners to go hungry. Joseph wanted to intervene, but hesitated because he was here as a guest, and was grateful to a young miners' representative who replied that their enemy was the capitalist class, not fellow miners from abroad. His words gave Joseph one of those uplifting moments when he truly believed they were joined in a struggle from which all humankind would benefit. He was instantly brought down, to his surprise, by Frank, who pronounced in an argumentative, barroom tone that it was one group of miners or the other, and that he personally would rather see the British mining communities survive. The comment jarred.

He chided Frank for it when they were back in Christine's house. Here, the rest of the company was all female. There was a woman who worked alongside Joseph all day, another who had once loved him, one who appeared to love him, and even the fourth and youngest gave him looks suggesting more than a passing interest. Such an abundance of female attention gave Joseph more than sufficient confidence to take on Frank.

They were at opposite ends of a semicircle on the floor into which four of the six people in the room were arranged, some on cushions, some on thick oriental rugs. Frank's back was to the wall, one forearm resting on a raised knee, the other knee pressed against the carpet, his eyes a little bloodshot from the strong northern beer he was drinking direct from a dark bottle, his thick eyebrows lowered in a heavy scowl. He was in no mood to be told he was in the wrong by someone younger and less hardened by campaigning in the class war.

A neutral umpire would have said that Frank put his case more competently and more forcefully. It was a version of the eternal argument between what is right and what is possible, and in this, his first head-to-head contest with Frank, Joseph was defending universal ideals while Frank addressed the world as it was. The women joined in, one by one, starting with Christine. She was in the centre of the semicircle, on a low leather-backed chair, sitting forward with her elbows resting on her legs, as if she were conducting a seminar for the four people at her feet.

'Surely, Frank, we should never address the problem of domestic unemployment by exporting it. The British worker doesn't gain if the European worker is out of work.'

She spoke calmly and analytically, as always, using hand movements to emphasize her words, her eyes wide with sincerity. As usual, this only provoked Frank to insult her. In no time, he had reminded her that she was middle-class.

Whether Frank himself was truly working-class was open to sociological challenge: his father was a prison warder, more oppressor than oppressed, and yet a wage earner and a union member – until he was dismissed for a series of disciplinary offences related to alcohol. Unlike the older Mr Rist, Frank had been through some form of higher education. Nevertheless, in a competition to be the more working-class, he certainly had the edge on Christine.

Deirdre, by contrast, had been brought up by her mother on a council estate in Paisley. She also was utterly fearless in arguments, as Joseph knew from working with her day by day. She burst into the discussion to tell Frank that he was being offensive and 'talking shit'. Little Marsha, the youngest in the room, joined the attack behind her friend, reddening and talking excitedly, backing Deirdre, as she always did. They were an unlikely-looking partnership – Marsha petite and pretty, Deirdre squat, overweight and with a head shaped like a turnip. Marsha's parents lived in a quiet Bedfordshire village, where they ran the local pub. She looked like someone who was well brought up. Deirdre looked like a feminist scruff. Yet Marsha looked up to Deirdre with excitable reverence.

The vehemence of their joint attack had the perverse effect of calming Frank down, as if he enjoyed their anger. His face lit up with unfriendly amusement when, within a few minutes, he was likened to a fascist.

'It's interesting how feminists, who say we should relate the personal to the political, can be ruder and more personal than anyone I've known,' he remarked.

'No,' said Christine. 'Deirdre didn't call you a fascist.'

'Wash your bloody ears out: that's exactly what she called me.' Christine's reasonableness exasperated Frank.

'Deirdre pointed out that you're advancing arguments that were also advanced and taken to their extreme conclusion by fascists, which is a perfectly valid, analytic argument.'

'She called me a fascist, as a matter of fact. I don't hear *her* deny it.'

'No, Frank, the meaning of *fascism* is very precise,' Christine persisted. 'It's not a synonym for any creed that's right-wing and nasty, though it's frequently misused in that sense.'

And off Christine went, into an exposition of integral nationalism in the twentieth century. Suddenly Frank had one of his mood changes. He raised a hand, as if surrendering to his wife's relentless erudition, swore under his breath, picked himself up off the floor, and crossed to the back of the room, where a sixth person was sitting half-forgotten. It was Angel, as she liked to be called, though the name mismatched her temperament – a temperament with which Joseph was well acquainted. He and Angel had once been lovers. He was sorry to see her turning into one of those people who seemed to want to create reasons to be unhappy. Sitting alone on the settee, Angel could complain to herself that she was being ignored, though nothing kept her on the perimeter but her own disinclination to join the company. She brightened up, however, when Frank joined her, and soon they were immersed in a murmured conversation.

The other women all changed positions, moving an arm or straightening a leg as if Frank's move was everyone's cue to relax. Christine sank back in her low leather armchair, and hunted for something in a shoulder bag. She produced cigarettes, which she tossed to Joseph. A Rizla packet and a small ball of silver foil followed.

'Next year, we'll all be revisionists,' she said, with an eye on Frank, to ensure that he was not listening. 'Deirdre,' she added, 'why don't you run for the council?' Deirdre pulled a face and shook her head. 'Then I think we should put Joseph up for the council, or even – better still – send him to Parliament. What do you think? Let's make Joseph an MP, because nobody rolls a spliff like Joseph.'

'Funny qualification for an MP,' Marsha said, looking at Joseph from the corner of her eye as if sizing him up.

'And it's not right on ideologically to get a man to roll the spliff,' Deirdre observed. 'I think you're guilty of perpetuating a gender stereotype there, Christine.'

'But he's so very good at it. Watch.'

Christine and Marsha watched closely. It made him nervous. He had to concentrate hard to avoid spilling the tobacco in his shaking hands. Despite this distraction, a tightly packed joint took shape between his fingers.

'It looks like a dick,' Deirdre said.

He lit up the joint, took a quick drag, and passed the joint to Marsha.

'We're getting disapproving looks,' Christine said.

Frank had broken off his conversation with Angel to stare at the joint, though it was not its phallic appearance that offended him. Some wordless understanding passed between him and Christine. She gathered up her shoulder bag and a paperback book from the table at her side.

'Let's go upstairs,' she said quietly.

Nobody else moved. When Christine saw that no one was following her, she went red with humiliation.

'I'll go and make sure the radiator's switched on and it's tidy, then you can all come up,' she said, and she left the room.

Frank watched her leave, then turned to continue his conversation with Angel.

'How's the mortgage?' Deirdre asked. 'I'm talking to Frank.'

'What about it?' Frank asked.

'Paid off, is it?'

'No.'

'Lucky that Christine pulls in a big salary then.'

This time, Frank was not amused. He brought very little money into the house, living off Christine for much of the time, and did not like to be reminded of it.

Seeing an unpleasant confrontation in the making, Joseph intervened. 'What was going on there?' he asked Frank. 'You looked as if you were trying to order Christine out of the room.'

'I was trying to order *her*?' Frank replied, as if he went through life taking orders from Christine.

'That stare, Frank.'

'I have an agreement with Christine, right, that anybody who's going to smoke dope – upstairs. *Spies* can see through this window.'

It was true that the ground-floor windows had no curtains, but it took a special paranoia to imagine police agents peeking in from the dark bushes on the steep bank across the street. Marsha, whose head was already lightened by the drug, burst out laughing, then put a hand guiltily over her mouth to stop herself.

Frank's eyes opened so that the whites were visible, above and below the pupils, and he stretched out an arm and shook his head violently, as if some horror had been revealed to him, requiring immediate action. He jerked himself to his feet with such a sudden movement that Marsha started and watched in alarm, as if she feared she was about to be attacked. Frank left the room with a heavy footfall.

Once he was out of sight, Deirdre leant forward, pointed at the window and whispered loudly, 'Spies!' This set Marsha off again, laughing without inhibition.

Joseph wondered if he ought to go to the back of the room and talk to Angel, who was alone again and was listening resentfully to the other women's mockery. He could not think what he would say. Their affair had not ended well, and he was not entirely sure why she paid these sporadic visits to Newcastle from her London home. Ostensibly, she came to see Joseph, but she plainly preferred Frank's company, and might have been hovering, buzzardlike, over the decay of the Rists' marriage.

Soon, Frank was back in the room, beckoning Angel. She made a little skip as she crossed the room, as if pleased to be escaping. Joseph noticed them holding hands as they left. Then he heard the sound of the front door closing, and voices on the pathway outside. A minute later, Christine was back in the room, her face flushed. The open-eyed stare she directed at Joseph and the accompanying forced smile warned him to ask no questions.

'We can put the music back on,' Christine said. 'Any requests? How about Nina – Nina Simone?'

'What about a man, for a change?' Joseph pleaded.

'Which one?'

'Anybody.'

'Jimmy Somerville or Tom Robinson,' Deirdre suggested. 'They're gay.'

'So, don't you think Joseph would be a good MP, Marsha?' Christine asked, as Bronski Beat came on. She had sufficient friends and contacts to make the idea of sending Joseph to

Parliament realistic. Marsha assented, with surprising emphasis, as she held her breath to let the drug take effect, turning puce around the cheeks.

'Are you ever going to pass that joint on?' Deirdre demanded.

'If the miners are defeated, and I think they will be, we'll go into a long cycle of consensual parliamentarianism. That's why we need our people in Parliament.'

'Just one problem,' Joseph said. 'I'd be useless at it.' It was Marsha, having now parted with the joint, who asked why. 'Well, I haven't got the egotistical self-regard,' he replied. He felt at ease with these three, the more so because the cannabis was taking effect.

'That's a good argument in your favour,' Christine said.

'Also, I've got no ambition.'

'I think you are ambitious,' Marsha said.

Secretly he was tempted, but in the end nothing came of it, except possibly that the conversation stayed in Joseph's mind, and affected the decision he made much later, many years after Christine had first put up the idea that he should be an MP.

After another half-hour, Deirdre announced that it was time for the party to break up. She and Marsha were taking the last bus. Joseph stood up to go too, but Christine pleaded with him to stay longer, hinting that she had something else to say to him. While she was showing the other women out, Joseph wondered idly where Frank and Angel had gone, and whether they would be back. Then he became more interested in Christine's book collection.

She came back into the room, bestowing a brilliant smile on him.

'Now, what music would *you* like? Somebody who's not gay, I expect.'

After the record had been changed, she added, 'She's a very strange woman, that Angel, but I'm glad Frank has found a friend.'

'You don't see her as any sort of threat?' Joseph asked. He had seen the way Angel looked at Frank.

Christine sat on the floor, gathering the hem of her dress under her knees, and gave him a loaded look. 'Baby won't run off with another woman,' she said in a peculiar voice. 'Baby' was a name she used for Frank when they were alone. 'Perhaps it would be easier if he could, but Baby can't do that. Baby don't care for shows, Baby don't care for clothes: I wonder what's wrong with Baby.'

Indeed, Frank Rist was a strange one.

·7·

A Constituency Surgery

Every fourth Saturday morning took Joseph to the High Street, a street more down than high, reduced to near dereliction by the suction of money away to the hypermarkets and shopping malls. High Street shoppers in the part of south London that was Joseph's constituency travelled in buses, not cars, and paid with paper money instead of plastic cards. They were people with problems. He drove to this sorry street, parked his car in a backyard where a locked gate protected it from vandals, and slipped through the back door of a building stained and cracked by age. He went into a small room where the only furniture was a folding chair at a folding wooden table which creaked under the weight of the only expensive item in the room, a new computer system paid for by the House of Commons Fees Office. The walls of this small room had been painted the colour of scrambled egg many years ago, and were decorated with posters from elections held in the sixties. The other piece of office equipment was a rusting green filing cabinet on which stood an electric kettle. He made himself a fortifying coffee before the first knock on the door.

'Come in, Thelma!'

The front of the old shop was already full of people queueing. They were the people who made Joseph feel useful. They brought him their problems and had faith in his capacity to find answers, and though that faith was mostly misplaced, they were the nearest he would ever get to fulfilling a boyhood dream. He had had a dream that he would be a great man who would see faces turned towards him in gratitude. Much of his life had been spent drifting through jobs, learning the familiar truism that there are no great causes any more, no more revolutions, no more Dunkirks, no more dawns in which it was glorious to be alive. All that is left for an idealistic dreamer is to rummage around in the infinite number of small things to do.

Thelma Driver, who ran his constituency office, did not come in when invited. Instead, she hovered by the open door, giving Joseph a view of one fat arm and fleshy shoulder clothed in a dark green cardigan, and a broad dark face in profile topped by thick, black, curly hair and sweat droplets along the hairline, her eyes moving from whatever lay beyond the portal to Joseph, and back. She was a solid woman, in every sense, who had worked for years for no reward until Joseph's election had enabled him to pay her a small salary. He found her demanding and difficult, but she was his solid defence against intrigue in his own backyard. The local Labour Party would never oust him for another candidate while he had Thelma watching his back. But this morning she seemed distracted. Standing by the door, she kept peering out into the waiting room with a frown, as if anticipating trouble out there.

'How many this morning?'

She took a deep breath and raised her eyebrows, but did not answer directly. 'There's a bit of crowd, Joseph. Sixteen, so far.'

'And I've told Margaret I hope to be home for lunch with the children. We'd better get on. Who's first?'

Case one was the Afzal family. They were different from the run of supplicants whose problems generally arose from poor education, poverty, physical frailty, or personal inadequacies. Mr Afzal and his tribe, by contrast, were sturdy, hardworking and well-to-do.

They ran a local tandoori. Mr Afzal was planning the wedding of his eldest daughter, and wanted to invite a host of aunts, uncles, cousins and other relatives from scattered villages in Kashmir but was being blocked by officials who behaved as if they suspected him of trafficking in illegal immigrants.

'Mr Pilgrim, I would gladly pay a £1,000 surety for each of my guests who is flying to England, and if they are not returning on the set day, the government may confiscate my money. That is how sure I am of my legitimate request,' Mr Afzal complained.

Joseph promised him a letter on House of Commons notepaper, addressed personally to the chief executive of the passport and immigration service.

Case two was a regular visitor. He was an elderly man with a wasted body and an oversized round head. The lines on his face and the poverty of his clothes were evidence of a life of hardship which must have been compounded by being so small and round-shouldered, when his life had been spent on the roughest council estate in the borough. Yet he never complained. He spoke gently, in precise, crisp sentences, and had piercingly alert eyes. Intelligent and resourceful, he had only one obvious character flaw: he was quite mad. He came to Joseph each week with a new story about aliens and high-tech conspiracies. There was nothing Joseph could do for him, but since he always waited patiently and caused no trouble, he was allocated five minutes on each visit.

Today, he was grappling with a new and disturbing mystery. He had been sitting on the sofa, in his tenth-floor flat, when a thought came to him. Later, he turned on his television, and there was the President of the United States, at a press conference in Washington, uttering the same thought, word for word.

'And it went on happening, Mr Pilgrim. The next day it happened. And the next day, and again the day after that. I ask myself, can this be coincidence? But it can't be coincidence. The road of reality is broad as it's wide with many a warp and wrinkle in it, Mr Pilgrim. You know that, I know that, but even taking that into account, this can't be assigned to natural causes: it's too frequental and recurative. It's the CIA.'

Here, he came to a halt, as was his occasional habit when he looked for a reaction. Joseph tried to appear sympathetic without actively encouraging him in his lunacy.

'The CIA?'

'Look at me, Mr Pilgrim: do I presume to be an important man? Why should the President of the United States need thought waves stolen from a plain, simple man? Do you believe that the President would steal the private thoughts of a private man? The CIA would, though.'

'And how in fact do they do this?'

'Don't you know?'

'No, I'm not an expert on the CIA.'

'Nor am I, Mr Pilgrim, but I read it. I forget where. They have a thingamy of some description. It might have come off the world wide web. I can't recall exactly how it functions or what its name is, but it's a thingamy of a nuclear nature, a nuclear particular of Japanese design, undetectable to the naked eye. You'll have to come in person to my flat and hear the clock on the wall. It has begun to tick in a most unnatural rhythm. Not your tick-tock, tick-tock, more like tick, tick, tickety, tick, tick, tickety – bloody tick, bloody tock, bloody odd, Mr Pilgrim. You'll have to come round and familiarize yourself. That's how I got radiation sickness . . .'

After five minutes – not a second more, not a second less – Thelma opened the door and announced firmly that time was up. Joseph's visitor never objected to being cut off in mid-sentence, but stood up, shook Joseph's hand, and took his leave.

'It's a Mrs Jones next.'

Thelma often accompanied these announcements with a look

that told Joseph something about the person he was to meet, particularly if it was a first-time visitor. Thelma would watch the visitors and sum them up as they waited outside. If they were drunk, they did not get past the door. The name 'Mrs Jones' did not convey anything to him, but neither did Thelma's expression. She was looking out into the waiting room, as if distracted by something happening out there.

Mrs Jones was younger than the usual visitor: she looked scarcely old enough to be married. Pretty in a rough way, she had her hair pulled tightly back, emphasizing the puppylike plumpness of her cheeks and a Gallic nose. Her almond hair colour did not look natural. She was tightly wrapped in a fake leather coat, and her head was thrown back, as if in defiance of the world. Without waiting to be asked, she took the seat across from Joseph, and from a shoulder bag she produced a pile of paper nearly an inch thick which she put in front of him. She then unbuttoned her coat, silently and fussily making herself comfortable. There were at least a hundred separate documents in the pile. She was evidently expecting him to read them.

It did not take long to draw the outlines of her life story and the problem that had brought her here. It was a dispute over children.

'How old are your daughters, Mrs Jones?'

'Sharon is twelve, Kayleigh is ten.'

His immediate thought was that it was not biologically possible. She was obviously too young to have a twelve-year-old daughter, but when he looked closely, he deduced that she might be older than he had first thought, possibly in her late twenties. There was something innocent about her expression that understated how much she had experienced. He discovered that one of the documents in front of him gave her year of birth as 1970. If the daughters took after their mother, Mrs Jones would be a grandmother in the first year of the next millennium.

Now that she had unbuttoned her coat, he noticed that she was wearing a smart tartan skirt and navy-blue blouse. He had already seen enough of the documentation to know that clothes like that must have cut deep into her budget. He deduced that she had dressed up to pay a call on her MP. He was reassured. Too many of the people who tramped through his surgery were so engulfed by their problems that they were past taking proper care of themselves, making them difficult to help. He was able to scrutinize her at will because she was taking no interest in him, staring instead into the corner of the room while chewing her lower lip, as if intensely preoccupied with her own thoughts

'So, you have custody of the girls, but your ex-husband has visiting rights,' he said, returning his attention to the documents. 'He is allowed to see them two weekends a month.'

'I'm not letting 'm.'

'Mrs Jones, there's a court order . . .'

'I know there's a court order, that's why I came.'

Now she was taking notice of him. She was sitting up straight, looking him in the eye, ready for an argument.

'What actually do you want me to do?'

'See to that order. An' I'm called Dawn, actually.'

'But as an MP I have no authority over the courts, Mrs Jones, Dawn.'

'But I'm not ever letting that *man* near my girls.'

From the defiant fury in her eyes and the venom she concentrated into the single word 'man', he guessed that she was used to using a stronger expression to describe her children's father.

'But is it reasonable to take the attitude that a father should never be allowed to see his daughters?'

Dawn Jones threw up a hand in a gesture of exasperation, as if it were beyond her comprehension that the world should contain people who thought her ex-husband had a right to see their children. She suddenly stood up. He feared that she was about to walk out in anger, but she turned a hip towards him and, to his surprise, pulled at her clothes, drawing up the blouse and lowering the skirt a fraction, to exhibit the flesh around her hip and stomach. In the middle of the white was a huge, vivid bruise, fully four inches in diameter. It had turned the colour of turpentine.

Having exhibited it for long enough to be sure that he had had a good look, Mrs Jones tidied her clothes and sat back down. In place of that earlier defiance, she now had the satisfied look of someone who thinks she has scored a decisive point. She was right. He was shocked.

'Your husband did that? How did he do it?'

'Fist.'

'He must pack a hard punch.'

'I've got a better one than that,' she announced. 'I'd show it you, if you were a lady MP. It's on one of me frontal assets.'

'Where?'

'Bosom.'

She had quite large breasts for a small woman. The thought that a powerfully built man might have punched her there was repellent.

She had taken out a cigarette and was looking for her matches. Tobacco smoke would draw a disapproving reaction from Thelma, but instead of trying to stop her, Joseph took a box of matches from a top drawer, declining the cigarette offered in return.

'And you're right,' she continued, 'he packs a very hard punch. They could stick him in a ring with Mike Tyson. I even wish they would.'

'Does he often hit you?'

She took a drag on her cigarette before answering. 'Soon as look at me.'

'And you're worried that he'll hit the girls?'

'No. He's never going to hit my girls, because he's never getting near enough, ever again. No discussion, that's it. So they can stuff their court order. I thought you might help, seeing as you're my MP.'

He liked this defiant manner. It was a relief from his too-frequent meetings with people who had lost the will to fight.

'Yes, of course I'll help. I'm not sure how, but I will. Can you leave all these documents with me?'

'I need them.'

'Yes. I'll have them photocopied and bring them round to you early next week.'

After Mrs Jones, there was a run of housing problems: badly built homes, bad street lighting, and badly behaved neighbours did more than anything else to fill up his surgery. The most difficult case in this morning's run was that of a youngish woman driven almost to the point of mental instability by a leak in her roof which had caused streaks of damp in her infant daughter's bedroom. The mother, who was almost in tears, explained that she and the child were now having to sleep in the same bed every night. The little girl was prone to bed-wetting. Joseph took down her details and promised a stiff letter to the Director of Housing, though he thereby risked a confrontation with Thelma. She did not believe that it was the job of an MP to interfere in the affairs of the local council.

'How many more?' he asked, three hours and a dozen complaints later. It was now very close to the time when he should be leaving if he was to keep his promise to be home for a family lunch.

Thelma drew a breath before answering. 'Five more, Joseph, or four.'

The telephone in the adjoining room rang. Thelma started.

'Is there something the matter today, Thelma?'

'There's a man who is constantly on the phone,' she said, obviously irritated by the caller.

'Did he give a name?'

Thelma frowned and looked out into the waiting room. Joseph thought for a moment that she was not going to answer.

'Mr Drucker,' she said.

The journalist: it was more than a week since he had been on the doorstep. Joseph had been wondering whether he would hear from him again. His reappearance would surely mean trouble.

'Put the call through, and give my apologies to the people waiting.'

A minute later, he was listening to Dave Drucker, whose south London accent sounded more menacing over the wire than it had when they were face to face.

'Sorry to disturb your constituency surgery, Mr Pilgrim: just a little thing I wanted to check, yeah. You did say that you and Frank Rist were friends when you were in Newcastle, didn't you? That's confirmed, yeah? What kind of circle did you, yeah, mix in?'

'I don't understand the question.'

'It was, like, a left-wing circle, yeah?'

'Yes.'

'And to relax, yeah, did you go down the pub? You must have relaxed somehow. Did you go to somebody's house – Mr Rist's house, like – and relax there, yeah, smoking dope?'

Thelma had returned and was standing by the open door again with that anxious look on her face, evidently wanting to break in to tell him something.

'Where is all this leading to? What's your point?'

'Wasn't it a bit hypocritical to vote how you did the other night, Mr Pilgrim?'

'Which night?'

He had lost any handle over what Dave Drucker might be talking about, and was distracted by Thelma's agitated manner.

'Tuesday night, Mr Pilgrim. The Hansard record is here in front of me . . .'

'Mr Rist.' That was Thelma's voice breaking in. She marched indignantly out into the next room, and Joseph heard her indignant exclamation: 'Mr Rist, excuse me!'

·8·

A Constituency Surgery (cont.)

Frank Rist was in the next room. Joseph could even hear that familiar voice, its staccato syllables drawn from deep in the larynx. He could not make out the words.

In his other ear, Dave Drucker was talking monotonously about Tuesday night's Hansard, but he wasn't making sense. Joseph put down the receiver and stepped through to the next room.

Frank was sitting on one of the folding chairs in the middle of the room, long hair falling in untidy waves on the shoulders of a black jacket made of fake leather. There was an air of battered authority to him, despite his scruffy clothes. He had taken charge. With a pad of paper on his knee, he had assembled the remaining supplicants in a circle, as if he were leading a discussion group.

'Ah, Joseph,' he said, as if he was resuming a briefly interrupted conversation. It was the first time they had spoken in twelve years. As he continued, Frank waved aloft the notepad in his hand. 'Mrs Baker here has been confronting the bureaucrats. You ought to listen to her story. It tells us that the offices of the borough council are infested with the worst degenerative socialism. Mrs Baker has been gobbed off and fobbed off by job's-worth after job's-worth, Joseph, and she is looking to you, her elected representative, to help. Isn't that right, Mrs Baker? This is the fourth time she has been to see you, and she was put at the back of the queue, by Thelma. And that's the second time Thelma has done that.'

'Three and a half hours, last time I was here,' Mrs Baker announced, with a triumphant nod.

Frank's allegation that Thelma was deliberately sending Mrs Baker to the back of the queue of visitors at his surgery was likely to be true. Thelma had known her for years, and was sure she was nothing but trouble. Joseph had been willing to believe the stories of official harassment the first time he received her in his surgery, but there were too many stories, too many people involved in a campaign against Mrs Baker to be believable. Joseph had since met several of her neighbours, all of whom seemed to be reasonable people, who relayed a catalogue of complaints about her spiteful, unpredictable behaviour. She was an aggressive and disturbed woman. The housing department was going through a painfully slow process of having her moved to another estate where her particular talent for falling out with those around her might find fewer outlets. It was an open question whether she would agree to move, or claim she was being persecuted.

Mrs Baker was now sitting with arms folded, her eyes fixed on Frank, in whom she seemed to have detected a kindred spirit.

Joseph cleared his throat and announced, 'Mrs Baker has been invited to accept a housing transfer . . .'

But Frank cut in. 'Joseph, Joseph, Joseph, Joseph Pilgrim, I know all about Mrs Baker's transfer, I know all about that. How convenient, how very bureaucratically convenient to shove this woman out of sight, on a sink estate. How degenerately socialist.'

Thelma, whom Frank had been resolutely ignoring, gasped with indignation, put her hands on her hips and raised her eyes to the ceiling.

'No, I'm not talking to you, Thelma,' Frank announced. 'I'm talking to Joseph Pilgrim, Mrs Baker's parliamentary representative, someone I know from way, way back, and who's not much changed – not hot, nor cold, but lukewarm, if you ask me. Here is Mrs Baker, an ordinary citizen, meeting nothing but obstruction and obfuscation from socialist bureaucrats, and do you feel any passion to right what's wrong? Neither hot nor cold, Joseph, but lukewarm.'

Here, Thelma emitted a snort so loud that it stopped Frank in mid-flow, and momentarily he had a struggle to remember what else he wanted to say. He waved his writing pad towards another complainant, a tiny little man with long, thin strands of white hair. 'And Mr Parker, here . . .'

'Frank,' Joseph said quietly.

Ignoring him, Frank stood up to rest a hand on the shoulder of Mr Parker, a small, elderly, submissive workingman. 'Mr Parker has told me a story which I find totally disturbing.'

'Frank –'

'Mr Parker went to Barking on a bus and while he was sitting on the upper deck . . .'

'Frank,' Joseph said for the third time, suddenly raising his voice. 'This is an MP's surgery. What are you doing here?'

'What are *you* doing, Joseph, my former friend?'

'Constituents should be allowed to come here, to meet their MP, without this sort of disruption.'

'These good people have been waiting for hours, and Mr Parker, as I say, was on the bus to Barking . . .'

'Mr Pilgrim can only see one person at a time,' Thelma interjected, at last breaking the silence she had maintained with reluctance. 'I told Mrs Baker that she needn't wait, she could go and do her shopping and come back, but she insisted on sitting here. And I don't know what *you're* doing here. As Mr Pilgrim says, it's an MP's surgery.'

'And look at the environment you make them wait in, Thelma, Joseph, look at this disgusting room. Is this how you treat the people who elected you?'

Frank was now standing in the centre of the room, orating like a fundamentalist, or like the narrator of *Kubla Khan*: his flashing eyes, his floating hair, the sweep of his arm across the patchy walls, bare floor, and old cheap chairs and folding wooden tables made his point powerfully. He was right: it was a disgusting environment.

Thelma opened her mouth, but Frank was not finished.

'No, Thelma, I'm still not talking to you: I'm talking to Joseph. I have worked-out reasons for talking to Joseph, because he is the elected representative of the people and he is answerable to these good people in a way that you're not. You're an employee; he's the representative. So, Joseph, let me tell you why Mr Parker's here, just briefly. It won't take more than a few minutes of your valuable time, Joseph.'

He looked defiantly at Joseph, daring him to say that his time was in fact too valuable. Joseph remembered the family lunch and felt his gastric juices bubble from hunger.

'But he's not the next in the queue,' Thelma cried.

'No, he's not, he's not, Thelma. Quite right. He's definitely not: I'm next in the queue,' said Frank. 'I've been next in the queue for at least an hour, Thelma, as you know, because I have been surrendering my place in the queue to one neglected person after another. As you know, I was here half an hour before your doors opened. I've seen everything. Now I'm giving up my place to Mr Parker. Joseph, my former friend, where are you going now?'

Joseph had crossed the room and was at the door leading out into the street. 'Can you step outside, please, and we'll talk there?' Seeing him hesitate, Joseph added, 'Out, or we call the police.'

'Ah, ha, ha, ha, the police, yes, the police; how keen exsocialists are to call the police.'

This implied a previous occasion when the police had been summoned to deal with Frank Rist by people he called 'exsocialists'. But Frank did not elaborate. With a swaggering walk marked by a slight limp, he followed Joseph out on to the pavement. They came face to face against the background noise of heavy traffic. It was the busiest time of the week on the High Street, but the pavement was not crowded and the few passing shoppers hardly seemed to notice the two men eyeing one another.

Seen close up, in daylight, Frank's face had been corroded by the years. The roots of his hair had greyed, the eyes were more sunken than before, the cheekbones more tight drawn, the nose had sharpened and the teeth were bared in an odd, rictus smile. Yet there was an energy in his gaze and in the low, strong cadence of his voice that suggested that the animal strength and obsessive sense of purpose was still in him. Yet though Frank was not afraid of eye contact, he was unable to hold it. His dark pupils bounced restlessly off Joseph's face to some point on a wall behind him, upwards to the roof, then back to Joseph, but without properly focusing before they started off on another perambulation.

It was important for Joseph's purposes to try to locate Frank politically; for there would certainly be a political motive of some kind behind his unexpected appearance. His obvious hostility to council officials, and his deliberately inaccurate description of them as 'socialists' implied a radical break with beliefs they had once held in common, but his taunts that Joseph was lukewarm implied a strong belief in something.

'I suppose you know I've had a journalist on my doorstep, bothering my wife and children. Dave Drucker is his name, and he has just rung me again.'

'No, I didn't know that. I'm sorry to hear it.'

That was not the reply Joseph had expected, but it came straight back, with a finality that was intended to close off conversation rather than to inform.

'Well, somebody has been talking to him, and I think it's you.'

'Not me, my friend: I don't talk to newspapers. Newspapers are corrupt. I write for *Spike*.'

'*Spike*? What the hell is *Spike*?'

'You don't know *Spike*? You should get linked up, my old china. It's the hot new web site and if you look at it, you might read something that concerns you. That's my friendliest advice to you, and I won't say more, if you don't mind, because you've already threatened me with the police.'

Frank Rist raised his hand and made a circular movement in the air in an exaggerated gesture of farewell. Joseph was on the point of grabbing his shoulder, furious that he should be walking away without giving a straight answer, but Mrs Baker had emerged from the surgery and was watching, with arms folded and an unpleasant smile. Through the murky glass of the shop front that served as a constituency office, the faces of Mr Parker and the other supplicants could be seen staring out. Rather than make a fool of himself in front of his clientele, Joseph allowed Frank to walk away, with limping gait, his long hair bobbing against his jacket.

Wherever Frank lived, the likelihood was that at least an hour's journey lay ahead of him, such were the difficulties of reaching this suburb from any other part of London. It would appear that Frank had sacrificed up to five hours to whatever purpose had brought him here. But there wasn't time to wonder why Frank had nothing better with which to fill his life. The last handful of constituents had to be interviewed, and there was the irritating puzzle of that unexplained call from Dave Drucker.

Tuesday night, the journalist had said – Tuesday was the evening he had spent drinking with Gerald Moon and Rachel.

Mumbling an apology, he hurried past the gaggle of waiting constituents into the privacy of the back room, and was dialling Never Evil's constituency office number when Thelma put her head round the door to ask if she should send in Mrs Baker. He replied testily that Mrs Baker could wait. 'If that journalist, Dave Drucker, rings back, I need to know at once.'

Never Evil, like Joseph, was holding his constituency surgery and could not be disturbed. His secretary took a message.

He remembered that Rachel owned a small mobile telephone, of which she seemed inordinately proud. She had made him take down the number. He dialled it with little expectation that she would answer, but soon he could hear her voice against a noisy background.

'Rachel, it's Joseph: do you know what a web site is?' he asked.

'Say that again: I can't hear you.'

'I said, have you ever heard of something called a web site?'

'A web site?'

'Yes.'

'Joseph, I can't believe you don't know what a web site is.'

'Well I don't. What is it? Nothing to do with spiders, presumably.'

'You really don't know what a web site is?'

'I really don't.'

'Switch on the computer.'

With some difficulty, Rachel explained to him, step by step, how to log into the world wide web. It emerged that Joseph had his own password, which she had set up for him on his office computer. Astonishingly, the same password applied although he was using a different computer fifteen miles away.

'What's the web site address?' Rachel asked.

'What?'

'The web site address?'

'What does that mean?'

'What web site are you looking for?'

'I don't know. He said something about *Spike.*'

'What?'

'*Spike.*'

'*Spike* what? *Spike* dot com, *Spike* dot org?'

'Is that English or another language?'

'Wait, I know what it is, I've heard of *Spike*. They're a bit loonie, aren't they?'

'Could be.'

In a few minutes, the problem was solved, and the printer stored beneath the trestle table had come alive. Meanwhile, in answer to the looks Thelma was giving him from the doorway, Joseph had to agree to see Mrs Baker. She, for one, had thoroughly enjoyed Frank Rist's peculiar performance. She sat opposite Joseph with a satisfied smile.

He was struggling to explain why it might be best for her to accept a housing transfer when Never Evil rang back. Though reluctant to hold a conversation in Mrs Baker's hearing, he feared she would take it badly if asked to leave the room. On the other hand, he did not want her listening, so he did not protest when she nosily picked up the sheets of paper he had taken from the printer and left on his desk.

'Neville, the late-night vote on Tuesday, the one you especially wanted me to be there for – what the hell was it about?'

'Tuesday, Tuesday, Tuesday,' Never Evil replied, evidently struggling to remember. 'Ah, Tuesday, I know – we had a plonker wanting to legalize cannabis. But with your help, we squashed it. *Muchas gracias* from me and the Chief.'

Mrs Baker was shaking her head and clucking. She gave Joseph a look filled with malicious amusement, and held up one of the pages from the web site. First, he took in the by-line – 'by Frank Rist' – then the headline:

HYPOCRITES' CORNER
The anti drugs reform MP who used to roll an expert spliff

His look of horror caused Mrs Baker to burst into cackling laughter. She sounded like the witch from *The Wizard of Oz*.

.9.

Lady Draycott

He had a fright, but in the end it was not too bad. Early on Saturday evening he beat a retreat into the back bedroom that served as a study, to minimize the disturbance to the rest of the family as he dealt with the telephone calls which came one upon another once the Sunday newspapers had exchanged their first editions. In addition to a dozen journalists, he had to deal with a highly stressed party press officer, and with Gerald Moon, who rang several times on behalf of someone much more important, whose name was not mentioned. Since there was no point in denying Joseph's youthful dalliance with marijuana, the Important Someone suggested that he issue a statement regretting this folly and strongly and firmly opposing any move to make cannabis legal or to reduce the penalties for its possession. Joseph did not want to sign up to anything so reactionary, because at heart he thought that the drugs laws were too strict, but he had put himself in a cleft stick by the way he had voted the previous Tuesday. (Twenty times he swore to himself that he would never again go through the division lobbies without knowing what he was voting for.) Having accidentally made a stand against legalizing cannabis, he had to put up some sort of case for keeping the law as it stood, at least for the time being. After negotiations that went backwards and forwards as Gerald Moon rang off to take further instructions from the Important Someone, they agreed a statement that avoided using the word 'legalization' but mentioned 'depenalization' as one option to be considered. Since no one knew what 'depenalization' meant, it was mutually agreed that the word could do no harm.

Margaret arrived with a glass of chilled wine. She seemed to find the situation funny, once the children were in bed. She was detached from his political life, having declined the role of full-time MP's wife – though, but for Margaret, he would never have been an MP. She was the one who had pushed him into offering himself as a candidate in their local constituency, after he had complained of being bored by his minor job as an executive in a publishing company. Since the seat had been held by the other side for a quarter of a century, no one really thought it was winnable – except Margaret, who had studied the opinion polls and the local election results and done the appropriate calculation. On election night, when Joseph was so astonished by the result that he was almost driven to apologize to the shattered man he had unseated, Margaret had been almost drunk with triumph. In the middle of the night, she rang her poor Conservative mother, dragging her out of bed to announce that not only were the Conservatives beaten more thoroughly than anyone had ever foreseen, but that the feckless son-in-law was an MP.

Since that triumphant night, Margaret had left him to get on with it as if politics were a private hobby.

A copy of Dave Drucker's article lay by the fax machine. Margaret picked it up, read it through, laughed, and said it made him sound like 'a right junky' – as if that was not a serious problem for a public figure. Then she added, presciently, 'Surely you can't be the only MP who has taken dope.'

And that, Joseph decided later, was what saved him. There were, in fact, an uncounted number of MPs in their forties or younger burdened by the same guilty secret, who watched with close interest and noted with relief how he had emerged with his career undamaged. Most of the mail Joseph received from the public was sympathetic too, though he also had a handful of abusive letters from people who believed he certainly ought to be out of public life and possibly inside a secure institution.

Margaret made one other comment, which he took seriously: that he ought to try to find out what had driven Frank to extend his activities from attacking Joseph on an obscure web site to collaborating with a tabloid journalist. 'I always thought Frank was quite strong-principled,' she remarked.

'What do you mean?' Joseph exclaimed. 'Have you seen this bloody web site? It's barking. Really, unpleasantly barking. And most of his barking ideas are a world away from what he was saying ten years ago.'

'But even people with funny ideas can have principles,' she said.

They tried to think of anyone they knew who might still be in contact with Frank, but he had fallen out with almost everyone. He had changed for the worse since Christine's death. The only possible exception was the person Margaret dismissively recalled as 'that weird woman who was in love with both of you'. Margaret had always resolutely refused to remember what Angel was called.

Angel was surprisingly easy to locate: she was in the telephone directory, still listed at the address in Clapham where Joseph used to visit her in the bad days when their relationship was breaking up. But having a worthwhile conversation with her over the phone proved to be a challenge beyond Joseph's reach. It started badly because he was expecting some sort of expression of pleasure, or surprise, or some variation on 'however many years has it been?' – but there was nothing like that, only the hurried 'hello' of one who has been interrupted at a bad moment. His apology for being out of touch for so long was met with an unnerving silence.

'So, how are you?' he asked.

'I'm all right,' Angel said.

He expected her to return the enquiry, but she seemed to be waiting for him to get to the point.

'Well, this will probably come as a bit of a surprise, but I'm an MP.'

'Yes, I know. Frank saw you on the news.'

'Frank Rist?'

'Yes. He saw you ask the Prime Minister a question.'

That told him the first thing he needed to know from her, that she and Frank were in touch.

'Well, how would you like to have tea with me in the House of Commons one day?'

In his brief experience, this was an invitation no one could resist; yet Angel hesitated. Finally, she accepted, and they arranged a time. He would have to hope she would be more forthcoming when they were face to face.

He was more disturbed by evidence that someone had been in his office in Millbank. The unknown visitor had pulled back his chair, apparently to sit on it, and had moved things on his desk. Messy though his desk was, he knew his own mess from somebody else's. At first he assumed it was Rachel, his assistant, who had free access to his room; but she denied it, and he had no reason to disbelieve her. This left him wondering uneasily whether Frank Rist might have found a way past the twenty-four-hour security at the building's entrance, which ought to have been impossible. He learnt the identity of his visitor about an hour before he was due to meet Angel, when he was disturbed by a light knock on his office door. His fellow MPs strode up and down and banged on doors with the loud confidence of people who were proud of their right to be there. This was the quiet approach of someone who did not want to be heard.

'Who is it?'

She entered with a rustle of expensive clothes: Diana, Lady Draycott, wife of Sir Peter, who closed the door quietly, stood with her back to it, tall, imposing and out of place, and said, 'I suppose all you New Labour puritans don't keep drink in the office.'

She had hidden the years well. He could still have taken her for a woman in early middle age, though he knew that the shining auburn of her hair must have been artificially preserved. She was dressed in a long, well-fitting lilac dress and an olive-green outdoor jacket with a thick fur collar like a scarf, which she wore as a man would, with buttons undone and her hands pressed down into the side pockets.

'I have some wine, if that'll do,' Joseph said, jumping to his feet. He indicated the sofa, and at once wanted to apologize for it. As she sat, she tested it by running a hand along its back.

The room seemed to be larger and sparser for her presence. It had been in Joseph's mind to throw out his old kettle and invest in a cafetière, to transfer some books and a few ornaments from his home to brighten the shelves full of featureless government documents, and to select some pictures and photographs for the walls. Now he wished he had made a priority of all that.

Then he wanted to apologize for the wine, which was in a bottle he had kept standing in a cupboard for several days. It was embarrassing to be serving white wine at room temperature. And then, for a bad moment, he thought that he had no glasses, until he remembered two that had accumulated dust at the back of another shelf. The office, fortunately, was equipped with a small sink in which to rinse them. This operation took time, time filled by a strained silence. But when he handed her a full glass, she looked him directly in the face and gave him a wide smile, as if to indicate that the sofa, the wine, the glasses and the decor were, indeed, substandard, but she thought none the worse of him for it.

He was not wholly surprised to see her. He assumed that every conversation he had with Sir Peter was relayed to her, enabling her to be kept informed of his affairs by proxy; but the old knight was too well bred to ask questions about something as personal as Joseph's former experimentation with drugs. Diana had therefore to come and find out for herself.

While he resumed his place at the desk, she took out a cigarette and a holder, and lit up without asking his permission, sentencing him to spend several working days amid the smell of stale ash. He was glad of the several feet of faded carpet between them. The cigarette holder was about two inches long and made of tortoiseshell-coloured plastic, and so oddly unfashionable that it made Diana look her age for the first time. *It can't be the same one,* Joseph thought. The smoke momentarily made her eyes water. She waved it away with a slow flick of a bony hand, and screwed up her eyes, emphasizing the crow's feet that spread across her cheekbones.

'I called by the other day,' she said. 'I meant to leave a note, but of all the ridiculous problems, I couldn't find anything to write with.' With a nod in the direction of the untidy heap of paper on his desk, she added, 'I do hope I didn't the spoil the arrangement.'

'Stop being sarcastic, and tell me why you're here.'

The time when he had been in awe of Diana Draycott had passed. She was still someone whose good opinion he valued highly, but he understood now that she was neither wealthy enough nor well enough placed to be the person she aspired to be. Years earlier, he had seen her name creep occasionally into gossip columns, where she was described as a hostess, in the days when Peter Draycott was being written of as a future Cabinet minister. Then they were Mr and Mrs Draycott. He became 'Sir Peter' as a consolation prize for not making it to the top.

Diana took a drag on her cigarette and flicked away the ash. 'Imagine my surprise: I had a phone call out of the blue, this morning, from Angel.'

Diana was distantly related to Angel's mother. It was through that connection that he had first met the Draycotts.

'That's probably because of me.'

'It's certainly because of you. The poor girl seems to have had a terrible shock hearing from you. I think my task is to chaperone you. You're due to meet her in Central Lobby in an hour. I'm going to walk across there with you, if that's all right. Her request.'

'That's a bit odd.'

'I thought it was rather appropriate. It will make up for my signal failure to protect the poor girl's honour years ago. Didn't you deflower her in my house? What I didn't know at the time, of course, was that you were a raving drug fiend as well.'

'Diana, I was an occasional user of cannabis, which I gave up years ago, and I didn't deflower her, at your place or anywhere else, though you did very kindly put us up for a night, I admit – oh bloody hell, I don't have to answer to you. Somebody is running a vendetta against me, and I thought Angel might be able to help.'

In a few words, he described Dave Drucker's visit to his house, Christine's death, and his recent encounter with Frank Rist.

'Didn't I tell you not to get involved in left-wing politics? You ignored me, and now it's landed you in trouble. You should have concentrated on womanizing. That was what you were good for.'

'That's not fair.'

'Really? *Really?* The world seems well enough populated with women who've had sexual relations with you.'

'No it isn't, that's not true,' he asserted. He could not tell whether she was still merely making fun of him, or whether an edge had crept into her voice, signalling some buried resentment. Whichever was true, he wished she would change her tone. 'Besides, all that kind of stuff. It's not remotely a matter of legitimate public interest.'

'That won't stop the blessed newspapers, my dear. We are not in an age when anything is private any more. It's forgotten that Western civilization was built by men with the appetites of rabbits.'

'Like George Washington.'

'Like George Washington. But now if the President of the United States has a strumpet in his office, they make it a constitutional crisis. But was Hitler faithful to his timid little mistress? Oh, very good, obviously the sort we need. It wasn't at all like this when Sir Peter and I were young. Fornicators fornicated in peace and private, and why not? The Prime Minister's wife was able to have a child by her lover, who was one of the most outrageous buggers in London and a liar and a friend of gangsters, but did it matter? All that the Conservative Party asked was that buggers should bugger discreetly and keep up the decencies in public life. When Peter went seat hunting, one was hawked around a hundred dreadful coffee mornings as a demonstration that Peter had lust, wholesome, properly channelled lust. It was bloody awful.'

There was colour in her cheeks, and for a moment she looked drawn and tired. The time Peter Draycott had spent battling to be adopted as a candidate in a suitable seat, twenty years earlier, was a bad memory. She held out a now-empty wineglass for Joseph to refill, and resumed talking as he poured.

'The tragedy is,' she continued, 'that one knows so many talented queers who have had to marry themselves to frightful women. And I suppose Margaret T. was a little to blame, though she was very good about fornicators. Do you know that she would have kept Cecil in the Cabinet, notwithstanding that he had fathered someone in office hours, until the great horde of semi-literates dragged him down? And then, of course, she was dragged down too. And in her place, we chose a drip.'

'I didn't think it was the press who finished off your friend Cecil,' Joseph said. 'It was the representatives at the Conservative annual conference.'

'That is *precisely* whom one was referring to,' said Diana.

Spoken with startling vehemence, this was the sort of remark a politician's wife would not normally make out loud, however heartily she thought it, and especially not to an MP from the opposing party. Like the use of obscenities in mixed company, it showed either that she thought she knew him exceptionally well, or that the wine had had such a rapid effect that she didn't know what she was saying. What it certainly demonstrated was that Diana was deeply, bitterly angry with people on her own side of the political divide – angry in a way that those who have given their lives to politics can be. He could not gauge whether her grievance was the downfall of Margaret Thatcher at the beginning of the decade, Peter Draycott's failure to reach the Cabinet, defeat at a general election, some purely personal hurt, or some combination of all four. She seemed to have come to Joseph as a man might go to a prostitute for favours he dare not ask of his wife, to express sentiments she would not utter among her own people.

Suddenly, she mentioned a name from the past, a long-dead Conservative MP much respected in his day by those who shared his narrow opinions, which Joseph did not.

'Didn't he die in mid-term?' Joseph said, recalling a parliamentary by-election that had marked the start of a famous career.

'On a couch such as this, my dear, in a room not far from where we speak,' she said, running her hand along the sofa's back. 'Do you know what was beneath him when he breathed his last? Sorry, I shouldn't say *what*. She was ghastly, but she was still a *who* not a what. Some women here seem to become besotted with the men who employ them. So, there they were, sealing her contract of employment, in a manner of speaking, when he tragically expired.'

Much as Diana disapproved of gossip, she had a shameless talent for collecting and disseminating it by word of mouth.

'And it didn't make the papers,' Joseph exclaimed, battling to stop himself forming a deeply sexist image of young Rachel.

'Those were the days. Those *were* the days. Has all the wine gone?'

'Not quite. You finish it.' As he poured, he remarked, 'This is all fascinating, Diana; but it doesn't help.'

'So, you have an obsessed man in pursuit. That is a bore.' She tapped her wineglass with her fingernails. 'Yes, that is a bore,' she repeated. 'Such a bore. This sort of thing has happened to several colleagues of Sir Peter, as you know.' There was a hint of mockery in the way she referred to her husband by his full title. 'There's always someone in the background with a grudge to work off. Not usually a man: the problem is usually an obsessed woman. Whether it helps that you have an obsessed man, I couldn't say. But since he's the nub of your problem, is there anything you can give him which he wants? What does he want? Alternatively, can he be frightened off?'

'I don't know quite what he wants; I doubt whether I can give it to him; and I have very strong reservations about making any attempt to frighten him.'

'So what's your strategy?'

'Strategy? Phew, strategy. In so far as I have a strategy, it's to avoid giving him another opening. I rather let myself in for it by voting the way I did on drugs legislation. In a way, once I've voted against legalizing cannabis, it's legitimate to expose the fact that I used to indulge in it. But anything else he knows about me has just got no public interest element in it at all. And if he's thinking of dragging up his own wife's death, that is just awful. And to imply that I was involved is downright slander.'

Lady Draycott was silent for a moment, except for the tinkle of a fingernail tapping her wineglass.

'I might be able to put you in touch with someone, someone with *le pouvoir*. I'm not sure quite how to approach him. I'll talk it over with Sir Peter and give you a ring.'

The wine was finished, and the business had been dealt with.

She stood up. 'Shall we go and wait for Angel? I'll stay to say hello, then I'll try to slip off.'

The pavement along Millbank had been rendered impassable by a party of Japanese enjoying their first sighting of Parliament. Joseph and Diana, walking arm in arm, had to step on to the road in face of oncoming traffic. Fortunately, in this part of the city, no vehicles ever move quickly. The pair's jagged progress towards the frontage of the House of Commons was almost completed when Diana stopped unexpectedly, pulled her arm away from Joseph's, and tapped him with the back of her hand.

'That man,' she said, pointing across the road towards Westminster Abbey.

'What of him?'

'What is he photographing?'

The man across the road turned on his heel and vanished down a walkway leading to the abbey, as if he knew they were talking about him.

'Wait!' said Joseph, taking off across the path of oncoming traffic, ignoring the blaring horn of an irate taxi driver. There was no sign of the photographer along the narrow pathway. He hurried down the full length of it, past neat flowerbeds. Outside the visitors' entrance to the abbey, which towered above to Joseph's left, two or three hundred people were crowded into a small space. Beyond them was another crowd. The pavement over to the right was also teeming with humanity. The man with the camera was not to be seen.

He rejoined Diana on the pavement outside the House of Lords. Her expression had changed. She was staring at him with an intense, almost accusing look.

'Well?'

'I lost him.'

'And what was he photographing?'

'I don't know. I didn't get a chance to ask.'

They resumed their walk, but Diana now clearly did not want to join arms with him again. As they approached the vast building, with its elaborate buttresses and its multitude of statues, she said, 'Joseph?'

The question stopped there.

'Yes?'

She stopped walking and turned to face him, the unspoken question now hanging heavily between them. She even succeeded in keeping her unwavering gaze on him when a trio of tourists pushed between them.

'Diana, there can't possibly be any reason why anyone should have photographed us. It just simply isn't possible.'

'Then why did you run after him like that?'

'I was just going to ask him what he was up to. I mean, how or why would anybody be waiting to catch a photograph of us together? Just think about it. There is no reason, and it isn't possible.'

But her suspicions were enough to spoil the atmosphere. They went on into the vast, crowded building, walking side by side in grim silence, as if they had quarrelled. They arrived in the same huge octagonal hall where Joseph and Rachel had spied Frank Rist. Exasperatingly, Angel was late. They sat and waited on one of the benches for twenty minutes, after which Diana stood up and sighed with exasperation.

'Angel has become very odd,' she announced, as if Angel's oddness was the source of all the tension between them. 'You know she lives like a recluse in that falling-down house. And she can't keep a bloody appointment. If you see her, give her my apologies, but tell her I couldn't wait a minute longer.'

Joseph stayed for another twenty minutes, but there was still no sign of Angel, so he gave up. Back in his office, he tried to ring her at home, but there was no answer.

·10·

Dinner at the Club

Lady Draycott was on the telephone within days of having promised to introduce him to 'someone with *le pouvoir*'. He was in a good mood even before he heard her voice. Rachel had been in his company for two or three hours, finding one reason after another not to go back to her shared office along the corridor. Their relations had dramatically improved during the recent excitement, which had convinced Rachel that working for Joseph was an experience worth living through. His files, his office shelves and his correspondence were sorted out as never before, as he indulged in the secret, unalloyed pleasure of talking to her and watching the way she moved. She looked so elegant today, in a dark brown rib rollneck sweater made of some sort of soft stuff – neither wool nor nylon, but a mix of yarns – a honey-coloured cavalry corduroy skirt reaching almost to the ankles, and long black boots with buckles on the outside, and with her black hair meticulously parted in the middle, that she could have posed for a fashion magazine. His rise to prominence had made him an employer worth dressing up for.

'Now, let me guess,' said Lady Draycott, 'what are the odds on you owning a presentable dinner jacket and black bow tie? A thousand to one?'

'Why the hell would I want a dinner jacket? What do you think I am, a Tory?'

'Then get out pen and paper. I'm going to give you the address of a good outfitter's shop. You're to hire a penguin suit with appropriate shirt and bow tie next Tuesday, for dinner with Sir Peter and friends at their club.'

'Tuesday I'm doing a live radio broadcast.'

'What time?'

'Late. Eleven till one in the morning.'

'That's all right then, you can do your broadcast on a full stomach. Frankly, I'm amazed they let you near a microphone. I hope you're not going to encourage impressionable young people to behave as badly as you did.'

'Don't worry, the party press office has given me a fat folder full of things I am allowed to say so that I don't express a wrong opinion. Tell me about this dinner. Will you be there?'

'Strictly boys only.'

'Then I don't want to go: I'd rather have dinner with you.'

Rachel, who was filling a black plastic refuse bag with old reports and minutes, turned her head to listen with interest.

'Yes very gallant, but you'll go anyway,' Diana replied. 'And don't go expecting a good time, because it's not your sort of thing at all. But somebody's going to be there, somebody who can help. Sir Peter will make the introduction. Forgive me if I don't say who, but I'm calling from somewhere slightly public. By the way, I'm told you feature rather prominently again in this web site called *Spike*. What a hoot. Have you *seen* the sites it's linked to?'

He was surprised that Diana should have visited *Spike*, though he had noticed before that she was an avid reader of any source of political gossip, no matter how outrageous. Frank Rist had posted a long description of his morning spent in Joseph's constituency surgery, under the headline

WAITING FOR GOD
– Because that's who my old comrade seems to think he is

When he first read it, Joseph had tried to convince himself that he did not mind. He told anyone who asked that it was more likely to upset his hardworking constituency organizer, Thelma, but this was politician's-speak. In reality, he was confused and distressed by the campaign Frank Rist was waging against him. He was not used to being disliked.

'Who was on the phone?' Rachel asked.

'Somebody you don't know about.'

'You seem to be very fond of her.'

'I didn't say it was a her.'

'But it was, though. Is she the visitor you had the other day, that you didn't tell me about, the one who smoked cigarettes with long thin filters, and used Nina Ricci L'Air Du Temps same as my mother?'

He arrived by taxi, flustered and late, at a large building that might have been impressive when first built many decades earlier, but now looked dark and empty between the brightly lit shops adjoining it. He had to climb dark stairs to enter. Inside, in a booth behind a glass panel, was an attendant in green uniform and top hat who called him 'sir'. Beyond, there was a spacious hallway whose high walls ahead were covered in large oil paintings, all portraits of men in Edwardian or Victorian dress. Beneath the portraits, a wide staircase turned round two walls, so wide that the space beneath had been converted into a small sitting room. The tiles of the hall floor were small black and white squares. Joseph would have liked to explore upstairs, but the attendant instructed him to turn left. A long corridor lined by more portraits ended at a door beyond which he heard male voices. Here he stopped and asked himself whether this was actually a good idea. He was uneasy about being in a club from which women were barred, and he felt idiotic and conspicuous in his hired dinner jacket, which had attracted ribald comments from other MPs. Because of his uneasiness, he had weakly allowed himself to be drawn into a drinking session in one of the cavernous bars below ground in the House of Commons, so that he was not entirely steady on his feet. He had also failed to find an opportunity to ask Sir Peter for the name of the special guest he was here to meet.

However, he went on in. The room was cramped at first sight, with almost its whole floor space taken up by a large dining table, around which men in dinner jackets had already gathered in groups of two or three. He was relieved to see Sir Peter among them. The dark walls were covered with yet more portraits: nearly all men, again, but there was one woman dressed in frills, evidently an actress. She was the only semblance of female company. Beneath these *oeuvres manqués* silver cutlery had been set out for a dozen places. A waiter was circulating with a silver tray bearing glasses of red and white wine; Joseph helped himself to what turned out to be good-quality champagne.

Sir Peter came directly over to introduce him to someone whose name he did not quite catch: Henry Hugely, or something phonetically similar, whose off-hand manner seemed to say 'I know this is a great honour for you, young man, but I will pretend that the pleasure is mine.' Joseph did not like to ask directly whether this was the 'somebody who can help' he had been brought here to meet, but soon deduced that he was not. Sir Peter also introduced him to a peer whom he remembered as a Cabinet minister from many years back. Again, this was not the 'somebody who can help'.

'Our star guest is late again, so let's begin anyway,' Sir Peter said.

At dinner, the peer was at the head of the table. Sir Peter was at his left, and the missing guest should have been at his right, but his place was empty throughout the meal. Joseph was placed next along, between the empty chair and Henry Hugely, whose conversation assailed his left ear through three tasty courses, though Joseph never discovered who he was. Sir Peter had warned Joseph that there would be 'larking about', but there was none while they were eating. He wanted to ask the identity of the missing guest, but was embarrassed by his own ignorance, and too far away from Sir Peter to lean over and whisper the question. The conversation was so serious and dull that Joseph was again overwhelmed by the feeling that he should not be here.

He took off his jacket because the room was stuffy, and was surprised to see the waiter advancing on him in a menacing fashion. Everyone was suddenly looking at him.

Sir Peter explained. 'Joseph, we leave our jackets on. Club rules.'

The pattern of conversation was that Hugely would air an opinion at formidable length, then halt to ask whether Joseph agreed. Having by now lost track of what he was being told, Joseph took the easy course and said that he did. Pleasantly surprised that a 'Labour man such as yourself' should share his point of view, Henry Hugely would set forth on another topic. Joseph had a blurred suspicion that he had spent the evening agreeing with propositions which, sober, he would have found repulsively reactionary. But despite the opinions pouring in one ear, he was able with the other to follow snatches of what Sir Peter Draycott was saying. 'Goodness me, they had stature,' Sir Peter exclaimed wistfully of the great men who led the Conservative Party in its glory days, men like the old peer sitting at the head of the table, who was listening with a self-satisfied expression. 'Men who proved their worth in and out of politics, men and Margaret, or am I *laudator temporis acti*?'

The old peer did not think so at all, whereas Joseph did not know because he did understand the Latin quotation.

Sir Peter was complaining about the 'young chaps' who now

controlled his party. Too many, in his opinion, had gone straight from university debating clubs into full-time politics without pausing to work in the world outside. 'Awfully good at talking the language of the leaders we admire, but the pith is never there. I'm afraid we're in the age of the epigoni,' he said.

Joseph wanted to join in with a description of the contrast in his own life, between the radicalism of his youth and the compromises he now accepted, but a glimpse of the benign, flabby face of the old peer made him think that tales of violent picket lines might not stir him to anything but chortling indignation. He did, however, make a cautious observation, struggling not to slur his words.

'Do you know, when I was young, someone I liked very much who was a radical from the class of 'sixty-eight told me how much more hard-headed we of the late-seventies generation seemed to be.' (He was referring to Christine, whose death had been much on his mind: she had in fact compared Joseph and his contemporaries to young Bolsheviks, but caution told him not to repeat the word.)

By the end of the meal, Sir Peter had moved on to the loss of public esteem for politicians generally, made worse, he believed, by the manner in which they were caricatured in contemporary fiction. 'There are only two kinds of politician in modern fiction: the out-and-out rogue, *à la* Francis Urquhart, or the politician as fathead, as in *Yes, Minister*. If only there were a Trollope or a C. P. Snow to catch us as we actually are, in all our imperfections, though I admit the result might be awfully dull: all jaw-jaw and nothing much happening, as in that very long novel by Anthony Powell.'

'Have you thought of writing your memoirs, Sir Peter?' someone called from across the table.

Sir Peter paused, as if considering the matter. 'To be quite candid, I already have,' he said. This caused a ripple of interest which he sought at once to dampen, raising a hand in demurral. 'One won't be putting them on the market, I'm afraid. After much blood and toil one discovered that one had nothing terribly new to say. There was a working title though, of which one was quite proud – "I Seem to Remember".'

He repeated 'I Seem to Remember' as if he were savouring its cadence, but quietly, so that no one except Joseph heard him. Joseph was overtaken by a rush of affection for the old Tory. Other ex-ministers would have filled the evening with self-justification and self-aggrandizement, but Sir Peter just did not have the conceit so common in the profession.

'May I read your memoirs?'

'Oh, I don't think you'll find them of any interest.'

'No, no, I would very much like to read your memoirs, please.' He was prepared to argue the point.

Sir Peter nodded, as if in assent, but before Joseph could exact a spoken promise, there was some sort of commotion at the door. A man who seemed to be an official of the club was whispering urgently to Sir Peter, who rose to his feet. Someone else arrived – a tall, solidly built, curly-haired man. Evidently he was the missing twelfth guest. He was dressed in a two-piece suit rather than one of the dinner jackets that made the others look like eleven penguins. Joseph could tell at once that this was 'somebody who can help'. His importance was manifest in the respectful silence that fell over the other guests as he was ushered to his place, though the look on his youngish, cherubic face conveyed more bewilderment than a sense of power.

Sir Peter remained standing, and tapped a wineglass with a spoon for silence. 'While Jonathan, our honoured guest, is waiting for his food to arrive, let's observe the formalities, shall we?'

To Joseph's surprise, somebody at the lower end of the table jeered. It seemed such a grossly rude reaction to an innocuous announcement, but no one else seemed shocked. Sir Peter even raised a hand in acknowledgement.

It was a joke, the first symptom of the evening's 'larking about'.

'First, I want to introduce someone who is dining at our club for the very first time.' He was interrupted by cries of 'hear, hear'. 'Joseph Pilgrim, sitting at my left, unusually for someone at our table, though it's not unusual in the House of Commons – he's a Labour man.' Jeers. 'That's why he's on my left.' More jeers. 'But he's a very good friend of mine, and I'm jolly glad he could come.'

Loud cheering erupted round the table. Palms were slapped against the tabletop. A bemused smile had come over the man called Jonathan.

'Now,' said Sir Peter, 'our President will present the report of the annual meeting.'

The ageing peer at the head of the table raised his substantial bulk off his seat to jeers and catcalls. He was holding a large, leather-bound book, and had put on bifocal spectacles. To judge by his beaming, rotund face, he was enjoying himself.

'The minutes of the annual meeting,' he announced, looking slowly from face to face as he spoke. 'I move. Minute one: our dining club shall be named Another Club.'

Loud, prolonged jeers.

'Two: the club shall be administered by a committee' – here he paused, giving his audience their cue to resume jeering, and he paused again after each noun – 'whose membership (*jeers*), meetings (*jeers*), documentation (*jeers*), administration (*jeers*), and adjudications (*jeers, booing, catcalls*) – shall be maintained NOW AND FOR EVER in utmost secrecy' (*loud, prolonged cheering*).

Amid the cheers, someone was heard to cry, 'Oh, very British!'

'Three, Another Club shall meet for one purpose, its main

purpose, and no subsidiary purpose shall interfere with this main purpose . . .'

There was some more jeering, but the noise quickly died away, as the mood appeared to turn suddenly solemn. He waited for complete silence.

'Four, the purpose of Another Club shall be . . .' The President paused again and threw back his head for the finale: '. . . TO DINE!'

The cheering, clapping, table slapping and foot stamping rose to a cacophonous climax. Even the man named Jonathan was caught up in it, applauding with enthusiasm. He could be heard crying, 'Oh, bloody good!' Later, when Joseph pulled together his sporadic recollections of the evening, he recalled to his dismay that he, too, was cheering loudly, with one hand executing a wild circle above his head.

Sir Peter, who was applauding with more restraint than the others, leant over to whisper, 'It's all frolics, as you can see. But you absolutely must speak to Jonathan as soon as you can.'

'Who the hell *is* Jonathan?' Joseph whispered back, but Sir Peter had already turned away.

'Jonathan, may I introduce Joseph Pilgrim? One of tomorrow's men, and a very, very old and dear friend of Diana's.'

'Diana?'

Not a good start: the great man, whoever he might be, did not recognize Diana's name.

'My wife Diana – Lady Draycott.'

'Lady Draycott! I do apologize. Yes, Lady Draycott, yes indeed. Wonderful woman.'

Correction: it was not Diana's identity that had confused the twelfth guest. He remembered Diana clearly, but did not recognize Sir Peter. Unfazed, Sir Peter continued, 'Joseph is enjoying a rather sudden rise to prominence, partly welcome, partly unwelcome. I'm sure he'll tell you more, but, if you'll excuse me, I must circulate.'

As Sir Peter stood up, Joseph suddenly felt furious with himself. He still had not done the single most important thing he had needed to do: he had not found out the identity of the important guest. Now it was too late. This was likely to be another of those critical moments like the day he questioned the Prime Minister, and once again he was hopelessly unprepared. All he could do was busk it. Last time, he had busked it and all had worked out well.

Making a quick guess, he inferred that the mysterious Jonathan must be a high-flying libel lawyer, one of those who attract six-figure fees.

'I was placed next to Lady Draycott at a Guild dinner,' Jonathan was saying. Joseph waited, expecting more, but the mysterious Jonathan only nodded, as if the seating arrangements at this distant dinner fully explained his intimacy with Lady Draycott.

'I met her twenty years ago,' Joseph replied. 'And I do agree: she's outstanding.'

'I ought to have remembered that she is married to, to . . .'

'Sir Peter.'

'Sir Peter, Sir Peter,' the man named Jonathan chanted. 'What's he like, actually?'

'Solid and honest. He should have been a Cabinet minister.'

'Should he? I didn't know that.' Jonathan seemed to have taken Joseph's expression of opinion as if it were fact.

'I think he should. He'll never be one now, of course.'

'No,' Jonathan said thoughtfully. 'No, I suppose not. Do you enjoy modern politics?'

'Well, it's full of variety. Do you enjoy being up in court?'

The question seemed to startle the man named Jonathan. Instead of replying, he gave Joseph a sharp look.

'What I *don't* enjoy,' Joseph added, 'is one of the bloody papers poking about in my life.'

'Oh? Which one?'

Joseph named Dave Drucker's newspaper. 'There is some quite good stuff in it, but some awful garbage.'

'Its circulation is healthy,' Jonathan said, sounding peeved.

'Yes, but then public taste is so bloody awful that you know what they say: no one ever went bust underestimating the taste of the public. Standards in the gutter, sales through the roof, tragic but true. Have you had any dealings with this wretched newspaper?'

The man named Jonathan broke apart a piece of bread before replying. 'Well, yes, in a manner of speaking. I own it.'

·11·

The Broadcast

He woke up with a blurred but worrying recollection of having said something very foolish. It tugged at him all the time he was helping to get the children dressed, breakfasted and out of the house. Margaret asked, as she stood by the open door, in a rush, if anything was wrong. He said no, and to avoid further questioning, declined her offer of a lift to the station. Alone in the house, he made a strong coffee and sat in the kitchen, trying to recall and assess.

It was not only that he had failed to recognize the man next to him at the dinner table as one of the country's wealthiest newspaper proprietors, Lord Canary, owner of the very newspaper that had been making his life miserable. That memory was ghastly enough, but it was overlaid by another, even worse, one wrapped in night, tiredness and alcohol. It seemed unreal, but it had happened, that he had made a remark so indiscreet that it was like opening the gates to his life and inviting disaster to step in.

A car had arrived soon after 10 p.m. to take him from the dining club to a studio. He had tumbled into the vast, brightly lit reception hall of a towering circular building near Oxford Circus. A man in uniform had made a telephone call to inform someone inside of his arrival, and a pretty girl appeared to escort him to a cavernous room along a bending corridor on an upper floor. It was a live, phone-in radio programme. Five guests and a professional broadcaster discussed issues of the day with any lonely insomniac out there who cared to call. The guests sat at a round table covered in soft felt, which was comfortable to lean on, giving the studio a homely feel. A large supply of free wine and sandwiches was to hand. The technicians sat in an adjoining room, watching through a glass panel and communicating by microphone. Joseph had his back to them. He had the illusion of taking part in a private chat among dinner guests, pleasanter and more private than the club dinner. The cramped studio, with its deep blue carpet, and the clocks and monitor screens overhead, was smaller and cosier, and the company was mixed. Having spent almost four hours drinking and eating in the company of men, Joseph was moved to tell the woman sitting opposite him, a good-looking Irish journalist with long curling black hair and dark eyes, how pleasant it was to have female company. Still bothered by his failure to recognize Lord Canary, he let slip where he had had dinner. That mistake earned him a look of cold disapproval. The Irish journalist obviously knew that this was a club from which women were barred. He shook his head to clear it, and poured himself a glass of water. The man next to him helpfully poured him a glass of red wine. He sipped each alternately.

Their host, the professional broadcaster, who had a clear deep voice which contrasted with his nervous, effeminate manner, addressed the five guests as if they were each uniquely fascinating, but every now and again he would clutch his ear as though in spasm, and would listen intently to something in the palm of his hand. The technicians in the adjoining room were talking to him through a tiny earpiece. Joseph turned to stare through the glass window, wondering what they were talking about. There was a problem with the equipment.

The first half-hour went well, discussing the National Health Service. Joseph had brought his bulging clip file full of briefing papers written by party officials which told him what to say, but he did not open it. He had read it carefully enough that afternoon to be confident of repeating the party line from memory. He did so quite adeptly, he thought, until he spotted the Irish woman looking at him with an expression that was far from friendly.

In the second half-hour, they discussed the ethics of arms sales. Joseph was less comfortable with this one, because he knew that some of the world's cruellest and least stable governments bought weapons from Britain, but he soldiered through a set piece about the importance of jobs in manufacturing industry, about honouring contracts, and about taking each case individually on its merits. He was suddenly interrupted in mid-sentence by the dark-eyed woman journalist, whose Irish accent became more pronounced when she was agitated. 'Does it ever cross your moind that people die through what you're doin'?' she demanded.

He did not immediately see her point. He was only sipping wine and drowsily parroting government policy in a womblike radio studio late at night: no one could die because of that.

But the Irish journalist launched into an argumentative monologue about a country across the other side of the world, whose fabulously corrupt government was collapsing in violent unrest, where she suspected that British weapons were being used against unarmed civilians. Now that he saw her point, Joseph had an uneasy suspicion she might be right, but there wasn't anything he could do about it. He wasn't a minister, he didn't make decisions, but he was obliged to defend those who did.

He tried to reply that the arms trade in itself cost no lives, because weapons themselves don't cause conflicts, but he was interrupted by mocking laughter.

'I went on CND marches when I was young,' he said, hurt by her mockery.

'And look at ye now, apologizing for a trade in death,' she replied.

Fortunately, no one else around the table took her side, and the broadcaster chairing their discussion cut her short by bringing a listener on to the line. The caller was so drunk that he could barely complete a sentence, and had to be replaced with another, a student who calumniated Joseph for being a 'disgusting sell-out'. He too was quickly disconnected.

The discussion of the arms trade was brought to an end, and they moved on to a simpler topic. Joseph relaxed and allowed himself to sample more wine, offering only brief contributions as the discussion waded through the shallows of other important matters. Across the table the Irish journalist continued giving him looks of concentrated fury. She evidently did not know the rules of the political game, did not seem to know that arguments fought out ferociously in public should not be taken personally. He gave her what was meant to be a warm, reassuring smile, but from the visual reaction, he feared it had the opposite effect. She was also knocking back the wine, with enthusiasm, and her handsome face was reddening.

By about 1.30 a.m., when Joseph was so tired that his surroundings were blurred, he was struck by a vivid thought that Frank Rist might be listening. Frank was the kind of obsessive who would tune in to a political discussion when anyone normal was asleep. The image of Frank, alone by a radio, hearing every word they said, was more real than the conversation in that little studio.

Struggling not to lose concentration, he listened to a male caller who was enlivening a desultory discussion about royalty with his bluntly stated view that various reported cases of adultery by royal princesses were sufficient reason to abolish the monarchy. This set the young Irish journalist off again.

'Why the princesses, though? Why them? Why the women? It takes two, doesn't it? So what about the men? And the Prince of Wales? Is he so perfect? Why do you condemn an unfaithful wife and not an unfaithful husband?'

Joseph thought it a vacuous point, but not wanting to take her on, he confined himself to a quiet snort. He assumed she was too drunk to pick it up. He was wrong.

'And sitting across from me here there's a Labour MP pulling a face and sneering. Why's that then?' she demanded.

The chairman broke in: 'Joseph Pilgrim – your views on morality and public life. Is a man or a woman who cheats in marriage unfit for public office?'

'Of course not, of course not. I could think of Lloyd George, or President Kennedy . . .'

Suddenly, their host seemed to have another spasm. His hand went to his ear and he listened intently to some complex instruction from the technicians in the adjoining room.

'And I suppose if you had an affair with a married woman which destroyed her marriage, that would be her responsibility, not yours?' the Irish journalist demanded, unaware that the discussion had temporarily lost its chairman.

Another voice, an MP from an opposing party sitting at Joseph's side, quipped, 'Have you had an affair with a married woman?'

It was a joke, one of those weak attempts at humour sometimes perpetrated by embarrassed onlookers when voices are raised in anger, but its effect on Joseph was similar to being hit in the stomach. In the momentary silence, he pictured Frank Rist alone by his radio set, sitting up to listen to his answer, hoping to hear him tell a palpable, provable lie.

'Yes I have, but I deny, I deny absolutely, that I destroyed anybody's marriage,' he declaimed.

The man who had asked the question winced as if Joseph had hit him, and looked round in alarm, his eyes protruding. Even the Irish journalist fell into an astonished silence.

The broadcaster who was chairing the discussion removed his hand from his ear, wondering why no one was speaking, and remarked cheerfully, 'I think we've exhausted that topic. We've got five minutes left for the latest reports on famine in Africa. Your thoughts, round the table, gentlemen and ladies, very quickly . . .'

That was the memory that assailed Joseph in the morning. Here he was, a married man, a public figure already under unfriendly scrutiny from predatory journalists, who had drunkenly told the nation that he had once had an affair with a married woman. His best hope lay in the lateness of the hour, and the tiny audience the programme must have by then. Perhaps no one who mattered had heard what he said.

In the Commons there was nothing: no messages, telephone calls or knowing remarks to worry him. Silence, in this case, bred hope. Diana Draycott rang to rebuke him for his lapse over dinner, but her tone was teasing, not angry. From the report back she had received from Sir Peter, it appeared that Joseph had made a good impression overall.

There was also an unexpected package from Sir Peter, who had remembered and acted on Joseph's request to read his memoirs. A short note accompanying the fat pile of closely typed A4 sheets advised him that he need not read it all if he was bored by it. Joseph read a few pages at random, and sadly concluded that his old friend was no Alan Clark. He had a plodding literary style, and was far too tactful to disclose any scandal, if he had any to disclose.

Despite what appeared to be a lucky reprieve, Joseph resolved – again – that there were things he must tell Margaret without delay, in case she read them first in the newspapers. At the back of his mind was a nagging worry that someone probably had photographs of him with Diana Draycott, whose name he had never mentioned to Margaret at all. More seriously, there was a lie he had once told, about Christine, which he had to put right.

But first he had to find a moment when they were alone – no

simple matter when he was working such long hours and there were inquisitive young children in their home. However, he made a special journey home late in the afternoon, explaining that he would have to go back in time for another seven o'clock vote, and managed to snatch some moments with Margaret at the kitchen table.

She had had a dreadful day. The health trust she administered was now so short of money that they had had to decide to suspend a programme of inoculation against TB for young children in one of the poorest parts of London. In addition, there had been a series of vexing arguments with the trust chairman, with whom Margaret had been at war for months. Joseph owed it to her to listen to her account of her day without interrupting or showing impatience.

As her narrative drew to a conclusion, the kitchen door was thrown open so forcefully that it banged against the adjoining cupboard, and Isobel made an entrance, her T-shirt smeared in tomato ketchup, a gap in her front teeth which had caused a recent visit from the tooth fairy, and holding a Walkman whose earphones trailed on the floor.

'Dad! Dad! What's official?'

Isobel was adding to her vocabulary every day. Patiently, Joseph tried to define *official*, a difficult word to explain to a six-year-old. However, as a politician's daughter, she was familiar with the term *Prime Minister*, and around that bobbin Joseph wound a reasonably simple exposition of the distinction between *official* and *unofficial*. Isobel listened with interest, head to one side, but was not satisfied.

'But what's official when it's eaten by a donkey?'

'Sorry?'

'On my Winnie the Pooh tape, yeah, it says Eeyore ate official.'

This took a moment to understand.

'No, darling, Eeyore ate a thistle. That's a plant that grows in the ground, which is covered in prickles.'

'But the prickles might hurt Eeyore's mouth,' Isobel protested.

As the discussion of Eeyore's culinary habits continued, it suddenly appeared that Margaret was having a convulsion. She had taken hold of his upper arm and was pinching it painfully, while her other hand covered her mouth. She was shaking, and tears were welling in her eyes. It was only after Isobel had skipped out of the room that he discovered, to his relief, that his wife was silently crying with laughter. He could not bring himself to spoil the mood, so he said nothing about the incident in the studio.

·12·

Dave Drucker at Work

Dave Drucker arrived by motorbike at the mouth of a cavernous underground car park in west London, switched off the engine, and allowed his machine to glide down in a sweeping spiral, past company limousines in the spaces reserved for top executives (whose busy schedule of meetings never let them leave the building), and past the four-door family estate cars of the newspaper's senior writers, all similar in appearance because they were all paid for by the company, until eventually, he reached a poky corner by a fire exit where there was a strip of tarmac too narrow for any car. Here, by special dispensation, Dave parked his motorbike. It was the only vehicle in the car park paid for by the person who rode it.

He was not senior enough to take the executive lift, so he walked back out into the sunlight and round to the front of the building, which looked like the façade of a covered shopping parade, and up wide stone steps into an entrance whose grandeur matched the reputation of the newspaper company whose headquarters it was. Its glass doors opened on to what looked like a marble hall, wide but not deep, where uniformed security men loitered. Two constantly moving escalators connected to the main part of the building, above. At the entrance to the 'up' escalator was a waist-high chrome metal pillar with three revolving arms which functioned as security barriers. The arrivals queued to get through, feeding their plastic identity cards into a slot in the chrome pillar. The human traffic was ceaseless: a card went into the slot, the card was extracted, the arm of the barrier unlocked, the human passed through. Every step of the rising escalator was occupied.

It was Friday, the most difficult day in the skewed rhythm of Sunday newspaper journalism. Saturday's deadlines were uncomfortably close, and Dave did not yet have a story to write, just a possibility on which he placed his hopes. A friend who worked in broadcasting had promised to send him a cassette tape, on which a man was to be heard saying something indiscreet. It ought to be waiting for him upstairs. If it said what he had been told it said, he would have a story to put up to the news desk. Otherwise, it was going to be a dreadful day trying to avert the looming white hell of a week without a by-line.

He was near the front of the queue by the chrome barrier when, to his surprise, one of the security men brusquely ordered him to stand back, gently pushing him with an outstretched arm to emphasize the urgency of the command. These security men were usually bored and laconic in their undemanding jobs, but the tense look on this man's face stopped Dave from protesting. Lost in his own thoughts, he had not noticed the change that had suddenly come over the bustling hall. There was no longer a queue for the 'up' escalator, and the 'down' escalator was quite empty. Everyone had crowded to the edges of the room to create a wide passageway. A senior security man was standing by the central glass door, evidently awaiting the arrival of someone exceptionally important. With an abrupt movement, he pulled the door open, and a tall, solidly built, youngish man in a sharp tailored suit stepped energetically through. His sharp, striped suit and leather shoes radiated money, but otherwise he did not convey any great sense of his own importance. Mildly abashed by the attention, he thanked the man who had held open the door for him, and made a beeline for an escalator, as if wanting to get out of everyone's way as quickly as possible. Behind him a greying executive scuttled, hurrying to keep up and obviously tense. Though the security man who had made Dave stand aside was waiting with a pass key, there was an instant's delay before the distinguished arrival could pass through, during which he was kept standing about a yard from Dave Drucker. They were looking into one another's faces. The cherubic cheeks and curly hair were familiar, but Dave did not instantly register who it was. The other man seemed momentarily startled by the way Dave stared at him. His ears reddened. He was through the barrier and away before Dave realized he had been staring into the face of Lord Canary. Everything here – the building, the equipment and the infinitely more valuable intangibles, including the copyright-protected names on the famous mastheads – was his, inherited from his father.

The short encounter left Dave shaken. That was not because of the lack of deference he had shown to the man who controlled all their lives. He had long since forgotten how to be deferential. They paid him to treat famous people with disrespect. No, what shook him was the recognition that he was older than his proprietor. In a competitive profession, that was a scaring thought.

The silent line of human traffic was now allowed back on the escalator. It ascended past large-leafed evergreen plants set in their individual windowboxes in the sloping space between the escalators, to be tipped out upon the hard polished floor of a vast atrium resembling an outdoor shopping mall. There was light, almost dazzling in its profusion, pouring through a billowing sequence of huge curved skylights. The highest was some ninety feet above the head of the escalator. Thousands of glass specks embedded in the marblelike floor tiles turned the light back up and outwards. Directly ahead, the open floor of the atrium ended in a layered arrangement of balconies, reached by spiral steps tucked in a corner, and topped by eucalyptus trees. A thin waterfall rode over the lip of the lowest balcony and down its shining black wall, disappearing into the floor. The tumbling water filled the huge atrium with a Mediterranean humidity.

Dave made directly for the lifts. There were two, held by great marblelike square pillars. The nearer lift was approaching the ground floor, but there was a small crowd already waiting. Dave watched it fill, and opted to wait for the other lift, which arrived within a matter of minutes. Pressed against its semicircular translucent exterior, he watched the atrium floor fall away as the lift glided noiselessly upwards. From above, the raised part could be seen as an interconnected sequence of terraces, each decorated by a shallow pool of clear water. There were koi carp swimming around below Dave's feet. The building had six floors. Lord Canary's office was at the very top, tucked demurely into the roof, as remote as the gates of heaven. Each floor had glass walls, but the people working within were hidden behind white venetian blinds, reflecting the light back into the brilliant atrium. Behind the blinds were hundreds of desks, chairs, telephones and computer terminals. There was a library holding hundreds of thousands of old press cuttings, meticulously selected and filed for ease of access. The database system accessed a volume of information many times greater. Hundreds of trained professionals serviced the daily operations of Lord Canary's newspapers. Yet sometimes a poor wretch whose name is to be mashed into raw material for this industrial operation, after encountering the likes of Dave Drucker in search of a story, will delude himself that the faint cough of reason and the gossamer of his good name will be an effective defence. A day in the luxuriant heartland of one of the great British newspaper companies might open his eyes to the power of the operation he is up against.

At the fourth floor, Dave made his way down a short corridor and turned left, through double doors that opened into a cramped, crowded newsroom with a low ceiling. The desks were in rows of four, pressed together so that pairs of journalists worked face to face, their views of each other obscured by the ubiquitous computer screens and by wire baskets piled high with papers and books. There was a terminal at every desk. The floor space, already overcrowded with desks, was reduced even further by square pillars whose sides were large enough to function as noticeboards. The room was so cluttered that almost no journalist was in any other's unimpeded line of sight, and yet no one was ever quite out of sight of the news desk – a cluster of workplaces in the centre of the chaos, where the usual batch of junior executives was all in place when Dave arrived, including the news editor, who was engrossed on the telephone.

On good days, Dave was keen to get the news desk's attention, to tell what he had and begin the battle to get his story placed at or near the front of that Sunday's newspaper. Today was not such a day. Helmet under one arm, Dave passed by them to get quickly to his desk, where he picked up the phone, dialled the direct line for a radio studio across town, and asked for an assistant producer there by name. No luck: his contact was out of the office, but was due back soon.

Dave divested himself of his nylon jacket, nylon overtrousers and leather boots. He changed into a pair of shoes he extracted from the bottom drawer of his desk, switched on his terminal, and sat back in his high-backed swivel chair, stroking his chin. All he had in his sights this week was this weird story about a new MP who was not yet famous. Grimacing, he opened up a file called 'Pilgrim' on his screen and reread his rough notes, adding to them here and there. As he typed, he muttered and shook his head, silently cursing the intractable gaps in the story. He was flicking back several pages through his notebook to check the name of the weirdo at the centre of it all – was it Freddie Rist, or Frank Rust? – when, from the corner of his eye, he was aware of someone standing over him. It was the news editor, a bulky man whose shoulder muscles threatened to burst out of his expensive navy-blue suit. He had one useless eye, which he was reputed to have lost from a kick on the rugby pitch, and a nose like a beak. His working eye moved independently, like a chameleon's.

'Do you propose to trouble the news desk this week, Dave?' he asked, in a low growl.

'Hope so, Ian. Hope so, Ian.' The news editor's name was Ian Smith.

It was an awful answer to have to give on a Friday morning. Dave nervously rubbed one hand up and down along his thigh, and could feel small droplets of cold sweat on his pate. He feared what the news editor might say next. But he was saved by a booming voice across the room: 'Ian, Ian Smith, get your arse across here – now.'

It was the editor, a diminutive, furious man named Richard Track, showing his usual courtesy as he called the news editor into his office.

Dave tried his contact in the radio studio again. Still not there. In the pit of his stomach, he could feel that Friday-morning panic take hold. Ahead of him, by the coffee machine against the wall, two of the younger reporters were holding a rapid-fire conversation, speaking so quietly that Dave could pick up only a few phrases: *chased the bastard along the pavement . . . tried to give me a hard time . . . the snapper was sweating like a pig . . .* Both were in their early twenties, tall, powerfully built, confident and bold. They would not hesitate to do the sort of thing Dave did so well – doorstep a politician, stalk a duchess around Antibes, bang on a front door to ask the couple cowering indoors about their murdered daughter, offer money by shouting through the letterbox, go wired up, pinch a photograph from a mantelpiece – but with the one difference: they were a decade younger, and did it all for £30,000 a year less than Dave was paid.

He had been a dirt merchant for the best part of twenty years. He had never had the cunning or the foresight to make the transfer to a desk job before he felt the passing of the years. He had pulled in good stories by the hundred, but had never won a journalism award. He had earned good money, but had spent it on good drink and bad divorces. He needed a big story, one to bring down a Cabinet minister or the captain of the England rugby team. And until the big story came his way, he could not afford to let a week pass by without producing something to remind them of his usefulness, or he might be washed up into some council office as a deputy director of communications.

At last, Dave's phone rang. It was his contact in the radio studio. 'But I posted it to you,' he exclaimed, in answer to Dave's question. 'I posted it yesterday, in a Jiffy bag, first-class, addressed personally to you. It has to have got there by now.'

'OK, mate, I'll check it out and let you know.'

Dave cut the connection and immediately dialled an internal number which put him through to the room somewhere in the depths where the daily post was received and sorted. He told them he was looking for a Jiffy bag addressed to him by name. After an anxious wait, the man down in the post room came back on the line.

'Sorry, Dave. Your package is here. Security didn't like the look of it, so they held it back to put through a scanner. Do you want it sent up?'

'No, I'll come and get it,' Dave replied. He could feel the relief coming over him like sunshine after rain, and did not want to risk having the precious package go astray en route to the fourth floor.

There was a smile over Dave's wide face an hour later when the conference in the editor's office ended and its participants fanned out over the newsroom floor. Ian Smith spotted it and guessed at once that Dave had something to tell. He strode across the newsroom floor, one eye on Dave, the other wandering sightlessly.

'I could kill for a smoke,' he said.

'Thought you'd given up.'

'Come on, come on,' Ian said impatiently, rubbing his fingers together as if he was demanding money. Dave, who was only an occasional smoker, surrendered a cigarette. The news editor lit up gratefully, pulled up a swivel chair and sank his bulk into it, putting one large polished black lace-up shoe on Dave's desktop. Smoking in the office was a breach of company policy, so it was better done in the discreet corner where Dave sat.

'You're looking pleased with yourself.'

'Hear this,' Dave said, switching on a cassette player. A woman's voice was heard, excited and argumentative, with a distinct Irish accent. 'Hang on,' Dave said. Now a man's voice was heard, asking a question, and another man, replying. Dave let the exchange play once, then stopped the machine, rewound, and played it over again:

Have you had an affair with a married woman?

Yes I have, but I deny, I deny absolutely, that I destroyed anybody's marriage.

'Your man Joseph Pilgrim, I presume?' Ian asked. Dave nodded. 'What a gent! Where did he say that?'

'Late-night radio, the night before last.'

'What a gent!' Ian repeated. 'You know, I was studying his face on TV the other night, and he could spoil a strong, reliable theory I have about politics.'

'What theory's that, Ian?'

'That the politicians who turn out to be serial shaggers are all physically, physiologically, follicularly challenged.'

'This one not ugly enough to fit your theory, then?'

Ian Smith took a long drag – then gazed at the cigarette, as if in wonderment that so small an object could cause such pleasure. His jocular tone put Dave at ease. If the news editor was relaxed, it meant that the story was good, and would appear at or near the front of the paper.

Suddenly, joking time was over, and Ian's one good eye was looking hawkishly at Dave. 'So, who's the lady? You can name her, I take it?'

'Yep.'

'And the husband?'

'Yep.'

'It's this nutter you've been telling me about, I assume. The one whose wife was killed?'

'No. My source says no, better than that. Better and better. Here, have a look at these.'

From a desk drawer, Dave produced a large reinforced envelope. Inside, there was a sequence of black-and-white photographs, printed in ten by eight inches format. Ian Smith examined them, one by one. They were of a man and woman walking together along a busy pavement, absorbed in conversation. The House of Lords was in the background. The man was Joseph Pilgrim.

'Who's the bird?'

'That,' Dave replied, 'is a Tory Lady named Diana Draycott.'

·13·

Mrs Draycott's House
1977

Joseph had found a half-empty carriage where he could settle down in a window seat and wrap himself in solitude and mild depression. He was on his way to visit a married woman. She was related to Angel in some distant way. In general, he would rather have been visiting Angel herself, who was the only person he knew of his own age who had a house all to herself. It had come to her as a consequence of a change in her parental firmament, some divorcing and/or remarrying by a parent or step-parent or two, which had endowed Angel with yet more adults who shared responsibility for her upbringing without providing her with a family home where she was actually welcome. But he had quarrelled with Angel so abrasively that he was not even sure he liked her any more, and even less sure that he was welcome at her place. He did not want her to think that he had no other social life, or that he wasn't getting on nicely without her. That was why he had taken up a long-standing invitation to call on Angel's relative.

After a two-minute wait on Cambridge station, he was startled to hear his name called out in a loud, confident county voice which carried well above the background hum of traffic. He looked around, in all directions, but could not see her in the darkness.

'I'm here,' the same voice announced. She was standing at the door of an estate car across the forecourt. As he hurried over, she waited, hands buried in her overcoat pockets, until they were face to face. 'Didn't you see me draw up? Off in a dream again?'

There was a hint of sarcasm in that word *again* that he did not like.

Mrs Draycott looked different from his sketchy memory of her. He had met her two or three times, and had dined at her house once, with Angel. She had a right-wing husband, an aspirant politician, whose greatest virtue was the longish intervals he spent listening instead of rehearsing his standard-issue right-wing opinions. Caught in the artificial light, against a shadowy backdrop, the size of her car, the extravagant collar on her black coat, which looked like real fur, and the scarlet and deep blue scarf tossed over one shoulder all spoke of money and social status.

'So, how very nice to meet again. How long have we got? When's your train?'

'There's one in quarter of an hour and one at midnight.' Unusually, he had taken the trouble to check.

'It seems a shame only to see you for a quarter of an hour. Do you mind awfully taking the late train?'

As she settled in the driver's seat, she hesitated before saying, 'I'm afraid you're going to have to see me in these.' From a glasses case on the dashboard she produced a pair of tortoiseshell spectacles which magnified her eyes. 'I only wear them to drive, which is why I really can't be bothered with contact lenses. No doubt I look dreadful.'

'No, they're rather nice.'

She laughed as she started up the car, obviously not believing him – but it was true: the spectacles made her less intimidating.

He had hoped to see the high walls of Cambridge's university colleges, but they passed through unfamiliar streets where there were only shopping parades and three-storey houses built close to the road.

'How's Angel?'

'She's all right.'

'Are you and she still getting along?'

'No.'

'Oh dear.' He was aware that she looked with curiosity, but to his relief, she asked no more questions.

The car halted outside the town house which he thought he remembered; but inside, like its occupant, it seemed to have subtly changed. This was because he had noticed almost nothing about it on his last visit, when the only thing on his mind was whether he would be able to get into the same bed as Angel. Now, the darkly polished table in the hall, the black-and-white reproduction of a Picasso drawing hanging over it, against blue-and-white striped wallpaper, or the way a raincoat had been left over the back of a chair and a pair of felt boots had been left untidily underneath the table (in Joseph's home, such items were always put away in their proper place) – all these details now were impressed upon him as extensions of Mrs Draycott's forceful personality.

As she took his coat to hang it up in the cupboard below the hall stairs, she was still wearing her 'only for driving' glasses, which made her look younger than she had seemed before. She tossed her head, which drew attention to a mass of auburn curls; but she was still beyond the age range that Joseph found sexually interesting, being at least in her mid-twenties. He experienced his first sharp stab of regret that his affair with Angel was over.

He was directed into a long room which at the flick of a switch was filled with yellowish light from wall-mounted bulbs concealed behind large, shell-shaped glass casings, and which evidently served as both dining room and sitting room. At one end, ringed by a set of eight red-upholstered chairs, was a dark, stained wood table covered with newspapers, shopping bags and other items, and at the other, a suite of two armchairs and a large sofa draped in a curtainlike brown-and-red throw. They, too, had domestic bric-à-brac on them. She apologized for the room's untidiness, housework not being her 'strong point', instructed him to sit, and offered him tea, coffee, or 'something stronger'. He chose whiskey. She asked whether he wanted it with anything, or neat. Not knowing how he liked it, he asked for soda water. A lifetime's aversion to anything with soda was soon to begin.

She left the whiskey bottle and soda fountain on the floor beside him, supplied herself with a gin bottle and several small bottles of tonic water, kicked off both shoes, removed her glasses, and sat almost sideways, her arm on the back of the sofa.

'So, has something gone wrong then, *vis-à-vis* Angel?' Seeing him hesitate, she added, 'I only ask because in the summer the two of you slept together under my roof, for which Virginia would probably kill me if she knew.'

'Who's Virginia?'

'Angel's mother.'

'I don't know her,' Joseph said, hoping that by taking this track he could evade any more questions.

She gave him a searching look, tapped her wineglass with the nail of her forefinger and, after a moment's reflection, said, 'I don't think Angel is quite as mature as you are. I can't remember: are you still at Oxford, or have you left?'

'I'm about to start my second year.'

'Your second year? Gosh, golly, gosh!' Joseph was not sure whether that was a point in his favour. She quickly put him right. 'I'm so glad to see you. I was sitting alone in our house wishing somebody would ring. Peter has been doggedly seat-seeking, which seems to take him somewhere different every week. Do you know that expression seat-seeking?'

'He wants to be a Conservative MP.'

'He wants to be a Conservative MP,' Mrs Draycott repeated. 'It was his idea, and I'm all for it. My only condition is that he must find an absolutely solid seat which we can hold in bad years as well as good. I don't want to see him unemployed in late middle age. But my god, it's a bind. We had no idea. He must have been in front of more than twenty committees. That's twenty ruined weekends. He often comes second, or third, but he might as well be five-hundredth, for all the use that is. However,' Mrs Draycott sighed, and controlled her voice, which had begun to rise, 'we shall persevere. He has got to do it this time, because the Labour government is going to fall in the next year or two, and if Peter is to get on and be a minister, he must be in there when it happens. But I'm sorry, I'm boring you.'

Joseph protested that he was not bored at all, which was true enough, because he had never heard anyone map out the future with such clarity. He was not bored, but indifferent. The plight of the Draycotts, with their spoiled weekends, did not rouse his sympathy.

She shook her head, a private gesture that seemed to convey disbelief over some unshared thought, then looked directly at him. Her expression was not entirely friendly. 'Yes, so I'm married to ambition. I believe in public service. And what about you? What's your ambition in life? *Have* you an ambition?'

Despite the unfriendliness of her tone, Joseph preferred the wording of the question to the usual 'What do you plan to do when you leave university?' – which was a middle-aged person's way of asking how he planned to cross the years from his age to theirs, as if he had nothing else in his sights. Either it was the unusual choice of phrase, or a reckless feeling that the evening was heading towards social disaster anyway, or the burning whiskey in his stomach – whichever was the reason, he blurted out an answer he would never normally have given to anyone older.

'I want to stay young and never be middle-aged, basically.'

'Gosh, golly, gosh. Don't we all? Well, you could die a romantic death before you get to my age, like Byron or Jimi Hendrix. That used to be quite the thing, lying in a ghastly mess in bed, or in a heap of smouldering metal wrapped around a tree, *hope I die before I get old*, but I thought that had gone out of style. But then, I don't claim to be particularly with it. In fact, I'm probably quite without it.'

'People don't really say with it any more,' Joseph pointed out.

'Golly, not with it to say with it. I am *passée*.'

There was a moment's awkward pause and Joseph feared that the conversation was slipping downwards to disaster, but he was wrong. Mrs Draycott was thinking about what he had said. After a moment, she tapped her glass with her fingers again, and began asking questions calculated to draw him out. She asked what he meant by staying young, since he could not avoid physical ageing, whether he could name people who had, by his definition, avoided ageing, and what it was that he admired about them. As she asked questions, Mrs Draycott shifted position, swinging her feet down on to the floor and removing her arm from the back of the sofa to lean forward, forearms resting on her legs, as if preparing to take him on in combat. He too sat forward, bringing their faces a foot or two closer together than before.

He had not intended to confide his private dreams, but there was something in her tone – attentive, challenging and bordering on sarcastic – that forced him on. Then, as another lengthy silence broke in, he regretted everything he had said. He thought she was going to laugh at him.

In fact, Mrs Draycott threw her arm over the back of the sofa again. 'Well, frankly,' she said, 'that's the most interesting ambition I've heard all week.'

Grateful and relieved, he took a long gulp of whiskey, felt the soda collide unpleasantly with the British Rail sandwich and crisps still loitering in his stomach, and hurried on talking, aware that his face was red and that his eyes were darting like a blind man's. She was sipping gin and looking at him so intently that Joseph wondered what could be going through her mind. When he stopped talking, he became aware of a noise, but it was only the ticking of a brass clock on the mantelpiece. The woman sat up straight, as if to stand, but then appeared to hesitate.

'Are you happy, generally?' she asked.

'I think that the importance of being happy is hugely overrated.'

'You know, I think I agree.' From the handbag she had left on the floor near her feet, she produced a packet of cigarettes and offered him one, which he accepted. No one older had ever offered him a cigarette before: it was like admitting him to maturity. As she leant down to hunt around in her bag for matches, she added, 'Excuse me, there's something I left in the kitchen.'

It wasn't the matches. As she stood up, she tossed them across the room for him to catch. He lit up while she was away, trying hard to remember how sophisticated people held their cigarettes. He settled for a conventional two-fingered hold, so loose that the cigarette almost drooped, and for slow hand movements and long, slow drags.

She returned from the kitchen with an object in her hand which he did not recognize, and embarked upon a mysterious operation: in one hand she held a long white piece of wire, which looked like a pipe cleaner, and in the other, a finger-shaped, tortoiseshell-coloured object about two inches long. She was delicately inserting the wire into one end of the finger-shaped object, which obviously had a hollow tube at its centre, and drawing it through. Each time it emerged, it had become dirtier, until it was covered in unpleasant brown stains and she tossed it in a wastepaper basket. He watched, fascinated, as she inserted a cigarette and lit up. He had never seen anyone use a holder before.

The ingestion of whiskey was causing the wall behind her to execute weird little sideways movements: sliding to the left, leaping to the right; sliding to the left, leaping to the right . . .

She emptied her glass and frowned, as if worried by something.

'Joseph, you look awfully relaxed and actually rather tired. Are you sure you want to catch a midnight train? You can borrow my spare room.'

'Yes. That's fine.'

'I'm sorry I can't lay on an Angel to keep you company.'

Standing up, he caught sight of himself in the mirror over her mantelpiece. He thought he looked moody and dangerous, though in truth his face was a little flushed and his eyes were a little bloodshot. In that moment, the silly thought took hold of him that she wanted to seduce him, but in reality, she escorted him prosaically to the same spare room that he had once shared with Angel, and with a polite smile, bade him goodnight . . .

. . . weird blue light had invaded the room. He was frightened of something looming in the dark. He was struggling to be free of it, fighting to be awake, when a woman's voice pierced his nocturnal terrors. She called him by name. Now he was somewhere else, in a dark room, and the silhouette of a strange, vampirelike woman was hovering above his bed. He shouted.

'Ssh, Joseph!' the woman said.

The room was flooded with real light, white electric light, and he remembered where he was, though he had no idea of the time, or of how long he had been asleep. Diana Draycott was leaning over him, with one hand still on the bedside lamp, wearing a thin, pink nightdress. He could see in the lamplight the outline of a breast and a nipple and the contours of her back. He was lying on his bed in his shirt and underpants. The duvet had disappeared, kicked on to the floor as he struggled with his nightmare.

'You gave me some fright,' she said. 'I thought the house had been broken into. You must have had a terrible dream.'

She sat on the bed next to him, like his mother's ghost made flesh. He thought that politeness required him to sit up, which he was reluctant to do, but when he raised his head, she told him in a soft voice to lie still. She was sitting at his waist, one leg tucked under her, the other dangling to the floor, hands on her lap, looking at him with interest. He did not dare let his eyes wander, because her thin nightdress might show him shapes and shadows that were not meant to be seen. They gazed at one another for a long time, like children playing a game of stare.

Eventually, thinking that it would be rude to maintain this motionless silence longer, he took a deep breath and put one hand under his head: his right hand, because she was sitting to his left and he did not want to show an armpit. 'I sometimes have a dream about being trapped in a room full of weird blue light. It goes back to something that happened . . .' He tailed off, reluctant to say more.

'Sounds dreadful.'

That hint of sarcasm again, but somehow not unpleasant. On the contrary, the combination of her voice, her skimpy nightdress and the drink still burning in his stomach had an alarming effect further down his body, where he had only the tail of his shirt and his tight pants for covering, and where he was appalled to see a mound stirring. It seemed to him to be abysmal manners to allow such a thing to interrupt a serious conversation with a married woman. Fortunately, there was no reaction from Mrs Draycott, who seemingly had not noticed.

'Can I get you anything?' she asked.

'A glass of water would be nice.'

She nodded and left, giving him a glimpse of bare, muscular calves. She was difficult to place: not young or available enough to be within the normal range of sexual interest, and yet there was something about her that had a disturbing effect. When she returned, she had on a dressing gown of blue towelling but was still barefoot; she was bearing a long glass of cold water.

'So, what happened to give you nightmares?' she asked.

He took a long draught of water.

'When I was in my teens, my parents went out for the evening, with my sister. I was woken up by a horrible noise, a terrible thud-thud-thudding. I went out on the landing. It was full of a weird light which went round and round the room, on and off, on and off, flickering all around me.'

'How spooky!'

'There was a police car parked in the drive, with the blue light going round on the roof. The police were banging on the door. There had been a crash.'

He was expecting her to ask questions, but Mrs Draycott simply sat still, waiting.

'My sister had been in the passenger seat. She went through the windscreen, face first. She's quite disfigured, scars all over her face, and terribly self-conscious.'

'How old was she?'

'Twelve.'

'Poor little thing.'

'It's probably ruined her life.'

Another silence. Taking care to control himself, and speaking unnaturally quietly, he went on, 'My father was all right. Outwardly all right. Not hurt physically. He was driving.'

He took a deep breath, exhaled, and took a sip of water. Mrs Draycott frowned and leant forward to stroke his forearm, up and down, with the tip of one finger. At first, he thought it was a motherly 'there, there' gesture, but she was not offering words of comfort, or even looking him in the eye any more. The frown was still there, as if she was concentrating hard on some private thought.

After a minute or two, she withdrew her hand and sat back. 'Forgive me for asking the obvious question: your mother was in the car when it crashed?'

He nodded. 'Eleanor, my sister, thinks that my mother's ghost comes back and talks to her about the family. She says that my mother doesn't completely approve of me. Anyway, ever since, I have hated the flashing blue lights on police cars. Whenever I see one, I want to run away.'

The story was true in every detail, and retelling it stirred truly painful emotion, and yet perhaps he was guilty of dramatizing. He wanted to convince her that he had known great emotions. He wanted her to think that he was out of the ordinary.

Mrs Draycott took his hand again, cupped it in both palms, squeezed tightly, and lapsed into another long silence. Inexorably, this bodily contact had the effect he dreaded: the bulge around his groin rose like an unwanted guest, harder than before. He decided, desperately, to resume the conversation, keep talking and keep an unwavering eye contact.

'So, so, so why did you decide to marry a politician?'

She looked straight ahead rather than at him, and sighed. 'He's not a politician. He's the manager of a small firm which manufactures cardboard boxes. I've said I want him to be a politician.' She stopped and took a deep breath. 'You see, if you go into politics, you won't ever be alone. You're in a tribe. Don't you agree?'

Then, without letting him answer, she patted his hand again. 'But I know you're not going to join our tribe: you'll probably join the enemy, so let's stay off politics.'

'Yes. Yes, of course. What would you like to talk about?'

She didn't have a ready answer. Still holding his hand tightly, she raised her eyebrows, and her eyes wandered until they alighted upon the bulge at his groin. There they lingered, too long for there to be any doubt that she had seen what he feared she would see. To him, it looked too enormous for anyone to miss it anyway. She then looked him in the eye. She had a rash of red around each cheekbone, and she looked somewhat shocked. She loosened her grip on his hand, without altogether letting go. Now, belatedly, the mountainous swelling sank and disappeared, too late. First his ears and then his cheeks burned with chagrin. He did not know what to say. He did not want to admit that he had lost control of himself; nor did he want her to think that he had deliberately answered her kindness with a towering erection. He embarked on a spluttering apology.

'Don't,' she said sharply. 'Don't say sorry.'

Diana breathed in and out, during an interval that seemed never to end, the longest, heaviest silence he had ever experienced.

'Well, this is unexpected . . . Isn't it?' she said eventually. He assumed that she was so hideously embarrassed by what she had seen that she did not know how to extricate herself. He was glad that she cared about him enough to share his humiliation.

'You're so young, very young,' she added, as if answering an unspoken question.

She turned her head again as if to check whether the tumescence was still on display. To Joseph's relief, it was gone, entirely. He wondered if polite conversation could now be resumed.

'Mrs Draycott . . .'

'Don't say that, you sound like Dustin Hoffman,' she said, half laughing.

'Is he the actor who looks like Al Pacino?'

This time, she did give a snort of laughter. Mercifully, it was not cruel laughter, and she rubbed the back of his hand for reassurance. 'Yes, he's the actor who looks like Al Pacino. We used to think that Al Pacino looked like Dustin Hoffman, but never mind. I was thinking of a film called *The Graduate*. Before your time.'

She squeezed his hand impulsively and said, 'You know, when you and Angel went off to bed together, I was jealous.'

He wanted to return the compliment, but could not think of anything to say. After another loaded silence, she turned her head to look again at his midriff. The problem was over, though. He relaxed. He felt acquitted.

But to his astonishment, Mrs Draycott moved her hand to where the incriminating mound had been, and lightly brushed it with her fingertip. He almost protested, but there was a look on her face that told him she was in the grip of an emotion as powerful as any he was experiencing. He was astonished. He thought women, especially older women, had more self-control. She touched him a second time, more boldly than before, and raised her eyebrows as he hardened under her fingertips. When she turned to look him in the face, her face was flushed with guilty delight. For that moment, she could have been his own age. She breathed out heavily, like someone who has just had a fright, and asked, 'Shall I put the light off?'

Now, at last, he thought he knew exactly what was happening, and saw his cue to be masculine. He sat up and raised an arm to put it protectively around her shoulders. To his surprise, she flinched and released her grip on his other hand. He dropped his arm and sat back.

'Sorry,' she said. 'Sorry, I'm not . . .'

Another sentence hovered uncompleted. She took off the blue dressing gown, folded it, and laid it rather fussily to one side. Then, with a visible effort, like someone trying to steel herself to jump into cold water, she stood up beside the bed, took the hem of her nightdress in both hands and, in a single movement, removed it and threw it on the floor. Joseph's pulse rate jumped and his breathing became so heavy that he almost choked as he gazed at her in amazement and guilty admiration.

And that was as good as it got. There were other snatched weekends, but something was wrong. He became obsessively afraid that he would not be able to hold on to Diana. Every difficulty that came in the way of their meetings felt like a personal injury. When he was not with her, he could not stop thinking about her; and when he was, he wanted to be in bed with her directly. He asked her repeatedly to visit him at university, so that his contemporaries would see his formidable mistress. When, eventually, she kept her promise, it was to buy him dinner and tell him gently that it was all over. Peter Draycott had secured a safe seat and would be an MP within a few months. This made it far too dangerous for her to be conducting an affair. She hoped he would understand.

He was still smarting from that loss a year later, on the night of the general election that brought the Conservatives back to power. By now, he had fallen in with Frank Rist, who had stumbled upon Angel's underused house in Clapham. Frank seemed a charismatic figure. He was in conflict with everyone, including – or rather especially – other members of the little organization that was absorbing his energies. The group seemed to exist to prove that a man who had been Trotsky's bodyguard in Mexico was a KGB and CIA agent, allegations disputed with matching vehemence by rival groups; Frank had questioned whether it really mattered, for which proceedings to expel him were under way. Seething with contempt for the capitalist system, the communist system, and Trotskyite sectarianism, Frank had drifted into the Labour Party, which he also despised. He and Joseph were part of a crowd in Angel's front room, watching the election results come in, when Peter Draycott's image appeared on screen, standing on a stage in some distant hall, in a line of candidates and candidates' wives. Diana was behind him, dressed in green, with a wide-brim hat.

Frank, who had been drinking hard, nudged Joseph and asked quietly, 'Is it true, then? You and that Tory lady – did you?'

Frank knew friends of Joseph's from university, and had heard rumours of his interesting liaison.

Frank was tough. Joseph, who was also drunk, wanted to sound tough. 'I bloody did, I fucked her, I fucked her good.'

He bit his lip when he noticed that Angel was within earshot, and for the rest of his life he was horrified by the memory of that gross bragging – though he could not help noticing the look of respect it brought to Frank's drink-fired face.

·14·

Exposed

Dave Drucker was on the doorstep again: no flash photography this time, but none the less unwelcome. The smile on his round, stubbled face did not reassure Joseph at all as he asked in that nasal south London accent of his whether they could step indoors.

'Let's talk here,' Joseph replied. A sensation in his stomach reminded him of how little he wanted to talk to Dave Drucker at all. He had lived with the fear that he would call again. Now he felt like one who has been awaiting bad news and finds the messenger on the doorstep: he wanted to be told the worst, without delay. He watched impatiently as the journalist drew a notebook and Biro from the pocket of a loose-fitting jacket, and scanned his notes pensively.

'Your decision, Mr Pilgrim, only I've heard a story, yeah, which I'd like to hear your side of, yeah.' Dave paused and looked enquiringly into Joseph's face, giving him time to change his mind. 'I won't beat about the bush then, Mr Pilgrim. Is your affair with Lady Draycott still ongoing?'

Yes, he had thought this might be it. Ever since the photographer had caught them on Millbank, and he had lied to Diana by telling her there was nothing to worry about, this is what he had half expected. He had feared worse; still, he was unprepared for it. He had rehearsed answers to questions he might be asked

about Christine's death, but not about this. He hesitated for perhaps five seconds before collecting his wits. The hesitation was
long enough to give him away.

'Sure you don't want to step indoors, Mr Pilgrim?' said Dave,
who was watching carefully, with predatory eyes.

It was later into the evening than on his last visit. The street
was empty; there would be no chance of being interrupted by
passing neighbours, when interruptions would have been a relief.
It was chilly and getting dark. But despite all these good reasons
for acceding to Dave's request, Joseph ignored it.

'I don't understand what the hell you're talking about. Why are
you asking me about Diana Draycott? Yes, I know Diana Draycott.
She's an old friend.'

'I didn't hear you properly, Mr Pilgrim. Did you say she's an old
flame?'

'What's that in your hand?' He had spotted an oblong object
half concealed by the sleeve of Dave's jacket.

'It's a tape machine, Mr Pilgrim.'

'You're recording this conversation?'

'I find it quite difficult to hear all you're saying, Mr Pilgrim.
You seem very upset at the mention of Lady Draycott. Is that
because of the effect on your family, yeah?'

'What do you mean?'

'Like you're worried about the upsetting effect of this revelation
on your wife and children, yeah?'

'Of course I'm worried about my wife and children.'

'Highly worried?'

'What is this? What is this line of questioning?' The man asked
such stilted questions.

'And are you saying the liaison with Lady Draycott is now over,
Mr Pilgrim?'

'No. No, I didn't say that.'

'So is it ongoing?'

'I'm not talking to you about Diana Draycott.'

'And that's because you're highly worried about the impact that the revelation of this affair could have on your children, yeah?'

'Oh course, I'm worried about that. How can you ask these questions? This could devastate my children. What do you think you're doing?'

'But you haven't denied that there was an affair?'

'That, as far as I can see, is none of your bloody business.'

'I'll take that as confirmation, Mr Pilgrim.'

Joseph only just heard the ending of the sentence, which was uttered as he slammed the door, leaving Dave's circular face outside in the cool of the evening. In his rage, Joseph pushed the door so hard that it whistled on its way to the doorframe and the patterned glass rattled. Standing in the hallway, he understood that there was no escape from this crisis which he had tried to pretend would never happen.

He went directly to the adjoining room and watched Dave through the window, loitering on the pavement, listening to the tape recording he had made. As he watched, he experienced something similar to carsickness. *What was he going to say to Diana?* It would have to be soon if he was to have any hope of warning her before the press arrived. It might even be too late.

He was surprised by the sound of Margaret's voice in the room, behind him. She must have come in silently.

'Was that you slamming that door?'

Being rebuked for slamming a door was so inappropriate to the moment that it was reassuring, as if their domestic routine had resumed, covering over the transient ghastliness.

'That damn reporter was here again.'

'What this time? More tales of your dope smoking?'

Outside, Dave was now talking to someone on a mobile phone, probably to another journalist, probably talking about Joseph, probably working out how to make malicious use of what they knew. In here, he was helpless.

'Not dope?' Margaret asked, thinking that he was shaking his head in reply to her question.

'It's something else. It's a thing that happened before we even met.'

'One of your *mistresses*?'

He turned about, surprised by her tone. She had her hand on her hip and her mouth curled in a gesture of disapproval – but no more than a gesture. This was a habit of hers. He had been given the same reproachful look when she first saw Rachel. 'And I suppose you picked her for her brilliant mind, and I suppose you didn't even notice while you were examining her knowledge of government policy that she's drop-dead gorgeous?' It was her method of attack: teasing, disbelieving and caustic, but good-humoured.

It had been much worse in the first months of their long relationship. Then, only recently out of her teens and perhaps emotionally still in them, Margaret had been like a green-eyed monster, with her explosive bursts of unreasoning suspicions, interrogations, sulks and tears, brought on at different times by almost every woman Joseph knew or ever had known. Anyone who knew her now, as the controlled, efficient and sometimes tyrannical NHS administrator, would find it impossible to recognize the ball of jealous fury she had once been. Having used a lifetime's supply of jealousy in a few months, she was more amused than threatened by his easy relations with other women, watchful but not possessive.

Still, he was wary of supplying her with combustible material. He had never mentioned Diana Draycott to her at all, either as an old lover or as an acquaintance renewed. It was going to be a long story to tell in one conversation, but he drew a deep breath, braced himself, and was about to begin when a child's howling called Margaret away.

On the pavement outside, Dave had completed his telephone call, and seemed to have lapsed into odd behaviour. From a box behind the seat of a motorbike parked on the kerbside he took a large pair of black plastic trousers, which he put on over the grey flannel trousers he was already wearing, hopping on one foot and then the other as he pulled them up. A black biker's jacket and helmet followed. Watching this mildly comical operation suddenly made Joseph think that perhaps this man who had invaded his life was not omnipotent. It might be possible to do something. As the noise of the motorbike engine assured Joseph that he had finally been left alone, he calculated that twenty-four hours remained before whatever Dave Drucker was writing would appear in print. There was time.

He slipped through the house into the cluttered upstairs study at the back, which had accumulated yet another cardboard box full of books and papers. Diana was the first person he ought to ring, but that was going to be a difficult conversation. He could not even think of an opening sentence. So he rang Rachel first, on her mobile. She answered from a noisy bar somewhere. He asked her to locate Gerald Moon for him.

Then he dialled the Draycotts' country home. The phone rang interminably, ten or twelve rings, until his dread of the impending conversation turned to a cowardly hope that he would be excused this ordeal. Then he heard Sir Peter's voice, sounding abrupt and unfriendly. The long, cold pause after Joseph had identified himself told him that the call was too late: they already knew.

'A reporter and a photographer have been here. I told the scoundrels to b— off,' Sir Peter said.

'Yes, they've been here too.'

He could not think of anything else to say. Sir Peter rescued him from a difficult silence by announcing that Diana wanted to speak. Her voice burst into his ear, in a tone he had never heard before.

'How the hell do they know?' He wished he knew. He thought carefully, trying to remember whether he had ever dropped a careless hint. 'Joseph, are you going to answer?' she demanded, after a moment's silence. 'Did you talk about me to this wretched Frank Rist – if that's his name?'

'I don't think I ever did.'

'I've never met him, have I?'

'No.'

'Did you tell someone else?'

'I told people at university.'

After all, he was then nineteen years old and desperate for the company of a woman who had seemed to be an aeon older.

Diana fell silent, breathing heavily, as if she wanted neither to talk to him nor to end the conversation. Suddenly she said, 'We've got two outside the house at this very moment, one with a camera. In twenty years in public life, this is the worst, the most distressing, the most painful – the worst of all.' She fell silent again.

'Diana . . .'

'Have you spoken to Angel? What does she have to say about it all?'

'No, I haven't spoken to her.'

'Don't you think you'd better?'

'Couldn't you speak to Lord Canary?'

'No.'

'But he has the power to stop it.'

'No, I can't. He's in the Far East. I had to explain myself to some *girl* who said she would pass on a message. It was quite the most humiliating conversation I've ever had. It's not like ringing to say, there's a bright new MP you should meet – this is like being a beggar.' She took a deep breath. 'If he rings, he rings. If he doesn't, he doesn't. I'd better go, I need to talk to my husband.'

It was the first time he had heard Peter Draycott so described. She sounded exhausted.

'How is Peter?'

He asked because he wanted to delay the moment when their conversation must end.

'Peter doesn't get angry, Peter doesn't raise his voice, Peter doesn't accuse, Peter doesn't complain, so I don't know how Peter is, but if you'll excuse me, I shall go and see. By the way, he would like his manuscript back, please.'

With that, she put the phone down, and he experienced the wrenching pain of lost friendship. For all he knew, they might never speak again. Their bantering exchanges had been woven around a shared secret of which they never spoke, a buried, guilty, agreeable memory. When next they met, it would be as strangers whose former love had been defiled by the cold curiosity of strangers.

Diana had left one suggestion and one request. He set to work on the request without delay, rummaging through the latest unpacked cardboard box cluttering the small study, looking for Sir Peter Draycott's memoirs. Though there were other, more urgent things he might have done, he felt that he owed their dead friendship this last rite.

The typescript of 'I Seem to Remember' was in its padded envelope, unread. It would always be unread. The supply of memoirs by former government ministers already far exceeded demand. Joseph fanned through its hundreds of pages – at first randomly, as if to reassure himself that the text was as uncompelling as he had first assessed it, but then methodically, kneeling on the floor, scanning one page after another, placing the discarded sheets in a neat pile face down, searching for any reference to the short period when he and Diana had been lovers. Suddenly, he wanted to know if there was anything more he could learn about their affair, any secret discovery to make it *his* private memory again, not the prostituted property of a million indifferent newspaper readers. At last, he alighted upon an extract covering the time when Sir Peter had been adopted for a safe seat.

As my life approached this crossroad, I became briefly concerned about my wife Diana. I was, of course, looking forward greatly to the new life awaiting me as a Member of Parliament, but she did not share my exhilaration. She appeared to be looking into the future with trepidation though, as usual for her, she did not complain. I asked her, 'Is there anything the matter, and can I help?' She confessed to me that she was not looking forward very much to the life of an MP's wife. The longer we talked, the more impressed I was by how clearly she had taken stock of our future. Diana was absolutely right: being the wife of an MP is a very demanding role, with all of the responsibility and few of the joys of elected office.

After we had discussed this problem frankly, I said to her, 'It's for you to choose. If you feel you can't face this life, then I shan't hesitate to renounce my position as a prospective parliamentary candidate and resume my business career.' But Diana, with that self-sacrificing spirit that has been the hallmark of women since the Creation, replied very firmly, 'No, Peter, you have given an undertaking to your party and to your future constituents and you must stick by that through thick and thin!'

In the years that followed, I would come to owe more to my wife than words can convey.

That was all. It did not tell him much, but he learnt for the first time that there had been an acknowledged crisis in the Draycotts' marriage. No doubt Sir Peter had brought to this marital conference the agenda-setting skills he was acquiring as he trained to be a professional politician. His offered sacrifice had been turned down, hers had been accepted, inevitably. But what had prompted the meeting? What did Peter suspect?

Before he could read any more, he was interrupted by a call from Rachel, who had tried Gerald Moon's home number, mobile and pager without success, and had been told he was out of the country. Joseph would have to cope without the spin doctor.

The noise from the children had died down. He could hear a murmur somewhere in the house. It was Margaret's voice: she was reading to them in one of the bedrooms. The routine within their household was proceeding normally, despite the threat outside. He could not immerse himself in it. He needed to act, to dull the pain and anxiety. There was Diana's suggestion to be acted upon. She had said that he ought to speak to Angel, and that was what he would do.

He rehearsed his opening words as he listened to the dialling tone. This would be only the second time he had spoken to her in twelve years. On the previous occasion, he had arranged to meet her, but she had not turned up. She had not contacted him since to explain or apologize. She would surely be surprised by his persistence. He decided to say *I'm sorry you weren't able to keep our last appointment, but never mind, are you by any chance free just this evening, because something has cropped up which I'd like to discuss face to face, if possible . . .*

After the phone had rung several times, she answered.

'Hello, Angel, I'm sorry you weren't able to keep our last appointment, but never mind . . .'

'Who is this?'

'Joseph Pilgrim.' From the other end came a long, disconcerting silence. 'As I say, I'm sorry you weren't able to keep our last appointment, but never mind – oh, for heaven's sake, I need to talk.'

'Now?' She sounded startled by the sudden change of tone.

'Yes, please.'

'Go on, then, talk.'

'Must we talk over the phone? Can I come over and see you? I'd like to see you again. Now?'

After another silence, Angel gave him directions to a nearby pub, without saying why she preferred to meet him there rather than at home. The whole conversation was over in two minutes.

Joseph looked into the children's bedroom to tell Margaret where he was going. She was sitting on the bed with a picture book on her knees and a child on either side, one in a woollen nightdress, the other in pyjamas with his thumb in his mouth.

'Please don't make a noise when you come in, because I need an early night. Perhaps you could sleep in the back room. And don't drink and drive,' she said.

There would be time in the morning to tell her about Diana.

·15·

Revisiting Angel

Forty-five minutes later, as his car approached Clapham, he had a depressing suspicion that Angel might have sent him to a pub as a ruse to avoid seeing him again. He decided that if she was not there, he would wait half an hour, ring her again at home, and then decide on his next move. As he heard the noise of voices coming from the pub, which had a wide, ornate frontage decorated with hanging baskets of greenery, he wondered if he would anyway ever recognize her in the crowd.

The inside of the pub was a long open room, with a low balustrade where a wall that once divided the lounge from the saloon had been knocked down. The clientele were in little social groups, either standing at the bar or sitting around one of the circular tables, like grass tufts on a sand dune. But across by the furthest wall, on a leather bench on the floor beyond the balustrade, a lone plant had taken root: a middle-aged woman whose long hair held streaks of iron grey, sitting alone with a pint of beer. In appearance she resembled one of those pungent, eccentric bagladies who walk the streets muttering to themselves, their clothes tied with string, but the prominent black eyebrows and glistening rotund face were unmistakably Angel's. Sitting back with folded arms, she watched him suspiciously as he found a path through the social clumps and approached her bench. At close range, he saw that her face had gained lines around the eyes and forehead, while the mouth had turned down, giving her the look of one for whom life had proved to be an irreversible disappointment.

They exchanged curt greetings before he went to the bar, returning with drinks for both of them. He apologized for his sudden visit. He said, half-truthfully, that he had intended to renew contact virtually from the day he and Margaret had moved south to London, many years ago. In fact, he recalled sending her a postcard notifying her of their new address, and another announcing the birth of Isobel. A nod from her confirmed that both had been received. He informed her that Tom had since been added to their family, and described in brief how his sudden career change had come about. She listened without a word. At first, her silence was encouraging, because she was looking him straight in the face with frank interest and evidently taking in every word; but in time it became unnerving. Thinking that she was expecting more explanation, he told her about Dave Drucker and the story about his old dope-smoking ways. Still there was no response. Her second drink was untouched. Her arms remained folded. Her stare was unwavering. The uncomfortable thought went through his mind that she might actually be mad, and that nothing he was saying was penetrating whatever dreamworld she inhabited.

'I'm talking too much.'

'Can I get you another drink?' Angel asked, reaching for her bag.

'I'll get them. Same again?'

'No, I'll have a Laphroaig with ice, please.'

'A what?'

'Whisky.'

He had her repeat the name, and muttered it to himself over and over again at the bar, fearful that it would slip from his memory before he had been served. He was trying his best to please, but she sat immovable, with folded arms, as he returned from the bar.

'Sorry, I've talked about myself a lot,' he said. 'How are you?'

'I'm all right.'

'And what are you doing? Have you a full-time job?'

'I'm getting by.'

'And what about your old house in Clapham? You're still there?'

That drew her longest answer yet. In several staccato sentences, she informed him that there was damp rising from the basement, rot in a windowledge, and two slates were missing from the roof. She also wanted to replace an electrical fitting, and had unfulfilled ambitions for the upstairs bathroom.

'You always seemed to find it a bit of a burden.'

'It's not a burden, but it costs a lot of money, a lot of money, and I haven't got much money. And I don't think it's right for you to grin as if it's funny.'

'Was I grinning? I'm so sorry.'

'Because everybody can't be a famous Member of Parliament, Joseph.'

Occasionally, Joseph came across this puzzling phenomenon, that old acquaintances seemed to resent his sudden rise to what they regarded as success. He found it hard to explain that being in the House of Commons did not feel like success to him. 'I'm not very famous, Angel.'

'You were on television.'

That was famous enough for Angel. He was lost for an answer. It was an evening for being made to feel dreadful by old lovers.

'Anyway, it's nice to see you again,' he said, wondering how he could steer the conversation back to Frank Rist's activities without causing offence. She gave him a look that he could not confidently interpret. It might have been saying that she did not believe it was nice to see her at all.

'How's your wife?' she asked in an unfriendly tone.

'She's fine.'

'Are you happy?'

At that moment, Joseph was anything but happy.

'Not happy?' Angel said, quickly sensing his mood.

It was the moment to go to the nub of the matter. Tugging at his ear from awkwardness, he replied, 'I don't know whether you ever knew about my relations with Diana Draycott.' Angel did not answer. He decided to march on; there was, after all, no point in concealment. 'I had an affair with Diana, you see. It started one night after we'd had an argument, and I thought you were ending our, our . . .' He could not think of the word covering what had passed between him and Angel.

'Love,' she said, as if she were giving an order.

'Yes, I thought you were ending it, because you didn't want me to stay at your house, so I went to Diana's. Something began between myself and Diana, which didn't last. And now the newspapers know, and I'm afraid that Diana's going to be terribly hurt.'

'Won't your wife be hurt?'

'Yes, she will too.'

'So why did you mention Diana but not your wife?'

He had thought that because Diana and Angel were distantly related, it might be the more effective way to draw Angel's sympathy, but apparently not.

'Is your wife jealous?'

'No. No. Well . . .' An image of Margaret as a young tigress came to mind, but he decided quickly that it would be disloyal to share it with Angel. 'No, she's not,' he asserted.

But he could see Angel looking hard into his face, and knew

that, unwittingly, he had given the impression that he was unhappily married to a jealous woman. Neither assertion was true, but like many people who are themselves unhappy Angel had a gift for drawing confessions of unhappiness from others.

She suddenly changed the subject, and began talking about an occasion when they had been together. The day stood out clearly in her memory, but not in his. From her description, it could have been any one of several days he half remembered.

'You don't remember?'

'I'm not sure.'

'You've forgotten what you said?'

'Remind me.'

'Well, if you've forgotten, it doesn't matter.'

'Just jog my memory. What subject were we discussing?'

'I said it doesn't matter.'

'Give me a chance, Angel.'

'You were talking about loving me.' He still did not remember. Angel sighed loudly, uncrossed her arms, and laid her hands on her lap. 'If you don't remember, that means you've forgotten.'

He had an uneasy feeling that this memory lapse counted heavily against him. Whatever he had said on the subject of loving Angel had evidently meant a lot to her.

'Anyway, I don't know if there's any way you could possibly help. I mean, about this Diana business, and the newspapers,' he said. Angel had crossed her arms again, and once again was staring at him in stubborn silence. 'I mean, I know who's behind it.'

'How?'

'Sorry?'

'How do you know?'

'It's obvious. It's Frank. He has written things about me on a web site, and it's as if he has been stalking me.'

He described seeing Frank late at night in the Commons, and

the subsequent incident in his constituency surgery. The story seemed to irritate Angel, who sighed impatiently and picked up the bag that was lying on the bench beside her.

'I'd like to go home now, please. Are you going to be a gentleman, and walk me to my door?'

He excused himself and took refuge in the gents, relieved to be away from her strange stares and impenetrable silences. Facing the porcelain, he reminded himself that he must stay with her until he had extracted an answer from her to indicate how much she knew about Frank's activities.

She had emptied her whisky glass in his absence, having hardly touched it in his presence. She must have swallowed it almost in one gulp. She declined his offer to fetch another, evidently wanting him to drink up quickly so that they could leave. Perhaps because it was getting late, his own beer had begun to taste odd.

He asked whether she was still in regular contact with Frank. She answered with a nod, watching him all the time with an air of detached curiosity.

'I'm facing exposure of this Diana thing in the Sunday papers,' he explained, surprised by the difficulty he was suddenly having in constructing coherent sentences. 'I don't mind for my sake, but it's very, very, very bad for Diana Draycott . . .'

'Has she got a jealous husband?'

'No, no, no, Sir Peter Draycott is the kindest, most caring, most understanding man . . .' Speech was becoming more difficult with each word. He took another long sip of beer, hoping that it would help. It still tasted odd.

'So why is it worse for her than it is for you?'

Joseph replied, laboriously, 'It's worse for her than it is for me because she's who she is and I'm who I am. Is that a taut–, taut–, taut–?' He shook his head. The word he wanted was *tautology* but the -*ology* had slipped away. Angel was still watching, arms folded. 'Anyway, I wondered if you can help.'

'How?'

'Can't you ask Frank not to do it?'

'Yes, I can ask.'

'Can you ask tomorrow? It's got to be tomorrow, because we've only got tomorrow, because it's Sunday's paper, you see.'

'Yes.'

'That's very, very, very kind of you, Angel. Very kind. Do you want to go, because if you want to go, I mean I don't want to go, unless you want to go, but . . . you follow. My car is, my car is parked. Out there.'

Angel watched, immobile, as he pulled himself to his feet, with unexpected difficulty. 'Has it occurred to you,' she asked, 'that if you drive a car in your present state, you'll be arrested? Won't that be a scandal, for a famous Member of Parliament?'

'Oh shit.'

He sat down abruptly. She was right, of course. He was blind drunk. That was why speaking, standing, thinking and other simple actions had become so challenging. Odd that he should be blind drunk on only a couple of glasses – but the second one had tasted peculiar. Should he complain? No. He could not risk the scandal. It was going to be a long, difficult journey home, and early in the morning he would have to come back to reclaim the car.

'You can stay and use my couch, if you want to,' Angel offered.

He looked into her face – or faces, because at least two images of her were swimming before his eyes – and wondered if there was anything wrong with this offer. He decided that he probably had no choice.

The cold air and light drizzle outside helped clear his brain a little, though for a moment he feared he would be sick. There was an odd taste of malt in his throat. He was surprised when she slipped her hand round his elbow and then at once withdrew it. He was sorry that she did that. The brief gesture was the first real sign that she still liked him.

'You're very quiet,' he said, after they had progressed in silence along several dark residential streets.

'I'm wondering.'

'Wondering what?'

'Whether you're completely naïve.' The question took him so much by surprise that it almost rendered him sober. Before he could reply, she asked, 'What do you actually suppose Frank wants?'

'Revenge.'

'No, he doesn't want revenge at all. He'd like to prove that he's right and you're wrong.'

'Then there's no need to drag Diana into it.'

That was rather a good answer considering the state he had been in only minutes earlier, he thought to himself.

He could not see her house well in the yellow half-light, but he had an impression that it was more run-down than on his first visit, twenty years earlier. He smelled the damp as soon as they were inside the long narrow hall. Beyond the stairway was a door that had not been there before, with a covering of cheap plywood, implying that the ground floor was now a self-contained flat. His feet thudded on bare wood.

'You've had the carpet taken up.'

'It rotted,' she replied, putting a sigh into the second word. She turned her back on him and headed upstairs. She was still a nice shape from the back.

There was damp on the wall going up the stairs, but in her sitting room on the first floor, there was a musty warmth rather like being wrapped in an unwashed old shawl. There was little furniture. The main items were a freestanding glass cabinet on the wall furthest from the door, and along the outside wall, a long leather sofa. Angel appeared with an armful of bedclothes.

'So, you have a downstairs lodger?'

'I have to.'

'A good tenant?'

'Yes.' She finished making up his bed, then added casually, 'It's Frank.'

'Frank! Frank Rist?'

'He has lived here since Christine died.'

'Jesus Christ. Why didn't you tell me?'

Joseph leapt to his feet, almost sending the armchair toppling backwards, thinking to himself that whatever the inconvenience, he had to get out of the house at once.

'It's all right, he's out for the night,' Angel said.

'But you should have told me he lived here.'

'I didn't realize you didn't know.'

Pacing the floor, Joseph considered again whether he should still make a quick exit. Eventually he decided against it, having weighed up the difficulty of persuading any cab driver to take him to outer London at this time of night, the possibility that he might be recognized the worse for drink, the inconvenience of getting up at dawn to collect the car and be back in time for his Saturday-morning surgery, and the risk of causing offence.

'Do you want to ring your wife?'

'No. No. I'd better not. She might be asleep.'

'I'm in the same bedroom as before if you want me,' Angel said as she left.

When he turned out the light, he discovered that the thin curtains allowed the bright moonlight into the room. The full moon perhaps affected his sleep: he had a restless night, punctuated by his standard nightmare featuring pulsating blue light, and police cars, and looming, undefined threat. He thought something had invaded his bed, and fought in his sleep to push it away. Awakened suddenly, he was surprised to see Angel walk through a door near his head and glide across the room stark naked, her back and bottom fluorescent in the moonglow. Then he realized he was not awake: he had slipped out of one disturbing dream into another, though the second was more realistic than the first. There was no door near his head.

In the morning, he found Angel at her kitchen table drinking tea, with both hands wrapped around the mug, dressed in a blue towelling dressing gown and leather slippers. He had no difficulty carrying out her invitation to help himself because the cupboards were organized as they had always been. He even recognized some of the old crockery and cutlery. She had taken pains to keep it all clean and tidy, but had been unable to prevent the kind of erosion that left chips missing from the sideboard and the cupboard doors.

'I'll show you where it's damp in Frank's room,' she said unexpectedly, as he was rinsing his breakfast things.

He did not want to see the damp in Frank's room, but she was intent on showing it to him. She led the way downstairs holding a key. The inside of Frank's lair was as sparse and spartan as he would have expected: low ceiling, poor lighting, one wooden chair at a work table, a single rug over part of the wooden floor, and bookshelves on every wall reaching to the ceiling. There was a library of Marxist texts familiar from their left-wing days, to which had been added editions of the Bible and religious tracts from Frank's next phase, and now books filled with warnings about the spread of the European superstate.

'Up there,' said Angel irritably, thinking that he was looking around for the damp but not seeing it. She was pointing up into one corner, with a sweep of the arm that caused her dressing gown to flap open. She had nothing on underneath, and since she was directly facing him, instead of seeing rising damp he was looking at a near-naked woman. As with the house, all the furnishings were where he remembered them, but the years had added to the roundness of the stomach and put sag into the breasts. He saw, guiltily, that she knew what he had been looking at. With unhurried movements, she wrapped her dressing gown back around herself and said, 'You'd better go.'

There was more awkwardness awaiting him outside. As he paused at the open door to say goodbye, a battered, cream-coloured Volkswagen pulled up by the gate at the end of the short garden path. Its driver was Frank Rist.

Both men halted in mutual recognition. Frank was on the pavement, one hand on his car door. Joseph was the first to move, turning his head to see if Angel was still behind him. She was. He stepped forward slowly, debating with himself whether to explain his presence. He decided against it: she would have time enough for any explanations she thought necessary.

The thought then went through his mind that it was odd that Frank could afford a car.

Suddenly, Frank raised a hand to ask Joseph to stop. He rummaged in the car, emerging with a small black object in his hand. Before Joseph had recognized it as a camera, Frank had taken at least one photograph.

'Don't, Frank!' Angel said.

She was in the doorway, arms folded. Her demeanour suggested that the balance of power between her and Frank had changed in her favour since they were young. Frank put the camera away without a word.

'Why did you do that?' Joseph asked.

Frank smiled that broad false-friendly smile that had ceased to deceive. 'For my album, Joseph, old mate, my personal album. Great moments in time: a Member of Parliament calls at our house.'

'Frank!' Angel called. She unfolded her arms and pushed the front door wide open to give him room to pass. He walked meekly into the house. It was like watching a housewife summon a ferocious-looking pet dog.

She gave Joseph a last hostile look, and shut him out.

·16·

The Siege

Isobel and Tom were happy all morning playing Count the Journalists. Stationed in the smaller front bedroom, one on either side of the window, they pressed their small faces to the corners of the pane thinking they could see without being seen.

'No, Tom! You've missed the nother one: not the big one, the nother one next to him, the other nother one.'

It fell to Isobel to supervise, because Tom's grasp of the numerical sequence collapsed somewhere around seven or eight. Periodically, one or other child would emerge from the bedroom to announce excitedly, 'There are *twelve* journalists at the end of the path.'

Their parents stayed in the kitchen or the back bedrooms, away from watchful eyes, because the little crowd that Isobel lumped together as 'journalists' included at least as many photographers as reporters. It was unpleasant having to hide away as if the house were under siege.

As usual for a time of crisis, Margaret was at the kitchen table, mug of tea in one hand. Unusually, she was smoking, although she knew better than most about the effects of tobacco. The alien smell added to Joseph's dislocated feeling that none of this was really happening. He searched Margaret's face for any sign that she blamed him for the disaster. There were reasons enough. These were not the best of circumstances in which to own up about an old affair, even though it had been over years before he had met Margaret. Moreover, he had to describe how he blurted out a self-incriminating remark on the radio. But Margaret did not appear to be angry, jealous, or even curious. He gave her only a minimal explanation and she asked no questions. She had lapsed into silent, weary gloom.

The children were getting on their nerves, running back and forth excitedly between the front room and the kitchen. Isobel arrived, breathless, to ask, 'Dad, Dad, what's a journalist?'

Her mother replied, 'Journalists are people who always ask a lot of questions about private things which are none of their business.'

Soon, there came a howl of distress from the small bedroom at the front. Tom lurched down the stairs, crying at full volume. His parents rushed to gather him in protective arms, fearful that a ghastly accident had been added to the day's dismal events. Between hot tears he protested, 'Isobel say I a bloody journalist!'

Isobel explained self-righteously that Tom had asked her why she wore a red hairband. That being none of his business, she had naturally likened him to a bloody journalist. She was told off for saying 'bloody'.

After a time, as Margaret's stoic silence became as oppressive as the manic screams of the children, Joseph retreated to his study, and to the telephone messages which had now filled a half-hour tape. Nearly all were from journalists. Some, from well-wishers, only lowered his spirits further because they were no practical help, but put him under an obligation to reply. It was a relief to hear Gerald Moon's voice in the middle of the tape. Irrespective of whether he liked Gerald, or approved of him, he certainly needed some expert advice now. He called the number Moon had left on the tape.

'Are you all right, mate?'

'Not really: the house is under siege.'

In a few sentences, Joseph described how the morning's events had begun, soon after nine o'clock, with a long, insistent ring on the doorbell. Joseph had been alert enough to shout a warning to the children not to answer the door. There was a stranger outside, holding a notebook. Minutes later, Joseph made the mistake of answering the telephone. It was the same journalist, using a mobile phone. Joseph gave him a determined 'no comment' and a warning that he would be trespassing if he did not retreat beyond the front gate – despite which the doorbell sounded about once every half-hour, either because another journalist had joined the vigil, or because one of those already there was bored. The telephone rang continuously, until the tape in the answering machine was full. Unable to go out to the newsagent, they still had not seen the newspaper that was the cause of the commotion, but Gerald had, of course.

'What's the damage, do you think?' Joseph asked.

'It might be bad; it might be all right. Is there any more to come out, mate?'

'About Diana and me? Nothing.'

Gerald was silent for a moment. 'I'm sorry, mate, but this is totally important: there's definitely nothing?'

'Nothing. It finished years ago.'

There was, of course, another story which Dave Drucker seemed to know but for some reason had never used – but that was not one to be shared with Gerald Moon.

'OK, mate, that should be all right. Did you say they're outside your house?'

'They've been here all morning.'

'Can I suggest something? Why don't you take out a flask of coffee?'

'Treat them to coffee? I'd rather shoot them.'

'Yes, but they're doing their job, mate. You know? They're going to waste a whole day hanging about, with no story, so they'll be pissed off. Yeah? So which is better, mate – to have them pissed off with you, or with their news desks? Better it's not you, surely.'

'I'll get a barrage of questions if I step out there.'

'Do you have to answer them, though? You can't be forced to. It's up to you, though, mate. It's just my advice.'

'Do you think the Draycotts are under siege? I can't ring and ask.'

'Well, neither can I, mate. I don't do media stuff for Tories. But I know a bloke who does. I can ask.'

'I'd be really grateful, Gerald. I would just very much like to know that Diana's all right.'

'All right, mate, I'll ask.'

There were also calls on the tape from members of his constituency party. He ought to reply to them, but weariness overcame him at the thought of having to explain his relationship with Diana separately to two borough councillors, a magistrate, a full-time trade union official, a deputy head teacher, two social workers, a computer programmer, a housepainter, an unemployed musician, and others whose occupations he did not know. Some would sympathize, but others certainly would not. Some took a fixed view that an MP is the servant of his party, nothing else, and that all of his actions and all the publicity he attracted should be judged only in terms of whether he was serving it well or not. By getting his name in the paper first as a reformed dope smoker and now this, Joseph plainly was not giving his party flawless service. He had been through it all with Thelma the previous day, so that she at least would be forewarned. She had made no comment, but he deduced from the look she gave him that too much publicity like this could be the end of his political career.

Outside, in the back garden, a squirrel was running along the top of their wooden fence. He was a familiar caller in their garden, with an annoying habit of digging up bulbs and biting into them greedily – squirrels were neither elegant, nor rare, nor much loved by the public, but at least the little mammal had one quality Joseph sorely lacked: he was sure-footed.

It took Gerald only a few minutes to ring back. That in itself was heartening. Gerald was a calculating young man, who did not take this much trouble out of sentiment, but because he continued to believe that Joseph might be useful in future. In other words, Joseph was not finished yet.

'My contact says they can't do much for Lady Draycott. She won't take advice. They're going to have to leave her to do it in her own way.'

Joseph took several deep breaths. For the first time that morning, he was angry. Now that he had stopped feeling useless and helpless, there was room for anger. The sensation rose in a single hot wave, making him want to strike out.

'I want to get Frank Rist,' he said. 'He's behind this. He's the little shit that tipped them off.'

'Right, yeah, tell me everything about him.'

As Joseph ran through a rapid account of recent events, he noticed Margaret out in the garden, talking over the fence to their next-door neighbour. Everyone in the street must know by now about the knot of journalists at the front of the house.

'What's this bloke's job, by the way?'

'I doubt if he's got one. On social security, probably. Can you do anything about him?'

'He's toast,' Gerald said, and hung up.

Something curious was happening down in the garden. Their neighbour had fetched an aluminium stepladder and was passing it across the fence. By the time Joseph had reached the garden, the ladder was in place and Isobel was ascending it, guided by her mother. It was explained to him that Margaret and the children were tired of being trapped in the house. Their neighbours were a retired accountant and his wife, kindly types with no noticeable political opinions, though sometimes a little too ready to involve themselves in Joseph's affairs. Now he was grateful for their nosiness, as the accountant's wife relayed excitedly how she had rung her neighbours on the far side, who in turn were contacting the people in the house beyond. With telephone calls and ladders, they would get Margaret and the children all the way to the end of the street, garden by garden. The only risk was that a journalist might peek round the side of the house at the wrong moment, in which case they might be photographed in an undignified pose.

'Wait, I'll create a diversion,' Joseph announced.

It took a few minutes to prepare a large flask of coffee and gather it and a dozen plastic cups on to a tray. He almost lost his nerve as he reached the front door, knowing that the simple act of opening it would bring him face to face with the mob outside. But he told himself that there is no point in consulting a spin doctor and then allowing cowardice to overrule his advice.

The photographers went into action at the instant he stepped into the sunlight; he had been snapped perhaps fifty or sixty times before he had covered the short distance to the front gate. The whir of cameras was quickly superseded by the babble of questions. Diana's name was thrown at him from six directions.

Pretending not to hear, he asked if anyone wanted coffee.

As the questions continued to fly at him, he looked enquiringly from face to face, wearing a fixed smile. He had overcome an initial attack of nerves, and was secretly starting to enjoy himself.

'Oh, come on, I'll have a coffee,' said one of them eventually.

Joseph handed the tray to the nearest journalist, asking if he would kindly hold it. Almost all of them eventually accepted his offer, thanking him with surprisingly good humour. They were a mixed bunch, about ten men and a couple of women. The reporters were all young and had taken some care over their appearance; the photographers were older and uglier.

'Can't you just give us one quote about Lady Draycott, just one quote?' one of the women pleaded, shamelessly giving him a look of doe-eyed helplessness. Joseph shook his head.

'Oh come on, Mr Pilgrim, we've been stuck here all bloody morning,' one of the men complained.

Joseph took the tray and the empty flask back into the house.

A minute later, he was in the back garden making a rapid ascent over the garden hedge. Next door's garden was neater than theirs, with small shrubs and bedding plants all around the narrow lawn. There were almost no hedges, as if the occupants objected to any plant more than knee-high, but at the halfway point one neatly clipped rose bush had been allowed to stand alone.

He thanked the accountant and the accountant's wife and used their ladder to climb into the garden beyond. This one was more extravagantly cultivated, with fruit trees and abundant small bushes, creepers which had wrapped themselves around climbing frames, and wistaria covering the back wall of the house. The occupants emerged through the patio doors as Joseph dropped down on to their lawn. They were a young, childless couple, whom he did not know well. For that reason, he was compelled to stay talking to them for several minutes, explaining the disturbance on the pavement. The man stood with folded arms, shaking his head, and the woman frowned continuously. Neither made any comment until he suggested that he ought to be moving on. With a wave of a hand, the man indicated a ladder already in place and invited Joseph to help himself.

The third garden was a shambles, disfigured by spreading weeds and builders' rubble. The man of the house had a savage appearance, with a ring in one ear and tattoos on the arms and shoulders, on display because above the waistline he wore nothing but a vest. He interrupted Joseph's brief speech of thanks as if he were too busy to listen, and directed him to a gap in the hedge leading to garden number four. This was less a garden than an outline, like the base of a pie without the filling. The grass was cropped neat and short, and the flowerbeds around the border had been raked and cleared of all rubbish, but nothing was growing. There was nothing but neat, bare soil.

He almost caught up with Margaret and the children, who were at the top of another ladder, preparing to jump down into the next garden, but politeness demanded that he introduce himself to the middle-aged couple and their adolescent son who had gathered at the foot of the ladder.

'We didn't know we had an MP living almost next door,' the mother announced. 'If we'd known that, we could have seen you about the pedestrian crossing . . .' And she launched into an unabridged history and analysis of the pedestrian crossing outside a nearby shopping parade. In the middle of this epic, her husband – who obviously made a practice of ignoring what his wife was saying – suddenly cut in to ask, 'Does this often happen in your line of work?'

Joseph shook his head, thinking it rude to speak. Eventually, he was released to clamber across the high hedge and down into garden number five, where he shook the hand of a slightly pompous-looking householder who had made a poor attempt to comb his hair so as to cover his bald patch.

Finally, in garden six, he caught up with Margaret. The brightly coloured slide, the tricycles and the garden toys carelessly scattered about told him at once that this was a home inhabited by young children, one of whom had made friends with Isobel and Tom. They were running in a circle, shouting primitive battle

cries. Another child was clinging to his mother's dress as she and
Margaret conducted a lively conversation. The mother was red in
the face, rotund, and wearing an old corduroy dress, apron and
pink bedroom slippers, but she had a pleasant, glowing smile.
Because of a bend in the road, this garden was smaller than the
others, five-sided rather than rectangular, as if a corner had been
sliced off.

'We're expressing amazement at the appalling behaviour of
journalists,' Margaret announced.

'Tell me about it,' Joseph replied.

From the glass veranda doors a small, balding man who was
evidently the children's father emerged carrying a newspaper,
which he handed to Joseph. 'Your wife said you'd not had the
chance to see this,' he said.

What first hit Joseph was the huge headline, across two pages,
and the large black-and-white photograph of a man and woman
walking along Millbank together, outside the House of Lords. He
had to look twice before he recognized himself. The story, billed
as an 'exclusive' by Dave Drucker, began:

A Labour MP is facing political ruin today over his 'passionate
fling' with a high-ranking Tory. High-flyer Joseph Pilgrim
stunned radio listeners last week when he BOASTED of his
affair with an unnamed married woman. The only detail he gave
of the affair, during a late-night radio phone-in programme, was
that the woman and her husband are still married.

But the sworn statement of a former close friend of 39-year-
old Mr Pilgrim has sensationally stripped the mask of anonymity
from his secret lover. She is Diana Draycott, a prominent
Conservative and wife of former Home Office minister Sir
Peter Draycott. Mr Pilgrim, married with two young children,
and Lady Draycott, pictured near the House of Commons, are
still 'very close' friends.

Thousands of listeners to a late-night radio phone-in heard Mr Pilgrim's astonishing admission, blurted out in answer to an unexpected question from a fellow panellist. The Labour MP added defiantly: 'I deny absolutely that I ever destroyed anyone's marriage.'

Sir Peter and Lady Draycott have been married for almost 25 years, with two teenage children. They are described by friends as a 'devoted' couple.

Asked to comment on his relationship with the 48-year-old Tory, a furious Mr Pilgrim exclaimed: 'It's none of your bloody business. I'm worried about my wife and children. This could devastate my children. What do you think you're doing?'

Yesterday, a friend who knew Pilgrim closely at the time of the affair said: 'He was completely infatuated with her. He used to go off for weekends in Cambridge (where the Draycotts then lived) without telling anyone. It was a short passionate fling which ended because she refused to leave her husband. It was supposed to be a secret, but lots of people guessed he was having an affair, though almost no one knew who with.'

'You'd think it all happened yesterday!' Joseph exclaimed, before he discovered the information, tucked away in about the fifteenth paragraph, that his affair with Diana had taken place in 1977.

Despite himself, Joseph was impressed by the skill with which a small number of facts had been organized for maximum effect. He now understood those oddly artificial questions Dave Drucker had asked on his doorstep, which had manoeuvred him into making replies that, when reproduced in cold print, read like the blustering of a guilty man unexpectedly caught out.

He could not feel angry. He could not feel wronged. This was what Dave Drucker did. It was in his nature, as it was in a wasp's nature to sting. He felt a fool.

Margaret had stepped over the toys scattered on their

neighbours' lawn to read the newspaper over his shoulder, frowning. Suddenly, with an angry gesture, she pulled it out of his hands.

'When did they take this picture?'

'The other day. God knows how they caught us.'

He realized as he spoke that Margaret had gone pale. She was looking at him with a shocked expression, as if she could not believe what she was seeing. Then Joseph noticed how falsely eloquent the photograph was. The camera had caught Diana with her head thrown back, her mouth open in a wide smile, looking at him from the far corners of her eyes, as if in adoration. Anyone seeing it could be forgiven for assuming they were lovers still. It was a stunning example of how a camera can lie.

He started to try to explain, but she abruptly handed the newspaper back to its owner and said, 'Can we get out to the front, please?'

The woman allowed Margaret to go through the house and out via the front door, while Joseph watched from her front room. The knot of journalists was just visible in the distance, still sipping their coffee. Margaret crossed the road, walked towards them, crossed back again, and slipped into the driving seat of the family car, which was parked only feet away from them. It was only after the car had moved off and stopped a few yards up the road that it attracted their curiosity. There was a shout of recognition as Joseph piled the children into the back seat, and journalists began running along the pavement. The car had pulled away before they had covered half the distance.

In the back of the car, the children continued to bubble with excitement. They had had so much fun that they tried to prolong it by pointing out pedestrians to one another and crying, 'That one's a journalist.' A policeman was thus transformed into a policeman journalist. When they saw a mother and pushchair,

Isobel declared, 'There's a mummy journalist with her icky bicky baby journalist.'

'I saw a rhinoceros journalist,' Tom claimed.

The more absurd the observation, the more it fed their hysterical amusement. Margaret drove in grim silence until she could tolerate no more, then turned to shout at them to be quiet.

'That photograph was very, very misleading,' Joseph said.

'Look, I've been a prisoner in my house, the whole country knows you've been seeing an old lover I've never even heard of – that's enough, I don't want to talk about it.'

·17·

Promotion

For the second time, he went into the House of Commons on Monday morning wondering if his reputation was ruined beyond repair. He had not been able to face reading any more newspapers after seeing Dave Drucker's offering, except for Monday morning's *Financial Times*, which he took on the train into work so that he could forget his problems by immersing himself in the ups and downs of multinational corporations.

Inside the Commons, he looked expectantly into the faces of everyone he recognized, wondering what he could read in their expressions. Everyone, oddly, behaved as normal. The policemen and the badge messengers said good morning, a couple of MPs exchanged pleasantries with him, and one stopped for a long conversation about a standing committee on which they both served, scrutinizing a dull but worthy piece of new legislation on the administration of juvenile courts. There was an amendment which he and Rachel had drafted, on the advice of a couple of helpful magistrates' clerks, which was now incorporated as page 17, line 11 of the amended Bill. Joseph and his fellow MP, a podgy, bald, earnest and unbelievably dull man, discussed the amendment for nearly half an hour, standing in hot sunlight in one of the inner courtyards. His companion evidently had no idea that Joseph's name was in that day's newspapers.

By mid-morning he had decided that nobody in the entire

Palace of Westminster read the tabloid newspapers anyway, so he skimmed through them himself, although he feared the mood they would plunge him in. In fact, he was pleasantly surprised. By the standards for which tabloid newspapers had become famous, the reporting was factual, brief, and buried in inside pages. Weeks later, he would learn that there had been a change of opinion across the newspaper office midway through the day, as happens in a fast-moving industry. At first, Dave Drucker's story had provoked excitement, when it was thought to have all the ingredients of an enduring scandal; but by lunchtime, the reporters who had been sent to the Pilgrims' and the Draycotts' homes to 'get a new angle' were ringing in to report failure. They owned up with grudging admiration that Joseph Pilgrim had outsmarted them all, serving them coffee before sneaking his family out the back way. The only 'new angle' to emerge was an outraged comment by a friend of Sir Peter, another Tory knight of the shires, who was accusing Drucker of unjustified intrusion into personal privacy.

Joseph was in a café inside the Commons, reading these surprisingly straight accounts of his old love affair, when he was slapped hard on the shoulder by a squat figure in a pinstriped suit. He looked up into the grizzled, bearded face of Denis Drummond, the Minister who was reputedly close to the Deputy Prime Minister and who had once cryptically told Joseph that he was 'OK'.

'Got a minute?' Denis asked.

'I was just reading about myself,' Joseph replied, closing the newspapers.

Denis set a half-finished cup of tea down on the table and sat opposite Joseph. He stared at him for a full minute, as if weighing him up, before taking a large spoonful of sugar and stirring it into what remained of his tea. 'Got a bit of a fucking problem in our department. There's four of us ministers sharing two PPSs. Did you know that?'

Joseph could not immediately remember what a PPS was, but was embarrassed to ask, so shook his head, hoping that it would come back to him quickly.

'It's not fucking working out,' said Denis. 'I need one to myself. Yes? We were throwing some names around and yours came up. What do you think? Do you want to be my PPS?'

'I can never remember what those initials stand for,' said Joseph.

Denis looked offended. 'If you're not interested, just say so.'

'Parliamentary Private Secretary,' Joseph suddenly exclaimed, as he realized what was offered. This was a job in the government. There are four levels to which an MP can aspire: Secretary of State, Minister of State, Parliamentary Under-Secretary of State, or Parliamentary Private Secretary. What was being held out to Joseph was the humblest of the four, but it was a start. It was what almost every new MP hungered for. And this was the day when he had come into work thinking he had been ruined by a hint of scandal.

'Sorry, Denis, I was distracted by this shit in the newspapers.'

'Yes, I've seen it,' said Denis. 'Load of fucking rubbish.'

'You wouldn't be bothered by having a PPS who has had all this garbage written about him?'

'I'm told you're getting good at handling the reptiles.'

'I'm gaining experience.'

'We need that. You know what you get, don't you? A load of extra bloody work, no money, and if you vote against the government on anything you're sacked. Nobody with any sense would do it.'

'Yes, but I'd like to.'

Denis Drummond put a hand on his shoulder. 'I've got to go, got a fucking meeting. Give it thought.'

When Joseph reached his office, his immediate impression was that Rachel already knew about his unexpected promotion, because she was excitedly congratulating him before he had time to remove his coat.

'This is really good,' Rachel exclaimed, pointing at a newspaper lying open on her desk. She was dressed today in a tight red top and a very short black skirt and black tights which invited his eyes to direct themselves to her legs.

Joseph had been reading the same newspaper in the café when he was interrupted, but had not reached the centre pages, where there was an opinion piece, prominently displayed, written by a former Conservative politician who had taken to journalism since losing her seat in the Commons. Above the text, there was a photograph of her. The camera had expertly caught a cruel smile befitting her reputation.

Joseph Pilgrim, up and coming Labour MP and one of the better-looking men in a House of Commons woefully short of male talent, has been exposed by a Sunday newspaper for his youthful fling with Diana Draycott, whose husband is an old, dear friend of mine. Sir Peter is now rightly doing what so many cheated Tory wives have done in the past: he is standing by his woman. That is no surprise to anyone who knows him. He was always decent, unselfish and incorruptible, in a government – and a profession – which fell a long way in public repute. But let's be honest, he was never a top-rank minister. He was never thought worth bringing into the Cabinet and, dear man though he is, he is not the most exciting prospect a woman might find in her marriage bed.

I'd say it is pretty obvious what actually happened when Joseph Pilgrim, a handsome teenager, met Diana Draycott, thirtyish and married to Mr Nice-but-dim. Bluntly, Mr Pilgrim was doing the lady a favour. Of course, he should have kept his mouth about it afterwards – but, hey, that's teenagers. End of story.

As he read the final paragraph, Joseph threw the newspaper down with a cry of disgust.

'No, that's good, Joseph,' Rachel exclaimed. 'That's a Tory woman on your side. That's really crucial. You've been attacked twice, and twice you've come out well. That's brilliant, Joseph.'

'But what if the Draycotts read that? I wasn't doing her a favour. Peter's not dim!'

Rachel conceded, 'Well, it's shabby on both of them, yeah.'

'What can have induced anyone to write something so nasty?' He intended it to be a rhetorical question. To his surprise, Rachel reacted with a guilty, defensive look. 'What?' he asked.

'Gerald's been working *so* hard!'

'Gerald's behind this?'

'He was on the phone for hours . . . on a Sunday, Joseph.'

He would have liked to have been angry. He would have liked to shout that Gerald was a professional liar in a trade suited for liars, but he was halted by the thought that Gerald might actually have saved his political life. How did he know what controlled the mood swings of the daily press? If all the newspapers had come out attacking him with one voice, there would have been no future for him.

The pager attached at his trouser belt tingled. On its screen, a message had appeared: GOOD BOY, IT'S WHAT WE'RE HERE FOR. RING ME ASAP – NEVILLE.

He rang the Whips' Office on an internal phone.

'What do you mean, "it's what we're here for"?' he demanded of Never Evil.

'Joseph, my boy, we're just having a good laugh about it. Did you really give the scumbags coffee?'

'Yes, I did. Is that why you wanted me to ring?'

'No, listen old boy, about this PPS position – Denis Drummond has spoken to you, yes? The whips' view is we don't object in principle, but we think it's a bit early. I hope you don't mind hearing this. You understand. It would be a big promotion for someone who's only been here a few months. It would put you right ahead. We think it's not the best place for you.'

'What, you're blocking the appointment?'

'No, what we thought was: do the job on an informal basis. That means do whatever Denis wants. Consider yourself unofficially informally on the payroll, but without an official announcement. Denis says that's OK with him. Is it OK with you?'

'So, I get a job for which I'm not paid, which no one knows I've got, which stops me from ever voting against the government, because if I do I get sacked.'

'That's about the long and the short of it,' Never Evil said.

'Neville, can we wind back to the beginning of the conversation? Forgive me if I'm being dense, but I still don't understand what you meant when you said, "it's what we're here for".'

'Just a joke, my boy, just a joke – inspired by all this complete crap in the papers, which we're completely overlooking. Our decision not to completely approve your appointment has nothing to do with what's in the press, I assure you. We *never* let the press set the agenda. In fact, the lads are saying you've done the job we're all here to do – to shaft the Tories! We're having a good laugh.'

Joseph put the phone down on him.

In a weird and tawdry way, he had achieved success. As he discovered over the next few days, he had begun to stand out among the new MPs. He saw it in the friendly approachability of people who had ignored him up until now. He discovered that he was having to waste less time sitting patiently on one of the green benches in the debating chamber hoping for a chance to speak. The Speaker and her deputies were quicker to call him, having found out who he was. Even a few journalists from upmarket newspapers approached him with words of sympathy. And there was an extraordinary encounter with a celebrated Cabinet Minister.

He spotted her walking along the pavement in front of the House of Commons, though he did not recognize her instantly because she could hardly have looked less like the occupant of high office. She was dressed in a cheap-looking overcoat, fur boots, and a pompom hat, and was walking slowly, as if her feet hurt, oblivious to those around her, not caring what impression she might be making.

As he recognized her, she noticed him. Rolling her eyes in his direction, she announced, 'I know who you are.'

He wondered whether it would be appropriate to reply in kind, but since a recent opinion poll had shown her to be the only member of the Cabinet more popular than the Prime Minister, she would expect him to know who she was.

She patted his arm and continued talking. Each word came out loudly and separately, as if she had deliberately slowed her own rate of speaking. Sometimes, she drew up her upper lip to use the tone of voice an adult might use to amuse a small child.

'I say that, my dear, because there are so many of you who arrived at the last election that half the time I don't know who most of you are. Which way are you going?'

'Seven Millbank.'

'I'm going past there to the building on the corner. Keep me company.' On the way, she remarked, 'I'm glad you owned up about cannabis. You'll get a lot of goodwill for that.'

They reached a crowded part of the pavement beyond the frontage of the House of Lords, where tourists were pouring in and out of a riverside park. Joseph watched their faces to see if any of them recognized his companion. Some did. She fell silent, as if the effort of walking required all her attention. Less than two years earlier, she had survived an operation to remove a brain tumour. The hat was there to conceal hair loss. Though it was reported that she had made a full recovery, she was taking care to conserve her energies.

'May I say that I think you have done an amazing job?' he said.

'Yes, you may.'

'You've done an amazing job.'

She had been sent to Northern Ireland, where she was having success persuading the hardline leaders on both sides to negotiate.

'Fuck 'em, I say. Loyalist troublemakers, republican troublemakers, fuck 'em. They can't go on like this for ever, so fuck 'em. They're used to dealing with posh ex-public-school boys from London who are very grand with them. They don't know how to deal with me, coz I ain't at all posh, and I got one of these.'

At the end of this sentence she pointed ostentatiously at her thighs. A middle-aged couple passing by the other way started with surprise. Joseph gave them a reassuring smile, to convince them that they could not really have seen a Cabinet Minister walking along the pavement pointing at her genitalia.

'Are the reptiles going to give you any more trouble?' the Cabinet Minister asked.

'Fuck 'em,' Joseph replied.

They parted at the entrance to Seven Millbank.

But if this was success, what was the point? He had clumsily brought untold distress and humiliation upon a couple from whom he had received nothing but kindness in twenty years, and he had surrendered the right to think for himself for the sake of a nebulous position. Of course, he could refuse to take it. He could become a rebel. He could announce to the world out there that politics is a tainted profession. But everyone out there already knew that, and meanwhile society's conflicts had to be resolved by someone.

There was another avenue open to him: he could use his influence for the people who tramped through his constituency surgeries every week seeking help. In this, he was scoring small successes. Half of the relatives whom Mr Afzal wanted to invite to his daughter's wedding had been issued their visitors' visas, after Joseph had complained to the Home Office. Even the egregious Mrs Baker had been offered a council house that seemed to meet her requirements. The case that worried him most was Dawn Jones and the two daughters she wanted to shield from their violent father. Joseph had convinced himself that if he could solve Mrs Jones's problem, he would have proved to himself that there was a purpose to being in Parliament.

Frustratingly, there had been no breakthrough in the case. The court order against Mrs Jones still stood, though unenforced. Joseph had made a discovery he had hoped would resolve the problem. He had learnt of the existence of special contact centres where estranged fathers and their children can meet. Dawn Jones need not fear for her daughters in one of these centres, because there would be adults on hand. The offer to meet in a contact centre had been forwarded to Mal Jones, through his solicitor, but there had been no reply.

Awaking one morning under a cloud of mild depression, he decided he could wait no longer: he would get into his car and seek out Mal Jones at home.

·18·

Mugged

Mr Jones at least lived at ground level, in a compact little council estate beyond the boundaries of Joseph's constituency, close to a wealthy suburb. The houses were small and pressed together like rows of redbrick boxes, each with its minuscule front garden. This was one of London's better council estates, despite its high density, and too far south to be as ethnically mixed as the inner-London estates. Some gardens were immaculately neat, but not the one in front of Mr Jones's house, which could not accurately be described as a garden at all: it was a few ugly square yards of churned-up concrete. There was a delay after Joseph knocked on the door, giving him a false moment of disappointment and relief before he was confronted by a wiry man with a tight red T-shirt over his jutting chest. His head had been shaved, but the dark hair had started to grow again, like a thin black skullcap. Mal Jones was smaller than Joseph had expected, in the light of Mrs Jones's claim that he could hold his own in the ring with Mike Tyson. He looked older than his wife, but there was a restlessness about him that suggested someone who could move quickly. He had a hard, narrow face, shifting eyes, and the unfriendly expression of someone expecting trouble.

Joseph asked if he was Mr Jones.

'Yes, who wants him?'

'*Are* you Mr Jones?'

'Are you?'

'No, I'm Joseph Pilgrim, Mrs Dawn Jones's constituency MP.'

He saw how the man's muscles tightened at the mention of that name. Though he was lithe, he had powerful arms which looked like the product of meticulous weight training. Mr Jones took a step forward, out of the doorframe. By coincidence or design, this gave him the space to swing either of those powerful arms in a punch.

'And?' he asked. His eyes had trouble meeting Joseph's. They seem to wander around his chest and lower jaw.

'And I'm here to see if there's a sensible compromise to be arrived at.'

Mr Jones stared at the roofs of the houses across the path as he weighed up this remark. Then he shook his head.

'It doesn't register. Don't know the name.'

'What, you've never heard of Mrs Dawn Jones?'

'I've heard of her, John: she's the cow I married. I never heard of you.'

'No, well, OK, I don't say I'm a household name, but if you look in the local paper, I'm usually there. I represent the constituency just a little to the north and east of here, Mrs Jones's constituency. I wondered if it might be possible to work out a compromise regarding your children. You will know, Mr Jones, that your wife has opposed any contact between you and your daughters.'

'Where's your identification?'

Joseph fumbled in his pocket, and produced a House of Commons pass. The wiry man took it from him and examined it, back and front. Joseph wondered about the wisdom of letting the precious plastic card out of his grasp. It was a relief when it was handed back. Mr Jones was impressed enough by this proof of status to look into Joseph's face for the first time.

'You see, Mr Jones, there are places known as contact centres which provide a facility for a father to meet with his children in a case like this, where the mother wants the reassurance of an adult presence. These places are staffed by professionals who would allow you to talk to your children, be with them, play with them, without anyone getting in your way, and Mrs Jones's worries would be set at rest. Does that seem like a possible compromise?'

In his nervousness, he could hear himself lapse into the jargon spoken by the sort of people who run contact centres.

'Is that her idea?'

'No, mine, but I have discussed this proposal with Mrs Jones, who has reservations about it, but is, I think, prepared to give it a try. Mrs Jones and I are in regular contact.'

Joseph had not expected Mal Jones to be impressed that he was so assiduous as to be in regular contact with a constituent (though he was impressed by it himself), but he believed he had gained a little of his trust, a foothold in the man's suspicious emotions. He could see that Mr Jones was thinking hard about what to say. His guard down, Joseph was all the more taken aback by the vehemence of what suddenly came out.

'You just tell that cow I want to see my kids. I don't want to see some knacker of an MP at my door; I want to see my kids. I want to see 'em at the arranged time, I don't want her to fuck me about, and if she does, I'll be round to see her. Right? And you f— off!'

Worse than the abrasive words was the menacing manner in which Mal Jones began advancing on him, with a look on his face that implied that violence was imminent. With a sweep of his arm, he pointed at the direction in which he expected Joseph to go. Caution told Joseph to leave as instructed.

Several yards down the pathway he realized he had made a mistake: he had set off obediently in the wrong direction. He turned round, and saw Mal Jones now talking to a neighbour, who had apparently emerged to find out what was happening. From the way they looked at him, they were discussing Joseph, and Mr Jones was working up a fine head of indignation. Caution told Joseph to keep walking, albeit the wrong way. He turned a corner in an attempt to double back, and found himself exploring a maze of narrow paths between the high wooden fences marking the backs of the properties. Unable to go in a straight line in what he believed to be the right direction, he was compelled to turn right and take a long detour which eventually brought him out on a wider path between the frontages of yet more compact council homes. It was wide enough for children to play in. There was a battered climbing frame in the distance, but the only people in sight were two boys who looked as if they were only just into their teens. They were dressed identically, in jeans and loose jackets, hands in pockets, staring at him in a manner he did not like.

'Shouldn't you be in school?'

He had meant to sound friendly, but the two boys first looked alarmed, then became aggressive. 'What? You what?' said one.

After the experience with Mr Jones, Joseph did not want another confrontation. He waved the boys away. As he passed, one stepped forward to touch his forearm, but let go at once as a woman appeared out of a nearby house. She gave the boys a dis-approving look, and they ran off.

'Good morning,' Joseph said. The woman smiled in reply, and set off, carrying a shopping bag.

Soon, he found his way back to a road that seemed to be the one he had driven along on his way here. He calculated that his car was parked about a quarter of a mile away. As he turned another corner, he was surprised when the same two boys emerged from an alley just ahead. They had been joined by a third. They all stood waiting as Joseph approached.

'What? You what?' the tallest of the boys repeated. Joseph was trying to think of a suitable reply, when the boy stepped forward, holding out his hand. The other two stepped forward. 'Give us your money!'

As Joseph shook his head, one of the other boys seized his arm again, while the biggest lad pushed him violently in the chest with both hands, forcing him to step back. A second push, more violent than the first, sent him staggering over sideways. As he reached out to stop his fall, grazing his fingers on tarmac, hands grabbed him and he felt his wallet leave his jacket. By the time he was back on his feet, the boys were running away. With a shout, he set off after them and, as if in reply, his wallet was hurled into the road. There was no one in sight: it was as if the estate was deserted. A quick calculation told him that it made more sense to retrieve his pillaged wallet than to chase fit young boys down alleyways they had probably known all their lives. Fortunately, they had taken only his money. The cards and his precious pass into the House of Commons were still there.

As he proceeded to his car, the estate repopulated itself. People looked at him with passing curiosity. He had been left bedraggled by the scuffle. One woman gave him a sympathetic look and was on the point of asking him a question, but he did not want to be questioned and hurried on to find his car and drive away quickly – back to the House of Commons, with its police officers, badge messengers and security staff to ward off predators and keep him safe, in a world in which people behaved in a way he was beginning to understand. He had left that familiar terrain hoping to do good, and was returning some fifty pounds poorer and feeling an abject failure.

He spotted Gerald Moon queueing in one of the cafés, in front of brightly lit hotplates of unappetizing food. The young man answered Joseph's greeting with a pained expression. 'I'm not really in the mood for conversation,' he said.

Telling himself not to take the rebuff personally, Joseph ordered tea and hot toast, and settled down at a table alone with the *Financial Times*. He had heard from Rachel about Gerald's mood swings: one day the champagne-swigging extrovert, another day morose and reclusive. He was surprised when Gerald joined him, to devour some strong-smelling crisps in surly silence, blinking sporadically. When the crisp packet was empty, he wiped his mouth with the back of his hand, frowned, and asked, 'Have you noticed any change in Rachel lately?'

'I find her easier to get on with, because I know her better,' he replied. 'Does that answer your question?'

'Listen, mate, I'm preparing something really big for her birthday, a big surprise, not a word, but I'd really appreciate it if you would overlook it if she's late in the next day.'

'When's her birthday?'

Gerald gave a date. Joseph wondered casually how old Rachel might be, and was supplied with the answer before he had asked the question. 'Twenty-three. She's a brilliant kid.'

Gerald stared out of the window at the view across the Thames with a look of such abject sadness that Joseph guessed something had gone wrong with his relationship with Rachel.

But in another minute, he had lost interest in Gerald and his problems. The room where they were sitting was separated from the area where food was served by a wall containing two large doorways. In one of the doorways, Joseph saw the familiar yet stranded figure of Sir Peter Draycott. He looked older. The expression on his face was harassed, humiliated and beaten. On catching sight of Joseph, he turned and walked away. Joseph could not blame Sir Peter for avoiding him, but this was a shocking and salutary reminder of how their friendship was ruptured.

He had heard reports about the Draycotts, all of which told him that the past few days had been much worse for them than for him.

He had read that Diana was being pursued vindictively by a pair of overbearing women from Sir Peter's constituency association, who wanted him to retire and make way for someone younger and tougher. They took the view that Diana owed a blameless private life to the party that had launched her husband's career, and had forfeited their trust. She reputedly had not helped by telling them high-handedly to mind their own business. (One rumour circulating in the tearoom said that she had described them as a couple of ghastly old hags.) Diana's chances of continuing to serve on the regional party executive were said to be diminishing by the day.

He had heard these things, but the worst of it was that he dared not make any attempt to contact either Diana or Sir Peter; and he could not discuss it with Gerald Moon or anyone else on his own side of the political divide. They would see Diana as a political opponent who had entered the rough world of politics voluntarily and must take the consequences. He wished he could be reassured that the Draycotts were all right and did not hate him.

If there was nothing else he could do, he could at least punish Frank Rist.

'Gerald, there is something you said you'd do for me.'

'Yeah, actually, mate, I want you to do something for me,' Gerald replied, and without giving Joseph an opening to put his request first, he continued, 'You see, my boss wants something out in the public arena, but I've got my head full of this Rachel stuff, mate, and I've got to be careful these days. I'm getting too much exposure. You could do it, mate. I mean, now you're Denis Drummond's PPS . . .'

'Is Denis involved?'

'Not directly, mate, but the Deputy Prime Minister is, and, well, you know about Denis and the Deputy PM. Have you heard about the Dome, mate?'

'What dome?'

'On the Greenwich peninsula, mate, there's some land that was wrecked by the gas board – really polluted. The Tories had an idea to clean it up and build a massive Dome.'

'Yes, I remember. We're going to scrap that, aren't we, as a waste of money?'

'No, we're not, mate.' Gerald looked around, his eyes sweeping the breadth of the café to ensure that no one was overhearing them. He leant forward and lowered his voice. 'We're going for it, big time. That's what we want out in the open, mate.'

Gerald gave another nervous look around the room, blinked several times, and picked up a paper napkin, which he began to tear into narrow strips. His manner added to Joseph's uneasy feeling that he was being drawn into something it would be wiser to stay clear of.

'When was this decision taken, Gerald?'

'At full Cabinet, Thursday of next week.'

'*Next* week?'

Gerald gestured frantically at him to keep his voice down. Then he fell silent, peering at Joseph over the rims of his spectacles and obviously wondering if he was to be trusted.

'I helped you, mate, when you were up to your neck in it,' he said, sounding hurt.

'All right, Gerald, I'll do as you ask,' Joseph replied, because there was no denying that he probably owed his political life to this strange, twitchy youth. 'But if the decision hasn't even been taken . . .'

Gerald shook his head, setting off a sequence of nervous blinks, and with another guilty look around the room, he produced a folded piece of paper which he handed across the table conspiratorially. 'For Christ's sake don't get caught with this, mate.'

It was a civil service minute of a ministerial meeting which had been held privately in Downing Street. Despite the sparse language and absence of detail, there was enough information on a single sheet to verify everything Gerald had said. The Cabinet was indeed divided over whether to proceed with the Millennium Dome, and would indeed be making a decision the following Thursday in favour of going ahead, despite the Chancellor of the Exchequer's reservations, though more than half the Cabinet might not yet know that.

He could also see now what was making Gerald so nervous. Leaking a Cabinet Office minute, especially one that pointed to a split in the Cabinet, was a great deal more serious than passing on political gossip.

'Some of the boys from the Sunday lobby are hanging about upstairs looking for a story,' said Gerald. 'Do it now, do it for the Deputy PM. You know how he hates the Chancellor.'

'I thought it was your boss he hated.'

'Yeah, a bit, sometimes.'

The lobby upstairs, with its high walls and the striking black life-size statues of former prime ministers glaring down from their plinths, looked bigger than usual because it was almost empty, apart from the half-dozen badge messengers forever on duty at its doors. Joseph could ignore them, because they saw everything, and saw nothing, but there was another MP holding a conversation with a pair of Sunday newspaper journalists whose faces Joseph recognized. They both had large stomachs, as if rotundity were a prerequisite of Sunday journalism, but while their girths were late middle-aged, their faces looked younger.

Joseph needed to wait for the other MP to depart. As a ruse, he lifted the receiver of one of the telephones that were located by an exit, and sat down on the short green bench pretending to be holding a conversation. During this hiatus, he was conscious of the enormity of what he was about to do. If it went wrong, his future as a potential government minister would be over, and for the rest of his career he would be remembered as the man who came close to where the power was, and screwed up. For a moment, his will deserted him and he imagined that he would slip away like a coward, but when he saw that the two journalists were now alone, he pulled himself to his feet and crossed the stone floor. They turned towards him, evidently happy enough to speak to anyone who had time to stop and talk.

'Are you looking for a story?' he asked.

'We're always looking for a story,' said one of the journalists, though his tone did not convey any great expectation that Joseph actually had one to offer.

With a quick look round to check for listeners, Joseph relayed what he had learnt from Gerald. He was answered by a moment's silence, then one of the fat journalists exclaimed, 'That's a fantastic bloody story.'

The other looked troubled. 'What's your involvement in this, Joseph, if you don't mind my asking?'

'I don't want to be involved in it in any way at all. OK?'

'Sure, sure. But with respect – you know – we'll get asked by our news desks about the provenance of our source – you know – is it copper-bottom? I mean, with great respect, Joseph, you're telling us some pretty inside-track stuff. I mean, can you steer us towards anything to stand up what you're saying?'

With another look around to ensure they were unobserved, Joseph handed them the civil service minute. The two fat journalists pressed their heads together to read it, emitting little gasps of astonishment and pleasure.

'Please don't be caught with that, whatever you do,' Joseph urged them.

One of the fat journalists hastily tucked it away in an inside pocket, then gratefully touched Joseph on the shoulder. 'That's a splasherozo, my friend. Fantastic. Definitely worth an expensive lunch.'

The other fat journalist, the one who had been less willing to accept his story, shook him by the hand, thanked him profusely, and also promised lunch. (They were as good as their word: later in the year, they treated Joseph to a meal that cost what an average earner would call a good week's wage.) Joseph left hurriedly, aware that the longer he stayed, the greater the risk of being seen. He made his way to one of the private phone booths on an upstairs corridor in order to ring Gerald, conscious that he had just stepped over a line from which there was no return. It was like losing his virginity again.

'The thing you ask for is done,' he told Gerald. 'Now I want you to do something for me. I've already said I want Frank Rist roasted alive. He has caused a lot of pain to two very good friends of mine, and he has got to pay for it. You know how to do it, you know how to get things into newspapers. Use your skills and get Frank Rist.'

·19·

'"Obsessed" activist "stalked" MP'

A right-wing activist was named yesterday as the 'stalker' who leaked details about an MP's private life. Fellow MPs leapt to the defence of high-flying Labour MP Joseph Pilgrim after a Sunday newspaper revealed details about a love affair with the wife of a Tory which ended 20 years ago.

Information about the affair is understood to have come from Mr Frank Rist, a member of the small splinter group the Independence Party of the United Kingdom. According to one report, he was paid £5,000 for revealing that Mr Pilgrim had once been the lover of Diana Draycott, wife of the Tory MP and former Home Office minister, Sir Peter Draycott.

Yesterday, Mr Rist refused to discuss the affair, saying: 'I don't talk to the gutter press. Read my web site if you want to know what I'm about.'

Mr Rist edits a web site which campaigns for 'libertarian' ideas, including legalisation of all hard drugs, the lowering of the age of consent to 12, and outright withdrawal from the EU. Recently, he posted information that Mr Pilgrim had experimented with soft drugs in the 1980s, a charge which the MP has admitted to be true.

Mr Pilgrim and Mr Rist are understood to have met when they were involved in left-wing politics together in Newcastle upon Tyne. They both campaigned in support of the miners' strike of 1984–85.

A close friend of Mr Pilgrim said: 'This character was far left, now he's far right – from Trotskyism to outer edge of Toryism, via god knows what other weird and wonderful ideas. He's completely obsessed with Joseph. He once followed him into the Commons and it's a mystery how he got past security. And he disrupted his constituency surgery. He's a stalker. It beggars belief that any newspaper should take him seriously.'

Thelma Driver, secretary of Mr Pilgrim's constituency party, added: 'We had this man in the constituency office for a whole morning being a nuisance and refusing to go away until he had spoken to Joseph. He was very threatening.'

A spokesman for the UK Independence Party said: 'I want to stress that the so-called IPUK has nothing to do with UKIP. It is a breakaway organisation by a very small group of extreme libertarians who seem to think it's all right for a man to have sex with a 13-year-old boy. Our understanding is that Rist used to be a member of a religious cult.'

The Willesden-based Millennial Church of Christ the Saviour confirmed yesterday that a Mr Frank Rist was formerly a member of their congregation, but stressed that he has cut his ties with the church.

A spokesman from the Labour Party's Millbank headquarters said: 'This shoddy story illustrates the quality of the sort of people who have been mounting a vicious personal campaign against a highly respected new MP.'

'Bollocks,' Dave Drucker exclaimed, in his newsroom fastness up in the citadel in Kensington. Dave's nerves had been set on edge by the Joseph Pilgrim story. He had set out to knock a little-known MP out of public life, but with each hit, Mr Pilgrim seemed to grow stronger. Dave would not have minded in any personal way, because he quite liked the man, but it was becoming an office joke at Dave's expense.

'So, he wants a big smear campaign against Frank Rist. Well, he'll wish he hadn't, he'll wish he hadn't. Because I'm getting ready to put together the big one, and it'll kill him. And he's just made it easier for me. Cheers, Joseph, cheers,' said Dave.

·20·

Public Meetings

'Public meetings! What do you want to do public meetings for?' said the wise MP in the tearoom. He was one of a grey-haired circle of little-known backbench MPs, all with solidly safe seats, whose political mission was to minimize their own workload and steer away from unnecessary effort. 'How many votes do you think you'll win at a public meeting? It takes – what? – twelve million votes to win a general election, but you won't see twelve uncommitted voters at a public meeting. What you'll find is the know-it-alls, the nuts, and the troublemakers. Anyone who takes the trouble to come to a public meeting has already decided how they're going to vote. And it'll be held in a horrible little hall, on a horrible night, because they always are. Do one public meeting every four or five years, in your constituency, during a general election – that's my advice.'

Notwithstanding these wise words, Joseph had allowed Margaret to talk him into attending a meeting of NHS staff who wanted a politician's take on the changes due to take place in the health service. Gripping his raincoat collar, Joseph struggled against the cold drizzle that flew almost horizontally into his face during the ten-minute brisk walk from an underground station to an old Methodist hall somewhere in north London.

He had anticipated an audience of a couple of dozen, but there was at least that number at the doorway alone, where they were jostling to escape the rain. The interior echoed with human voices. Puddles were forming on the stone floor from umbrellas being shaken and folded and raincoats being removed. The crowd was large enough for Joseph to have lost himself in it, but he heard Margaret calling, urgency in her voice. She was at the large door-way separating the hall from the main hallway, dressed in a severe corduroy suit she wore on workdays. As soon as he was within reach, she was straightening his tie, a gesture so habit-driven that she scarcely knew she was doing it. It certainly did not cross her mind that she risked making the top-billed speaker look ridiculous by adjusting his dress in full view of his audience as they filed to their seats.

'What happened?' Margaret asked, in a whisper. 'Did your taxi driver lose the way?'

'I came on the Northern Line.'

'On the Northern Line!' She looked at him as if he had committed an act of madness.

'Yes, you know – we support public transport.'

'Joseph, there are nearly three hundred people here to listen to you. They don't want to wait while you're stuck on the Northern Line.'

'Why so many?'

'Because of you, stupid. I hope you don't let them down. I'm going to take you to meet the chairman, then I'll go and sit in the audience. Have you got your speech notes?'

'I'll do it without notes,' Joseph replied, thinking that if he had foreseen the size of the audience, he would have come better prepared.

Margaret gave him a reproachful look as she steered him towards the hall, in which the first thing he noticed was the purple stage curtains, then the gold-embossed pillars at the edge of the wooden stage topped by hideous masques. It looked like an old music hall theatre. Margaret pointed out someone in a crowd whom, apparently, they had both known in Newcastle, but Joseph did not recognize the face or the name.

At the foot of the wooden stage, she introduced him to an immensely fat man with sweat dripping from his thinning hair and a wet but powerful handshake. This was the chairman. Having introduced them, Margaret slipped back into the crowd. The chairman guided Joseph to a back room, where free refreshments were on offer, and introduced him to various hospital administrators and union officials, describing him as 'the man of whom we're hearing so much' without specifying what they were hearing. No one made any direct reference to Diana. Thus a pattern was set that would last through the evening. Everyone had heard of him; no one said why.

As they filed out on the boards to take their places along a single wooden table, bare except for a jug of water, four glasses and one microphone, the hum of conversation quietened. Joseph took his place at the far end of the table, and was delighted to spot Rachel in the front row. She had not said she was coming. She managed to look striking even in the plain white raincoat she had wrapped around herself for warmth. He was so captivated by the sight that he forgot to look for Margaret. It was not until the end of the chairman's opening remarks – during which Joseph was billed as 'a new MP who has been making a big impact' – that he spotted her, several rows back. She was signalling to him, trying to mouth a message. He thought for a moment she might be telling him to keep his eyes off Rachel, but she was pointing towards the back of the hall. He shook his head to convey that he could not understand. She scribbled a note, which was passed forward to him by someone from the front. Unfolding it, he read the warning *Frank Rist is here*. The lighting prevented him from seeing to the back of the hall, where he suspected Frank must be.

There was nothing to be done but soldier through the speech he had mentally prepared. He opened with words of regret that those who had expected the new government to be more generous than the old in its expenditure on health care had been disappointed. After the apology, came a suitably vague promise for the future. He was interrupted in mid-sentence by a shout from the back. He could not see the heckler, who was hidden in shadows, nor could he make out what he was saying; but he recognized Frank Rist's voice without any difficulty.

His first impression was that the audience did not like the interruption. In general, people are more likely to side with the person they have come to hear against the one who is demanding their attention. Even so, it was awkward to be barracked by someone he could not see, but whose talent for causing trouble was painfully well known.

'The Brussels conspiracy,' Frank shouted.

Joseph now regretted that he had not taken time to study Frank's web site and get a proper measure of him. He could not tell whether the voice from the shadows was making a serious claim about a genuine conspiracy, or being obscurely sarcastic. He decided to risk an attempt at humour. With arms outstretched, he replied, 'I don't know anything about this Brussels conspiracy, but if this is a plot to ruin the appetites of patients by feeding them too many sprouts, it sounds very serious indeed.'

Perhaps it was not that funny, he reflected ruefully, as his joke fell flat. Even Rachel had turned her beautiful head to look at the man at the back, who was shouting a string of sentences which were being lost in the noise of others exhorting him to be quiet.

The fat chairman was on his feet. 'Excuse me, order, order – could the gentleman at the back please be quiet, because we're here for a meeting about the National Health Service and Mr Pilgrim is speaking, so let's listen to him with courtesy, please.'

That produced a round of applause, neither loud nor long, but enough to silence Frank for the moment. Joseph completed his speech in a few words, and treated himself to a glass of water.

The first member of the audience to speak was a large woman with a strong Jamaican accent, who announced that she had been a practising midwife for twenty-three years, and was on the same salary as someone newly qualified. He feared that she was about to allege racial discrimination, but in fact she was delivering a general complaint on behalf of all midwives. She said that they had no way to better themselves financially except to give up delivering babies and become managers. Very soon, Joseph realized that he had a much worse problem before him than Frank Rist: he had placed himself in the gruelling situation of facing an audience who knew what they were talking about. He could see from the reactions of other people in the hall that everything the elderly Jamaican midwife said accorded with their experience. If there was one person in the hall who had not a clue how midwives' salaries are structured, that was Joseph.

He fell back on the ploy of blaming the old government, and promising to take up the midwife's points with the Secretary of State for Health. That was unoriginal, but it got him through question one unscathed.

Next came a junior doctor, whose contribution was supposed to be a question but actually was a well-argued and well-informed attack on the government's policy of signing contracts with private firms to build new hospitals which were then leased to the NHS. He described it as a disguised way of borrowing money expensively: in the short term, it provided new hospitals for which the current government paid almost nothing, but in a generation's time, taxpayers would be paying 'through the nose' for commitments signed now. He sat down to applause, and every head turned towards Joseph. He could see by their expressions that they had listened with interest to a well-informed argument, intelligently put, and expected to hear a reply of equal quality.

Joseph could be thankful in this moment of distress for the many hours he had spent at the kitchen table hearing Margaret talking about the realities of administering the NHS. She too was adamantly opposed to these private finance initiative deals, so he was already acquainted with the arguments against them. Sadly, he could not remember whether there was an argument in their favour, so he struggled by with the line that it was a choice between hospitals financed in this way or no hospitals at all.

He had a suspicion that this was a thin argument even as he presented it. The next contribution was from a medical student, who made two points: one, that government can borrow money at below-market rates, so it would cost less for the government to pay a contractor to build a hospital, paying on delivery with borrowed money, than to lease a building that belonged to the firm that had built it; two, that the Chancellor of the Exchequer had instituted a 'golden rule' that the government could borrow for investment but not to cover current expenditure, but since a hospital building is undeniably an investment, what was to stop the government from borrowing to build hospitals?

What indeed? Joseph had a terrible feeling that he was cornered, and that his mind was being stripped in public, leaving his ignorance exposed. Suddenly, with what seemed like a life-saving flash of inspiration, he remembered something he had once heard a health minister saying about penalty clauses and how they applied in private finance initiative contracts. Wrenching the argument from his memory as best he could, he was serving it up to his attentive audience when he was interrupted again by Frank Rist's voice at the back. This time, it was a hearty cry of 'Bollocks!'

Joseph could see the wave of irritation as it went through the audience, and saw that Frank had clumsily rescued him. People who were following the ebb and flow of the exchanges did not want them vulgarly interrupted. They were all on Joseph's side. Dealing with a heckler would be much easier than answering polite, intelligent questions.

He decided to use humour again, because he knew of old the difficulty that Frank Rist had coping with humour at his expense.

'Actually, no, we were talking about the private finance initiative, but I am sure we can come on to your particular hobby later,' he said. This time, he raised a decent laugh, making Frank Rist's next shouted comment unintelligible.

'Can the brother at the back either stop this heckling or leave the hall?' the chairman said.

There was a kerfuffle in the darkness at the back, as if people were pushing one another. As Joseph had half anticipated, the sound of laughter had triggered a reaction from Frank. Another man was on his feet, pointing towards the disturbance and shouting, 'I'd like to ask a question, chairman, on a point of order. I read in the paper that Mr Pilgrim is being stalked by a madman who used to be in a religious cult. I'd like to know if the man at the back is the same man who is stalking Mr Pilgrim.'

Others jumped to their feet as Frank emerged from the shadows, having successfully fought off those who were trying to hold him back. The chairman was shouting, 'Will the heckler leave the hall, please? Can we have the heckler out of the hall, please?'

'No, no, listen, please brothers and sisters, listen,' Frank Rist shouted, as he marched down the central aisle waving an accusing finger. The audience was in no mind to listen. Most of what Frank said could not be heard, but above the shouts of 'Sit down!', Joseph caught a few phrases: 'We can't do anything as a country. We're not a nation, we're in a state called Europe.'

But no one wanted to hear his warnings. Only his long greying hair was visible as he was evicted bodily by half a dozen men who had encircled him. An exit at the side of the hall was opened, Frank was shoved through it, and the doors were shut behind him. The chairman did his best to restart the meeting where it had left off, but the continuity was broken, and the last twenty or thirty minutes were taken up with desultory exchanges.

When it was over, Margaret slipped away to go home and pay the babysitter, while Joseph stayed with the crowd as it drifted across the road. Rachel came too. Joseph wondered if it was wise to be seen in the company of someone so strikingly lovely, given the reputation attaching itself to him. Under the white raincoat, she was wearing a short black skirt and a dark blouse which was so short that it left an exposed circle of tanned skin. The wearer of such an outfit needed a faultless waistline and a nice-looking navel. Rachel had both. He was grateful that she stayed tactfully in the crowd.

He had shaken a dozen hands and had struggled to memorize a dozen names when he noticed that something across the room was attracting attention. The premises had an unusual layout, more like a wine bar than a pub: the long counter down the length of one wall, and a large, uninterrupted floor space, crammed with little round wooden tables. The whole of the wall adjoining the street was of plate glass. Outside, a man in a brown leather jacket with long, greying hair wet from rain was staring in, hands in pockets and a wildly aggressive look in his eyes. It was Frank Rist.

Rachel walked quickly over to Joseph, gathering up her raincoat on the way. 'Stay here: I'll talk to him,' she said.

He was reluctant to have her cope with his problem, but there were people jostling to speak to him whom it would have been rude to abandon. While they discussed the financing of the National Health Service, Joseph watched from the corner of his eye. He saw Rachel intercept Frank at the door, saw him mouth a question along the lines of *Who the fuck are you?* and saw him recoil the first time she touched his sleeve, before allowing himself to be steered back out on to the pavement.

'Has it stopped raining?' Joseph asked the semicircle around him. One of the women went over to the window to take a look, and returned to announce that the rain had indeed stopped. Rachel and Frank were settled at wooden slatted tables, set in a row on the pavement alongside the window.

A buzzing sensation in Joseph's pocket warned him of a message on his bleeper. It was from Margaret, who was already home. To escape the hubbub, he slipped into the men's toilet, and rang on his mobile phone.

'I tried to ring you on the mobile. Didn't you hear me?'

'No, sorry, I'm not used to the bloody gadget. I didn't hear it ring. Must be the noise in the pub.'

'What are you doing in a pub?'

'Networking with your colleagues from the world's finest health service.'

'Well, don't get drunk and say something stupid, and don't ogle Rachel. Did George speak to you?'

'George?'

'George from Newcastle. I told you he was there.'

'Oh, right. Well I don't know what George from Newcastle looks like, Margaret. I don't remember any George from Newcastle.'

'It sounds quite important, Joseph. He says he recognized Frank.'

'Anyone who was on the left in Newcastle in those days would recognize Frank.'

'But he wasn't on the left, he was a psychiatrist.'

'The two are not incompatible, Margaret. There are left-wing psychiatrists, just as for that matter there are left-wing people who need psychiatrists.'

'You're not listening properly. Frank was his patient.'

'Frank wasn't a psychiatric patient. He may have needed a psychiatrist, but I don't think he ever saw one.'

'Ask George.'

'But I don't know George.'

'Well, find him then, Joseph. It sounds important.'

'OK. I'll look out for George from Newcastle.'

He ended the call, muttering to himself that he did not know how he was going to look out for George without knowing what George looked like. He was actually more interested in looking out for Rachel. The possibility that Frank might have been a psychiatric patient was one of many reasons for not leaving the two of them alone any longer. Ignoring the hurt looks from the people he had been speaking to, he walked straight out of the pub.

Although the rain had finished, the air was biting cold. Rachel had wrapped her raincoat tightly around herself and was hunched up from the cold, but Frank had removed his leather jacket and was sitting motionless in an open-neck shirt. Only the trace of blue on his long fingers and in his thin, pointed face suggested that he experienced the cold at all. He stared hard at Joseph. Acknowledging him with a brief nod, Joseph sat opposite him, next to Rachel. They were sharing a narrow bench, and their thighs pressed together. She did not try to draw away.

Frank broke the silence. 'Why did you slander me? I've never slandered you. You called me a stalker.' Joseph shook his head, but before he could reply properly, Frank exclaimed, his voice rising: 'It said I'm a stalker. They called me a stalker. Am I a stalker? Do I stalk? Did I ever stalk you?'

'Frank, ignore what it says in the paper. I have to ignore what it says about me. You do the same. I'll tell you who has been worst affected by this: my friend Diana Draycott. She has been worse hurt than you have, or I have. I cannot understand the mentality of someone who would sell a story like that to a tabloid newspaper. How much did they pay?'

As soon as Joseph raised his voice, Frank watched with silent respect. He seemed to be placated by other people's anger. After Joseph had finished, Frank roused himself with a shake of the head and pointed at Rachel. 'She's intelligent – but she's brainwashed.'

'How much was it worth, to ruin Diana's life?'

'She says the euro is not a threat to the sovereignty of Britain,' Frank continued, resolutely evading the question.

'It's not necessarily,' said Rachel.

'Frank, would you like to tell me why you've been running this campaign against me? Why were you here tonight? Why did you come to my surgery, and write all that on your web site?'

This prompted a jeering laugh. 'Because thou art lukewarm, and neither cold nor hot, I will spew thee out of my mouth. Would you like me off your back, Joseph Pilgrim? Would you like me to leave you alone, completely?'

'That would be a relief.'

Frank set off on a ranting monologue. Perhaps it only lasted three or four minutes, but it seemed endless. The words came in hard, staccato sentences, each following logically, one upon another. Joseph had heard similar sentiments in the mouths of rational and successful politicians, but spoken in Frank's belligerent tone, they sounded like paranoia rampant. Frank believed that England faced destruction as a nation, its Protestant individualism sacrificed to Catholic and Teutonic bureaucracy. Unusually, he accused Margaret Thatcher of playing a guilty part. (He vehemently objected to having been called a Tory in the press.) He saw the destruction of the mining communities in the 1980s as a prelude to the destruction of England. Seemingly, he was offering to leave Joseph alone in future, if Joseph would stand up and call for England's withdrawal from the European Union.

'I'm afraid I can't join you in this crusade, Frank. I think you're deeply mistaken.'

This provoked another morose silence. Frank's eyes moved constantly, like the eyes of a hunted animal watching for predators, but he seemed to see nothing. Rachel fidgeted. She appeared to be more amused than intimidated by Frank's outburst.

'May I ask you a personal question,' Joseph said. 'While we were in Newcastle, did you ever see a psychiatrist?'

'No,' Frank said, seeming surprised by the question. His surprise turned almost at once to suspicion, and he shook his head scornfully. 'Oh yes, oh yes, is that the new political smear? A stalker yesterday, a mental patient today. That's Soviet-type black propaganda.'

'No, Frank, it's just something someone said to me; but if you say it's not true, I believe you.'

'It's because I was in a cult,' Frank replied, unexpectedly. This reference to his own recent past was so unusual that Joseph could think of nothing to say in reply, and waited silently for Frank to continue. He felt an elbow dig his ribs. It was Rachel silently signalling to him to keep the conversation flowing.

'Do you feel you have entirely shaken off the influence of this cult, Frank?'

'They're mad,' Frank said. 'You've got to find a way; you've got to find a way, but that's not it – trying to put a date on the end of the world. Like waiting for the world revolution. It'll be the Great Disappointment all over again – 1844, the twenty-second of October, Adventists up on the roof in their ascension robes, property sold, staring up, wondering when the Saviour would step out of the sky. How do these people face the next day? There's a web site with a live camera fixed on Jerusalem's Golden Gate in Jerusalem, because they think Christ will return at the end of the Millennium. Mad. Mad, mad, mad. And it makes people laugh.'

'And is that why you left the cult?'

'I believe that societies destroy themselves. I *know* that societies destroy themselves. Not in the Marxist way, not in the Adventist way, but they do: Rome, Babylon, the Union of Soviet Socialist Republics. *Nothing beside remains round the decay of that colossal wreck.* And our society will be destroyed. It is being destroyed. We have lost it.'

'So, what drew you to the cult in the first place?' Rachel asked, with obvious interest. She sat forward, leaning on her elbows.

A look of extreme pain went through Frank's face, as if he were being eaten by cancer. Instead of a reply, there was a long morose silence, until Frank uttered a single word: 'Christine . . .' It came as a low hiss. Then suddenly, Frank's body was convulsed by a violent shudder. He shook his head and, rousing himself, gave them both a look as if they were about to attack him.

'It's got to be stopped, Joseph. Some people say it's not deliberate, but I say it's as malicious as the Third Reich. What do the Belgians care if they lose their country? They never had a country. There is no Belgium, except a bit of flat ground where the Flemings and Walloons live. And the Germans are so ridden by guilt that they daren't be independent again. But we have two thousand years. We are the cradle of the industrial world.'

'So you haven't changed your views about the miners' strike?'

'Why should I? It's the same person who did the damage. Her. She did that – she did this. She signed us in. We must never allow this country to be run by a woman.'

Joseph glanced at Rachel to see how she would react to this outburst of misogyny. To judge by the sparkling look in her eye, she was thoroughly enjoying herself.

'All right,' Joseph said, 'you're a man with a mission, and you think it helps your cause to run a vendetta against me. If you won't answer any other questions, answer this one: how can it help to bring Christine into it? Some people still read her books. What good does it do to drag her name through the tabloids?'

He expected an answer, but Frank only stared, his expression at once hostile, suspicious and utterly bemused, as if Joseph had been speaking in tongues.

Rachel intervened: 'Do you see yourself as someone who is doing this out of principle, or because the newspapers pay you a lot of money for it?'

Still there was no answer. Frank seemed immobilized. Suddenly he shook his head a second time, punched his thigh, picked up his jacket, and without another word, set off across the road with his swift, limping gait, and vanished from sight.

'He is seriously sick,' Rachel said with a hint of glee. 'Definitely a pineapple short of a picnic.'

With the release of tension, she sat back, letting her raincoat flap open and giving him a tantalizing glimpse of the band of bare flesh around her waist. Joseph gave a gasp of pain. He had been so tense during this exchange that he had been pressing his elbows against his rib cage, unaware of doing so. The mobile phone in his inside jacket pocket had been digging painfully into his armpit. He pulled it out and laid it on the table.

'Everything all right?' a voice behind him asked. Joseph turned. It was the fat chairman, leaning out through the door, sweat running down his pate despite the cold air.

'Yes, problem solved, thank you very much. I'll rejoin you in a moment.'

In truth, he did not want to rejoin them at all, these people who assumed that his interest in their affairs was inexhaustible. He would rather have spent the evening with Rachel. With Frank gone, he felt almost light-headed, and ready to enjoy himself.

'Rachel, my wife has put me on notice about you,' he announced, causing her to start.

'I haven't met your wife.'

'No, but she knows you by sight. She says I mustn't ogle. So if you catch me looking at you as if I think you're possibly one of the most gorgeous women who ever adorned the human race, give me a kick.'

He was gratified to see the colour come to her cheeks. She gave him a look that was suspicious and questioning, but not angry.

'Yes, well, it's cold, so let's go inside,' she said, standing up. 'Don't forget your mobile.'

When he picked the gadget off the table, Joseph noticed to his surprise that there were numbers on the dial, exactly as if it was in use. He pressed the button marked 'No', and the numbers disappeared. He was going to ask Rachel what that signified, but she was already at the pub door, where she stopped and looked over her shoulder.

'And why "possibly"?' she asked, but stepped indoors without giving him time to reply. He had momentarily feared that he might have offended her. He was glad it was all right.

·21·

The Reckoning

All was not all right when he got home to Margaret. As he closed the front door, he called out for her – softly, so that the children would not hear. There was no reply. He made a quick search upstairs, where both the children were tucked up in bed. He finally located Margaret in the kitchen. She was standing with one hand on her hip, the other clutching the kitchen table, watching him with an expression that reminded him of the early, stormy days of their relationship – lips tight together, chin forward, and eyes staring. She did not reply to his greeting, but continued to stare as at a stranger. When he drew near, she flinched and put up a hand to stop him from touching her.

'Give me your phone,' she said. 'Your mobile phone.'

Baffled, he handed it over. Margaret took the gadget in her left hand and poked it twice with her right forefinger, as if she were trying to stab it to death. Out in the hall, the telephone rang.

'Don't bother answering,' Margaret said. Her finger stabbed the mobile phone again. Outside, the ringing stopped. She handed the phone back to him. 'You don't even understand how it works, do you?' He shook his head. 'Press "Yes" – twice.'

He followed her orders, baffled, and saw his own home number come up on the mobile phone's luminous screen, and then heard the phone in the hall ring. On her instruction, he then pressed 'No', and the ringing stopped. He tried again. As if by magic, it

·214·

happened again: one button made the phone in the hall ring, the other made it stop. But when he looked at her in boyish delight, her face was still white with anger. Her lower lip trembled. He could not imagine what was the matter.

'You'd better be more careful, hadn't you?' she said. 'And don't give me that injured innocent look.' Suddenly, she lapsed into a caustically accurate impersonation of him. '"If you catch me looking at you as if I think you're possibly one of the most gorgeous women who ever adorned the human race, give me a kick . . ."'

He was stupefied. It was as if she were performing some extraordinary act of telepathy. Then it all came in a rush: the pain when he had accidentally pressed the mobile phone in his pocket, the numbers on the screen which implied that a call was in progress . . .

'Oh shit.'

'Well, have you fucked her, or are you just working on it?'

'No, Margaret, honestly, no – fuck Rachel? – good God – I mean – oh, what a misunderstanding! I mean, if the idea ever went through my mind, for one nano-second – look at the situation, Margaret: she's scarcely half my age!'

'Oh, you're put off by her youth,' Margaret said, with heavy sarcasm. 'And what about her looks, and the way she dresses, and the flirty flirty way she talks to you, are all of those a turn-off too?'

'She never flirts with me.'

'Joseph, are you completely stupid? Or do you think I am? Is that your story, that *that girl* doesn't flirt with you?'

'But she doesn't,' Joseph insisted, surprised that Margaret could have imagined that she did.

'I think he really is stupid,' Margaret told their general surroundings. She threw up an arm, as if orating to an unseen audience, then stared at him with wild round eyes, hunched in a pose that seemed to take inches from her height. 'And what is this story about Christine? Is this another scandal, like the last one?'

'Why are we talking about Christine?'

'Why were you talking to Frank Rist about Christine? What have the newspapers got hold of that you haven't told me about? Was she another of your mistresses? Is that the next scandal to bring a hoard of hacks to our doorstep, trapping us in the house?'

He had not seen her like this since the earliest days of their relationship. She was staring at him as if she were drunk.

'Must we talk about this tonight?'

'What, you'd rather wait until it's all in the papers, and I can read about it – as I read about Diana Draycott? Shall I take the papers every Sunday, to learn your sordid sexual history?'

As he reached for the fridge door, she lifted her hand in the shape of a claw, and for a moment he thought she would spring at him to scratch his face. She looked demented.

'I need a drink, Margaret,' he said. 'I'll answer all your questions, but I do need a drink in my hand, please. Can I get you one?'

She did not answer, except to lower her hand and take a step back, her eyes still fixed on him. He took out a beer and drank from the can. The cold liquid gave him a sharp, short headache above one eye.

'Christine was your lover, I take it.'

'Why do I need to talk about her?'

'Why do you need to talk about her?' Margaret countered scornfully. 'Because I want to know what the bloody newspapers know. What about the night she died? Are you the mystery witness who ran away from the scene?'

'No, absolutely not, no: I'm sure it wasn't me. Nobody saw me.' Joseph sat at the kitchen table and took another long swig of beer to fortify himself to tell her what he should have told her twelve years earlier.

'Nobody saw you? So you were there?'

'I didn't see anything.'

'Why didn't you tell the police you were there?'

'I didn't see anything. I couldn't tell them anything. Except that Christine was doing this weird pirouette, like a sort of St Vitus's dance, in her nightclothes, in the middle of the main road. I don't know why. She obviously didn't see the lorry.'

'You saw her being killed. You witnessed a fatal accident, and you walked away.'

'I hate those blue lights that flash on top of police cars.'

'Joseph, this will destroy you. You'll be ruined. The family will be ruined. The scandal will be on every front page, on every bulletin: you will *never* live it down.'

'No, no, no, that's not going to happen, Margaret. Believe me. Trust me.'

'I'm sorry, but I don't trust you. You've kept this from me for twelve years, and when I think about it, when I think of how we started . . .'

'I have never spoken about it to anyone. Frank can't possibly know. He can't have seen me. He was hundreds of miles away.'

'Did you talk to George, the psychiatrist?' Margaret asked, suddenly dropping the accusing tone.

'Is that important?'

Margaret raised her arms in a gesture of cosmic despair. 'I don't want you in this house while this is happening. I'm worried about the effect on the children if there's going to be another hundred hacks at the door. And you'd better find George the psychiatrist and talk to him. I'll leave your toothbrush and pyjamas on the landing.'

On that typically practical note, she went to bed, closing the door behind her.

·22·

After Christine Died

1985

White-faced, fragile, with hands trembling, and almost drunken for lack of sleep, Joseph pulled himself into work on the morning after Christine's death. Deirdre was already removing the shutters from the shop windows. Red from the effort, she grunted hello. Fortunately, she did not yet know what had happened. That gave him time to calculate.

After falling between two different jobs in publishing, he had wound up working with Deirdre – temporarily – running a tiny left-wing bookshop in Newcastle's West End. His morning had already been set aside for a monthly audit. With cheque stubs, bank statements and unpaid bills to hand, he beavered in the back office, writing columns of figures, adding them mentally, checking his answers by calculator, until he had established that the business was deeper in deficit than ever before. And yet, though the bottom line had never looked so bad, with the summer lull over and, since much of the excess of liabilities over assets derived from stocking up for the autumn, the little bookshop would survive and improve. This cerebral drudgery brought forgetfulness for as long as his mind was fully focused. Then he would remember, suddenly and painfully, as if he been violently stabbed by recollection.

Deirdre was occupied in the front of the shop but occasionally showed herself in the back office to speak to him about this and that. Once, because of the pallor in his face and the weakness of his voice, she asked if anything was wrong.

Sooner or later someone would say 'Christine is dead' and he might have to admit that he already knew, because he might not be capable of simulating, convincingly, the disbelieving reaction of someone hearing the news for the first time. Such a lie, once made, is irretrievable. But to admit he had crept away from the scene like a coward, when he should have stopped to speak to someone in authority and not worried about the inevitable questions about what he was doing in Christine's house at that time of night, and then to explain why – this was the appalling difficulty that had been stalking him since he had woken, shivering, at 6.00 a.m. It wasn't that he couldn't think straight: in this, he could not think at all. A cloudy pain blocked his brain. He would have to stare at the wall until the pain subsided. Then he would find his hands trembling. He would feel sick. It was easier, much easier, to be buried in his columns of figures than to address the question *How much will I tell them that I already know?*

In the afternoon, he heard Deirdre's friend Marsha come in to help out on the till. Having just finished her finals, Marsha had time on her hands.

Deirdre's loud exclamation – 'No. Fuck. You're joking' – gave Joseph a few seconds' warning before Deirdre was in the back of the shop with pounds of excitable shock packed into her glistening, fleshy face.

'Have you heard this? Have you heard about Christine? . . .' Now a dash of suspicion entered her expression, bringing her eyebrows together and causing her voice to quieten. 'Marsha, when was it?'

'Just after midnight,' Marsha said, joining them. She leant against the doorframe, fiddling with her fingernails and watching Joseph closely. Both women seemed to expect the next comment to come from him, but he felt nauseous. There was a real risk he would be sick if he opened his mouth. He was rescued by another remark from Marsha, though it was frustratingly brief. 'She ran out into the road in her nightclothes.'

'But that's weird! Utterly, utterly weird. Joseph, that's incredibly weird.'

As if the shock had just hit her, Deirdre took a step back and sat abruptly on the folding wooden chair by the card table beside the door. The fragile chair creaked under the shuddering collision with the seat of her dungarees.

'That's what it said on the radio,' Marsha added, 'but they didn't give her name out. The police have been looking for Frank Rist all morning, all over the place.'

'Why? What has he done?'

With an effort, Joseph said, 'Frank's been missing for days' – then he noted with inward relief that at least his first comment on Christine's death was true.

'Well, he's turned up,' Marsha announced.

'Where?'

'London. He rang the college. Christine's professor had to ring him back and break the news.'

The question of when Joseph first knew about Christine's death seemed to have passed unaddressed. He thought that perhaps the women were too shocked to be observing his reactions, but then he saw Deirdre watching him closely.

'Let's make him a coffee, shall we, Marsha? He looks like death.' Deirdre's tone implied that Joseph had some cheek to expect women to look after him, but it was kindly, and she went directly into action.

While Deirdre was in the kitchen waiting for the kettle to boil, Marsha pulled off a loose sliver of fingernail between her teeth, threw it in the bin, and gave Joseph a conspiratorial smile. It implied something, but he did not know what.

'You're very discreet,' she said.

'Why am I discreet?'

'Tactful.'

He still could not see why. It worried him that he could not see why. 'I'm sorry, but why am I discreet and tactful?'

Marsha shrugged, as if to imply that he could consider the words withdrawn. After a moment's silence, she asked, 'How did you know Frank was missing?'

'Christine told me.' This, the second piece of information he had let slip, was more carefully calculated than the first.

'When?'

'Last night.'

'You talked to her last night?'

'You talked to her last night?' echoed Deirdre, emerging from the little kitchen with three mugs of instant coffee. 'Then you must be about the last person she spoke to, Joseph. What sort of state was she in?'

'Rather worried. Frank had gone. She didn't know where.'

'Is this some bloody weird coincidence, or is it connected?' Deirdre asked, resuming her seat, both hands wrapped around her coffee mug. She continued, answering her own question: 'But it can't be connected, if Frank's in London. If something spooked her, it wasn't him.'

'Poor Christine,' said Marsha. 'Perhaps she was stressed out and sleepwalked.'

'It might be just as well Frank was in London, because people would be asking. Will we ever know? Joseph, you look like shit warmed up: do you want to go home?'

·221·

'No, I'm OK. Better, thank you. Both of you, thank you. I feel better.'

Suddenly, Deirdre put down the coffee mug, so abruptly that a brown geyser erupted over its lip and made a stain on the card table. 'I just can't believe she isn't going to ring up again. She rang every bloody day, didn't she, Joseph? It's a basic feature of life in this shop, the daily call from Christine, twenty minutes every time, during which she puts in an order for a totally arse-aching book with a brain-destroying title like *Deconstructionalism and Community Media*, or whatever. I'm going to miss her so much.'

She had reddened all around the cheeks and neck, as she always did at times of stress, and tears welled in her eyes, which set Marsha off. With one hand, Marsha flicked a droplet from each cheekbone. Deirdre took out a tissue to wipe her nose. Marsha too took out a tissue to wipe her nose. Joseph gripped the back of his chair till his knuckles turned white, fearful that he too might burst into sobs.

Once she had recovered, Deirdre sat forward, elbows on her knees, and for a minute resumed sipping her coffee. In the background, Marsha sipped hers, with an occasional glance over her shoulder to ensure that there was no one in the shop. Then, as if synchronized, both women looked directly at Joseph.

'What did she say about Frank, actually?' Deirdre asked.

'He disappeared without telling her where he was. I mean, he'd done it before.'

The women looked at one another, as if some silent understanding was being exchanged, as if Deirdre had asked a question and Marsha had assented. He braced himself, dreading the questions he might yet have to face. Deirdre brushed a piece of dust from the knee of her jeans and began speaking without making eye contact. 'It's not usual to talk to a bloke about things said in the women's meeting, Joseph, but since she's dead, I suppose it's all right. Your *friend* is a woman-hater. Did you know?'

'Yes, I'm afraid he probably is.'

'There's no "probably" about it. Frank's not sexist in the usual way: he's worse, he's misogynistic. He was violent with Christine, and she was afraid of him. I mean physically afraid of him. Did you know?'

'Sort of.'

'Sort of,' Deirdre repeated sarcastically. 'It's amazing what blokes sort of know. They know enough, but not enough – not enough to be any help.'

'You'd think, as a feminist, she'd have coped,' Joseph replied, not wishing to get into an argument.

'Yes, well – as they say – every woman's got a fifth column in her head. Christine sympathized with Frank, she related to him, and she loved him: that was Christine's fifth column.'

'He'll have to come back, won't he?' said Marsha. 'Won't they want him to identify her, and sign things?'

Again, the women looked at one another as if they were communicating in silence, but at that moment the shop door was heard to open. Marsha hastened round the front. In the back office, a heavy silence prevailed as Joseph and Deirdre resumed work. He could sense that there was something else she wanted to ask, but he was reluctant to find out what.

Later, when there were no customers around the front, Deirdre went out for a whispered conversation with Marsha. She rejoined Joseph with the air of one who has something important to say, and sat down at the card table so that she could speak with her back to him. He realized later she did so to spare him embarrassment.

'Can I just say something, Joseph?' Deirdre asked. 'I know you stayed a bit late at that party. That's all I know, that's all I want to know. I don't know what Marsha knows: probably nothing. But that little shit Victor Pauley made some comment at the end.'

Victor Pauley was a strange, unprepossessing obsessive who hung around the bookshop and Christine's house. No one really liked him, though no one quite knew why.

'He had an idea you were still in the house when everyone else was leaving. I don't care, Joseph, only if Frank comes back to identify Christine's body and stuff – you know, what sort of mental state will he be in? Do you think maybe you ought not to be here? Frank's unpredictable, Joseph. I don't want anything that shouldn't happen to happen in the shop. It's going to be hard enough keeping going anyway without Christine. Anyway, Marsha here has had a brilliant idea, which she'll tell you about.'

Marsha had reappeared, leaning on the doorframe, looking at him with the eagerness of someone waiting for an answer to an important question.

'I'm going youth hostelling tomorrow,' she said. 'I'm going to walk Hadrian's Wall from Heddon to Carlisle. You could come, if you like.'

He was surprised to see Marsha redden.

'I can manage without both of you for a week, so why not get out of it into the fresh air, and ring in on Saturday,' Deirdre said.

In fact, they were gone a fortnight. By calling in from country phone boxes, they learnt that Frank was back in town, moody, morose and unwilling to say very much to anyone, but curious to know Joseph's whereabouts. There was a short preliminary inquest, which revealed nothing. Police enquiries were continuing. An appeal on local radio for a missing witness had had no effect so far. Another hearing was to be held before a coroner's jury at an unspecified date, likely to be six months into the future. There was also a funeral, featuring about twenty members of

Christine's extended family, an equal number of her college students, and a larger turnout by the Tyneside left. Frank had cut a lonely figure. Not one member of his own family was there, he did not know the students, and the activists were predominantly feminists who looked upon him as if he were, in some unspecified way, to blame for Christine's death. Joseph heard all this over a crackling line as he stood at twilight in a phone box in an empty country lane overlooked by a forest-covered peak called Greenrigg, and was thankful to be away. A few days later, they had confirmation that Frank was back in London.

By then, he and Marsha had trudged across half the breadth of rural England, spending their nights in cheap youth hostels. There was no embarrassment about their daily arrangements, because the sexes were separated at night anyway, and by day they walked side by side or one behind the other. Yet people they encountered here and there took them for a couple, and they were enjoying each other's company so much that they decided to prolong their walk. At Gilsland, they abandoned the westward course of Hadrian's Wall and turned south, along the Pennine Way, to Alston.

She did not mention Christine until he did. He wondered how she would react if she knew that he had gone to bed with his friend's wife, and that half the reason that he mourned Christine so was that he wished he could have done it again, and again. She asked no questions, but treated him with a kind of amused respect. At the start of their expedition, she had inspected his rucksack, ticked him off, and instructed him to discard certain useless items like his hardback history of the Spanish Civil War, which were replaced by mundanities such as sun cream and spare socks. There was a demure bossiness about her that flattered him, and spared him the trouble of taking care of himself. During their week away, he was impressed by her sturdy good health. He discovered that she had never had a day's serious illness. She had never even had a tooth filled. Although she was small, her short legs easily allowed her to walk twenty miles across open, hilly country without tiring. She was fitter than he was. After a few days of watching her muscular calves gleaming in the hot sunlight, he began to think that there was something about her small, athletic body that he wanted.

She was sitting on a tussock, her knees drawn up, biting through a tomato sandwich and trying to catch the juice that dribbled down her chin. She was dressed in a loose-fitting T-shirt with thin horizontal stripes, alternating mauve and light green, and tight navy-blue shorts, and had her socks rolled down over the rim of her walking boots so that almost the entire length of her bare legs was on display. Little hairs were visible on her shins. (He would find out later that she shaved her legs, but not in youth hostels.) The sun reflecting off her short fair hair as she moved her head up and down, wrestling with the tomato sandwich, appealed to him. There was no one anywhere in sight. This spot, on a Cumberland peak overlooking a valley stretching into the far distance like a patchwork counterpane in shades of green, was as private as a locked bedroom.

Conscious that he was examining her, she looked directly into his face and raised her eyebrows as if questioning him.

He said, 'I wonder if she had a premonition . . .'

They both understood who 'she' was. On the night of Christine's death, Joseph had been woken by a deep kiss on the mouth. Christine said something he did not hear properly, and slipped out of bed. Then he heard voices whispering in venomous hostility. He believed that there had been someone else in the house, but when he wandered sleepily on to the upper landing, there was no one. Even Christine had gone. There was only a cold draught from the open front door. But he did not tell Marsha any of these details: he did not say he had been in Christine's bed, and she never asked.

'. . . she gave me a kiss, like a goodbye kiss.'

'And what does a goodbye kiss feel like?'

'Um, how do you describe a goodbye kiss? It's firm and definite, but not long and lingering like a lover's kiss – none of the tongue-in-the-back-of-the-throat stuff. A kiss in which the lips take the lead role. Sort of emphatic. Do I make sense?'

Marsha cocked her head to one side, in a gesture that seemed to say that yes, he was making a limited quantity of sense; but the gesture was also coquettish.

He asked, 'Shall I . . .?'

'OK,' she said at once. But after what was – Joseph admitted later – a tentative, timid landing, she shook her head. 'That wasn't emphatic.'

'Sorry, let me, um . . .'

He shifted nearer to her, and kissed her hard on the mouth, not yet venturing to touch her.

'Well, I don't really . . .' she said.

'All right: but may I put my hand on the back of your head?'

'If you think that will be explanatory.'

This time, he not only kissed her hard and long, but also risked a hand on her breast. It felt squashy. She was wearing nothing under her shirt. She winced, and the colour came up in her startled face. He moved away, anticipating a sarcastic warning to desist, but Marsha picked a blade of glass and brushed her cheek with it. 'She kissed you like that?'

'Yes. Well, yes, I think I got it right.'

'You *think* you got it right?'

'Yes, I think so. Shall I . . .?'

'Don't you dare. Oh, go on, but don't . . .'

This time, Marsha broke away, shaking her head very firmly. 'She wasn't having a premonition, at all.'

'No? What then?'

'She must have fancied you, and she must wanted you to stay with her, if she really kissed you like that.' Her cheeks were still flushed and she had lowered her head. Then she raised her eyes to give him a discreet but unmistakable look.

He did not feel he really knew Marsha very well, though he knew that she came from a dull village in Bedfordshire. Though people who live in such places must beget children, he doubted they ever had sex, real sex, and thought it impossible that they would enjoy it if they did – especially in the open countryside with the sun beating on their shoulders. He assumed that, coming from such a drab place, she would stop him before he had gone half as far as he would like. She would not, for instance, let him slip her clothes off, one item at a time, until there was none left to remove. She would not wriggle with pleasure as he explored her sun-heated skin with his fingertips, or be persuaded to roll on to her tummy so that he could rub her bottom roughly, walk his fingers up her spine, tickle her between the shoulder blades with the tip of his tongue, kiss the nape of her neck and nip her on the shoulder blades; nor would she roll over in the grass and allow him to knead and squeeze her breasts, teasing the nipples with his tongue and biting hard enough for it almost to hurt, first one breast then the other; nor arch her back and give cries of pleasure when he buried his face between her legs; nor allow him to have her in three different positions, one after another – all, so to speak, on a first date – which, all in all, shows how wrong you can be about people who come from boring villages in Bedfordshire.

Afterwards, her face was very red and she told him he was 'bad'. He was interested to learn that her parents called her Margaret, which in those years was the unsexiest name in the parish register. She had stopped using it in disgust in May 1979. 'You can call me Margaret when *she*'s not Prime Minister,' Joseph was told, on the implied assumption that they would be together after that era, though it seemed then to be an era fated to last for ever.

After much discussion, Marsha reluctantly agreed that Frank and Angel should be invited to their wedding, which took place the following spring. Neither turned up.

·23·

Jonners at the Club

Jonathan James Carew Delahuntley, the second Viscount Canary, walked with lumbering strides, swinging his left arm but not his right because the fingers of his right hand were making a tight ball out of sweet paper. He was aged over thirty, but with the face of an undergraduate. His double-breasted, tailor-made, navy-blue, pinstriped suit and shining black leather lace-up shoes, the look of mild bewilderment on his chubby face, which was accentuated by a half-open mouth with pouting red lips, the cherubic cheeks and curly hair, the way he stooped as he walked, one shoulder lower than the other, as if embarrassed by his impressive height, gave him the demeanour of a young man anxious to please, someone for whom career success had preceded maturity. But the lot that had befallen the young Viscount was far more extraordinary than that: he was one of the richest and most powerful men in England.

The Daimler that crawled silently a few feet behind him was his. The Viscount had lunched in Covent Garden and was proceeding to his club on foot to allow a meal of pheasant pie and summer pudding to settle. His head was full of agreeable afternoon thoughts. Every shop across this prosperous street had a new frontage and a smartly designed window. There were so many riches attracting the eye that many people would walk past the sole unmarked, unrenovated old building without noticing it. Its peeling, faded brickwork was ludicrously decorated with an empty sloping flagpole. This was his London club. There are more expensive, more exclusive clubs than this in central London, but he liked this one best. As he turned to ascend the steps, he was startled when his chauffeur called, 'Shall I wait, sir?' He had forgotten the car was there.

'Oh yes. Yes, do: if you don't mind.'

Inside, the uniformed doorman sitting behind a glass screen greeted him by name. Viscount Canary breathed deeply as if he were inhaling the smell of floor polish across the large hall, with its chequered black and white tiles and the oil paintings covering its high walls. The Viscount's long legs took him up the stairs two at a time and across the landing to an upstairs lounge full of leather armchairs, a couple of which had become afternoon resting places for greying heads. The room was long, but not wide. He strode directly to the nearest corner, to a particular chair, upholstered in wine-coloured leather, which overlooked the street. From an inside pocket, he produced a gadget that his father had never used, a powerful mobile telephone with which he could dial anywhere in the world. Viscount Canary was alone, relaxing; yet he was in contact with the global economy.

It would be wrong to say he felt at home here; home had been Eaton Square, Lausanne and the Faubourg St Germain. No, the club was more familiar, more enclosing, safer than home: he felt *at school* here. The paintings covering the walls and the wide staircase with wooden banisters were very like the dark panelled walls and wide wooden staircase of his first boarding school. The room where he now sat was reminiscent of the sixth-form sweat room in which he had spent his pubescence among sons of City brokers, sheikhs, rock legends, Hong Kong bankers and other possessors of new money. They called him Jonners. They were the nearest to a peer group he ever had.

One of the pleasures of this perch was watching the women in the street below, particularly those with time on their hands who stopped to inspect the shop windows. Window-shopping was his favourite pastime too, though the goods on which he liked to gaze could not be bought with money. Being so rich had deprived him of the pleasure of spending.

Viscount Canary sighed. He took a crumpled sweet paper from his pocket and flattened it out, ironing the creases with his fingertip. Sometimes he felt old, as old as his dead grandfather; sometimes he felt as young as a lost schoolboy.

He had been in place just a few minutes when his mobile telephone rang. It had a quiet ring, which did not disturb anyone else in the room, and a volume control that allowed Jonners to talk in a murmur and yet be heard across the world. The call was from Vancouver, where an early-rising executive needed to discuss the price of newsprint. Jonners knew that a man who gives orders need not say much: he certainly did not need to explain where he was. Let the man think he was in the boardroom or his penthouse office, or over the Atlantic in his private jet, anywhere, surrounded by staff and pressed for time. Silences and curt answers would be his idiom; but he was already learning to remember every important detail from every business conversation.

Seven words were all he expended: 'Yes? When? How much? Yes, go ahead' – and thus the man from Vancouver was given clearance to spend almost a million Canadian dollars. If the money was misspent, the man in Vancouver would lose his job.

Viscount Canary sat forward to watch a group of four young Japanese women. Tourists, obviously, on a shopping spree. One in particular, with very long black hair and thick black-rimmed glasses, was wearing slacks and soft shoes, without socks. Something about her suggested to Viscount Canary that she would have gorgeous ankles.

The phone again. Time for the Viscount to be updated on the cost implications of the special photographic feature planned for the colour supplement of Sunday's newspaper. 'How much? I shall need that figure. Where's the extra advertising?'

His father's life and his grandfather's life had been like this: telephones ringing every few minutes throughout the day, every day, every year. From his earliest consciousness, they had been the only sources of power and authority in the world as seen by Jonners. First, his terrifying grandfather, before whom all had trembled: visitors, friends, headmasters, prime ministers, policemen and Jonners's father. (It was said that Gramps's father, Albert Huntley, a print compositor's son from Manchester, had been yet more terrifying. Gramps's first wife, who was French, had instigated the change of name to Delahuntley.) Then Gramps died, and all of a sudden Jonners's father, who had never seemed like a large figure, who was not so much a father as a feckless older brother living in the same shadow cast by Gramps, stepped out of the shade and became the most important, the most interesting, the most influential man in the world. Jonners grasped that it happened that way, and that it would happen to him. And now it had. His path was paved.

If Jonners had a close friend, he might have whispered that it was not easy to be born a tycoon. Everyone in his new milieu was older, tougher and more knowledgeable about the world. Even the women he encountered – or was it especially the women? – were hardbitten and determined. They had to be, to meet Jonners. Jonners was the peak of a rock face constructed of careerists scrambling one upon another; only the ablest, the most determined and the most ruthless reached Jonners. Being Jonners was an entirely different experience. He was Jonners by chance. It could have happened to anyone.

It tired him to be surrounded by the cacophony of ambition. So he enjoyed his occasional escapes into this sleepy room where the only noise was the rustling of newspapers, the clink of coffee spoons and the silence of retirement. He would have liked to spend every afternoon here quietly, almost secretly, directing the affairs of his billion-pound multinational conglomerate, but sadly the pressures of the boardroom made his visits rare.

A moment of triumph. The long-haired Japanese tourist on the pavement below had something in her shoe. She lifted one leg to adjust it, and a few inches of ankle were briefly displayed. At moments like this, Jonners wished he had a pocket telescope.

He sat back and closed his eyes. The phone was sure to ring in a minute, but it was pleasant to let his consciousness drift away.

When he opened his eyes, he was astonished to find someone standing directly before him, a man in late middle age, smartly dressed in a double-breasted suit, with a square face which he recognized but could not immediately place. The oddest thing was the man's expression: his eyes were wide open and staring with almost mad intensity. There was no colour in his face, and his lower jaw was trembling. He was evidently in the grip of a powerful emotion.

'Lord Canary?'

'Yes. Would you care to . . .?'

'No, I would not, sir, no, not at all. I would not care to sit down in your company, because, sir, you disgust me,' the man exclaimed.

The Viscount, who had risen from his chair half intending to shake the visitor's hand, gawped in astonishment. No one spoke to him in this manner. He looked about him. He expected someone to do something. At every minute of every day, since the first day he could remember, there had always been someone to do whatever needed doing, but now, though every head across the sleepy room had turned towards the sound of a raised voice, no one made a move to help the Viscount.

The extraordinary man continued his tirade. 'You are a charlatan, Lord Canary. You are the lowest of the low. You're fifth-class!'

The strange man looked so wild with fury that Lord Canary feared he was about to be assaulted, and decided to leave at once. Clutching his mobile phone, he beat a lumbering retreat, in his haste knocking his thigh painfully against a teak table.

'Hell's teeth, don't turn your back on me,' the madman shouted.

'For God's sake, sir, I have to go,' the Viscount cried, looking over his shoulder, as he escaped to the landing.

His assailant strode menacingly behind him. The Viscount halted before he reached the top of the stairs, fearing that the madman might push him. He stood uncertainly on the landing.

'What kind of animals do you keep in your employment, might I ask? Do you know what these people do, the hurt and ruin they bring? Do you care?'

At last, a member of staff appeared from the club bar, wringing his hands with anxiety at the sound of an angry voice in this somnolent club.

'What in God's name is all this about?' the astonished Viscount exclaimed.

The attendant, still wringing his hands, turned to the unknown assailant and asked, with what seemed to the Viscount quite undeserved respect, 'Sir Peter, I wonder if perhaps you might . . .'

The man named Sir Peter gave the Viscount another look of fury and contempt, and stomped away into a side room.

'Bloody hell!' shouted the Viscount, no longer caring about how they were raping the quiet of a London club. He was beginning to recover from his astonishment, and if there was one thing he was good at, one thing he had been born to do, it was to shout at employees. Angrily, he dialled his chauffeur. 'Bring the car to the front,' he ordered.

As he descended the stairs, he was intercepted by the attendant. 'Viscount Canary, I do most profoundly apologize.'

'Who the hell is that, and how did he get in?'

'That was Sir Peter Draycott,' the other replied.

'Draycott. The MP, Sir Peter Draycott? Lady Draycott's husband? What the hell is the matter with him?'

The attendant shook his head despairingly, having no more idea than Jonners what could have prompted such unclublike behaviour. He said something about the club committee.

However, a thought came to Jonners some minutes later as he sat in the back of his car, and he called his secretary on the carphone.

'Delia, would you be kind enough to dig out anything we've carried in any of the titles about an MP named Sir Peter Draycott – that's D-r-a-y-c-o-double-t. Say in the last month.'

Dave Drucker was at one of the tables on the main floor of the atrium when Lord Canary walked by to take a lift to his office. Dave saw the distracted look on the media mogul's brow, but did not give it another thought. The concerns of the proprietor were not his concerns. Dave was on a high. He had the last piece in place to pull off his coup, and had already called the news editor on an internal phone to ask him to come down.

Opposite Dave sat a man who at first glance had the personal appeal of a train spotter. Of slim build, with short dark greasy hair and dressed in an old checked jacket, he had unusually sharp eyes set close together, and a general appearance that might make anyone unwilling to trust him. But Dave, as a seasoned journalist, was used to interviewing people he would never trust outside his professional life.

They were talking intently when the bulky figure of one-eyed Ian Smith appeared beside them.

Dave saw at first glance that the news editor was in a bad temper, and guessed why. While Ian was in a conference with the editor, Dave had left a note for him, asking him to come down to the atrium as soon as possible without explaining why. Ian would not like that. He was status-conscious, as newspaper executives tend to be, and would not like being summoned by a mere general reporter. Dave did not care. Deference was his weak suit. When he was in possession of a good story, he could afford to amuse himself by winding up the news editor.

Pulling back an empty chair, Dave announced with forced heartiness, 'Ian, meet Victor. Victor Pauley. Victor used to be a Trot.'

Ian did not sit on the proffered chair, but put one hand on the back of it and nodded at Dave's guest, who peered up at him without acknowledging the greeting.

'I'm not of that persuasion any more,' Victor Pauley said. 'I'm the other way now.'

'Yeah, from far left to far right.'

'No,' said Victor. 'I stand for anti-fascism, but I have adopted a theory of markets that's directly contrapositive to Marxism.'

'Whatever,' said Dave, who had already had Victor's economic views expounded to him once. 'Don't worry about that, Victor. That's tangential, yeah. The point is, Ian, that on the night Christine Rist was killed, yeah, she threw a party at her house and Victor was a guest, yeah. And he has given me a sworn statement, which he'll repeat in court if he has to, that when the last of the other guests left, our boy was still there, tucked up in her bed. Isn't that right, Victor?'

Victor nodded.

Ian took a deep breath. 'How many years ago?'

'Yeah, it was a long time ago.'

'MP shagged somebody else's wife a long time ago: not a bollock-grabbing headline, is it?'

The remark was directed at Dave, as if there were no one else present. It was not actually what Ian Smith thought, but he was annoyed by the disrespectful manner in which he had been summoned and he wanted to give his reporter a hard time. Also, this was Dave's third attempt at Joseph Pilgrim. The first two had been disappointing.

'Come on, Ian. This is the man who said on radio that he'd slept with a married woman, *a* married woman – note: so we now know he's been through a brace, at the very least. This is the man who claimed he had never broken up anyone's marriage. Mr Frank Rist might beg to differ.'

'Joseph Pilgrim broke up their marriage,' the man named Victor Pauley asserted, as if the thought had only just come to him.

'But, bigger than that, Ian, yeah – there was the mystery witness who never materialized. I checked with the Newcastle cop shop, who tell me their file on the case was never closed. It's fucking obvious, Ian. Joe Pilgrim was humping her the night she was killed. He was the witness who never came forward, and he did a runner. Straight after her death he disappeared from Newcastle altogether, and didn't turn up again until the heat was off. Isn't that right, Victor?'

'Absolutely.'

'It's mega, mega.'

'Mega,' echoed Victor.

Ian looked hard at the man named Victor, weighing him up. 'You don't mind signing an affidavit, Mr Pauley?'

'He could do with some readies, a small consideration,' Dave said.

Ian nodded curtly, and walked back to the lift, thinking to himself that Dave was an irritating bastard, one of whose many bad habits was to mention payment with the source sitting there listening; but there again, he was a resourceful and persistent irritating bastard.

·24·

Meeting the Deputy Prime Minister

Too much was happening. He could not understand how his relations with Margaret were suddenly so bad. One argument set off by a wretched mobile phone that switched itself on had sent their marriage tumbling from secure to irretrievable without passing through any intermediate stage. He had hoped she would abandon the idea of making him move out. His hopes were raised when she did not mention it over breakfast on the morning after their argument, but in the evening she asked him pointedly whether he had thought about looking for somewhere else. Then he knew she meant it, but he yet hoped that if he went through the necessary procedures, she might relent before the day of decision. The unasked question hung in the air for days. It affected the children. Isobel complained of nightmares. Tom reverted to wetting himself and to demanding to watch the same Thomas the Tank Engine video over and over again, taking refuge in repetition.

One morning, there was a journalist waiting on the pavement outside as they came down to breakfast. He was there to check a rumour that Joseph was about to resign his seat to avoid being implicated in a major sex scandal. What Joseph would have liked was some expression of solidarity from Margaret after he had sent the man away – just a word or a gesture that conveyed that they were in this together, Joseph and Margaret v. the fourth estate. There was none. She gave him that tired look, as if he had brought trouble on her household again. That evening, Joseph promised to move out and the following day, he found a new flat. There were no expressions of reproach or regret: only a businesslike conversation about how Joseph would find somewhere else to live, and what he should take with him, as if they were making arrangements to have the car serviced.

They also left unsaid whether this was a temporary separation until the crisis provoked by Frank Rist was played out, or divorce. Joseph did not push the point. He did not even ask about arrangements for him to see the children, fearful that once negotiations began, solicitors would be in and they would be down a slope from which there be no climbing back up.

So he moved in to a house in Lambeth, shared with two other MPs and a peer. It was like being propelled back towards the student life, except that his new housemates were older, uglier and less fun than any students he had ever met. They were not surprised or moved by his circumstances. He soon learnt how commonly marriages fall apart when one partner enters the Commons.

At first, he guiltily experienced the thrill of freedom, because he could return to bed as late as he chose, and could have brought back anyone who could be persuaded to join him. Soon, he was being reminded how oppressive this kind of freedom can be. He desperately missed the children. He spoke to both of them on the telephone every teatime, and found it painfully difficult to answer Isobel's questions about how long it would be until he came home. The pain of separation was made worse by his anxiety that their emotional lives might be permanently damaged. He would not have thought it possible that human beings so small, whom he had known so briefly, could take such a hold on his emotions.

He wondered about telling Rachel that he had separated from his wife. If there was one obvious benefit to separation, it was that it freed him to have an affair with Rachel, if she would have him;

but he decided not to raise the subject at all in case it appeared he was appealing for sympathy. She found out anyway.

Meanwhile, he was being harassed by daily telephone calls from Gerald Moon, who was becoming more and more obsessive about the secret party he was organizing for Rachel. Joseph could not help but be heartened by this bombardment. Gerald's rising insecurity was a source of hope, for he noticed how the more often Gerald rang him about Rachel, the less frequently Rachel mentioned Gerald. He had a recurring fear that Joseph was either going to compel Rachel to work that evening, preventing her from going to the party, or would insist on her being at her desk early the following morning, inhibiting her from enjoying herself. Gerald also wanted Joseph's advice about male guests. He mentioned several names, mostly journalists or political researchers who were all young and formidably successful in their chosen fields. (Joseph was not invited – either because he was too old, married, insufficiently successful, or all three). There was no mention of women guests. It seemed that Rachel was to be plunged alone into a room full of eligible young men.

More seriously, Dawn Jones's problems had worsened since Joseph's clumsy attempt to resolve them. She had been on the telephone in tears, fearful that she was about to be sent to prison. Her situation certainly looked bad. Not only had she received a summons for contempt of court; a solicitor's letter had also arrived for Joseph. He was astonished to see himself accused of making 'threatening' remarks. The implication of the letter was clear enough: if he approached Mr Jones again, he could be the next one accused of contempt of court. Then there came a handwritten note through the House of Commons internal delivery system, signed by a Tory MP whom Joseph knew by sight, a youngish man on the way up, who was said to have a sharp tongue and a well-developed sense of his own importance.

In view of your gross discourtesy, in visiting my constituency without prior warning to me, and your abusive and inexplicable behaviour towards my constituent, Mr Mal Jones, I am giving you notice of my intention to complain about your actions to the Speaker, as a point of order, at the commencement of this afternoon's business.

He had known, of course, that the estate where Mal Jones lived was outside his own constituency. It followed logically that it must be within another MP's, but he had not given that matter a moment's thought.

'I'm afraid you're in the wrong, my boy,' Never Evil said cheerily, when Joseph rang the Whips' Office for advice. 'Go into the chamber, listen to the point of order, get on your hind legs, say sorry very 'umbly, and forget all about it.'

The complainant was a small man with a strange repertoire of body movements. As he stood up in the back row of the opposition benches across the way, his jaw jutted forward jerkily, then retracted; his mouth pursed, creating an angry, spiteful look on his narrow face; a shoulder twitched and an arm set out in a direction all its own, before he clasped his hands together in front of him. But though his body language was disjointed and inarticulate, he spoke like an accomplished veteran of student debates.

'On a point of order, Madam Speaker, I want to raise a point of order of which I have given you prior notice, and have also notified the Member opposite, the Honourable Member for Ladyford North. I have received a complaint, Madam Speaker, from a constituent, Mr Mal Jones, who lives in the Broadacre Estate in my constituency. Mr Jones informs me that on Wednesday last week, he was disturbed by a visitor who arrived uninvited at his door and behaved in an abusive and threatening manner.' At this point, other Tory MPs cried *Oh! Oh!* in mock horror. 'This was the

Honourable Member for Ladyford North, who raised a matter with him concerning his estranged wife, Mrs Jones. I was not notified, Madam Speaker, that the Honourable Member opposite proposed to visit my constituency on a matter such as this, and had I been so notified I would have made the strongest possible representations to the Member opposite not to conduct this visit . . .'

'He's making a fucking meal of it,' a voice muttered on the bench in front of Joseph. He had been watching the Tory MP's jerky body movements so intently that he had not noticed Denis Drummond slip into the chamber.

'Would I be right in believing that it is still the custom of this House for one Honourable Member to show another Honourable Member the courtesy of notifying him before visiting his constituency?'

'Order! Mr Pilgrim!' called the Speaker, seeing Joseph rise to his feet.

Joseph did as he had been advised. In a few words he explained what had taken him to Mr Jones's house and he pleaded inexperience in overlooking the courtesies of the House. These brief remarks were delivered to the embarrassing accompaniment of a rumbling 'hear, hear' from the bench in front.

He sat down thinking that would be the end of the matter, but was surprised when a second Tory MP leapt up with a cry of 'further to that point of order, Madam Speaker!', to which Denis Drummond reacted by sweeping his arm in the air and shouting at the man to sit down.

'Order, order,' cried the Speaker. Joseph was sitting quite close to her. Her face was red, her fine robe was slipping from her shoulder, and her spectacles threatened to tumble off her nose. 'There will be no further points of order further to the point of order. Order! We have heard the point of order and the apology from the Honourable – Order! – the Honourable Member for

Ladyford North. I would remind all Honourable Members that there are courtesies which we observe in the House, particularly in matters – order! – relating to other Honourable Members' constituencies. Order! There being no further points of order, the Clerk will now proceed to read the orders of the day.'

And that was it. A few minutes later, Denis Drummond caught Joseph's eyes and indicated with a nod of the head that he should leave. They slipped out together through the door behind the Speaker's chair, which led into the lobbies where MPs gathered to vote.

'What a load of bollocks,' Denis said. 'Have you got a fucking minute? Come and meet the Deputy PM. I told him you could help him out.'

'How?' Joseph asked.

Beyond the voting lobby was a wide aisle, running from left to right, which MPs regularly used as a thoroughfare, and straight ahead was a narrow corridor leading deep into the building. Joseph had seen it, but did not know where it led.

'He's got a fucking climate conference coming up. Big stuff. He's got a whole fucking programme of ideas to fight for and he wants a bit of backbench support. I said you could do some lobbying among the new MPs.'

'I'd be f— very glad to.'

A few steps down the corridor there was a door on the left, set back so that it was concealed from the sight of anyone passing on the main corridor. It opened on to a cramped, thickly carpeted staircase. The staircase was so quiet that it seemed to be deserted. There were closed doors set along little corridors at each level reached by the staircase. On each door was a printed name. Each name was a Cabinet minister's. That explained the silence: generally, Cabinet ministers are not to be found in the Commons.

As they ascended the stairs, Denis Drummond started singing to himself in a low bass. The tune was instantly recognizable as 'John Brown's Body', but the lyrics were different. After a moment, Joseph was able to make them out:

Oh, the Clerk will now proceed to read the orders of the day.
Yes, the Clerk proceeds to read the fucking orders of the day.
All the fucking orders that the Clerk proceeds today
Can all get fucking stuffed.

Denis Drummond had risen to his position from a standing start on the factory floor, by a life devoted first to the trade union movement and second to the Labour Party. Some said he was a good minister. Others questioned whether his approach was as serious as it ought to be.

The door marked with the Deputy Prime Minister's name led into an outer office where a woman was waiting alone at a closed door leading to a second office. She raised a warning hand as they entered, and she indicated to them both to wait.

'It could be a few minutes,' she said.

In fact they waited nearly twenty minutes. Twice, the woman at the door slipped through to the other room, only to return and give an apologetic shrug. Whenever she opened the door, the sound of a powerful voice raised in anger could be heard in the other room. On the third occasion, she stayed in the other room for several minutes before ushering them in. They went through into another office which struck Joseph as surprisingly small considering the seniority of its occupant. It had all the usual trappings of an office: a desk at the end near the window, crammed bookshelves, two reclining chairs, and a small fridge, all contained in a space about half the size of Joseph's office across the road.

It also appeared at first sight that no one was there. The Deputy

Prime Minister was actually standing at the far side of the desk; his back was to the door, and he was staring out of the window, his shoulders hunched tight together and raised so that his bull neck had disappeared beneath his collar. At first glance, he seemed to be utterly alone. Though not exceptionally tall, he was a stockily built man, and his jacket was stretched hard around the shoulder muscles within. He was holding a metal ruler in his right hand, which he had slipped under his left armpit so it protruded out. There was no mistaking that the Deputy Prime Minister was shaking with rage.

This was confirmed when, after a pause, he swung round to face his visitors. His fleshy face and prominent eyebrows were a picture of concentrated fury.

None of this bothered Denis Drummond, who had casually helped himself to a cold drink from the fridge, offering one to Joseph and indicating to him to take one of the comfortable chairs. Denis took a swig and said, 'Joseph has agreed to help with Kyoto.'

The Deputy Prime Minister looked at Joseph and nodded, as if to convey that his presence in the room was tolerable, though possibly no better than tolerable. Without further ceremony, he began talking, pacing the floor furiously as he spoke about his negotiations with foreign governments and various world bodies, and the agreement he hoped to secure on greenhouse gases and global emissions at the impending world summit in Japan. The monologue continued without interruption or pause for at least a quarter of an hour, during which he dragged up dates and statistics from memory. His tone was at first only mildly gruff, until something triggered the memory of whatever it was that had put him in a fury, and he began to raise his voice as if he were enraged by the need to revise worldwide targets on carbon dioxide emissions. As the Deputy Prime Minister's fury approached a climax, he began beating the desktop with his metal ruler, so that each word was expelled against the crash of metal on wood. Though his anger was alarming at first, Joseph was calmed by the casual behaviour of Denis Drummond, who continued sipping coke as if nothing unusual were happening. The Deputy Prime Minister was a man with a famously short temper, who had spent the greater part of his life in meetings or in broadcasting studios where he was compelled to appear calm while inwardly boiling with rage. He had been compelled, perforce, to learn how to sound calm and optimistic while being baited into a fury by an opponent or an interviewer. Now, in private, in company he trusted, he could shout and bellow about a topic that fascinated him.

'So what can you do?' he asked, having come to an abrupt halt.

Joseph had had a struggle not to be put off by the extraordinary mode of delivery, but he had followed what was being said with care, and it was interesting. It concerned issues that, by the sound of them, could render much of the planet uninhabitable for their grandchildren.

'It seems to me there were six main points in what you said,' he replied, and he listed them one after another, repeating the Deputy Prime Minister's words as faithfully as he could. Denis leant forward to take a piece of headed paper from a side table and scribbled notes.

'No!' cried the Deputy Prime Minister. He disagreed with the interpretation Joseph had put on his words on one of the six points, and repeated his earlier remarks with all the same raging emphasis. When he had finished, he snatched the piece of paper from Denis's hand, read it, and scribbled some corrections before handing it over to Joseph, who was now holding the government's policy on global warming, summarized in about a hundred words in two different hands.

'So what can you do?' the Deputy Prime Minister asked again.

'One possibility,' Joseph suggested, 'is that I could draw up an open letter, addressed to you, and get a few other MPs, new MPs, to sign it with me, and we could send a copy to every Labour MP. And it would say that we're concerned about the forthcoming global summit, and we particularly hope the Deputy Prime Minister will address six particular points, which will be these six points, which is what you're going to do anyway. So, when you get back and report to the parliamentary party, you're bound to get asked about the very things that you've done, and you'll be seen to be on the case and responding to backbench opinion . . .

'Of course, it's only an idea,' Joseph added hastily, as he spotted a fearsome scowl on the Deputy Prime Minister's face.

The Deputy Prime Minister chortled, and turned to Denis Drummond. 'You said he was sharp.'

'Fucking sharp.'

The Deputy Prime Minister looked at the clock, swore, and hurried back to his desk. With an urgent wave, Denis signalled to Joseph to follow him out of the room.

'That was good,' Denis said as they returned down the deserted staircase. 'By the way, you may have noticed he was in a bit of a fucking brown study.'

'No, I hadn't noticed,' Joseph said.

It was meant as a joke. The tension had lifted and he was in the mood for banter. To his surprise, Denis took him literally.

'No, well you get fucking used to his moods when you know him as I know him. He's a great man. There's nobody better, or straighter, anywhere in the fucking movement, but his mood gets a bit bucolic. Did you notice a story in the papers about the Greenwich Dome?'

Joseph could scarcely have missed the story even if he had not been looking out for it: it had been blazoned across the front of two Sunday newspapers, after which few news bulletins had passed without a mention of it. A top-level inquiry was under way into the source of the leak.

'But should the DPM be so angry?' Joseph asked in alarm. 'He came rather well out of the story, didn't he?'

'Some clever cunt leaked a civil service memo,' Denis said. 'I think it was Gerald Moon. Do you know Gerald? He's a fucking head case.'

Unbeknown to Denis Drummond there was an affidavit on the Cabinet Secretary's desk, in which Gerald Moon swore on oath that he had never passed the disputed minute to any journalist, or discussed its content or its existence with any journalist, or discussed it with anyone other than members of the government.

'I know of him,' said Joseph, silently recalling how he had been led by Gerald to believe that the Deputy Prime Minister would want the memo leaked.

'The worst of it is that Downing Street think it was us that fucking leaked it,' Denis explained. 'That's what's really made him angry.'

·25·

The Rachel Party

'So, apart from the way it has wrecked your marriage, how do you like the life of an MP, Joseph?' Deirdre asked. The crisis had brought her back into their lives as an intermediary in all matters relating to Frank Rist. This was important because of the signs that something else was about to happen. They were out at the terrace on a table close to the one where he had drunk champagne with Gerald Moon, enjoying a pleasantly cool evening.

'I was hoping to see you on television the night you were elected, but I fell asleep after Portillo,' she continued. 'Then I thought you'd disappeared off the face of the earth, until you asked the Prime Minister that interesting question. I quite admired you for that.'

He had not talked to her properly for years, but there had been enough sporadic contact to keep them abreast of her adventures. Others had mellowed since the wild militancy of the eighties, but not Deirdre. She had been to prison during the poll tax protests, had been fined for publicly burning a US flag during the Gulf War, and had been spotted living in a makeshift wooden hut, with people years younger than herself, up a tree along the line of a proposed by-pass. Now Deirdre was down from her tree, scrubbed, and employed by a charity that concerned itself with preserving rainforests.

Her weight problem was as steadfast as her socialism. It was rumoured that she had emerged from Styal prison quite thin, but that was long ago and this wavering from her fixed path had since been corrected. She was chunky in the legs, rotund of stomach, and red in the face, but in the intervening years she had allowed her hair to grow down to the shoulders, making her look less defiantly feminist. She was sitting back with her left leg resting on her right knee, one hand on her ankle, the other holding a cigarette, dressed androgynously in a pale open-neck shirt and black trousers. At her side sat a dumpy young woman, with short hair, stud earrings and a vulnerable look on her fleshy face, who behaved like a bored teenager in the company of adults, staring gloomily into the middle distance and saying nothing. She was strangely attractive, despite her sulky expression, because she seemed to need protecting. The older woman was obviously fond of her, but would speak to her sharply, as to a difficult teenage daughter. Joseph could not pinpoint what the relationship between the two women was, and did not ask. He had never thought of Deirdre as a lesbian. In fact, he remembered tales of entanglements with men, all large in body but not necessarily in intelligence.

'If Marsha really didn't know you were having a scene with Christine, she must be more naïve than you are,' Deirdre said suddenly.

No one else had used the name Marsha since the 1980s.

'That's not really the reason why we're apart,' Joseph replied. As soon as he had spoken, he wondered what made him want to leap to his estranged wife's defence, or indeed why, with a stranger at the table, he was discussing his marriage at all. But not even the hint of scandal interested Deirdre's young girlfriend, who stared indifferently out over the Thames, working her jaw as if there was chewing gum in her mouth.

'I don't think you'll necessarily get on with Gerald Moon,' he added, hastily changing the subject.

'I'm confident that he's a complete arse,' Deirdre replied.

While they were waiting for Gerald, Joseph told her about the case of Dawn Jones. The latest development was that she had decamped from her home and was living with a friend, hoping to evade the court order against her.

'Why don't you let me talk to her,' Deirdre suggested. 'I know people who are really good at evading court orders.'

Joseph had made a point of not knowing where Mrs Jones was, in case he was asked by the police, but he gave Deirdre an idea of how to set about finding her, with little expectation that anything would come of it.

Gerald Moon appeared on the ramp leading up to the terrace. He seemed gloomy at first, but he brightened up on being introduced to Deirdre's girlfriend. The possibility that her tastes might be Sapphic in no way diminished Gerald's obvious pleasure at being at the same table as someone young and nice-looking. He leant over to shake her hand, talking volubly about how his arrival had been delayed by a telephone call from a political adviser to a member of the Cabinet. Surprised by the heartiness of his hand-shake, she reddened, sat up, and made an effort to smile pleasantly. Deirdre seemed neither surprised nor interested by her behaviour.

'OK – council of war,' said Joseph. 'I have one piece of new information to throw into the pot. I've had a letter from the Millennial Church which Frank belonged to. They say he didn't leave voluntarily: he was asked to go.'

This prompted a snort of laughter from Deirdre. 'Not another. It started with Socky Wocky.'

'No, it was the WRP first,' Joseph said. 'Then the Socialist Workers' Party, and I think it was the International Marxist Group after that.'

'No, you're wrong, Joseph,' Deirdre insisted. 'Socky Wocky was definitely the first. They expelled him in the seventies. And the Migs wouldn't even let him in, so that's when he got in with the Healy–Redgrave lot. No wait, not them, another group – an off-shoot of the WRP. That's what he got expelled from. Then he bluffed his way into the Labour Party, until he got expelled under Kinnock. And the trades council expelled him for not being in a union.'

'That was because the Tobacco Workers expelled him for not being a tobacco worker.'

'Or a worker of any description. Now guess who he has fallen out with? That weird woman who has become his landlady. Angel. I spoke to her on the phone, and she and Frank have had a bad rift.'

That was news to Joseph. He wondered if the cause of their quarrel was connected with the night he had spent under Angel's roof.

'Can I tempt anyone to champagne?' asked Gerald, who had become increasingly fidgety as he was compelled to listen to a conversation about times and events that meant nothing to him.

'You can certainly tempt me,' said Deirdre, without even a glance in Gerald's direction. Her young girlfriend made up for this lack of attention by rising from her chair to accompany Gerald to the bar, but Deirdre's hand descended firmly on her shoulder and pushed her back into her seat. The girl resumed her earlier sulky expression.

'What I can't understand,' Deirdre continued, 'is why did we listen to this arse? How were we taken in by him? How could someone with Christine's brain be taken in by him – never mind marrying him?'

'Because when Frank is immersed in something, he is com-pletely convincing because he believes in it totally, because he has leadership qualities, and because he's a charismatic public speaker, and he has physical courage.'

'But apart from that, he's an arse. Why did this church get rid of him?'

'It sounds quite serious. Apparently, he had an argument with a woman in the congregation and nearly broke her jaw.'

The information did not appear to surprise Deirdre, who looked across the Thames as she absorbed it, nodding to herself. 'Some women found him physically intimidating, though I have to say I wasn't one of them,' she remarked. Considering the way Deirdre was built, Joseph found that plausible.

'Do you remember a man named Victor Pauley?' Deirdre asked. 'You probably don't. He was a very suspicious little rascal who claimed to be in contact with the IRA. In his bloody dreams! I mention him because he's around, and I think he's up to no good.'

'I can't remember anything about him.'

'He was at Christine's house on the evening before her death. I know because he talked to me about it afterwards.'

'There were a lot of people there that night. There usually were. They had all gone by about eleven o'clock.'

'Except you,' said Deirdre.

There was a birdlike sound in Joseph's pocket. It was his mobile phone, an object he kept about him although he blamed it for the misery that had overtaken his life. To his surprise, the caller was Gerald, who had stepped out of sight only a minute earlier, asking him plaintively to abandon his guests and come to the bar for a private word.

The bar was in a marquee at the end of the terrace. Its interior was laid out like a cramped pub, and Gerald was sitting at one of the tables, with a bottle of champagne and four glasses, his soft face a picture of abject misery. As Joseph sat opposite him, he blinked – not swiftly, as normal, but as if he had deliberately closed his eyes to shut out something painful. He fidgeted with one of the wineglasses, sniffed, and said, 'Sorry to drag you in here, mate, but I need to ask – has Rach said anything?'

The day of Rachel's surprise birthday party, to which Gerald had paid such obsessive attention, had passed by unremarked. Far from nursing a hangover on the morning afterwards, Rachel had arrived at work early and had worked hard all day. She had not mentioned Gerald on that day or since.

'Not a word.'

'Not a word? It's that bad, then, it's that bad.' This set off a sequence of six or seven blinks. 'I've been awake the whole bloody night, mate: I can't sleep, I can't eat. This is destroying me. I need Rachel. I need her so badly. Is it right you've split with your wife? I know what you're going through.'

It was a symptom of Gerald's limitless egotism that he should equate the frustration of his sexual designs on Rachel to a rupture in a marriage that had lasted more than a decade. In the circumstances, however, Joseph was impressed that Gerald had managed to lift his thoughts off his own concerns even to that small extent.

He wanted to rejoin Deirdre, but Gerald looked so downcast that kindness compelled Joseph to continue the conversation. 'The party wasn't a success, then?'

'A bit of a failure, actually. The concept didn't work.'

'Perhaps you should have invited some other women.'

'That's where the concept fell down,' Gerald concurred.

'I think that being the only woman in a room full of men is not necessarily much fun.'

Suddenly, Gerald sat bolt upright and blinked repeatedly. 'What do you mean, the only woman? Why? Where are you coming from?'

He looked so offended that Joseph hastily apologized. 'I'm sorry, I thought you went for a male-only guest list.'

'No, there were women,' Gerald said. He fiddled with the neck of the champagne bottle and blinked a few times more before adding, 'They were all called Rachel.'

Joseph repeated the words very slowly and clearly, to be sure that he had understood. 'They were all called Rachel?'

'You see, mate, I've always loved that name. Haven't you noticed the phenomenon that the most beautiful, most alluring, most mysterious women in the world are all called Rachel? It's since *One Million Years BC* when I was a kid. I wanted Rachel to know that she's the Rachel out of all the Rachels, so I invited all my favourite Rachels.'

'You threw a party at which all the female guests had the same name?'

'Not exactly the same. One spelt her name R-a-c-h-*a*-e-l.'

'Let me get a handle on this. How many Rachels did you invite?'

'Half a dozen.'

Joseph would have burst out laughing had Gerald looked less dejected. His mouth had formed a perfect crescent, its edges pointing down.

'And Rachel – Rachel, Rachel – our Rachel – didn't like it?'

'It wasn't a great evening, to be honest with you, mate.'

Later, he would hear more from Rachel about the evening. The men, in her estimation, were all young, gifted, successful and nerdy. All the Rachels were glamorous. They arrived one at a time. She felt mildly let down when introduced to the first Rachel, as if meeting another woman of her own age with the same name had taken a little of her individuality. The arrival of the next Rachel was embarrassing. They could not avoid having a conversation about being called Rachel. By now, Gerald had vanished into the kitchen, but the men hung on the edge of the conversation trying to say the right thing. One man, who spoke with a lisp, assured them, 'I can tell you all apart. I think you've all got lot-th of individuality.' But the arrival of two more Rachels in quick succession pushed them beyond the point of polite conversation. There were cries of dismay and screams of protest. Gerald was still in the kitchen. When the Rachels shouted for him to come out and give an account of himself, he emerged, beaming proudly, carrying a home-made birthday cake on which he had written the word *Rachel* in pink icing.

'It was so naff, I thought I was going to die,' Rachel said.

But that was all to come. Immediately, he had to steer Gerald back to their guests on the terrace so that they could have a serious talk.

'Why *One Million Years BC*?'

'It's a film I saw on TV as a kid. There's a fantastic actress named Rachel Welch.'

'Raquel.'

'What?'

'Her name was Raquel Welch, not Rachel.'

A look of unutterable dismay came over Gerald's face, as if he had seen crumble the pedestal upon which the edifice of his erotic fantasies had been constructed.

Nevertheless, he rallied when his eyes fell again upon Deirdre's young companion, and he opened the champagne bottle and filled the four glasses, simultaneously keeping up a flow of talk. 'I've acted unilaterally, Joseph, mate. Hope you don't mind. I was thinking about this Frank Rist bloke when I was lying awake, and what he does, and I was thinking he can't possibly make a living out of one pathetic web site. So it's likely that he's drawing benefits. Yeah? So I passed the word along.'

'Who to?'

'DSS. They're having a fraud crackdown.'

'God, you nark!' Deirdre exclaimed. The look of contempt she gave Gerald did not inhibit her, or her friend, from accepting his champagne.

'I haven't been able to get a grasp of this business about George the Shrink who turned up at a meeting and recognized Frank,' Joseph said. 'Should I know who he is, and does he matter?'

'I remember him because he came into the bookshop to order books by people like Erich Fromm and Flora Rheta Schreiber, but maybe you didn't meet him,' Deirdre replied. 'It sounds as if what he says could matter a lot, if we could find him. I know someone who knows his wife, so I'm hoping to turn him up.'

'Anyway, Mr Brains,' Deirdre added, suddenly turning on Gerald, whose mood was beginning to sink again as he failed to elicit the hoped-for response from Deirdre's girlfriend. 'You aren't saying anything. Haven't you got a suggestion?'

'Could we use this letter from the church to get Frank worked over by another newspaper?' Joseph said.

'No point, mate. We did it once. It didn't stop him. If you do it again, you risk giving him credibility.'

'Is there anything we can do?'

'Hit them with a lawyer's letter at lunchtime on Saturday.'

'Why leave it so late?'

'Because on a Sunday paper, Saturday lunchtime is close to production time. That's when you'll cause maximum panic. I've got to go.'

As he stood up, Joseph asked him, 'When you rang the DSS about Frank, did you use my name?'

'Yes I did, mate. I hope that's all right.'

Joseph muttered to Gerald's retreating back, 'No, it isn't all right, actually, Gerald, but thank you for asking.'

·26·

Dave Drucker Meets the Editor

The premonition that it might all go wrong came suddenly to Dave Drucker in the middle of Saturday afternoon, when the news editor remarked casually, in passing, that Joseph Pilgrim's lawyers had been on the phone.

'I hope they were told to get stuffed,' Dave said, but Ian Smith pulled a face and made some noncommittal remark about 'upstairs', as if someone high up in the building was involved. By the time Dave had returned to his desk, he was heating up with anger. The story, as written, was watertight. He knew, because he had been through it with an in-house lawyer, showing him documents and affidavits to back up every line. Suddenly, in that part of the late afternoon when most of the writers' work is over, and other reporters were congregating in groups to exchange gossip and jokes, and Dave himself had risked putting a pint or two into his stomach to augment that agreeable glow that comes from having a strong story prominently placed – suddenly, he faced this.

Dave saw himself as a frontline soldier at the mercy of staff officers stationed comfortably away from danger. No executive had to do what Dave had done: front up Joseph Pilgrim, and seek out other sources, not knowing whether he would meet co-operation or shit. Shit was what he had got, by the cartload, from a dreadful woman named Deirdre. Now he asked only that the staff officers in the rear should hold their nerve, yet they were negotiating with the other side's lawyers. Why?

A woman from the features department was working her way around the news room, talking to one reporter after another. Dave did not like her. She was a woman rising rapidly in what he regarded as a male profession – young, overdressed, heavily made up, and already better paid than he was. It was rumoured that her early success owed more to where she slept than to what she had written. Her voice was loud enough for him to hear her conversation from across the room.

'We're going to run Shit of the Year, everybody – Cad of the Year, to give it its proper title.' She was involved in planning ahead for the empty week between Christmas and the New Year. 'I need names, please, and *don't* say James Hewitt because a hundred people have said him already. Fred West is out because we need people who are alive. Somebody said Saddam Hussein, somebody said Mick Jagger, and somebody said a Yugoslav with a name that begins with M who's a bit of a shit too, apparently. Any other nominations, anybody?'

Sometimes, Dave like to take the mickey out of people like her, who lived in a mental world in which the man who made money talking about his love affair with the Princess of Wales was a bigger 'cad' than the man whose ambitions were drowning the Balkans in blood; but for the moment, he had bigger things on his mind. After he had brooded for several minutes, Dave stood up so abruptly that his chair almost tipped over, correcting itself with a rattling thump. Other journalists turned their heads in surprise.

'Dave! Dave Drucker! – don't you dare sneak off till I've spoken to you,' the woman from Features cried. She bounced across the floor cuddling a clipboard, and thrust her pelvis forward. 'Now, you're always a man with ideas, I know you can think of a Shit of the Year.'

Dave sat down, putting one foot on his desk, raised his head to gaze at the polystyrene tiles on the low ceiling, lowered it to gaze into her questioning face, and said thoughtfully, 'Just give the curry I had for lunch time to work through, my love, and you can come and see it happen.'

For a moment, she only shook her head in bewilderment. Then the import of his words properly registered, and with a grimace she retreated, shaking her head as she left.

On Dave's round face there was an angry, determined look. He stood up, more slowly than before, and strode over to the news desk, where Ian Smith sat.

'Why have you shown my fucking copy to Joseph Pilgrim's lawyer? Are we running the story, or aren't we? If we aren't, I want the fucking editor to tell me why.'

'Let's talk to the fucking editor then,' Ian replied calmly.

His reaction left Dave with a queasy feeling that something had happened that he did not know about. He was guided into the editor's office, a separate room off the main news room, its white walls decorated by framed copies of old front pages. Richard Track was a diminutive, waspish man with an inflamed face and powerful voice. His small, squat stature did not prevent him from terrorizing the middle-ranking executives who usually surrounded him even when, as with Ian Smith, they were taller by a foot or so. He was hunched over his desk, engrossed in a telephone call, and signalled to them to sit at the oval table that filled most of the floor space. Before the door had closed, another executive had slipped in, because any conversation involving the editor invariably attracted a supporting cast. This one was around forty, but the morass of wrinkles and care lines about the eyes and across the forehead, below a fast-receding hairline, made him looker older. He had a set expression which conveyed that he respected who-ever was speaking and sympathized with their position. Everyone knew that he was not to be trusted.

The editor slammed down the phone, swore, and rose to his feet. 'Dave, you prick, what are you up to?'

'The story stands up, Richard. I've double-checked every shitting detail.' Respect for Richard's office deterred him from saying 'fucking'.

'Every shitting detail,' the editor echoed, reaching into a low fridge to pull himself out a can of lager, which he flicked open. It made a gentle fizzing noise as he poured the contents into a plastic cup. He sat opposite Dave and looked hard into his face. The two lesser executives sat with elbows on the table and eyes on the editor. '*Every* shitting detail?'

'Every shitting detail, Richard.'

The man with the furrowed forehead frowned in a way that made all the wrinkles across his brow take a downward dive towards the bridge of his nose. He looked at Dave and shook his head as if to show how sorry he was to see a reporter caught in this predicament, not getting the editor's drift.

'OK, Mr Every-shitting-detail, why has Lord Canary been on the shitting phone? Why?'

'Don't know, Richard.'

'But aren't you the clever cunt who checked every detail? Aren't you? Is Lady Draycott's name in your copy?'

'Yes.'

The executive with the sympathetic face drew a sharp breath.

'Take her name out. That's point one . . .'

'Why, Richard?'

At this, even Ian Smith looked startled. It was reckless to question the editor, but Dave was so angry that he was past caring.

'Because you're a fuckwit, Dave. Question answered?'

The lined brow of the sympathetic executive was rotating from side to side.

'No it isn't answered, if you don't mind me saying so,' Dave replied, with a wild disregard for caution. 'So, I'm a fuckwit. I've got a degree in total fuckwittery, but why is that a material fact, Richard? Nobody has denied that Lady Draycott was Joseph Pilgrim's mistress. *Nobody* doubts it. This is a guy who has fucked two married women, if not more, a serial shagger, a proven bonkeromo. Where's our problem?'

Richard Track's expression softened. To answer him back was a risk. Sometimes on a Saturday, he would fire someone just to keep the others in awe of him; but at heart he liked Dave Drucker, and respected him for his gall. 'You don't give up, do you, cunt? Anyone want a lager?' he asked.

The two executives nodded gratefully, but Dave was in a mood for an argument. 'I'd prefer a beer, personally, if there's any on offer.'

'I haven't fucking got it. Do you want a lager, or don't you?'

'Cheers.'

The editor stood and passed around the cold cans. 'All right, Dave, Mr I've-checked-every-shit-gobbling-detail, I suppose we'll have to forgive the massive detail you overlooked in your hunt for a headline. Lady Draycott is a dear friend of Lord Canary.'

'Oh shit,' Dave exclaimed.

He looked shocked, but secretly, he was thrilled. It would be a fantastic story to retell in the pub, how he had shafted a dear friend of the Proprietor. He struggled to maintain a solemn, concerned expression, like the look upon the wrinkled brow of the subservient executive, while wanting desperately to burst out laughing. 'Oh shit. I have to admit I didn't know that, Richard. Lord Canary doesn't make me privy to his Christmas card list, so I wouldn't know whether Lady Draycott is his dear friend or what she is to him, I have to admit.'

'Don't get clever, cunt. Tell me: who the fuck is Frank Rist?'

'I keep being asked whether Frank Rist is my source, Richard.

I haven't named my source to anyone. I've arranged for the source to be paid without anyone knowing who it is, by agreement. If you say you've got to know my source, I'll tell you who my main source is, but not with other people in the room – no disrespect.'

'I said, who is Frank Rist?'

'Frank Rist is a gentleman who manages a weird little web site, who has known Joseph Pilgrim a long time, whose wife was killed in Newcastle . . .'

'Where was he, on the night?'

'In London, so I understand.'

'Or not, as the case may be,' Richard Track replied, half to himself, picking up a document from the table in front of him.

'That's verified, Richard – witness statements. He was staying with a woman who has a house in Clapham. It emerged at the inquest.'

Richard Track fell silent. He was one of those noisy people whose silences can be more daunting than sound. Everyone in the room waited while the editor read the document, frowning heavily and tapping the table with his finger. Finally, he put the papers to one side.

'We're going to have to pull the story. It's not worth the risk,' he announced. 'Give the pregnant nun some extra welly instead.'

'But why, Richard? Why?'

'Because there's something very wrong about Mr Frank Rist. The law up in Newcastle upon Tyne think he may have killed his wife.'

·27·

The Blackout
1985

As he felt the pressure under his shoulders from a pair of strong arms raising him up, he first thought that he had fallen asleep with his shoes on: lace-up shoes, soft but uncomfortably tight. Someone else had taken him by the ankles. He spoke; or he thought he did. He thought he asked to be left alone.

Other people were about, trying to wake him. He was lying on a very hard bed.

There was a dazzling light, which became less unpleasant after he had screwed his eyes tight shut and reopened them slowly, allowing only a slit between the eyelids. It was daylight from a greyish sky scoured by the black roofs of high buildings.

He was lying on the pavement. Two men in uniform were trying to lift him. One, whose face was close to his, smelt of tobacco. He tried to order the man to let go, but no sound came. Then his breath returned in a rush, and he emitted a bellowing noise which caused both men to pause, but not to loosen their grip. Struggling hard now, he took hold of an uniformed arm and dug in his nails as hard as he could, intending to inflict pain.

'All right, all right, bonny lad, easy now.'

They still did not intend to let go. He kicked. To his annoyance, his foot met nothing but open air, but at least he prised his ankles free from the grip of one of the uniformed men. The other had pulled his shoulders a foot or so from the ground, so that he was half reclining, his legs paddling frantically, hitting the pavement until his heels throbbed. The man who was holding him muttered words which were meant to be calming but actually had the opposite effect, enraging him. Rolling his head, he found bare flesh at the end of a uniform sleeve, and sank his teeth in. With a grunt, the other man let go.

He was on his feet. There were two ambulancemen, one on either side of him, both smaller than he was. The one whom he had bitten was rubbing his pained wrist and giving him resentful looks. The other was shaking his head.

'Are ye all right, Barry?'

The one named Barry nodded. 'Except the teeth marks.'

'He didna' draw blood?'

Barry shook his head.

Indifferent to their conversation, he looked about, wondering where he was and how he came to be there. It was a side street, a familiar street, away from the shopping centre, bordered by warehouses, offices, derelict land and advertising hoardings, nothing of interest. It was not far from the little bookshop. There was a tiredness in his legs that suggested that he had been walking for a long time. He must have been on his way to the bookshop.

There were people, staring. As many as twenty. Some on the pavement on this side of the road, and more across the road. There was a stretcher at his feet, on the pavement, and parked a few feet away was an ambulance with its blue light flashing. He was surrounded.

'Hey, there's no call for violence, like,' the ambulanceman named Barry was saying sternly, still clutching his wrist. 'We was trying to move youse off the pavement. Right?'

Something like this had happened before: a sensation of being crushed by an invisible malignancy.

He could remember walking alongside the Tyne, hating the vast iron girders of the Tyne Bridge far overhead. Something had gone wrong between there and here.

He did not like so many eyes.

He took a few steps. People backed away, respectfully. Biting the ambulanceman named Barry had taught them respect. But such a weariness, such a desolate exhaustion had descended upon him that his knees could not bear its weight. He had to put out an arm to lean on the brick wall. The ambulancemen approached gingerly, one on either side.

'You was out, bonny lad. Right out. Dead to the world. Did ye know that?'

He turned about to face them, resting his back against the brick wall. The crowd of onlookers had drawn nearer. There were too many of them. A woman at the front of the curious crowd, in a black-and-white-check overcoat with a faded scarf around her head, lifted an arm and pointed at him, saying something about him being found on the pavement but not looking like a drunk.

Yes, that had happened before. Toppling over in the street. When the grey mist descended and he could not see and could not think, sometimes he met the pavement. But he always got up and carried on. He had never been surrounded in this manner.

The man named Barry said, 'All right, bonny lad, if you don't want us to handle ye, like, why not get yours'n on to the stretcher, and we won't touch youse. All right?'

Seeing him hesitate, the ambulanceman stretched his arms out in a 'trust-me' gesture and added, 'Look, we don't know what's wrong with ye, like, what's on your mind, what's causing youse consternation, or why ye want to walk away, we just wanted to move you, like, to where you can be looked at. Right?'

Nothing to do but let them guide him into the ambulance. His friend Joseph had once confessed to having a horror of the flashing blue lights on ambulances and police cars, but for his own part, he did not mind them.

It was only a van with a large first aid cupboard. He would have liked to lie down, but had to sit as they set off up the steep hill and out into west Newcastle. He felt a drowsy kind of strength returning to him. His chin dropped against his chest.

He slept heavily. They managed to walk him into the hospital, but the moment they sat him down, on a wooden-backed chair, he was asleep again. He woke momentarily as they lifted him on to a trolley, and again when they transferred him to a bed in what he just barely noticed was a long hospital ward. He was drowsily aware of nurses undressing him. It was very pleasant. They were nice women. They put him into striped pyjamas.

Once in bed, he slept. An older woman in a different style of nurse's uniform woke him to ask him questions: his name, first of all. He shook his head, and went back to sleep.

A doctor roused him to ask him if he felt all right, and he only nodded and fell back to sleep. He was woken by a sharp pain in his arm, to see his own blood flowing into a small plastic tube. A very deep red. A nurse apologized, removed the needle, and wiped the wound with a piece of cold cotton which smelt of disinfectant. He fell back to sleep.

They put food in front of him, but he ignored it and slept on.

It might have been the following morning when they came and insisted that he get out of bed and sit at a long table, with a collection of old men in pyjamas and dressing gowns, to eat breakfast. He was hungry by now. He ate wolfishly. The old men stared at him. Soon, he was back in bed asleep.

A man was sitting at his bedside. Too young to be a figure of authority, even with a dark suit, clean white shirt, short hair and professional qualifications to fortify him, probably in his late twenties, and with the pale face and thin body of the sort of boy it would have been easy to bully at school, he none the less had an irritatingly important air.

'Now, Mr er um,' he said, presently, 'how are we feeling?'

We did not feel like answering.

'I shall ask some questions, which I would like you to answer, please. First, your name?'

No, they couldn't have his name.

'Your name?' he repeated. 'Don't you want to tell me your name?'

Silence.

'But we do need to know your name. All right, can we start with your address? Your date of birth?'

The doctor – or was he a psychiatrist? – raised his eyebrows, tilted his head, shifted in his seat, and wrote something on the clipboard in his lap. The pallor of his face was emphasized both by his sandy hair, and by the fact that he was sitting with his back to a large window, through which was visible the roof of some distant tower block.

'Let me ask another question. Are you aware, Mr um, that you have slept for almost twenty-four hours since your admission to hospital?'

'That's good.'

The medical man looked up, curious that this should be the first question to be received with anything but silence.

'Good. Good, you say. You say good, but is it good? Is it good, or is it unusual?'

'Whichever.'

The sandy-haired young medic blinked, as if startled. He had eyes as blue as the Mediterranean, but there was no sympathetic human life behind them. 'Whichever?'

'You're the expert.'

'I suppose I am, but you know about your sleep pattern. I don't know whether you usually sleep for twenty-four hours at a time, or whether you have ever slept for twenty-four hours at a time before your admission here. Has your sleep pattern been very disturbed recently?'

'What pattern?'

'Your sleep pattern. The pattern of your sleep. You must have a sleep pattern, even if it's a very disturbed and irregular pattern. How many hours do you sleep at night? How many hours' sleep do you think you have averaged, say in the past week?'

'Not many.'

'You sleep badly?'

'I sleep fine.'

'But you said that you don't sleep many hours.'

'I sleep fine, when I sleep.'

'But when you're not sleeping, what about when you're not sleeping?'

'I'm awake.'

A look of glazed exasperation came over the young medic's face.

For the first time, the patient began noticing other beds nearby, in each of which lay or sat a silent, immobile figure. The man directly across the way had blue-striped pyjamas, an old man with an almost perfectly round head, his skin almost brown, his hair ghostly white and thin. He was making a chewing motion with his lower jaw as he stared absently across the bare ward, apparently listening to the questions and answers. They were all listening. He remembered them from breakfast, these physical derelicts, these smelly, sickly old men dressed in striped pyjamas.

'Would you say three hours a night on average? More than three hours?'

'No.'

'Not more than three hours a night?'

'Why?'

'Why? Do you mean why do I ask these questions? I have to ask you these questions because I have a form which has to be filled in. The questions are on the form. Will you please answer them? I need to know about your sleep pattern.'

A silence followed, broken by a sigh from the medical man.

'All right, if you don't want to talk about that, perhaps I ought to introduce myself. My name is George. Yours is?'

'Cunt.'

'I'm sorry?'

'I said cunt.'

The medical man named George shifted in his seat again. Little beads of sweat had formed at his hairline. 'Mr er um, you've refused to give your name to the ward sister, you have nothing on your person to identify you, nothing like a driving licence, and now I believe you're refusing to give me your name. Am I right about that?'

Silence.

'All right. Let me ask you something else. Do you find that generally you have trouble applying yourself to whatever task you have to do?'

'No.'

Pleased to get a straight answer, the medic scribbled it down on his form.

'Do you find it easy or difficult to make decisions?'

'Oh god, I don't know what to say.'

George looked puzzled, until inspired lateral thinking warned him that the patient was taking the mickey. He shook his head, began to make a note, then changed his mind. Definitely a psychiatrist.

'I must ask you to answer sensibly, please. Do you suffer from feelings of guilt?'

'I've tried to, but I can't.'

'You've tried to suffer from guilt?'

'I can't. It makes me feel terrible.'

'Do you suffer from loss of memory?'

'Not so far as I can recall.'

'These are, these are not questions to be joked at, please. Are you interested in sex?'

'Not now. Thanks for asking.'

George the shrink sighed a longer, louder sigh. 'Have you ever had thoughts of suicide?' he asked, in a pleading tone.

'That's the last thing I'd do.'

'I'm relieved to hear that.'

But as he spoke, the young psychiatrist saw the joke. He gathered himself to his feet, gave the patient a murderous look, and left in silence.

At first, he couldn't go back to sleep, because he had been put on his guard. He suffered about ten minutes of wakefulness, enough for him to consider that a night of insomnia in a strange hospital ward would be unbearable. Worse even than that, there was the risk that he might be revisited by nightmares.

Actually, apart from waking in the small hours, frightened and unsure where he was, he slept so fitfully that when he was dragged out of bed to take breakfast for the second time, his back ached from having lain down for so long. Then, when he had floated back to sleep, the dreams began. The first was like a trick with mirrors: he dreamt that he had fallen asleep in an unfamiliar place. It was a nightmare about lying in a hospital, having a nightmare. After that, the nightmares trampled through his unconscious like a marauding army. He was back in his boyhood home, a rage in his heart, trampling through the rooms one by one, trying to kill the occupants. He tried to kill his father, hitting him over and over again, but could not hit him enough. He tried to kill his sister, too, but she also seemed resistant to death. Then he floated into the kitchen, covered with blood, and found his mother at work. She told him calmly that the whole family had been talking about him only that day and they all were sorry he was dead. That was why he had not been able to kill any of them: he was the one who had died.

He was in bed in a room the size of an aircraft hangar, full of strange noises, standing in the middle of the cold, concrete floor. Other people were there. This was embarrassing, because he was naked below the waist. At the far end, a colossal, stainless vacuum cleaner was threatening to suck something out of him. He touched the hangar wall. His fingertips met the unmistakable texture of cold plaster. Then he was out in some barren place resembling *The Waste Land*, in which there was only one undamaged building: a narrow, five-storey house standing amid the rubble, imposing and alone. Still embarrassingly exposed below the waist, he floated through the door and made for the basement, down a concrete staircase. At the bottom was a cellar with whitewashed plaster walls, empty except for a door, made of iron, and a woman dressed entirely in black, including gloves and a round-rimmed hat from which hung a veil that hid her face, if she had one. She pushed open the iron door and beckoned him to pass through it. The room beyond was pitch-dark. He was afraid. Rescued by his own fear, he was sucked backwards across the bare cellar, up the stone stair, out of the front door of the grim house, out of his dream and out of his sleep, all in one gliding movement, so that he awoke with a start, and was forced to take several deep breaths. His lungs were empty of oxygen, as if he had been suffocating.

After that, he slept lightly and restlessly, afraid to fall back into another dream.

Now there were two of them by his bedside: two conservatively dressed shrinks. One he had encountered already. In the foreground was an older man, old enough to have been his father, small and balding, in a pinstriped three-piece suit and with streaks of grey in his smoothed-back hair. He was the one who did all the talking, after pulling up a chair for himself. He had an impatient manner, and seemed to be giving his younger colleague a demonstration of how to be firm. The conversation, in retrospect, was less real than a dream. Though the older man paused frequently to give him an opportunity to speak, it was actually a monologue which must have lasted twenty minutes.

'So, the ambulance service, responding to a 999 call, discovered you on the pavement, in broad daylight, in a suspected coma. You were said to have been unconscious for at least twenty minutes, possibly longer. In the two days since, you've done nothing but sleep. So that's probably all the sleep you need for now. Now to make some progress in your case, Mr . . . Mr . . . yes, the man who refuses to give his name. We wondered if you were amnesiac. You understand that word? We wondered if you didn't give your name because you can't remember, but actually, you're just withholding it, aren't you? Why? Do you want us to think you're a fugitive, because we have checked with the police and they have no reports to tell us who you might be. Isn't someone worried that you've been missing for two days?

'Well, my colleague's view, and mine, is that you are ill. Clearly ill. It's very likely that you've been suffering for years. You may already know that. Perhaps you've seen a psychiatrist before and been diagnosed. But since we can't identify you, we can't check. And essentially, what happens is up to you. You can co-operate, help us to help you, and we can give you medication, and you will feel a great deal better. We don't have to section you. Or you can refuse help, and carry on suffering what you've been suffering, until the next time you faint in the street. That doesn't seem very clever to me, but you might think it is.

'What you can't do, I'm afraid, is stay here occupying a hospital bed for ever. You can stay one more night, and in the morning you'll have to go, or we'll have to move you to St Nicholas's Hospital, where they have facilities to deal with patients of your type. I think you understand. We'll see you in the morning, and decide then.'

They obviously expected him to know – as, indeed, he did know – that St Nicholas's was a psychiatric hospital.

They were threatening him with internment, like McMurphy, the Jack Nicholson character in *One Flew Over the Cuckoo's Nest*. The KGB did it too. Everywhere where authoritarian power met dissent.

They were asking for his name now. Then they would go after the thoughts in his mind. But they could not hold him, because he was like Trotsky, who always escaped, not like Lenin, who used his time in Siberia to write *What is to be Done*. He had been watching when they thought he was asleep and had seen the nurses fold his clothes away in the low cupboard beside his bed. He had also spotted that there was a time in the early evening when different nurses arrived ready for the night shift. It was a sociable time. The nurses left the ward and gathered in a little office next to it to talk before they called out their goodnights.

It was simple. He waited until there were no nurses in sight, got up, dressed quietly and quickly, and walked off the ward. He had difficulty finding his way out, and there was an awkward moment out in a corridor when he passed a nurse, who looked at him in surprise, but a reassuring smile and a nod of the head was enough to forestall questions. Before long, he had found the exit.

It was dark outside. There was a light rain. This was inconvenient, because he was dressed only in a thin jacket. He was talking to himself out loud as he left the hospital, gesticulating to emphasize his own words: 'Amazing, incredible: didn't answer a question – walked out.' He was imagining what the hospital staff might be saying, and the tributes due from revolutionary comrades. (Due, but unlikely to be received: other comrades were not as committed to the revolution as he was.)

'. . . Didn't tell them anything, not even his name. Incredible. And he got out. They couldn't tamper with him. Wonder who he was . . .'

There was a long walk ahead. He did not absolutely need to walk: he could have taken a bus, but he wanted to tire himself out. It was abnormal to be full of energy, from a combination of a long sleep and the triumph of his daring escape, and he wanted to lower himself into a more manageable mood.

As a precaution against the admittedly remote possibility that they were already looking for him, he started out in the wrong direction. He went further uphill to where the road levelled out and was bound on both sides by long rows of shops, all shut, with grilles over their windows. Only the pubs were doing business. After a few minutes, he was calmer. He had stopped gesticulating, and continued the dialogue with himself in a low mutter, hurrying along the pavement at speed until to his right, the sudden appearance of an expanse of green – a school playing field – told him that he had walked far enough. He crossed the road and headed into one of the side streets lined with terraced brick houses descending steeply towards the north bank of the Tyne far below. There were few people about. In these crammed yet desolate residential side streets, he could resume his train of thought, making no sound, though a close observer would have seen his lips moving.

Now that the elation brought on by his escape had faded, he faced the nagging problem of why he should have been found unconscious in the street. Months ago, there had been a bewildering incident when a complete stranger accosted him on the pavement, demanding to know if he was all right. He could not understand why.

'You just fell over, man. Did ye not know that? You landed there with a right crack. You hit your head something serious.'

Had he? He pushed the man off and hurried away.

But now he was forced to reflect that if the stranger had not told him, he would never have known. Perhaps it was happening frequently. They had wondered if he was amnesiac. The short answer was no, *but he didn't know who he was.*

At the age of seventeen, he had been the cleverest boy in school, and tough too; not popular, but an object of respect and envy. Where had all that envy gone? There was nothing in his life but conflict. Nobody wanted to be him. *He* did not want to be himself; he wanted the self he used to have. Must concentrate on something else. He decided to take a bus after all. He got off near the Central Station and could not decide to continue. Fortunately, there was money in his pocket for a round, and a pub nearby, full of strangers.

Hours later, when it was nearly midnight, he was standing, soaked by the light rain, outside his own house – or, more accurately, Christine's house. Its dark door resisted his first effort to insert a key. That small failure took on a symbolic significance, filling him with resentment. He could have shouted to her, because there was a light on in her bedroom, overlooking the front door, but he did not want to speak to her. He wanted to secrete himself in his own spartan bedroom at the back, on the top floor. The door yielded at the second attempt.

The hall was so dark that he guided himself by keeping one

hand on the wall. As usual, the floorboards creaked under foot, particularly as he started up the bare wooden stairs. Suddenly, someone flushed the toilet at the top of the stairs. A door opened, letting light on to the landing, and a shadowy figure with long hair stepped out only feet away from him. It was Christine, in pyjamas and dressing gown. She started and gasped from shock, staggering several steps back until she was against a wall, her right hand on her chest.

'Frank! You gave me such a fright!' She took several deep breaths before she continued, shaking her head. 'How long have you been here? I didn't hear the door. Where have you been?'

'It doesn't matter.'

'It doesn't matter! Frank, I've spent two days wondering where you were and if I was going to hear from you. You could have told me.' She dropped her hand to her side. 'Well, anyway, welcome home, baby. I was in bed. Are you going to your room?'

There was no reproach in her voice, and no real pleasure at seeing him either. Her eyes were shifting. Something else was on her mind other than his sudden return. He looked over his shoulder at the strip of light under her bedroom door.

'Oh well, I'm up now,' Christine said, with sudden decisiveness. 'Do you want to go down to the kitchen? We could have a Horlicks.'

She took two steps down and patted him on the shoulder, smiling and nodding her head. She spoke to him with the forced friendliness she would use to a newly arrived guest. 'Come, let's go downstairs and have a Horlicks in the kitchen and you can tell me where you've been, if you want to tell me, and I'll tell you all about my day at work, if you're interested.'

For just a second, perhaps less than a second, her eyes shifted again, a tiny, barely perceptible flicker of the eyeballs, a furtive glance at the crack of light under her bedroom door, then she took his upper arm to steer him downstairs, manhandling him as the ambulancemen had manhandled him. He dug his nails into her hand.

'Ow!'

She looked startled, but did not say another word, even when he dug his nails in harder. Something in that room was so important to her that she was prepared to bear pain without complaint.

'Frank, please . . .'

He yanked her arm across her body and crooked his elbow under her chin to push her back against the wall, and with his right hand he burrowed into her pyjamas, shoving his finger into her vagina. He had to push harder than expected, drawing a low cry of pain. He was feeling inside for evidence of another man, but his mind would not concentrate. He pressed himself against her, listening to her strangulated breathing. It was as though no one was there. He was alone. There was nothing but his own animal rage.

She had started to speak, the words pouring out in a fast whisper: 'Please, you're hurting, Frank, please, please let go.'

What to do? He could march smartly up into her bedroom to attack her lover, or he could beat her up, or drag her downstairs and rape her in the hall, to see how lover boy reacted. He was surprised by the calm with which he considered the options. What would a great hero have done? *No more heroes any more . . .*

'Frank, I didn't know where you were or when you were coming back . . .'

Trotsky would have walked away contemptuously.

He wiped his finger dry on her nightclothes and marched downstairs to throw open the front door, letting in cold air and rain, leaving her cowering on the staircase, her mouth open from shock. At the threshold, he turned to point an accusing finger.

'I have been in hospital,' he announced, and left.

There was no traffic now. He walked down the grass bank in front of their house and straight across, without any idea of which way to turn next. He had a sudden wish to go and see Angel, take refuge in her bed, but he could not remember whether there were trains to London after midnight.

He was surprised to hear Christine calling.

She was hurrying down the grass bank, in the rain, in her night-clothes, her right hand clutching her dressing gown for warmth. She slipped and almost fell on the wet grass in her hurry. She ran directly across the road.

There was traffic. He could hear the rumble of an approaching lorry.

'Why have you been in hospital, Frank? Don't just say you've been in hospital and walk off. I didn't know!'

Her face – concerned, guilty and hurt – and in the back-ground, over her head, against the backcloth of a black sky tinted orange, the light in her bedroom window triggered something that seemed to rise from the ground, a primal rage, a spasm of concentrated, uncontrollable, hate-filled fury. He had to hit her. He clenched his fist, and with a great sweep of his arm he landed one on her jaw, a sideways punch which was answered by a sat-isfying crack of knuckle on bone, which instantly calmed him. Christine staggered, danced a pirouette and went down on one knee in the road, letting out an extraordinary noise like the bellow of an animal.

Of course, she could not speak properly: her jaw was broken. Now he was sorry he had hurt her. He wondered what to do to make amends.

Something else passed across his sight – a wall of metal, moving fast, accompanied by a whistling sound, a long, loud note like a screech which he instinctively associated with fear and danger before he had identified it as the noise made by brakes.

The lorry. In the calm that followed his rage, he had forgotten the lorry, a colossal container lorry moving at speed. With its brakes full on, it thundered past under its own momentum, right over the spot where she was kneeling, passing so close to him that his legs were soaked by the fine spray from its massive tyres, and he staggered in its slipstream, taking several steps back to find his balance. Then he ran, away from the lorry and the horror it left behind, ran for forty or fifty feet to hide in a shop doorway.

He stayed there unseen for several minutes, shivering, his head throbbing as if his brain were on fire. Christine was dead, obviously dead. He had heard a sound like the snapping of twigs as her bones broke.

Hidden in the doorway, over a faint smell of urine, he listened to the sounds of death's aftermath. The lorry came to a halt after skidding for a quarter of a mile. Once it had stopped, there was a moment's silence. The cabin door slammed as the driver emerged. He called out in a weak, puzzled voice, once or twice: 'Hello? Hello?'

A moment later, the lorry's horn began blaring. It screamed out in an urgent distress signal over and over again, until a half-light cast itself across the pavement from an upstairs room above one of the nearby shops. The lorry driver had a shouted conversation with somebody leaning from a window. A car drew up from the opposite direction from the lorry and stopped. Conversations began as three or four people gathered. The lorry driver was talking in a voice sharpened by fright and self-justification. Not all of what he was saying was audible, but one extract came over distinctly: 'Are you the lad that was standing next to her? The lad that shoved her. So where has he gone? There was a lad there, right there, where you's standing now, right by her. I saw him, man!'

Someone else said something about the police.

He had to get out of this doorway and away from the scene, or the police would find him.

Memory loss.

If they found him, he would pretend to have no memory of the accident. They would find him shivering and trembling. But it would not look good, after what the shrinks had said in the hospital. They would lock him up in St Nick's, for sure, if they found him.

But they didn't come to look. The driver was beginning to whimper. The gathering crowd was trying to calm him. No one appeared to believe his claim that there had been a witness. And no one noticed that across the far side of the road, in the upper floor of the house atop the embankment, the light in Christine's bedroom went off.

When Frank saw the light go off, he knew he could not afford another minute in the sanctuary of the doorway. He slipped out with only the briefest glance at the little knot of people gathered by the mangled morass of bones and torn nightclothes on the tarmac. Keeping in the shadow, he took himself further away from the scene of the accident, and before long he had reached a side road. He was only just in time. As he was turning the corner, the first police car appeared, its blue light flashing. He ducked out of sight. Another police car came, closely followed by an ambulance, all moving fast but in eerie silence. He let them pass, then, with his head lowered and hands in his pockets, he nipped across the main road to make his way quickly up a stone stairway at the edge of the embankment.

The streetlights were on along the frontages of the houses on the far side of the road at the top, so he kept to the grass bank, weaving his way past bushes, minimizing the risk of being seen by the gathering crowd below, until he was stopped about thirty yards from the door of the house he had shared with Christine. The throbbing blue light from the police cars and ambulances parked down below were playing over the front of the house, so that it was alternately in darkness and then eerily lit. There was no sign that anyone was inside, but he had no doubt that Christine's lover was still there.

Suddenly, it was a strange-looking house, as if he had never seen it before. It occurred to him now that he would never live there again. The house had belonged to Christine: she paid the mortgage from her lecturer's salary, he had lodged there at her expense. Her family would turn him out, for sure. This was the end of an eight-year run which had begun when he met Christine. It had not been a bad relationship in many ways, and he found himself able to think about it with a numb absence of feeling: no guilt, no grief, no shock – all the night's weird events were occurring in an alien world outside his emotions.

As he watched, the door of Christine's house was opened from the inside. A man emerged, closing the door quietly, stealthily behind him. That was what Frank expected. It only remained for him to confirm his suspicion as to the man's identity. He waited in the darkness.

The man at Christine's doorstep was visibly distressed, and unsure of what to do. He was biting his hand, and standing on tiptoe for a better look at the scene on the roadway. He seemed to be upset by the blue light. He put an arm across his eyes, staggered back, then scuttled along the road, away from the scene of the accident, shielding his eyes with a raised hand like a guilty man being bundled into court, a man who did not like flashing blue lights.

Frank had planned to intercept him, to prevent him talking to the police, but that was not going to be necessary. By scurrying away, the second witness was acting as guiltily as the first; and as he passed under a streetlight, his face was visible for a second. It was Joseph Pilgrim, of course.

·28·

Fallen Angel

It was staggering how indiscreet Frank had been. Bearing that guilty secret, he should have stayed hidden away in Angel's house until Christine's death had passed into forgetfulness, instead of throwing off twelve years' anonymity on an insane impulse. Of course, he could not have guessed that George the Shrink would be at that public meeting and would recognize the heckler, after so many years, as the same disturbed young man who had been brought in for observation and had done a runner from the hospital. After Deirdre had at last located him, George was persuaded to sign an affidavit which proved that Frank Rist had lied on oath at Christine's inquest when he had claimed to have been in London on the night of her death. George felt able to do this because Frank had not, strictly, been his patient, having refused treatment. Angel was also going to have to explain why she had supplied Frank with a false alibi. They had quarrelled violently, and she had ordered Frank to move out of the house which had been his refuge for so many years. And Gerald Moon's telephone call to the Social Security Department hotline had had its effect. The inspectors established that Frank had been operating a web site while drawing income support, and had stopped his benefits altogether. There was a possibility that he could be charged with fraud. So far as anyone knew, he was now living rough, sleeping in the back of his car with all his possessions in the boot. If convicted of fraud, he would probably lose the car too. But, most seriously of all, the Newcastle police – who had never closed their file on Christine – wanted to question him about a possible charge of murder or manslaughter. In all, the disaster he had visited upon himself was comprehensive. He should have known better than to campaign against someone like Joseph, with access to influential people. Joseph was now a Somebody; Frank was a Nobody; and as Gerald Moon had once observed, 'in this game, somebody always beats nobody'.

It made Joseph uncomfortable to try to imagine what had prompted such folly. Frank had had a comfortable nobody's life, cheating the welfare state and cutting a little bit of a figure on the outermost fringe of politics until one evening, perhaps, when he had been sitting watching television alone, in that compact flat on the ground floor of Angel's house, and had seen someone he had recognized in the crowded debating chamber in the House of Commons addressing a question to the Prime Minister – his old friend Joseph, whom he had once looked down on as a protégé. Then he had spotted the same Joseph Pilgrim, who had slept with Christine, talking to a beautiful woman in the Central Lobby of the House of Commons, where he was a habitué and Frank was but a visitor. Perhaps it was then that he was overcome by a rancour so powerful that it destroyed any sense of self-preservation.

'Well, I don't feel sorry for him,' said Rachel.

As usual, she looked glitteringly beautiful. She was reclining, relaxed, in Joseph's Millbank office, with an arm casually stretched along the back of the sofa, wearing a plain white blouse and long grey skirt with a slit down the side. She had sat and crossed her legs in a single movement, without any apparent guile, but the effect was to leave her legs on view well above the knee. It was a struggle to focus on her character rather than her calves.

Now that neither of them had a home or social life to occupy their evenings, they were being seen together more often than discretion dictated in bars and restaurants around Westminster. There had already been an unsettling paragraph in a diary column, remarking that the MP who had achieved notoriety through his former affair with the wife of a Tory was courting it again, being seen with a young woman of striking good looks. Fortunately, it was in a publication that almost certainly would not cross Margaret's field of vision.

Yet for all the time they spent together, he did not feel he knew Rachel any better than when she had first come to work with him. He had not been with a woman as young as Rachel since Margaret was that age, in far-off days when 'as young as Rachel' did not seem young at all. She knew how to draw him out, listening to him with infinite patience, watching him with unnerving directness as he spoke, always making him say more than he intended; but about herself, she was habitually reserved. For himself, he had no doubt that any sexual involvement with Rachel would churn up dangerous emotions. In the longer term, she would almost certainly leave him and until she did, he would have to live with the fear of losing her, but he needed her so much that she must know – he thought – that she had only to beckon him with one finger and he would come to her like an obedient dog. She certainly knew how he hated going back to his lonely digs at night. Perhaps she was indifferently weighing up whether she wanted to sleep with him or not.

It all fell simply into place when he told her she could have Friday off. When she protested that she didn't want the day off, he explained that he had already promised Thelma that she could spend the day running his parliamentary office. For her, it was a perk, and he needed to keep on the right side of Thelma.

'So, where will you be?' Rachel asked.

'I'm going to call in on my father, who isn't well, and then I'm going to go and leave a bouquet on my mother's grave. It'll be the anniversary of her death.'

'Where is she buried?'

'In a little cemetery outside a rural village in the middle of nowhere.'

'I love cemeteries,' Rachel said. She had stopped looking at him, and was using one hand to straighten a cushion behind her back, making the comment almost over-casual. 'I used to do a bit of genealogy. You can find out such a lot from headstones. It would be interesting to see what's on your mother's headstone.'

He scarcely hesitated before saying, 'If you want, you can come with me.'

He could see an opportunity opening before him: it would be so simple, as the afternoon became evening and they were a hundred miles from London, to check in to a quiet hotel somewhere after supper in a country pub. He was certain that the same thought was in her mind. That certainty caused his pulse rate to increase alarmingly. He felt something equivalent to a pain in the chest as his heart pumped.

As he explained, there was another tiresome duty to perform before they set out on Friday. He felt responsible for Angel, who had been dragged unwillingly into the police investigation of Christine's death. That was partly her own fault, but Joseph did not believe she had intended to help conceal a possible homicide; and now that she had fallen out bitterly with Frank, she was on her own and she was, willy-nilly, on Joseph's side. When he rang to suggest a visit, she was no more enthusiastic than on the last occasion, but they fixed a time on Friday morning.

After a sleepless Thursday, he drove to Rachel's flat to collect her after breakfast. On the way to Angel's house, they stopped to buy two bouquets, one twice as expensive as the other. As a matter of delicacy, he felt obliged to ask Rachel to wait in the car while he called on Angel. He did not want to have to explain why. He tried to say just enough to avoid seem impolite but eventually, as usual, Rachel extracted more from him than he would have liked. He parked outside Angel's house, gathered up the cheaper of the two bouquets, and rang on her doorbell, several times, until he realized that no one was going to answer. This was the second time she had made an arrangement to meet him and then broken it. This was so irritatingly typical of Angel. It spoiled his sunny mood.

He was turning to leave when the door eerily opened itself, as in a horror story, when a light breeze started up. It had been unlocked all the time he was standing at it.

He stepped into the hall, where the look of dark disuse emphasized the unnatural silence. He called out for Angel. There was no reply.

But there was a sound coming from the kitchen, like a malfunctioning machine. At second hearing, it sounded like a human voice, but was making no sense. It was a short breathy sound, like an acute attack of asthma.

He found Angel on the tiled floor on the far side of the kitchen table, her back against a cupboard door. She was rolling her eyes in pain, and had one hand on her cheek. Her jaw was out of line with the rest of her face, having been knocked sideways by some powerful force.

'My god, Angel, what happened? Did you fall?'

Her eyes focused on him, and she gave a scarcely perceptible shake of the head. He could see that this tiny movement caused her a wave of intense pain.

'I'd better call an ambulance.'

Angel answered with a vigorous wave of the hand, which clearly meant that she did not want him to.

'But you've got to go to hospital,' he protested.

Angel was now struggling to her feet, pushing herself up with one hand while the other nursed her jutting jaw. He stepped forward to give her a helping hand, which she accepted; but as soon as she was steadily on her feet, she gave him a push and pointed to the door, evidently wanting him to leave. A wave of the hand emphasized the urgency.

He was trying to fathom why she might want him out of the house when there was a ringing sound in his pocket, from his wretched mobile phone. It was Deirdre calling him.

'Where are you?'

'Out of the office.'

'Great news. You know that woman Dawn Jones you were worried about: we've got her in a refuge and someone I know is on the case.'

'Deirdre, that's wonderful, but it's a bad moment.'

'OK. Just one more thing. Frank rang late last night, from a telephone box. He's really angry with Angel, and I'm not surprised. She's the bitch who sold your story to the newspaper, not him. He was covering up for her.'

At that moment, Angel was hobbling past Joseph, apparently heading for the kitchen door. She looked at him sideways on hearing the mention of her name, but did not stop. He took a step back to let her by.

'What are you saying?'

'Apparently, she needed the money to get some work done on her house.'

Angel was walking away from him, slow and stooped like an old woman. Her dishevelled hair compounded the impression of age. He stared at her back, and now he understood those resentful looks and cryptic comments, and the mystery of how he had been photographed with Diana. They had been on their way to see Angel, who did not keep the appointment – it was so obvious, he did not know why he had not seen it earlier.

'Frank has had a terrible row with her, because he thought she was going to drag Christine's death into it,' Deirdre went on. 'He's also really angry with you, Joseph. You'd better keep out of his way.'

Joseph thanked her, and weighed up how angrily he could confront a woman who was in such obvious pain.

'Angel, did Frank Rist attack you?'

She stopped, turned slowly around, and nodded, grimacing with pain, then again waved at him to leave. This time, she gave him an imploring look.

'You need medical attention, Angel. Why are you so anxious to get me out of here?'

As if in answer, there were heavy footsteps in the hallway, and a familiar voice called out Angel's name. She threw up a hand in a gesture of despair and sank back on to a wooden kitchen chair where she doubled up in pain. The kitchen door was pushed open and round it peered the circular face of Dave Drucker.

'Shit!' said Drucker, as he saw Angel rocking slowly, hand on jaw. He seemed neither surprised nor interested to see Joseph. 'Shit!' he repeated. 'It's the London traffic, love. It was the fastest I could get here.'

Drucker crouched and sat on his heels to take a closer look at Angel's face, then took out a mobile phone and began efficiently summoning an ambulance and the police, explaining to them that a woman had been assaulted and her jaw broken. In between giving instructions, he looked in Joseph's direction and explained: 'She rang us in the office to say Frank Rist was on the rampage. The bastard obviously got here first.'

'Where is he now? Is he in the house?'

Angel shook her head.

'His VW's not outside,' said Dave.

It was odd to be talking to Dave Drucker as if they were allies dealing with a shared problem.

At a signal from Angel, Dave crouched again and put his ear to her mouth as she whispered. Joseph could see that they were talking about him.

'The lady thinks you should get yourself out of her house,' he said. 'And I'd strongly second that.'

'Now just a minute . . .'

'Like before the law gets here. Trust me, Mr Pilgrim.'

'Trust you? Trust you? Either of you? I know what's been going on. She's been selling you information.'

'Yes, true, we paid her a good wad of cash,' said Dave Drucker, without a hint of embarrassment or shame. 'Now, Mr Pilgrim, can I seriously ask you to make yourself scarce? If you stay, you could have to make a statement to the law.'

'Are you asking me to withhold evidence of a serious assault?'

Dave Drucker shook his head, as if exasperated by Joseph's stupidity.

'I wouldn't worry about the evidence, Mr Pilgrim: it's everywhere. I'll make a statement. She'll make a statement. Let's just step into the hall. Yeah? Excuse us, love.'

The shadows in the dark hall closed over Dave Drucker's face.

'What are you going to write about all this?' Joseph demanded.

'Just now, Mr Pilgrim, I'm making sure nobody else gets a story out of it. That's why you've got to be off the premises. Yeah?'

'Let's just remind ourselves: you are the man who has pursued me for weeks with stories about my private life. My home has been under siege because of you, my family disrupted, a good friend has been humiliated – why the bloody hell should I do anything you ask?'

'Oh come on, Mr Pilgrim, you've seen *The Godfather*. It's nothing personal.'

'Then why the hell did you do it?'

Dave Drucker paused and inhaled through his nostrils before

answering. 'I suppose you could say that I'm a dog and you're a lamppost.'

Despite himself, Joseph was inclined to trust him, not least because trusting Dave would let him escape from an awkward situation and be alone with Rachel.

'I'm not going to be pilloried for walking away from the scene?' he asked.

Dave raised one hand. 'Mr Pilgrim, I swear – scouts' honour.'

The ambulance was drawing up as Joseph came down the path. He nodded to them and pointed into the house, and returned to his car. The police arrived as he was driving away.

·29·

Frank Reappears

By the end of his visit to his boyhood home, hours later, he was irritated with himself, his father, the world – everyone and everything but Rachel. His relations with his elderly father had never been easy, but they had improved since his marriage and with the appearance of grandchildren, and again when he was elected to Parliament, but now – like so much else in his life – they had regressed. The old man talked pointedly about Margaret throughout the visit, although Joseph had explained from the outset that his marriage had broken down. He could feel himself getting angry, but caught a look from Rachel warning him not to exacerbate a difficult situation.

Clearly, his father did not like Rachel. Perhaps he suspected her of being the cause of his estrangement from Margaret. The nearest he came to speaking to her was when she offered to fetch him a glass of water after one outburst had climaxed in a coughing fit. He accepted the offer with a nod, watching her as she left the room. At this point, Joseph expected that his father might make some remark that would grudgingly acknowledge her good manners or good looks; and he did, indeed, mention Rachel's physique, but not at all in the tone his son was anticipating.

'A rump that size belongs on a horse,' he said.

That was more hurtful by far than any insult he could have directed at Joseph.

As Joseph was drawing out of the drive, still shaken by his father's rudeness, he almost hit a parked car, a battered old cream-coloured Volkswagen tucked into the hedge across the road. There was a man at its wheel, a somewhat unkempt man with long greying hair, but Joseph did not feel the need to step out to apologize for a near miss, which he partly blamed on the other driver for parking in a stupid place. He drove slowly, however, lest his distracted state of mind should cause a real accident somewhere else along the five-mile journey to the cemetery.

At its entrance was a wide car park with a gravel surface, empty at that time in the afternoon. They parked on the far side and walked through a wooden gateway into a silent field, studded with long rows of grey and black gravestones. The grass around the graves was damp from recent rainfall and everywhere there was a smell of decaying flowers. No more than half a dozen people were scattered among the graves, which were so numerous and so uniformly laid out that Joseph came upon a wholly unexpected problem. He set out confidently in what he thought was the right direction, only to find that he could not remember where his mother's grave actually was. He was standing amid row upon indistinguishable row of gravestones.

'Can't you find it?' Rachel asked.

Every detail of the day they buried his mother was imprinted on his memory: the loneliness, the brightness of the sun and the cooling head wind, the subdued crowd, his sister crying uncontrollably, her scarred face glistening red: every detail, except this one.

They split up and scanned several rows until Rachel found the grave they were looking for and called to him. He was shocked by how *uneventful* his mother's resting-place was. Between two ornate plots, one an array of white marble, the other a neat gravel bed with a large pepperpot-shaped metal vase full of freshly cut carnations, it looked like the burial site for the poor relation, no more than a grassed-over hump. There was a single bunch of flowers placed across it, so old and withered that Rachel threw it away.

He had not been to this spot for nearly twenty years. At least the gravestone was unharmed by a quarter of a century outdoors: the inscription was as vivid as on the day of her funeral. The words carved into the face of the marble slab were exactly the words he had read with eyes that ached with grief when he was fifteen years old, but suddenly, shockingly, they had a different meaning:

Patricia Pilgrim
Beloved wife of Henry
Mother of Joseph and Eleanor
Born 2 April 1935
Died after a road accident 12 November 1973

She was only thirty-nine years old when she died. His age. That eternal mirage of human perfection he remembered as the centrepiece of a lost, happy childhood had still been young when tearing metal put an end to her possibilities.

He experienced the painful sensation of liquid forcing its way through tear ducts. Blinking heavily, he was relieved by moistening in his eyes. Soon his face was wet. A film of water obscured his vision, and there was a little rivulet rolling down over his cheekbones. He had not cried for years. It was comforting that, for once, he had something to grieve over that was not his fault.

He stood in silence for a minute or two, avoiding eye contact with Rachel. Finally he sniffed, wiped his face with the back of his hand, and forced a smile.

'She was only thirty-nine!'

Rachel looked at the epitaph and nodded. 'That's young,' she said, without conviction.

They found an iron bench to one side, from which the grave was just out of sight. He would have liked to hold Rachel's hand, but the moment was too important for sensuality.

He said, 'I suppose, no matter how bad it gets, it's better to be alive than dead.'

Rachel did not say anything. She looked more amused than concerned.

'I've done a terrible thing. Truly terrible. I've broken a home. Isobel and Tom will grow up with problems, because their father and their mother . . .'

He had not meant to end the sentence there, but his voice seemed to disappear in the ubiquitous silence. It was interrupted by sporadic sounds: birdsong, the wind, someone sobbing far away in some part of the graveyard beyond their sight. Or was that also the wind?

He was startled when Rachel's voice broke in, though she spoke quietly. 'Should you go back to her?'

Before he answered, he drew a mental sketch of how he might present himself, shamefaced, in Margaret's kitchen, in a house he no longer regarded as home; he imagined his badly rehearsed explanation, and her reaction. Why should Margaret be grateful? She might not want him back at all.

'I couldn't.'

Rachel nodded and then gave a furtive smile, which he understood to mean that she was relieved he had said no.

'How good is your knowledge of medieval history?' he asked. She shook her head. 'When the king was scourged, who actually did the deed? Was it done by virtuous men? Monks?'

'Don't know. Who was it?' She was looking amused again.

'Suppose it wasn't the king but a lesser figure, a minor-ranking noble in need of being flogged until the bones showed through:

did it have to be a good Christian wielding the scourge, or would they delegate it to the worst scumbag in town?'

'I don't know, Joseph. What do you think?'

'I've done things I shouldn't have done in my life, I'm not perfect, but these people who have been pursuing me – Dave Drucker and the like, they're worse than I am.'

'That's ridiculous,' she said, with sudden emphasis. 'Newspapers are driven by profit, and that's all there is to it, so it's stupid to wallow in guilt. It doesn't help you, it doesn't help your children, and it annoys me.'

There was an implied threat in her tone and in the look she gave him. *She's tough,* he thought.

Something reminded him that he had switched off his mobile phone, accursed instrument that it was. He switched it on, and almost at once, it rang. He snapped out the word 'hello' at the woman caller, only to discover that he was addressing a recording which informed him that he had three messages. Rachel wandered away to explore the cemetery while he listened. All the voices were female. First there was Thelma, to say that 'that horrible man who came to the surgery' had been on the telephone wanting to know Joseph's whereabouts. The next caller was Deirdre, exhorting him to ring as soon as possible. Then there was a similar message from Margaret. Her tone of voice lacked that cold irritability with which she had taken to addressing him since their quarrel began. He wanted to ring her at once, but the phone was ringing before he had finished dialling. This time, he was surprised to recognize the voice of Dawn Jones.

'Joseph – guess what,' she asked, sounding almost flirtatious. Hitherto, he had always been 'Mr Pilgrim'. 'They've found an important guideline.'

He did not know what to make of this announcement, but Dawn sounded pleased by it. 'Who has found a guideline, Dawn?'

'I don't know. One of these women that I'm with.'

'Who are they?'

'You know. You put them on to me. Somebody called Deirdre and her friends. They're a bit unusual but they really know how to help.'

'Yes, I can imagine,' Joseph replied, as a vision crossed his mind of what Deirdre's friends might be like: tough dykes with cropped hair wearing men's clothes. (Of course Deirdre's female friends might all perpetually dress in party frocks for all he actually knew.)

'Isn't it good, though, about the guideline?'

'What does this guideline actually say?'

'I can't remember.'

'Roughly?'

Across the cemetery he saw something that did not fit.

'Well, whatever it said, the judge thought it was impressive.'

'You've been in front of a judge? Why didn't somebody tell me?'

'Couldn't get you on the phone.'

'And what did the judge say?'

'I don't got to go to prison, and Shithead isn't allowed near my girls unless at one of those contact centres.'

'Because of a guideline?'

'That's right. I wish I could remember what it said.'

'It sounds like an outstandingly efficacious guideline. That's brilliant, Dawn. I'm so pleased.'

He rang Deirdre. 'What's this guideline your friends dug up?'

'Never mind that, I'll tell you later. Have you seen your father?'

'How did you know about that?'

'Marsha told me.' So, Margaret knew where he had been. He wondered if she also knew who had been there with him.

'Listen, Joseph,' Deirdre continued, with unusual urgency in her tone. 'Does Frank Rist know where your father lives? That assistant of yours – Thelma, or whatever her name is – may have let on where you are, by mistake.'

Joseph saw it again – the object in the car park by the cemetery that should not be there – the old cream VW had been outside his father's house. He had seen it before, outside Angel's house.

In a few words, he ended the conversation with Deirdre, caught up Rachel across the cemetery and took her by the upper arm. It was only later that he realized this was the first physical contact he had ever made with her. She started.

'Walk with me back to the car. Don't stop for any reason.'

Rachel looked for a minute as if she would protest, but her eye caught something in the distance that changed her expression to one of alarm. The tall figure of Frank Rist, oddly dressed in a large sheepskin jacket with upturned collar partially obscuring his face, was stepping from the VW on to the gravel. He placed himself at the car park entrance. So they would have to pass by him as they left.

'My god,' Rachel whispered.

There was a purposeful look about Frank. His head was drawn back. He did not take his eyes off them as they approached. When they were close enough, he slowly raised a hand, palm upwards, like a man with something important to say. Joseph kept his tight grip on Rachel's arm and, without altering their pace, steered her in a semicircle around Frank, whose expression turned from intent to surprise.

'Hey, Joseph,' he said, already addressing their backs. 'Hey, I want to talk. You wanker, Joseph, I need to talk! She's totally evil, you know. Do you know what she was telling that journalist – for money? Joseph, I'm speaking to you, wanker. Fuck you.'

Everything seemed to have been going in slow motion, but at last Joseph's leaden limbs had taken him to the car door, where he sneaked a sideways look at Frank. Rachel, standing by the passenger door with an arm on the car roof, was also watching Frank stomp angrily back to his VW.

'Shouldn't you just find out what he wants?' she asked.

'Believe me, that's not a good idea,' Joseph said, beckoning her to get in the car. Not wanting to spoil their day out, he had not told Rachel about finding Angel sprawled on the floor with her jaw broken. He started to explain as they drove off. From a glance in the rear-view mirror, he noted nervously that Frank was starting the VW.

There was a large lorry approaching from the right as he reached the car park entrance. Joseph almost failed to see it, and had to brake hurriedly. To his horror, he saw the VW's reflection filling the driving mirror until suddenly, there was a terrible noise of metal on metal and their heads were thrown back violently against the headrests.

In retrospect, Joseph allowed that the first shunting was an accident. The second was not. He saw in the mirror how Frank threw up his hands, and then seemed to give way to uncontrolled anger as he threw the VW into reverse and rammed them again. They were thrown backwards even more violently than before, causing Joseph an atrocious pain around the neck and shoulder blades. His eyes closed. He was not aware that he had taken his foot off the brake until a scream from Rachel alerted him to the danger that they could be shunted into the path of the oncoming lorry.

The lorry's horn howled and there was a ripping sound as it clipped the corner of their car, pushing it sideways and sending glass and metal fragments bouncing over the tarmac.

Rachel was frantically struggling to retrieve something from the bag that had been at her feet, so she was leaning forward at the moment of impact. Her forehead hit the windscreen, but not hard, and a second later she had thrown herself back in her chair and was punching the keys on her mobile phone. Joseph tried to drive off, but the engine had stalled. He heard the words *madman, cemetery, trying to kill us* . . . as he tried to recover from a drowsiness that had suddenly come over him, following the spreading pain around his neck like a score of needle pricks. He put the car into first gear and let it drift forwards, but did not dare accelerate.

'I said he is a Member of Parliament,' Rachel was shouting as the VW hit them for the third time. This time, Joseph's car and the pursuant VW lurched forwards together across the width of the road, ramming the trunk of a silver birch tree. The tree shuddered as if in pain but stayed upright. The two cars now straddled both lanes like a barricade.

Groggily, Joseph saw Rachel struggling to open the passenger door. She was unable to; it must have buckled under the impact. He deduced that getting out of the car was a sensible thing to do, though he could not work out why. He tried his own door, which obligingly opened, allowing him to stagger on to the road, gasping and groaning and unsure what to do next.

Frank Rist was still in the driving seat of the VW, holding the top part of the driving wheel with both hands, swaying backwards and forwards, watching Joseph.

Must talk to him, sort it out.

Suddenly, he was interrupted by a wholly unfamiliar voice, a rather self-important voice, calling, 'Excuse me.'

Over on the other side of the car, inside which Rachel was climbing over into the back seat to escape, there was a short, chubby, mildly ridiculous man in a light blue suit, who seemed to have appeared from nowhere like a leprechaun.

'Excuse me, are you injured?'

Joseph shook his head, a movement that sent a wave of pain down his spine, so acute that he almost cried out.

'Well, if you aren't injured, do you mind very much clearing the way? I can see you've had an accident, and I'm sorry to have to insist, but I'm in a hurry, I have a meeting to get to, and as you can see, you're blocking the road. This is a public highway.'

Joseph now saw a car behind the self-important little man. Its engine was running, and the driver's door was open. Further away, at least a quarter of a mile away on the far side of the road, the lorry had halted. Its driver was climbing out of the cabin.

Impatient at Joseph's failure to reply, the thwarted driver tapped the windscreen of the Volkswagen imperiously with his knuckle and gestured to tell Frank to clear the road. Joseph shook his head, hoping to warn the self-important little driver that provoking Frank could be a bad idea, but too late. With a jerky movement, Frank emerged from the car wielding a long shiny metallic object. A moment later, Joseph identified it as a long-handled car jack.

'Don't wave that thing!' the little man said, with a little less certainty than before.

With a single movement, Frank smashed the back windscreen of Joseph's car, which folded inwards like a blanket, splintering from side to side. Inside the car, Rachel cried out. Moving at remarkable pace, the indignant little man ran back to his car, turned it about, and departed at speed back whence he had come.

Frank seemed to be unsettled by the sound of Rachel shouting inside the car as she writhed around trying to force the passenger door open. He shook his head and began muttering to himself, his lips moving almost soundlessly, and with an apelike movement he walked around in a complete circle on the roadway, the car jack swinging at his side. He stopped and stared directly at Joseph, his bewildered face lined with suffering. At that moment, with his sheepskin jacket and unkempt long greying hair, he looked like a holy fool from the steppes.

This is Frank Rist: we were young together. Poor, mad Frank!

Joseph wanted to talk to him. He took an unsteady step forward, arms opened, but that was a wrong move. Something happened behind Frank's staring eyes – not the flash of recognition, the *you're-Joseph-Pilgrim-we-were-young-together* look he had hoped for; instead, all life seemed to leave those eyes, and Frank was like a jerkily moving wax model. Shuddering convulsively, he shook his head as if to expel a thought that caused him pain, adjusted his grip on the handle of the car jack and took a step forward. Joseph just had time to put his left arm across his forehead as he saw the car jack swing upwards and bear down towards his skull. He heard the crack of breaking bone and felt a hot sensation in his forearm, as if he had been stung by a particularly virulent nettle.

I deserve this for leaving my children . . .

The next blow hit him sideways on the shoulder, pushing him hard against the car and pinning his right arm. He felt the force, but surprisingly it hardly hurt at all. The next blow was to the chest, and sent him staggering backwards.

The light was performing strange effects. First, there was bright daylight, colours and movement, then in the next instant he was standing in pitch-darkness, though he could still hear indistinguishable sounds. His legs appeared to be having a misunderstanding with his knees and might have liked to lie down, if he only knew where down was.

During one of the short intervals of daylight, he saw Frank Rist watching with curiosity, as if weighing up where to land the next blow, and he realized that he no longer had a serviceable arm to raise over his skull. He wondered, without any real sense of alarm, whether he was about to be killed.

All went dark, and something different happened. When the light returned, he was looking at the back of Rachel's head. Her beautiful dark hair hung down, as usual, to her shoulder blades. She was shouting as if demented. Over her shoulder, he could see Frank Rist take a step back. In a confused sort of way, Joseph worked out that Rachel was risking serious injury, or even death, to save him from further punishment. It crossed his mind that, possibly, she loved him.

A man was running towards them shouting. There was another distant sound, very like the siren of a police car. Joseph's legs gave way.

·30·

The Patient

He woke up in hospital, remembering in scraps that he had been brought there in an ambulance and injected with something that had put him into a deep sleep. One arm was in plaster, there was a brace around his neck, and he felt groggy, sick and in pain. It was the sound of a mobile that had woken him. Not really knowing where he was, he focused his weakened mental resources on dealing with it. His one good arm rummaged through clothing in a locker beside his bed until he was holding the object that was making the noise. He discovered that he was being spoken to by Gerald Moon.

'Joseph, my mate, have you got a TV there?'

He looked around as best he could. He was on a high bed constructed like an oversize dinner trolley with long metal handles on either side, in a cubicle cordoned off by a single blue curtain on a curved railing. There was a small cupboard at his side, a miniature washbasin and, in one corner, high up, a television mounted on brackets. It was showing pictures without sound.

'You didn't see her then – Rachel? She's a natural, that girl. She should be a presenter.'

'Rachel was on television?'

'You were lead item on the six, mate. The police are holding the maniac. It's a great story. Have you really got a broken arm?'

Joseph's right arm was encased in heavy white plaster. 'I think so.'

'When you're up, mate, we've got to do a photo-op of you with your arm in a sling. Crime-prevention-type message.'

'Gerald, I'm a bit tired.'

Gerald rapidly apologized, but no sooner had he rung off than the telephone chirped again. This time, Joseph recognized the voice of Never Evil, asking how he was. He gave a noncommittal reply.

'OK, my son, one quickie while you're on: will you be back on your feet Wednesday, do you think? Well, work on the assumption that you are. You're third on the order paper again, my old son. Another chance for you to question the PM. So, let's get this one right, shall we? No surprises this time, if that's agreeable.'

This was how it had all started.

'Can you write out the question? I'll memorize it.'

'You won't pull a stunt?'

'No, I won't do that.'

A black woman in a blue nurse's uniform had entered the cubicle and was shaking her head disapprovingly. 'We don't permit those mobile telephones in the hospital, my lovey: they might interfere with our equipment. Will you turn it off, please.'

Joseph obeyed without protest, not wanting another call like either of the last two.

'You have a lady visitor, now that you're awake . . .' the nurse added, breaking off in mid-sentence to read a message on the pager at her hip. With an apology, she hurried away before Joseph could ask a question about the lady visitor.

He wondered if the visitor was Rachel – or was Rachel too busy giving television interviews? If not Rachel, perhaps Margaret. To his own surprise, he quite hoped it was Margaret. But could she have made the journey in this short time? Would she even want to? If Margaret really was outside waiting to see him, perhaps they could gather up the severed ends of their marriage.

Or if it was Rachel, that was another future.

After a moment, the bustling nurse was back, her starched uniform creaking as she walked. 'Mr Pilgrim, I apologize, I was called away for a minute there. When I said you had a lady visitor, I had wrong information. You're the lucky man, you have *two* lady visitors . . .'

Rachel came first, striding across the ward as models walk, unaware of the older woman behind her. Margaret stopped near the door, head on one side, obviously curious. Rachel was in a voluble mood. She began talking even as she sat down, about the calls she had had from television producers, politicians, newspapers, and many others. She had been chauffeur-driven to the hospital in a car belonging to a television company which was setting up an outside broadcast camera in the car park so that Rachel could be interviewed live as she came away from Joseph's bedside. He hardly heard her. Her chatter was like a distracting background noise against the silence radiating from Margaret. He found that he did not care about the outside broadcast camera waiting in the hospital car park, or the tributes paid to him in the House of Commons by a Home Office minister to cries of 'hear, hear' from both sides of the aisle. He was indifferent to the message Rachel was relaying from Downing Street. He wanted only to listen to Margaret's silence.

The look he threw in her direction must have given something away, because Rachel abruptly stopped talking and stared at the older woman, wondering who she was. Margaret approached and drew up a second chair. Introducing the two women to one another presented a small physical difficulty when one arm was buried in plaster, which eased the social embarrassment. The colour came to Rachel's face and she put a hand to her mouth, as if she had been caught committing a dreadful *faux pas*.

'I'm so sorry,' she exclaimed, touching Margaret on the wrist. 'I didn't recognize you. We've spoken hundreds of times on the phone.'

Margaret looked at Rachel sideways and smiled indulgently, but more eloquent than her smile was the involuntary arm movement that drew it away to prevent Rachel from touching her again.

After a moment's awkward silence, Margaret began talking. Suddenly she was as voluble as Rachel had been, except that she was speaking quietly, without the excited nervous edge to her voice of someone who is running on adrenaline. She was speaking about their children, about how Tom was in trouble at the nursery because he had punched another boy in a dispute over a toy dinosaur; whereas Isobel, by contrast, was developing an interest in books, children's books, a genre on which Margaret seemed to have developed an expertise overnight.

'Who's Harry Potter?' Joseph asked, bemused.

Margaret went into a convoluted explanation which featured boarding-school children with magical powers. The idea that Isobel was imbibing this nonsense delighted Joseph so much that he feared his eyes would water. Even the image of Tom deploying his golfball-sized fist in an infant territorial dispute was as poignant as it was worrying.

While Margaret talked, Rachel threw him a discreet smile and noiselessly left the ward. He threw one longing look after her. If Frank Rist had not struck on that day, of all days, Joseph might have had a sight and feel of the flesh below those carefully selected, expensive clothes.

Rachel was back minutes later, but only as an image: she materialized on the screen of the television. Her poise and her looks perfectly suited the medium. Gerald was right: she was a natural. She was talking to an unseen interviewer, talking about Joseph, who was visited again by the strange detachment which came upon him when he was being discussed on the airwaves, as if the person they were talking about was no one he knew. The person he knew as himself was sitting up, in some pain, talking to Margaret.

They talked for an hour in low tones. Nothing was said about what was uppermost in his mind: would he be returning from hospital to his old home, where he could be a father to his children? They did not touch on these questions, because there was no need. They knew one another too well.

Two police officers called on him in his office in Millbank in the middle of the following week. They were dressed in cheap raincoats and wrote in tatty notebooks. One was almost hairless, the other had a shaggy crop of thick black hair. He sat them on his sofa, then placed his swivel chair where it faced them. That meant he was looking down on them, giving himself the edge. Rachel sat and listened, as a witness to one of the events relevant to their investigation. Like a true politician, Joseph monopolized the conversation.

'I am very pleased indeed to co-operate with your inquiry in any way I can. As you know, I was one of the last to see Christine Rist alive. It has come as a considerable surprise to me, after so much time, to learn that Frank Rist was in the vicinity at the time. I believe he has given you a statement. There is not much I can add to it, because I simply don't know what happened, but if I may be allowed to express an opinion, I don't believe Mr Rist did anything to harm his wife.'

The pager on his belt vibrated. It was the thirty-seventh message he had received that day congratulating him on his safe return to the House. If events had worked out just a little differently and he had been driven from public life in abject disgrace, not one of the thirty-seven would have felt any loss; but today, the thoughts of the House were with him.

'I know that there are circumstances counting against Mr Rist,' Joseph continued, conscious of the advantage he enjoyed by meeting the detectives on home ground. They were making occasional notes as they listened with expressions that gave nothing away.

'There is his violent assault on myself and Rachel, the assault on Angel, and his absenting himself from the scene after Christine was killed. On the last point, I think the explanation is quite clear. Mr Rist had absconded from a hospital ward where he was under psychiatric observation. He was afraid that he would be sent back. That is the simple explanation of his behaviour, though why Angel supplied him with a false alibi mystifies me.'

The pager went off again. This time, it was Downing Street wanting him to ring, to rehearse the question he would be putting to the Prime Minister that afternoon.

'I have to say I think she was the author of her own misfortune. Mr Rist was very provoked. I understand that she is not anxious to see him prosecuted for that attack?' The detectives exchanged looks and indicated that he was right. 'Well, that doesn't surprise me. And this brings me to what I consider to be the real scandal: the story she was concocting, in league with a journalist from the gutter press. It's a story which, I am pleased to say, the newspaper in question has utterly rejected.'

His victory over Dave Drucker was complete. He knew this, though he did not know how it had happened. He surmised that Diana Draycott had had something to do with it, but could not ask.

'The lady claims that Mr Rist himself told her this story,' said one of the detectives.

'Did anyone else hear him say it? Has anyone else received this astonishing confession? I think not. And I, for one, would not take the word of someone who has been caught concocting an utter lie. Where could she have got this appalling story of my alleged affair with Christine Rist?'

As he said this, he saw how closely the detectives were listening, and wondered if they despised him, for he despised himself and the lie he was telling. Yet he had no hesitation about it: the

·310·

alternative would bring ruin upon himself, Margaret and the children, without any benefit to anyone.

It did not matter too much what the detectives thought of him, so long as his story held.

'I'm sure there were problems in the Rist marriage, as in any marriage, but I know they were devoted to each other. Perhaps I'm wrong, but I find it impossible to believe that Frank Rist would have deliberately harmed his wife. I suppose it was the stress of this false accusation that triggered the bizarre attack on me. He is to be pitied rather than condemned. Frank needs help.'

After the detectives had left, he turned to Rachel, anticipating that she would show him the contempt he felt he deserved. Instead, he was greeted with that smile she used to deploy when she first worked for him, one that paid regard to his status as her employer.

'That was very noble of you,' she said. 'Have you memorized your question?'

'I'm not making that mistake again,' he said.

Silence fell over the packed gallery of the House of Commons when Joseph's name was called. The question the whips had supplied for him was so obsequious that he frankly would not have complained if the opposition had jeered and barracked, but there was no question of this while his arm was swathed in a sling. Indeed, he sat to a roar of approval. The House makes its collective judgements. Some are harsh, some generous. They paid respect to Joseph as the MP who had endured a violent assault by a madman, and a similarly noxious intrusion by the tabloid press. He was innocent, in the House.